Dragon's Heart

The DragonFate Novels #3

DEBORAH COOKE

ISBN-13: 978-1-989367-41-4

Books by Deborah Cooke

Dear Reader;

Welcome back to the world of *DragonFate* and more of my dragon shifter heroes called the *Pyr*. Rhys and Lila's book features their firestorm, of course, but in the *DragonFate* series, the heroines all have powers of their own. Lila is a selkie and another kind of shifter hunted by Maeve, the Dark Queen of Fae. She also distrusts men and determined to defend her independence. She seeks out Rhys after their first kiss, but Rhys is skeptical. He thinks their firestorm is another spell of Maeve's, like Kristofer's firestorm, and means to ignore it. Unfortunately for Rhys' plans, Lila is hard for him to ignore, especially with the firestorm on her side. I love how these two challenge each other and examine the secrets of the past. Their romance is a powerful one for me, and I hope you enjoy it.

I'm finding with this series that all of the other *Pyr* want their cameos—I should have known that they wouldn't stay out of a quest to defend their kind from Maeve's plan to eliminate all shifters! You'll catch a glimpse of some old friends in this book. Be sure to check the family trees on the Dragonfire website to discover the books about any of the *Pyr* you've missed.

http://DragonfireNovels.com

You'll also find a link there for the Pinterest pages for *DragonFate* where you can see some of my inspiration for this book and for the series as a whole. Finally, there's a new DragonFate List of Characters on the Dragonfire website, which will be updated after each addition to the series.

Next in the *DragonFate* series will be **Dragon's Mate**, which is Hadrian's story. He has a vision of Rania in this book, which shakes him up. Like the other *Pyr* caught in the war against Maeve, he's uncertain whether to trust the enchanting beauty or the apparent firestorm and I'm excited about writing his and Rania's story.

To keep up to date with my books, please sign up for my monthly paranormal romance newsletter, *Dragons & Angels*. You'll hear about sales on ebooks, be notified of new releases, and have the chance to download free bonus content exclusively for subscribers.

I hope you enjoy Rhys and Lila's story!

Until next time, I hope you have lots of good books to read.

All my best,
Deborah

Dragon's Heart

The DragonFate Novels #3

PROLOGUE

Manhattan—Monday, October 28, 2019

hys watched in astonishment as the portal opened in the wall of the bar called Bones. What he saw made no sense at all: never mind that the *Pyr* were in the company of vampires and a werewolf with attitude who wanted to make an alliance. Kristofer's firestorm had ignited, his mate had vanished through a solid brick wall, then Kade had drawn a doorway on the wall and it had opened.

He wasn't nearly drunk enough to be imagining things.

In fact, Rhys didn't think it was possible to be drunk enough to have hallucinations like this. It must really be happening. There didn't seem to be anything beyond the door that had opened in the wall, just darkness and the glow of Kristofer's firestorm.

Kristofer was already heading for the doorway, a flame dancing on his fingertip. It was a beacon, leading him to his destined mate, and Rhys knew Kristofer would feel compelled to follow it.

Rhys would have hesitated and asked questions: he was the skeptic of the group of friends. Kristofer was the believer—but Rhys would have Kristofer's back. Rhys wouldn't have gone through that door voluntarily for himself, but he'd go without hesitation in support of a friend.

Alasdair had stepped back with caution, while Hadrian, also in his dragon form, was crossing the threshold right behind Kristofer. Kade was staring down at the stylus he'd used to make the doorway, as if he was astonished by its powers, too. Rhys heard Theo shout a warning in old-speak, but he had to stay with Kristofer.

1

There was no telling what they'd find on the other side.

He'd already shifted and was glad to be in his dragon form. His senses were keener and he thought he could smell danger. An icy shiver slipped over him as he crossed the threshold. Rhys spread his wings, sensing that the ground fell away beneath him and took flight. There was no sign of either Kristofer or Hadrian and he turned in the air when he realized he couldn't even see the light of the firestorm anymore. He looked back toward the door and the bar.

There was no door.

He was surrounded by darkness and all alone.

Rhys didn't panic. That was how others made mistakes. He calmly flew onward, pretty sure of his direction. It only made sense that he'd catch up to his companions. Kristofer must have raced on ahead to meet his mate, and Rhys already knew that Kristofer flew faster than he did.

To his relief, in half a dozen beats of his wings, something glimmered ahead. The firestorm! Rhys swooped low, hoping he arrived in time to help Kristofer, only to discover that he'd seen light reflected on the sea.

What sea?

He should be in the building adjacent to the bar, Bones, in Manhattan. It should be the basement of a warehouse, or another bar, or a tunnel—not an ocean. Despite his conviction, water spread to the horizon in every direction, lit by a glow.

What was going on?

Rhys flew in a wide circle, unable to explain his situation. He remained beyond the glow of light, distrusting it. He swooped down to dip his toes in the water, but nothing changed. The sea was silvery blue and calm, with just a slight undulation of waves. There were small islands in the distance and the crescent of a rocky beach on the closest one.

And that glow. It was golden, not like moonlight at all.

It was more like a firestorm's light. From this distance, it was just a golden light, one that didn't illuminate anything specific.

Rhys barely discerned a splash, coming from the direction of the glow. The sound was faint, even with his keen *Pyr* hearing, and he guessed that someone hadn't wanted to make a sound. It had to be Kristofer's firestorm. He sped toward the light silently, flying close to the water to avoid detection. The light dipped beneath the waves and dimmed. Rhys spotted a dark silhouette surrounded by a golden glow in the water. Whatever it was went deeper and the light faded.

Rhys dove into the sea in pursuit, expecting to find his friends.

To his astonishment, a spark lit at the end of his own talon. It glowed orange, radiant even in the water, which only gave him more questions. The flame sent a heat through him that couldn't be denied, heating him as well as filling him with desire.

But this was supposed to be Kristofer's firestorm.

Was his own destined mate nearby? That would be a coincidence beyond belief.

The flame was brighter when Rhys held his claw down toward the dark depths. The yearning and desire that filled him could only be explained by the firestorm. That form had to be his destined mate. He returned to the surface, took a deep breath, and dove. He held his claw before himself, following the glow like a beacon.

How could his mate swim so deep?

Rhys swam harder and spotted a silhouette, once more framed in that golden glow. The shape surprised him. Was his mate a seal? How could that be? The light was brightest around the creature. Rhys gave chase, his chest tight. He didn't dare return to the surface and lose sight of her. He had a strange conviction that if he did, he'd never find his way back again.

The light drove him on, but his mate had no intention of being caught. Rhys swam as quickly as he could, ducking around coral and rocks, swimming deeper and deeper. His chest ached for lack of air, but he forced himself to continue. The water became as dark as midnight, especially in contrast to the golden light of the firestorm. That glow startled eels and fish that never saw such bright light, but didn't illuminate much else. Just when Rhys thought his lungs would burst, the flame flared to golden brilliance, illuminating the entry to a cave, then winked out.

She must have taken refuge there.

Rhys reached inside, knowing he could manage only one grab before he had to return to the surface. His talons closed around something—or someone. It felt suspiciously like a woman's waist and the contact sent a fire through his veins that could only be the result of the firestorm. She struggled and squirmed, but she had to be in need of air, too. Rhys knew that people who were drowning often fought their rescuers. He gripped her with resolve and surged toward the surface.

On the way, he changed to his human form, reasoning that he could still hold on to her but would require less air. The water was lit with a blue shimmer during his transformation. He kept one arm around his mate's waist and used the other to haul them up to salvation. They were surrounded by a golden glow, but Rhys didn't look at her, not yet. He broke the surface with a gasp and took a greedy gulp of air.

Then he looked.

Rhys held a seal, a creature with large dark eyes that stared back at him fearlessly. He would have thought he'd made a mistake if it hadn't been for the thousands of little sparks of the firestorm, the tiny blazes that illuminated every point of contact between them.

This was his mate?

She squirmed in his grip and he saw a blue shimmer that was more than familiar. He watched, incredulous, as her shape began to change. He held tightly, uncertain what she would become but having his hopes. She drew back her skin quickly, as if removing a hood. If he had blinked, he would have missed her transformation.

She was a woman, a naked one, with fair skin and long dark hair that hung down her back, slick and wet. Her eyes remained thickly lashed and expressive, just as dark and mysterious as those of the seal. There was no sign of her skin, but Rhys understood about hiding one's truth. She braced her hands on his shoulders and pushed, flames erupting from the flats of her palms against his skin.

"Let me go!" she said, struggling against him. She spared a glance at the sky. "I have to hide!" She had a Scottish accent and a low sultry voice, but her fear was real.

She didn't yet know that he would do anything to protect her.

She maybe didn't realize his capabilities.

Rhys changed shape again, soaring high with her captive in his embrace. It felt good to carry his mate in his dragon form, to feel the wind beneath his wings and the power in his body. If anything, the firestorm was stronger and hotter, driving all other thoughts from his mind. He wanted to kiss her, to seduce her, to pleasure her—but she seemed to have the opposite reaction to his presence.

"Please, release me! You're being a shifter just means she'll get two for the price of one." She fought him hard, but without success. "If you want to be captured, leave me out of it."

"Captured by who?"

She gave him a look, as if he was an idiot. "The Dark Queen, of course. I won't say her name. She means to kill us all, and I intend to live."

"But this is the firestorm. Can't you feel its heat? The firestorm trumps everything."

"The firestorm?" Her tone became curious and she stopped struggling. She frowned a little, examining the light that flared between them, placing her hand on him then moving it away. She repeated the move, as if testing that the result was consistent. It was a delicious torment that turned Rhys' thoughts in a predictable direction.

"You're right. The light of Fae is silver, not gold." She stroked his chest and the light flared to brilliance between her hand and his scales. They both caught their breath simultaneously and Rhys felt the acceleration of her heartbeat. His own matched its pace, a sensation that left him dizzy and he flew in a spiral with his eyes closed, wallowing in the pleasure of her touch.

His firestorm.

It was a dream come true. He would have a family again.

"What exactly is a firestorm?" she asked, her tone more practical than Rhys felt.

"An ancient power," he replied in a low rumble. "The mark of one of my kind finding his destined mate." Their gazes clung and Rhys felt his mouth go dry. She was beautiful.

To his surprise, she laughed. It was a wonderful sound, like a thousand silver bells. She surveyed him with amazement. "Destiny? I'm not sure I believe in that."

"I'm not sure you need to." Rhys pulled her closer, creating a flurry of sparks between them and sending a simmering heat through his veins. He watched her take a deep breath, savoring the sensation, then she considered him with sparkling eyes.

"So, this is how a dragon is brought to his knees," she said, teasing him.

"Absolutely," he agreed. "You're beautiful." He meant it. Even without the firestorm, he would have been struck by her beauty. She was naked, so he could see a lot of her skin. As he glanced down, her nipples tightened but she didn't blush or avert her gaze.

"You aren't so bad yourself," she said and ran a hand across his chest, creating a line of flames that made them inhale in unison. She met his gaze and lifted a brow. "Although, a dragon. That sounds like playing with fire." Her lips twisted at her own joke and he hoped she might laugh again.

"*Pyr* is what we call ourselves." He recalled that she had powers of her own. "What do you call your kind?"

"Selkies."

He hadn't imagined it, then. She had turned to a seal. "I didn't think selkies were real."

"We nearly aren't," she replied, a little sharply, then eyed him. "I was pretty sure dragons weren't real," she continued with that same wry humor. He could have listened to her, with that accent, all day—or all night. "But you look pretty solid."

"I am." They were flying over the water, but Rhys heard waves on that beach ahead of them. He changed his course, wanting a kiss.

"But turn out the light," she urged. "We don't want to be seen by *her*."

"I can't. There's only one thing that extinguishes the light of the firestorm."

She started to ask, then their gazes met and he saw that she understood. "You're kidding me. Not while you're a dragon."

"Not while I'm a dragon." Rhys soared toward the beach, landing with a flourish. He felt filled with new power and grace, and he knew his shift to human form was perfect. He landed on his feet in the shallows with his mate cradled in his arms.

"Wow," she said, running a hand over his shoulder as if she couldn't stop herself. A sizzle of fire trailed after her touch, leaving Rhys sizzling. "Very impressive."

"Thank you."

Her eyes danced as she met his gaze. "Although the red and silver scales were very striking."

Rhys grinned. "I'm glad you approve."

There was a distant boom of thunder and her panic returned. She spared a glance upward. "She *is* watching! I have to go." She wriggled against him again. If she wanted him to release her, the movement had exactly the opposite effect. Rhys' embrace tightened and his desire rose.

"It's just a storm," he said, trying to soothe her.

"She certainly is," she said, her eyes flashing. It was clear that she meant to flee, but Rhys wanted that kiss first.

"Just one kiss before you go," he entreated. "For the firestorm."

She caught her breath, looked at his mouth, then glanced up again. "Or you'll hold me captive until I do?" There was a warning in her tone and Rhys understood that she liked her freedom.

He loosened his grip deliberately. "Of course not. The decision is yours."

She inhaled, her eyes sparkling, and ran her hands over him again, as if she couldn't resist temptation. "You are a surprise. I thought dragons just grabbed the damsels they wanted."

"I like women who choose to be with me."

She smiled at him, her approval clear. "Maybe just one kiss," she agreed, a little breathless. "I've never kissed a dragon shifter before."

Rhys smiled. "Then we'll have to make it count," he whispered, then bent his head and captured her lips beneath his own.

"Oh," she murmured and he swallowed the sound, slanting his mouth over hers to deepen his kiss. She made a little growl in her throat, as if she couldn't decide whether to fight him or to surrender. Then she sighed and melted against him, parting her lips to welcome him. Her fingers slid into his hair and tangled in it, drawing him closer. She wrapped her arms around his neck, taking control of the kiss in a thrilling way.

The firestorm blazed through him, setting his very blood on fire, hot and hungry and demanding, just the way they'd always said it would be. Desire obliterated every other thought from his mind. Rhys was aware of nothing but his mate and her perfection.

Her kiss—and her hunger for his touch.

He felt her arch her back to rub her breasts against his chest, and felt the tip of her teasing tongue. She wasn't shy, and he liked that, too. This time, it was Rhys who growled in frustration. He pivoted without lifting his head and strode toward the beach.

"No!" she said, breaking their kiss. "There can't be more."

"There must be more," Rhys replied. "The firestorm can't be stopped."

"This one has to wait," she said as lightning flashed across the sky again. She kicked hard, suddenly. Her move surprised Rhys enough that he loosened his grip. She didn't wait for a second chance. She jumped from his embrace and splashed into the water, diving for the depths again.

"No!" Rhys roared and dove after her. He saw a blue shimmer in the water ahead of him and knew what it meant. He snatched and caught the tip of her tail in one hand, and she paused to look back at him. She had half-changed, her lower body the tail of a seal, but her upper body still human. Her skin was gathered around her waist, like a cloak. She was like a mermaid but not. Her hair swirled around her and her gaze softened, the light of the firestorm glowing all around them. She reached back and touched his hand, so lithe and lovely that his heart squeezed.

"She's coming," she whispered, and he was amazed that she could communicate with him beneath the water. He heard her words, like old-speak but gentler. There was an entreaty in her gaze. *"Hide yourself while you can."*

"Who?" Rhys used old-speak and she must have understood.

She shook her head. *"I can't say her name. I won't say it."* She was fierce. Then she smiled at him. *"One day, maybe you can tell me about your firestorm, dragon man."* She swam closer and Rhys released her tail, unable to bear the idea of her being injured because of him. She touched her lips to his cheek.

"Thank you for the kiss. It was one to remember." Then with a flick of her tail, she was gone. Rhys saw her pale skin disappear and knew she'd completed the shift to her other form, then he had to take a breath of air. He surged for the surface, his chest tight, wishing he had the ability to swim after her and argue his case.

There was a brilliant flash of light above the water just as Rhys broke the surface again. It cracked like lightning, illuminating the surface of the sea and the beach as if it was midday. It was silver light, though, and the sight made him shiver. He spotted a pair of high-heeled sandals at the high tide mark on the beach, but there was no one else in sight. He turned in place, wondering who had abandoned the shoes, as the light faded away. Could it have been his mate? Would they lead her to him somehow? He began to move toward the beach, wanting any clue to her identity.

Then the lightning flashed again, cracking loudly as it struck Rhys between his shoulders. He cried out at the searing pain that shot through him and closed his eyes as the world spun. He summoned the change but his body betrayed him and he remained in human form.

He couldn't shift.

Rhys was the one to panic then. Nothing interfered with his ability to change forms, and his hidden dragon gave him the confidence to face any foe.

But he couldn't shift. It was terrifying.

There was a red string knotted around his wrist, one that burned. It hadn't been there before the lightning struck. Even though it was thin, he couldn't snap it. Rhys struggled to break it, then suddenly found himself in a court of glittering Fae, Hadrian sprawled beside him with a similar string on his wrist. He was soaking wet and his clothes smelled of salt water, but there was no spark of the firestorm.

Where was the ocean cove?

Where was Kristofer?

He hoped his mate had escaped.

Then the music started, infectious merry music, and his feet began to twitch of their own accord. Rhys found himself dancing a jig without having made any decision to do so. Hadrian awakened and lunged to his feet, seizing Rhys' hands as he joined the dance. The two of them circled, their feet pounding against the ground, compelled to dance against their will. The court around them blurred into streaks of silver and red, the music melded with raucous laughter, and his feet began to hurt. Rhys was breathless, his heart thundering, but he couldn't stop dancing. The red cord burned and the music went on and on and on.

All the while, he wondered about the selkie and her kiss. She had warned him, but he hadn't taken her advice. He could only hope that didn't mean he'd never see her again.

As his feet began to bleed, Rhys could only hope she was never snared like this.

CHAPTER ONE

November 9

hys wasn't in a good mood.

It wasn't just that his plans had been disrupted. He didn't like surprises, but he'd do anything for his fellow *Pyr*, even drive to Vermont for Kristofer's scale repair with very little warning. He was only slightly irked that he'd had to leave his beloved restaurant in the hands of his capable staff.

Okay, he was more than a little concerned about that.

The issue wasn't that there was snow in the forecast and he hated winter with a passion.

It was his firestorm.

If that's what it had been.

Rhys hadn't told his fellow dragon shifters one key detail about his sojourn in Fae. He hadn't mentioned the selkie and her kiss, much less the glorious burn of his firestorm. He would have, but learning that Kristofer's firestorm in Fae had been fake ended the confession before it started. What if his firestorm had been a spell, as well? It had sparked after he'd entered the portal to Fae, which fed his suspicions.

Kristofer's so-called destined mate had tried to kill him, too, which left Rhys wondering about the selkie's goals. Why had she gone so deep into the ocean? Had she been luring him to his death?

She *had* warned him about Maeve, but the firestorm still could have been a spell. She could have warned him then summoned the Dark Queen to harvest him, just to make herself look trustworthy. Rhys didn't like it. No matter how he looked at it, he'd followed Kristofer into Fae, been distracted by the spark of an apparent firestorm, indicating the proximity of his apparent mate, and had ended up dancing until his feet bled at the command of the Fae Queen.

That glorious selkie maiden might have been involved in the deception. She could be in league with Maeve, or she could have been snared into doing Maeve's will, like Bree had been. Even though the *Pyr* had managed to save Rhys, his survival certainly hadn't been part of anyone's plans in Fae, and he liked being alive.

It was preferable to the alternative.

Trick me once, shame on you; trick me twice, shame on me.

Rhys had been taught that by his father, and it was a mantra that guided his life. He wasn't going to tell the *Pyr* about the selkie, because they'd encourage him to pursue her, given that they were all protective romantics. Rhys had been spared that inclination. He was practical and he wasn't going to take the chance that she was part of Maeve's scheme.

Even if he had dreamed about her every single night since his escape from Fae.

But that was proof that there was something magickal afoot: Rhys never dreamed. Ever.

He could still feel the prickle of the firestorm, sparking in his veins, but she must be far away. He could ignore the summons when it came from such a distance, and he only hoped that his fellow *Pyr* didn't notice its subtle glow.

He certainly wasn't going after the selkie, wherever she was.

Rhys turned into Kristofer's farm just as the first flakes of snow began to fall and saw that he was one of the last to arrive. He knew there must have already been a lot of discussion about the Others and the path forward, but he'd decided on his own course. Arriving later was strategic—it gave his fellow *Pyr* less time to notice the firestorm and try to change his mind. Rhys parked his black pick-up beside Quinn's and Kristofer strode to meet him.

"Did you find that maple syrup place?" Kristofer asked, surveying the coolers in the back of the truck.

"Yes, thanks. I bought all they had." Rhys laughed at Kristofer's shocked expression. "I'll take most of it back to the restaurant, but some is for tonight. You were right: it's really good. Pure."

"So you tasted it?"

"When they found out that I was interested in a large quantity, they opened a bottle for me." Rhys smiled. "I think they were as shocked as you that I bought it all, though." He opened a large cooler to display the fresh salmon he'd bought in Manhattan that morning. "Look at these beauties. You won't believe how the maple syrup glaze transforms the flavor when the salmon is grilled."

"We're going to feast tonight," Hadrian said, clapping Rhys on the back as he joined them. He glanced at his hand with a frown and inhaled, then studied Rhys. So much for none of the *Pyr* noticing the firestorm's faint spark.

"Look at you!" Rhys said, pretending the glow of heat was from Hadrian. "Picking up tips from the Smith already?" Hadrian was an artisan blacksmith like Quinn, although his studio was in Northumberland. He did a lot of historical restoration work.

Hadrian grinned. "Trying. Do you ever worry that we invite you just to ensure we eat well?"

Rhys shook his head. "No, because I make you work for it."

"True enough. Mr. Perfection with his prep."

"Everyone's ready to be sous to your chef," Kristofer said, lifting out the cooler of fish with a grunt. "Just tell us what to do."

"You're on," Rhys said. "But it looks like Quinn is ready to get down to business first.

"He says the forge is ready," Kristofer admitted.

Rhys cleared his throat, knowing he needed to ask one question. "What happened with the gem of the hoard?" He kept his tone light, as if the answer was less important to him than it was. He knew that Kristofer's mate, Bree, had held the piece of amber for centuries without realizing its importance to the ancient dragon prince, Embron, who had recently been awakened. He also knew that it was the responsibility of the mate to give a gift to ensure the repair of her dragon's missing scale.

If Bree had offered the gem of the hoard, that would make Kristofer a target for the dragon prince forever—and it would feed all of Rhys' suspicions about Bree's true intentions.

"Rafferty brought it back," Kristofer said easily. "He said we should have all the tools we might need to succeed against Embron."

"But where is it?" Rhys insisted, aware that Hadrian was watching closely.

"Safe in my hoard. We'll decide tonight who's going to take charge of it until this is over." Kristofer's expression lit as Bree came out of the house. Rhys watched the way the new couple smiled at each other and wondered if his friend really did know enough about his new mate.

It had been only ten days since they'd met, after all.

And she had been a Valkyrie. It had been her task for centuries to harvest souls.

There was no spark of the firestorm when Bree stood beside Kristofer, which meant the genuine one that had sparked between them had been satisfied, and that she'd already conceived. They were in it together now, Rhys thought, for better or for worse, and he silently wished them well.

He still had his doubts, though.

"At least there's that," Hadrian muttered to Rhys as they carried groceries into the house.

"What do you mean?"

"The firestorm is satisfied," Hadrian said quietly. "She surrendered her immortality to be with him. Both good signs, even if I'm not quite convinced."

Rhys met his gaze and nodded, knowing that his suspicions were shared by at least one other *Pyr*. Then Hadrian surveyed him again, his expression becoming puzzled, and Rhys strode ahead, keeping his secret to himself.

"I never thought I'd see the day that you came into a city for anything," Nyssa said. "Never mind leaving North Rona in the fall. Don't you have seal pups to count?"

Lila felt her fellow-selkie studying her and didn't meet her gaze. She was too busy trying to hide the faint golden glow that had brightened around her fingertips since landing at JFK. The heat of the firestorm had definitely increased since she had reached the U.S., which made it harder to concentrate on her mission.

She was burning up and only one thing would satisfy her.

She hoped the brighter light meant her dragon shifter was close, because she'd found it impossible to think about anything other than sex since they'd met. She'd been skeptical of his claims about the firestorm, but this constant glow fed her desire and kept her awake at night. She wasn't exactly chaste, but she'd never thought so obsessively about sex before. She'd relived that kiss a thousand times, if not more, and literally burned for his touch. The firestorm clearly didn't take no for an answer.

Why hadn't he come to her? He could have followed the spark as easily as Lila had. It was the mark of *his* kind in finding their destined mate, after all. Wasn't the feeling mutual? Didn't he find her attractive? He was mortal, after all, and mortals usually felt an urgency to ensure that their lineage survived.

But she hadn't seen him since she'd fled into the depths, hoping to escape Maeve. Had the Dark Queen captured him after all? As soon as Lila thought of that, she'd decided to seek him out immediately.

She'd ensure that he was okay, seduce him, then go back to her work.

Nyssa had told her ages ago that she'd moved to Manhattan because there were many Others in the city. It had seemed like a good place to start to hunt her dragon, and Lila was relieved that the glow of the firestorm had brightened in the airport.

She must have made a good guess.

Lila could see him in her memory, his dark hair and dark eyes, his muscled build. His aura had been brilliant, all fiery red and yellow, an indication of his vitality and his confidence. There had been a shadow upon it, not the kind that indicated a physical wound but one that hinted he grieved a loss. Even though she could seldom heal that kind of injury, Lila found those shadows appealing. They meant that he had a heart.

He was beautiful in his dragon form—majestic, even—and obviously powerful, with scales as red as garnets, seemingly bordered in silver. He'd glittered and shone, like a jeweled treasure as he flew through the sky. Yet he was powerful, too, and clearly a warrior. When his bright gaze met hers, Lila had felt warm right to her toes.

And that kiss had been the stuff of fantasies. She was looking forward to another one, and a whole lot more. One night should be enough—a very active night—then she could get back to work.

It was the middle of the afternoon on a Saturday, a sunny day that had warmed the air a bit. It was still chilly and Lila was glad of her down-filled coat. She was trudging through a concrete wasteland with Nyssa, and totally out of her element. There wasn't a drop of water in sight, except the glimpses she caught of the Hudson River between the buildings. Lila lived on a remote island, with her own company and sometimes that of the seals: Manhattan didn't even feel like an island to her and it was jam-packed with humanity. How did Nyssa survive in such a place?

"Time for a change," Lila said lightly, choosing not to tell Nyssa all of the truth. Her sister-selkie was notoriously indiscrete, as well as in possession of passionate urges of her own. "Plus most of the seal pups have been delivered by now, and the count is even higher than last year."

Lila was a marine biologist in human society, which gave her the perfect excuse to remain on a remote windswept island in the middle of the sea and study her distant cousins, the grey seals. Each fall, the seals came ashore at North Rona Island to bear their young and she managed the count of new pups. Nyssa was right: Lila never left the ocean without good cause, but too many nights of burning with unsatisfied desire counted as an excellent reason.

Lila spared a glance at Nyssa, remembering her manners, and saw the small shadow on her aura that she should have anticipated—and would have, if she hadn't been consumed with the idea of a certain dragon shifter. "I was sorry to hear about Aquinas," she said softly, referring to Nyssa's long-time partner and mate. "My condolences."

Nyssa winced. "Thank you, but I wish it upset me more." She sighed. "I miss him, of course, but he was so much in love and it was never quite mutual. I liked him, but I always knew I was disappointing him. I don't miss that."

Nyssa was nothing if not honest.

And there was a reason why selkies were reputed to be cold-hearted. In Lila's view, her kind had a gift for star-crossed love. She'd made that mistake herself, and she knew Nyssa yearned for someone other than Aquinas, who had adored her. No wonder they all avoided emotional entanglements. Romance was always unsatisfactory for selkies.

Lila was well aware of all the people looking at them—mostly men, checking them out—but Nyssa was as oblivious of her surroundings as ever.

Or maybe it was just humans she ignored so well.

Maybe that was how she managed to live amongst them so easily.

Nyssa shook her head, which made her dark hair flow around her shoulders as if it had a life of its own. "And Nereus let you leave," she said. "That's incredible!"

Lila bit her tongue with an effort. She hadn't told Nereus, the King Under the Seas, about her trip, the plan being that she'd be back on North Rona before he noticed. The leader of their kind could be a bit tedious about his insistence on knowing everything about his subjects. Lila didn't think her personal life was his business, and she doubted he'd approve of her seducing a dragon shifter, given his persistent pursuit of her in the past.

"Isn't it?" she said instead of revealing the truth.

"He'll decide he doesn't approve," Nyssa said, laughing a little. "He'll decide that you're defiant and he is outraged."

"Probably."

"The ocean will roar, the waves surging toward the sky as he vents his wrath." Nyssa flung her hands toward the sky. "Ships will be tossed and turned, coasts will be deluged..."

She was joking, but not really. Nereus did have a temper and he did hold the trident that caused earthquakes.

"He's not that bad," Lila protested. "But he can be a bit overbearing."

"He doesn't have enough to do," Nyssa said with a shake of her head.

"Give him some more children," Lila suggested. "He always wants to increase our numbers."

"You first," Nyssa replied. "Hasn't he been in love with you forever?"

"I don't want to talk about that."

To Lila's relief, Nyssa changed the subject.

"I'm glad you finally *did* leave that island, even if I need to help you find dragon shifters. What do you want with them anyway?"

"Just curious," Lila lied, bunching her hands in her pockets. The wind suddenly felt colder to her, and she suspected it was because she wasn't coming clean with Nyssa. She wanted as few people as possible to know about the firestorm. "You said they'd come to the meeting of Others and I've never seen one."

"You're not likely to see one at the bottom of the ocean, or on a remote island north of the Orkneys," Nyssa ceded. "Still, it's a long trip for the sake of curiosity." She gave Lila a hard look that was difficult to hold.

"Don't you think it's surprising that you saw them in Manhattan?"

"Nothing surprises me in Manhattan anymore." Nyssa rolled her eyes. "But I didn't get a good look at them at the Halloween meeting. They hurried into the back."

"Why?"

"Because other dragons had showed up previously, on a night when no one expected them, and then everything went to hell." Nyssa reached for the handle on a steel door, then winced as she corrected herself. "Not literally Hell. Just Fae. And not everyone—just four of the dragon shifters and the bartender."

"I knew what you meant. Four dragon shifters?"

Nyssa nodded. "They went into Fae."

"Did they come back?" Lila asked with alarm. She'd worried that her dragon shifter had been captured by Maeve, but what if he'd willingly entered Fae? Maeve would demand something of him in exchange for leaving her realm—if she let him leave at all.

But surely she was burning for him because he was back. Lila didn't really know. She hoped she didn't have to endure this need forever.

"I don't think so," Nyssa said with an indifference that Lila didn't share. "It was different dragon shifters who came on Halloween, and they conferred with Murray and Caleb and the vampires. I didn't get to hear." Nyssa pulled open the door and Lila realized they must have reached their destination.

If this was a restaurant, it didn't look very inviting. Lila glanced up and read the sign. Bones. She guessed they served meat. Too bad. She was hungry but only ate fish and vegetables. She looked up and down the street and couldn't imagine there was a lot of clientele in such a rough neighborhood.

Meanwhile, Nyssa had opened the door and stepped into the darkness beyond. Lila smelled something burning that wasn't food and heard power tools. She narrowed her eyes against a flurry of sparks on the opposite side of the dance floor and resisted her urge to flee. Buildings were bad enough and paved streets crowded with vehicles, but tools and motors were not her thing at all.

The shooting sparks made her think of her dragon and her mouth went dry.

Let him be in Manhattan.

"They're only installing the steel wall now?" Nyssa asked of the hostess. "It's been almost two weeks!" They obviously knew each other.

The hostess had black hair, black eyeliner and black lipstick. She was dressed all in black, with multiple tattoos on her arms. Lila got a whiff of Other and thought she might be a Medusa. If so, she apparently didn't want to talk about old times or the Isle of the Blessed. Maybe she was too young to remember. Her aura was pale and youthful.

She rolled her eyes at Nyssa's question. "You know Murray. He has to find just the right person for the job. Besides, the wizard can't come until tomorrow."

"Why does he need a wizard?" Lila asked Nyssa.

"Because that's a portal to Fae," the hostess said, matter-of-factly, then nodded at Nyssa. "You eating or just drinking?"

Lila tried to hide her shudder and didn't look at the wall in question. She didn't like any suggestion that the Dark Queen or her powers were close.

"We just want to talk to Murray," Nyssa said. "We're looking for a dragon shifter."

"Aren't we all?" the hostess said, then smiled and shivered. "Did you see them?" She made a growling sound in her throat then rolled her eyes and Nyssa laughed.

Lila didn't say anything because she totally agreed. It was all too easy to remember that red dragon, the way he flew and bore down on her, the way he sliced through the ocean—the way he shifted shape to a gorgeous man then kissed her until she couldn't remember her own name.

That kiss. What would satisfying the firestorm be like? The best sex ever, she had to guess, and was impatient to find him all over again. She pushed her hands deeper into her pockets, trying to hide that golden glow.

"Hey, Murray!" the hostess turned and shouted across the virtually-empty restaurant. "Nyssa's looking for the *Pyr*."

A short stocky man covered with tattoos, his brows furrowed, left the workmen installing the steel barrier and came to meet them at the bar. A dwarf. Of course, he would be fastidious about hiring the right craftsperson for any job, regardless of how long that might take. Dwarves were more inclined to focus on practical concerns. He'd probably gotten at least three competing bids and checked their previous jobs before deciding. A selkie would have had that wall faced with steel in no time flat.

His aura was a deep blue that hinted at his reliability. It was intact, so he had no injuries. Lila suspected his loyalty would be as robust as his health. It also had a taint of grief, though, a deep shadow that spoke of a devastating loss.

He surveyed Lila with suspicion then inhaled. "Friend of yours?" he asked Nyssa, even though his wariness had diminished.

"Sister," Nyssa said, which was the easiest explanation if not precisely the truth. Lila and Nyssa were probably third or fourth cousins. Selkies weren't fastidious about keeping track of such details.

Murray nodded, unsurprised. "Why the *Pyr*?"

"Lila's never met one."

"Some people would be good with that situation," Murray said.

"Maybe she feels like playing with fire," the hostess said, then laughed at her own joke before she went to set tables.

Nyssa leaned on the bar. "Do you know who any of them are in real life?"

"Well, the one who introduced himself the first time was Theo Stephens, but he's the one who's missing along with Mel." Murray flicked an apprehensive glance at the wall being faced with steel. "He didn't tell me the names of the others who showed up with him later." He gave Nyssa a look. "The ones who went through the portal."

"But there were three different ones who came on Halloween," Nyssa reminded him.

Murray nodded agreement again, then counted them off on his fingers. "Drake Stephanos, Arach Knight and Balthasar Marino.

Stephanos lives in Virginia but I don't know about the other two." He folded his arms across his chest and looked stubborn. "And I don't know how to get a hold of them either."

Lila wasn't sure about that. His attitude made her suspect that he knew more than he was prepared to tell. "What about the ones who went into Fae?" she asked. "Did they get out again?"

"That was the thing," Murray conceded with reluctance. "On Halloween, Drake figured out that they were still alive, and went to find out more." He drummed his fingers on the bar. "He read their names out of the book, but I don't remember what they were."

Nyssa sighed.

"The book?" Lila asked.

Nyssa looked left and right, then whispered. "*Her* book of beasts. It's an inventory. Or a To Do list, depending how you look at it." She grimaced then shivered. "We're both there."

Lila grimaced. She knew the Dark Queen intended to eliminate all of the Others, but not that there was a list of outstanding creatures to annihilate.

It was so easy to despise Maeve.

The dwarf cleared his throat. "There were more who were added to the list. Seven, I think. They figured out that the book updates itself and that Maeve was trapped in Fae." Murray mused for a second then snapped his fingers. "But another one called yesterday and left a message, saying they were okay but didn't know any more about Mel yet." Murray tapped a finger on the glossy black bar. "He had a Scottish accent."

Not her shifter.

"That doesn't narrow it down much, Murray," Nyssa said, then pointed at Lila. "My sister has a Scottish accent."

"Right." Murray went around the bar and picked up the receiver on the phone there. He punched in a code and Lila guessed that he was going to access the message in the voice mail. He tapped a code again, then put it on speaker.

The man did indeed have a Scottish accent. "Hi, Murray. This is Alasdair MacEwan. We met briefly on the night of October 28th. You might recall my friends leaving...rather abruptly with your bartender." Lila smiled that he didn't specify their destination. He cleared his throat before continuing. "I wanted to let you know that all but one of them are safely home. We're still trying to get in touch with Theo, and I hope that he's with your bartender. I'll stop by on Monday to bring you up to date on what we know." He paused. "We all hope they're both okay."

Her dragon wasn't trapped in Fae. Lila was relieved.

"He didn't leave a number," Nyssa said with disappointment.

"I didn't need him to," Murray said. "It's displayed right here. He was calling from some fancy restaurant down in Tribeca. Everyman Epicure." He grimaced. "Sounds like one of those snotty places where you get a quail egg, a lettuce leaf and a raspberry on a huge plate for twenty bucks." He widened his eyes and nodded, as if trusting them with a secret. "It's organic, though." Then he frowned and shook his head. "I guess you can come back on Monday to find out more."

Nyssa was already looking up the restaurant on her phone. Lila would have done the same if hers hadn't turned into an expensive paperweight as soon as she'd entered U.S. airspace. She traveled so seldom that she hadn't thought to buy a connection package. Nyssa turned the phone to show the website for the restaurant, which featured one hot chef with his arms folded across his chest looking straight out at the viewer.

Lila caught her breath and smiled. She would have recognized her dragon shifter anywhere.

"That's one of them," Murray said. "He went through that wall into Fae."

"So, he's one of the ones who came back?" Lila demanded and Murray shrugged agreement.

The chances of success had definitely improved.

"Didn't you say you were hungry?" she asked Nyssa.

"Starving," she agreed.

Lila wasn't hungry for a quail egg or even a lettuce leaf. She wanted fiery hot dragon and she wanted him all night long.

"Then let's go," she said, looping her arm through Nyssa's. "I'm buying."

"Thanks, Murray!" Nyssa called as they headed out the door.

The *Pyr* gathered in the clearing between Kristofer's house and his barn. Kristofer's parcel of land was shaped like a great broad bowl, with the house at the very bottom. They were surrounded by fields dusted in fresh snow and a mixed forest that rose to the summit of the surrounding hills. A long winding drive led through the forest from the secondary highway a good distance away. A lively stream splashed down from the north, cutting a path through the fields, then continuing alongside the drive. It also ran through the closest town, and had been used to drive the mill there for over a hundred years. The sun was setting: the sky was streaked with orange in the west, and Rhys could already see the stars in the darker eastern sky. Except for the line of parked trucks and cars, they could have been in another time.

It certainly seemed like a scene from another era when Quinn, the Smith of the *Pyr*, shifted shape. He stood beside the jeweler's forge he had brought with him, blew the flames so they danced higher and sent sparks into the darkening sky. He shimmered blue around his perimeter, then shifted to his dragon form, rearing back and breathing a plume of dragonfire into the sky in a celebratory gesture. Quinn was sapphire and steel in his dragon form and the firelight was reflected in his scales like a constellation of flickering orange stars. His mate, Sara, had come with him, along with their five sons, and Rhys noticed how closely the eldest, Garrett, watched his father.

He would be the next Smith.

Kristofer shifted shape next, becoming a sleek dragon of peridot and gold. There was a new ruddiness behind his scales, a burgundy hue that had never been there before and that made his scales look more brilliantly green. He was missing a scale on his lower chest and the skin was exposed there. He coiled his tail around Bree protectively as he faced Quinn and she smiled up at him.

Drake was there with Ronnie and her two sons: the older one, Timmy, was by her first husband and the younger son, Eric, was the result of her firestorm with Drake. Drake had been the leader of the Dragon Legion and was considered by Rhys and his fellows to be their primary commander. They'd worked together to defend Drake's mate, Veronica, during their firestorm, as well as her son Timmy. Timmy had to be fifteen by now, Rhys thought, noting how tall the boy had grown. Drake shimmered blue around his perimeter, a precursor to the change, then shifted into an obsidian dragon of great power. Rhys saw Veronica run an admiring hand over him before he stepped toward Kristofer and Quinn, his eyes glinting with pride.

The leader of the *Pyr*, Erik Sorensson, shifted shape next. He'd come alone, leaving his wife and daughter in Chicago. Rhys admired Erik, seeing him as a kindred spirit in many ways. Erik was pragmatic and decisive, even though he had the gift of foresight. In his human form, he was wiry and tall, his dark hair touched with silver at the temples, with a British accent that became more crisp when he was annoyed. In his dragon form, he was onyx and pewter, and fearsome. He, too, breathed dragonfire at the sky, his green eyes flashing as he surveyed their surroundings for potential predators or observers. He began to breathe a protective barrier of dragonsmoke and it glittered as it unfurled.

The five *Pyr* who were closest to Kristofer shifted shape next and did so in unison. The blue shimmer of their pending transformation was blinding in its brilliance. Alasdair became a dragon of hematite and silver while Hadrian was emerald and silver in his dragon form. Arach was dazzling as a dragon scaled in aquamarine and silver. Balthasar's dragon form was citrine and gold. Rhys himself summoned the change and roared with satisfaction as he took his dragon form, proud of his garnet and silver scales.

Last of all the *Pyr* who shifted shape was Rafferty, who had been Kristofer's mentor. That blue shimmer flashed and Rafferty became a massive dragon scaled in opal and gold, one that moved with deliberation and power. His mate, Melissa, looked on with pride. Their adopted daughter, Isabelle, had remained in school in England and Rhys didn't doubt there'd been an argument about that.

Kade was conspicuously missing, although no one mentioned it. He'd been the one to provide the stylus that opened the portal to Fae, and Rhys knew he wasn't alone in thinking that the danger they'd recently escaped had been partly Kade's fault. Kade had left the *Pyr* when compelled to surrender the stylus and hadn't contacted them since.

Ten dragons gathered in a circle as Quinn coaxed his forge to burn hotter and brighter. Without discussing the matter, the younger *Pyr* left a space for Theo, the descendant of Drake and their informal leader, who hadn't been seen since he'd stepped through the portal to Fae.

"How shall the scale be repaired?" Quinn demanded. He had a scale in his talons and heated it in the fire of the forge. It was made of gold and heated to brilliant yellow as he turned it in the flames.

"With this," Bree stepped forward and offered two black feathers. They gleamed in the light of the forge, touched with blue and purple iridescence. "One from Huginn and one from Muginn," she added as Quinn accepted them.

"Foresight and memory," Kristofer supplied.

"A gift evoking the element of air," Quinn said. He heated the scale until it glowed white, then pressed one feather into it at an angle. The feather was immediately incinerated, but the shape of it was left in the gold. He did the same with the second feather, creating a relief of the crossed feathers in the scale. He raised the scale and exhaled dragonfire on it. Kristofer reared back, exposing the space where the scale was missing, and Quinn pressed the replacement into position.

Rhys winced at the smell of burning flesh and the wisp of smoke that rose from the spot. He saw Kristofer tip back his head and bare his teeth at the pain.

"Air," the *Pyr* and their mates said as one.

Bree leaned forward and blew on the new scale. It made sense to Rhys that a former Valkyrie brought the quality of air to her union with a dragon shifter. She had been able to fly. She was intuitive. She understood magick and spells—which was a good reason to steer clear of her, in Rhys' view—and she had given the feathers to heal Kristofer's armor.

"Earth," intoned Rafferty, the other *Pyr* joining him, and Quinn tapped the scale with a stone from Kristofer's land. The signs of Kristofer's affinity with the earth were all around them, both in his practicality—an expression of that affinity which Rhys shared—and his work as a stone mason.

"Water," was the next cry and Bree caught her breath. As Kristofer looked down at her with obvious pride, she lifted a tear from each of her cheeks with her fingertips and dropped them on the new scale. They sizzled and the scale glowed brighter for a moment. "I'm sorry you lost a scale for me and have to endure this," she whispered, but Rhys heard her words clearly.

"I'm not," Kristofer said, his tail curling a little more tightly around her.

"Fire!" was the final cry and all of the *Pyr* breathed dragonfire into the night sky, including Kristofer. The fire in the forge leaped high as if it couldn't have done otherwise and the very night seemed to be ablaze.

Drake raised his claws. "On this night, we repair the armor of our fellow dragon warrior, but we also form a new union to join forces with the Others in the battle against the Dark Queen. Our fate, indeed our very survival, and that of many other kinds, hangs in the balance and we cannot honorably stand aside."

"DragonFate," Hadrian cried. "We will defend the treasures of the earth and the future."

"DragonFate," Drake agreed. "I ask for a core group to take command, although all the *Pyr* will be at this quest's disposal."

Hadrian, Kristofer, Alasdair, Balthasar, Arach and Rhys stepped forward. Their movement sent a thunder through the land, as if even the earth approved.

"No matter what it takes, we'll bring Theo back." Rhys said. He wasn't looking forward to entering Fae again, but he would do what had to be done. There was no telling what Theo was suffering.

"Leave no dragon behind," Timmy said with a smile and his mom hugged him close.

Drake smiled down at his adopted son. "It is a universal desire amongst those who go to war and a noble impulse." He nodded at the *Pyr* volunteers, as did Erik. "Your offer is accepted."

"Know that we can be summoned with a word," Erik added.

"The DragonFate Warriors!" Hadrian cried and the six of them took flight together. They flew in a tight triumphant circle overhead as the stars brightened overhead.

"I will return to Fae," Rhys vowed and Kristofer tossed him Kade's stylus. He snatched it out of the air.

"I will be your second," Hadrian said. "We know the peril and the price."

"I will interrogate the Others," Alasdair said.

"We will hunt the ancient dragon prince, Embron," Balthasar said.

"We will send him to join his dead brother, Blazion," Arach added.

"Then it's left to me to defend the gem of the hoard," Kristofer said.

At least it wasn't fused onto his scale.

"We will remain with you," Erik said and Quinn nodded agreement.

The DragonFate team roared together and breathed another torrent of dragonfire, before landing again. The *Pyr* all shifted shape at once in a flash of shimmering blue, then shook hands all around. Kristofer kissed Bree then the others clapped him on the back. There was a celebratory rumble, then Quinn's son Garrett raised his voice.

"Is anyone else hungry?" he asked and they all looked at Rhys expectantly.

"I've got this covered," Rhys said and they laughed together.

Rafferty inhaled sharply, his bright gaze darting to Rhys. "Has anyone felt a firestorm spark?"

"Maybe it was ours," Kristofer said, drawing Bree against his side. She smiled up at him and another moment passed, although Rafferty looked thoughtful. Rhys felt a stronger simmer of fire in his veins, as if his destined mate was closer, but headed for the kitchen to disguise the golden glow.

Maybe Maeve had turned up the power on her spell.

Either way, Rhys decided that he wouldn't stay the night.

CHAPTER TWO

ila couldn't believe it. Saturday night and the restaurant was packed, yet she didn't think her dragon shifter was there. If she'd been the owner of Everyman Epicure, she would have been watching over everything on what had to be one of their busiest nights of the week. When they approached the restaurant, though, that flame around her fingertips hadn't gotten any brighter and the heat in her veins hadn't simmered any hotter.

He wasn't there. She refused to be disappointed. It would be easier to leave afterward if they had nothing in common except mutual attraction.

She might have left immediately, but Nyssa got in the line.

"I don't think he's here," Lila said.

"I think we should check to be sure."

Lila shook her head. "I already know."

Nyssa sighed. "I'm still hungry, and you promised me dinner. It's busy so it has to be good. Besides I want the whole story as well as a great meal."

"Not too demanding," Lila teased.

"Where *did* you meet?"

Lila hadn't decided whether to tell Nyssa about the firestorm or not. She nodded at the wall behind the hostess station and changed the subject. "Think he's worth waiting for?"

There was a huge image of her dragon on the wall, the same picture as was on the website. The image was more imposing when it filled an entire wall. He was dressed in his chef's whites, his sleeves rolled up to reveal powerful forearms, arms folded over his chest. He looked decisive. He was staring straight out at the viewer with those gorgeous dark eyes, almost as intense in the image as he'd been in real life, and the barest smile lifted one corner of that deliciously firm mouth.

"Hot," Nyssa said, then giggled. "Definitely worth a transatlantic flight."

"If we can find him."

There was a slogan on the sign, too:

Enjoy the best of the best at Everyman Epicure.
You have my guarantee on every bite.
—Rhys Lewis, owner and chef.

"Modesty isn't a problem, then," Nyssa said and Lila laughed.

"No, he didn't seem to suffer from a lack of confidence," she agreed, then dropped her voice to a whisper. "Maybe it's a dragon thing."

"So you did meet him in person?"

Lila nodded. "I kissed him. Well, he kissed me first and I kissed him back."

"Good?"

"What do you think?"

"I think it must have been amazing to have brought you so far. There's no shortage of hotties in Scotland."

"Ha ha."

There was a line of people waiting for tables, but Nyssa turned on the charm and they were soon ushered to a table. The hostess removed a *Reserved* sign from it before putting down the menus and gesturing to the table with a smile. She had a lovely yellow aura which matched her cheerful competence.

"You really shouldn't do that," Lila chided. She hated using her powers to influence situations, unless it really mattered. Nyssa had never shared that view.

"Oh, I'm sorry. I didn't realize you wanted to stand in line for an hour. You said you were hungry, too." Nyssa opened her menu, unapologetic. "Besides, I need to stay in practice." She looked over her menu at Lila. "That's your problem. You never practice, so you can't charm when you need to."

"Not a lot of candidates on North Rona."

"You might be wishing you'd kept in practice when you meet your dragon. He looks a bit stubborn, maybe even fixed in his ways."

Lila didn't reply. It had been so long since she'd charmed anyone that she wasn't even sure she could do it anymore. She was hoping the firestorm would make her irresistible by itself, but she didn't know much about it.

"Well?" Nyssa asked. "Do you see him?"

"I still don't think he's here."

It felt good to sit down and the little patter of water from the fountain by the door was particularly soothing. People would probably notice if she jumped right in, though. Lila was already feeling a bit parched from being out of the water for so long.

She surveyed the restaurant, wondering how much of the design Rhys had done. She'd guess a lot. He seemed like someone who liked to manage all the details. So much earthy pragmatism.

Rhys. She liked his name.

They'd passed an outdoor patio on their way in, fenced off from the street with a railing. There were window boxes of herbs and flowers all around the perimeter of the patio, obviously pampered since they were still in bloom this late in the year. She'd guess the plants had been changed with the season, as the planters were thick with blooming chrysanthemums. There was a roof over half of the patio, and wooden tables with steel chairs. The street and busy traffic seemed very distant, so just approaching the restaurant gave the sense that you'd found a haven.

The interior was a big square, with that patio outside the wall that led to the street. The kitchen was at the back: the wall was open to display it and the people at work there. The dining room had Saltillo tile floors, and a long bar of dark wood with stools on one side. There were exposed wooden beams overhead and red brick walls on either side. The palette was earthy, and it was both welcoming and cozy. Lila thought they might have been invited into a dragon's lair. The food smelled wonderful. There was a chalkboard beside them on the one long wall with the specials written on it. The restaurant was packed but not as noisy as Lila expected. She realized the ceiling was covered with cork to absorb the sound and the sound of that fountain definitely helped.

Their waiter was young and handsome, a cheerful foodie in his twenties. He had a healthy radiant pink aura and the easy manners to match. He introduced himself and Nyssa soon charmed him into revealing that the chef was away for the weekend. Ryan admitted this was very unusual, that Chef was always in every day. He recommended the special and two other options then went to get their drinks.

Lila knew for sure then that her dragon wasn't still in Fae. That was good news. And she'd been right about him wanting to manage every little detail. Lila had a similar fondness for staying on top of everything, and she always had a plan when she had to be absent. There had to be an easy way for the staff to contact Rhys, and she could guess what that might be.

"Plan B?" Nyssa asked but Lila was already on her feet.

She went to the end of the bar where she'd noticed there was a phone. Time to try that charm factor. The bartender came to her with a smile, another handsome guy in his twenties. His aura was orange, tinged with some of the confidence that Rhys shared.

"I'm so sorry," she said. "I changed my mind about the kind of wine I'd like and Ryan has already put in the order."

"That's no trouble. What would you prefer instead of the Chardonnay?" He put the glass aside, because he'd already poured it. "We have a nice Pinot Grigio by the glass, or a Semillon Blanc..."

As he reviewed the wines, Lila leaned over the counter as if trying to see the labels on the bottles. Actually, she was reading the labels on the phone for the programmed numbers.

Rhys' Cell was the first one.

Perfect.

She realized the bartender was waiting for her reply. "I had something wonderful recently but I forget the name of it. It was kind of grapefruity."

"A Gewürstraminer," he said with assurance. "That's really popular in the summer. Good match with fish but also with turkey." He bent and surveyed the bottles. "I'll have to get one from the cellar. It'll just take a moment."

"Thank you!" As soon as he left, Lila reached across the counter, lifted the receiver off the hook and pressed the first button. She could hear it ringing somewhere and hoped Rhys answered before the bartender returned.

"Rhys Lewis," a familiar deep voice replied. Lila smiled at the sound. Rhys' voice sharpened. "Hello? What's wrong? What's happened? Justin? Alexandra?"

"Neither," Lila said softly. "It's Lila Isbister." She thought she saw a little spark dance out of the receiver.

There was a moment of dead silence. "Do I know you?" he asked warily and she knew he'd recognized her accent, if not her voice.

"I was hoping you'd tell me more about the firestorm. It sounded intriguing, and this little spark has become a bit distracting. Maybe we should do something about it."

He caught his breath. "You can't be there. Not now."

"But I am. I came looking for you since you didn't come looking for me."

He made a little growl of frustration and Lila felt a simmering heat.

"I thought this mark of destiny was supposed to be irresistible," she said.

"If it's real," Rhys snapped and Lila understood his concern. "This is the house phone," he informed her tersely just as the bartender returned. The bartender's eyes widened when he saw Lila on the phone. "You can't use it for personal calls. It's my rule and I follow it, too."

"Then call me back," she said, and gave him the number for Nyssa's phone. She hung up then, hoping he had a good memory. "It rang," she said to the bartender with a smile, charming with everything she had. "I didn't know what to do so I answered, but it was a wrong number. Someone wanting Chinese food delivery." She shrugged and to her relief, her charm seemed to hold up.

"We get wrong numbers all the time," the bartender said easily, then uncorked the bottle. He poured a little into a glass and presented it to her. "Is this what you meant?"

Lila sniffed the bouquet, then took a little taste, rolling the wine around in her mouth. It was what she'd meant, but she would have taken this glass either way. "Oh, that's wonderful! Thank you so much."

He showed her the label. "I'll change it on your tab, in case you want a second glass. Leave the glass here and Ryan can bring it to your table."

"Thank you so much." Lila returned to the table with a bounce in her step.

Nyssa smiled. "Mission accomplished?" she asked just as her phone rang. She glanced at the call display, then laughed and offered the phone. "This would be for you."

"Yes. It would be." Lila took the phone. "I do like men with good memories."

"You'd have to expect that from a dragon shifter," Nyssa said lightly.

"Don't say that!" Rhys hissed, obviously having heard Nyssa.

"It's only the truth," Lila protested, realizing that he kept his powers secret in human society. They had that in common, probably for similar reasons.

"What the hell are you doing in my restaurant anyway?"

"Having dinner." Lila met Nyssa's gaze. Her sister smiled. "But really, I'm looking for you. Isn't that what I was supposed to do?"

"No!"

"I thought we could satisfy this firestorm of yours."

"I'm not sure that's such a good idea."

"Then you shouldn't have kissed me," Lila replied. "That kiss was an invitation if ever I've had one. It was a particularly tempting invitation, actually."

He made a little incoherent sound of frustration. "It was good," he acknowledged, sounding grumpy. "But I'm in Vermont!"

"Ooops," Lila said.

"Lila Isbister," he said. "Is that really your name?"

"Actually, it's Dr. Lila Isbister, of the North Rona Research Project based in Kirkwall, Orkney, Scotland."

"Call display says the phone belongs to Nyssa Macleod."

"I'm stealing my sister's cell phone because it works in New York while mine doesn't. I'd like to pick up where we left off, Rhys Lewis, and I've come a long way for that very purpose. How soon will you be back?"

He sputtered. "You can't expect me to come back to New York, just to seduce you..."

"Why not? I've come all the way from Scotland just to seduce you." Nyssa laughed at that. Lila hoped Rhys didn't have an issue with women who were direct. She always thought honesty was the best policy, plus it saved a lot of time. "I very seldom leave my research, you know, but this firestorm was the proverbial offer I couldn't refuse."

"It's a once-in-a-lifetime opportunity," he acknowledged. "If it's real."

"You said that before. How could it possibly be faked?"

"By magick." He spat the words, so they had a distrust of that in common. "I can't talk to you about this now."

"You're suspicious," Lila said. "What did *she* demand to let you return?"

He inhaled sharply. "I don't know what you're talking about."

"She was coming when we were on the beach. She was targeting us, maybe because of the firestorm. I got away. Did you?"

Rhys made a choking sound instead of answering.

"So, you're afraid I was involved, that maybe I lured her closer. But then you went into Fae by your own choice."

"Don't talk about it!"

Lila had a thought. "Which happened first?"

"Look," he said flatly. "I don't know your plan or your motivation. I don't trust you because of the timing of our meeting, and so I don't trust this apparent firestorm. Why don't you leave my restaurant and go back where you came from?"

Lila realized they were both inclined to be forthright. "That makes three things we have in common," she said. "You speak your mind, just like I do. You distrust magick, just like I do. You hide your nature from humans, just like I do. For a phone date, I think it's starting off well, don't you?"

Rhys growled with an annoyance that he apparently couldn't articulate.

Maybe the firestorm was messing with his sleep as much as it was with hers. She felt encouraged, even though it looked like their firestorm needed some healing before it could start. "Here's some honesty for you. I had nothing to do with her appearance on that beach," she said. "I thought maybe you'd summoned her."

"I would never..."

"It was incredibly brave that you entered her realm with your friend and I admire that. I'm glad you got out of there."

He inhaled sharply. "We have each other's backs," he said gruffly.

"That must be a wonderful thing," Lila said, even though she didn't know anything similar. She took care of the seals, but she wouldn't have said that anyone she knew would risk their own welfare to defend her.

Rhys wasn't talking but he hadn't hung up.

Lila would take progress where she found it. "The menu is enormous," she said, changing the subject. "What do you recommend?"

"Everything," he said with conviction. "It wouldn't be on the menu otherwise."

"Good. At least I know where to collect on that guarantee. I hope to see you soon, Rhys Lewis. You know where to find me." She ended the call and added his phone number to Nyssa's contact list. She checked the time, wanting to track just how long it took him to call back, then picked up the menu.

"Seared tuna?" she asked Nyssa. "Or poached halibut?"

"I can't decide between them either," Nyssa admitted.

"You get one and I'll get the other so we can share," Lila suggested.

"I want dessert," Nyssa said. "A reward for tracking down your elusive dragon."

"I don't think he's that elusive, but I want dessert, too. It's the first time we've been together in ages. Let's celebrate." They toasted each other just as Ryan brought the salads, then dug in.

Of course, it was delicious. Lila hadn't expected anything less.

Rhys stared at his phone.

The selkie who might be his destined mate was in his restaurant. She'd used the house phone to let him know. And she'd come to consummate the firestorm. Part of him was thrilled and desperate to return to the city before she changed her mind. The other part of him was deeply suspicious. She'd traveled all the way from Scotland on a whim? She'd tracked him down to his restaurant?

He felt targeted. Stalked.

Again.

They'd finished dinner and cleaned up by the time she'd called, and Kristofer had lit a bonfire in his fire pit. The *Pyr* and their families in attendance were sitting around it, and Quinn's boys were roasting marshmallows under Timmy's supervision. The air was cold and the stars had come out. Rhys had been watching the sparks shoot from the fire into the sky before his phone rang and shook his world.

His phone still sizzled in his hand, like the firestorm had followed even an electronic connection between them. How much did Lila know about Fae? What were her alliances—or those of her kind?

Dr. Lila Isbister. Well, he had a name and a WiFi connection. A quick search turned up a c.v. with a picture, proof that the researcher was his selkie. He'd never forget those eyes and that alluring smile—in fact, he'd recognized her voice immediately, and not just because of her accent. His heart was pounding and he was filled with rare anticipation, even though she was miles away and the firestorm was still only a very faint glow.

He wanted so much for it to be genuine.

"Something wrong?" Alasdair asked, obviously having noticed the change in his expression. He inhaled and his eyes glittered a bit, as if he'd caught a whiff of the firestorm.

"A bit of a crisis at the restaurant," Rhys said, disliking that he wasn't sharing all of the truth. He knew that if he told his fellow *Pyr* that his destined mate was in New York, in his restaurant, they'd be determined to help. Rhys didn't want to endanger them until he knew for sure that it was the real thing.

Rafferty joined them then, closing his eyes and taking a deep breath of the evening air. "Again, I feel like a firestorm has sparked," he said, then gave Rhys an intent look. "You were glowing while on that call."

"Just angry," Rhys said with a smile. "I hate when things happen at the restaurant and I'm not there to sort them out."

Rafferty's eyes narrowed slightly and Rhys knew the older *Pyr* wasn't convinced.

"I'll see if I can fix it over the phone," Rhys said before Rafferty could ask more questions. He walked into the dark pasture and called Lila, well aware that both Alasdair and Rafferty were watching him. He walked further, and resolved to keep his voice very low in the hope that they wouldn't be able to overhear.

It was a long shot.

Lila answered on the first ring. "I like a man with resolve," she said lightly. "And I love that you can cook. This salad is fantastic, everything in perfect balance. Kudos to you and your team."

Rhys felt his reserve melting under a bit of flattery. "Thank you."

"Although," she said with a sensual sigh. "I was looking forward to collecting on that guarantee."

Rhys had to close his eyes as a tide of desire swept through him. That voice. She could read the phone book to him and he'd be enthralled. "What did you order for a main?"

"Why?"

"Because I can tell a lot about someone by their menu choices."

She laughed. "Just as I can tell a lot about you by this restaurant."

"Like what?"

"It's organized. Even in your absence, the staff know exactly what to do when. That also means you're a fair boss and a good one, with reasonable expectations, and also that they're well compensated. They do as you want even when you're not here. It's clean, really clean, and very welcoming. Everything has its place, which tells me that you're orderly, and the dishes are both attractive and delicious. They're nutritionally balanced, too. That means you appreciate what's around you and make the most of each ingredient. I suspect that means you pay close attentions to the details, and I find that a very good trait in the bedroom. How am I doing so far?"

Rhys felt a stab of heat at her mention of the bedroom. "It would sound vain if I said you were doing well."

"You might be humble but you don't have a lack of confidence."

"I know how things should be."

"You have a strong affinity to the earth," she said, startling him with the accuracy of her guess. "Shown by your pragmatism and practicality, your focus on sensation, your ability to make this restaurant seem like a safe haven. I'll bet people linger over their desserts and coffees, reluctant to have to face the real world again."

Rhys didn't know what to say because it was true.

"And fire, because there's passion in this place, in both details and the little bit of unexpected in each dish. You're nurturing and protective, which seems like an excellent trait for a dragon shifter, probably noble, too."

"Don't say that out loud," he warned again. "We stay hidden. We have a Covenant."

"And you like to follow the rules," she continued. "What's the Covenant?"

"A pledge we take, to not reveal ourselves in both forms to any humans outside our immediate circle."

"Does a destined mate count?

"A real one does."

"And that's the root of the problem, isn't it? You're not sure of my objectives, even though the sex is going to be amazing—provided we ever get to it. When are you coming back to the city? I'm not sure I can stand this much longer."

She mused for a minute as Rhys kept silent, his gut clenching at her easy manner. She knew too much.

"What did she demand of you in exchange for your release?"

Rhys' heart stopped for a second. "Nothing. We escaped," he admitted tightly.

"Then that's not the issue. Is it me?" she asked, her tone indicating that she wouldn't be surprised or offended if that was the case. "Am I breaking the rules? Is it your role to swoop down and carry me off as your prize? Are you having a problem with me seeking you out instead of the other way around? Because I should warn you that I'm not very good at being a damsel in distress."

"That's not it. The firestorm is supposed to be a sign that one of my kind has met his destined mate, which is the woman who can bear his child when the firestorm is consummated." He heard her think about that.

"There will be a child?"

"Always."

"Always," she echoed.

Rhys continued. "Many of my friends believe that mate is also his perfect partner, and that her skills complement his."

"If you're worried about custody, don't be. If there's a child, it's all yours."

He was stunned by her attitude. "Excuse me?"

"I'm not a very maternal type. I work a lot and my nurturing energies are maxed out already. No time in my life for kids." She dropped her voice to chide him. "There's nothing wrong with admitting our strengths and weaknesses, Rhys. I believe in honesty."

He nodded once, her words adding to his suspicions. "Okay, I'll be honest in return."

"Please do."

"I had my doubts that this was a real firestorm and now I know for sure. You can't possibly be the mate for me."

"Why don't you come back to the city and we'll find out?"

"It's a long drive and it's already late."

"That's an excuse," she charged. "Be honest, Rhys."

"I don't think that a woman who would surrender a child so easily could possibly be my destined mate," he said, surprising himself with the confession. "I want a family."

"I don't," she said. "I came for sex. I don't see any problem with our having different long-term objectives."

"I do. There isn't going to be any sex."

"Are you afraid?" she asked in a wicked whisper. "That doesn't sound like a dragon choice."

"Don't say that!"

She continued as if he hadn't spoken, but Rhys hadn't expected otherwise. She seemed to like breaking rules, which was more proof that they didn't belong together. "What's the worst case scenario? We have a wonderful night, it's not a real firestorm, I go home, and you keep waiting for your destined mate. Or we have a wonderful night, it *is* a real firestorm, there's a child, I go home and nine months from now, you take custody of your child. Neither sounds very dire, Rhys."

But that wasn't the worst case scenario. The worst possibility was Rhys was deceived by a fake firestorm, just as Kristofer had been, and that he could imperil his fellow *Pyr*. Before he could decide whether he wanted to confide that in Lila, she made a little coo of delight.

"Score on the poached halibut," she said with pleasure and Rhys felt a surge of pride. "What a beautiful presentation." It was one of their signature dishes and he was particularly proud of it. "Oh!" she said with enthusiasm. "Oh! This is fabulous, possibly the best ever. What did you do to the beans?"

Rhys smiled. "I'll never tell."

She laughed, a seductive sound that almost made him forget his reservations. "Maybe I'll have to work it out of you," she threatened. "I've been known to be very persuasive."

"About beans?"

"About learning anything I really want to know. Charming even."

Someone laughed at that, a woman. Maybe Lila was with a friend.

Rhys frowned as he heard the waiter's voice. "Something special for you from Chef, miss." It was Ryan.

"Are you trying to get me drunk before you get here?" Lila asked Rhys, so it must have been a drink. "Oh, that is sweet." Maybe a cocktail.

"It's called a Firestorm," Ryan explained. "I didn't even know we served them here."

They didn't serve a cocktail called the Firestorm. "Where did that come from?" Rhys demanded.

"The bar, silly," Lila said and audibly sipped.

"The secret menu," that other woman said, laughter in her voice.

"Maybe," Ryan conceded with a laugh.

"It's powerful but so delicious. Wow." Lila audibly took another drink. "Maybe you're mad, bad and dangerous to know, Rhys Lewis."

"That was someone else," her companion said. "Let me taste it since we're sharing."

"But I didn't order anything for you," Rhys protested. He had a sense that things were slipping from his control and he didn't like it one bit. He wanted to be back in his restaurant immediately. He was too far away and something was going wrong.

Too bad he couldn't spontaneously manifest elsewhere, as Rafferty could.

"Of course, you did," Lila argued. "No need to be shy since Ryan already spilled the truth. Give it back, Nyssa!"

The other woman laughed. "It's irresistible."

"Just like my dragon shifter," Lila said.

"Don't say that!" Rhys complained, his voice rising in frustration.

"Oh, Ryan's gone. Don't worry," Lila chided and sipped again. "Looks like the firestorm is a multi-faceted adventure." Her words slurred and Rhys' attention sharpened. "This is really strong," she said, each word obviously requiring an effort to enunciate. "You are trying to get me wasted."

"We don't have a drink called a Firestorm," Rhys repeated, just as he heard the phone clatter to the table. It might have even fallen to the floor. He heard running feet, then the call was ended.

What had just happened?

He called back but was immediately directed to the voice mail of Nyssa Macleod. He recognized her voice as that of Lila's companion. He left a message, having no confidence that his call would be returned, then called again.

A man answered, a man with a deep voice that gave him shivers.

"I have your mate," he said, speaking with precision and authority. "I will trade her for the gem of the hoard. No more and no less."

Rhys was horrified. "But who are you? Where are you?"

"You have one solar day, beginning now," the man said instead of answering Rhys' questions.

Rhys heard a crushing sound, then the line went dead. He called again, and once more was directed to voice mail. He called the restaurant and asked to speak to Ryan. "What happened to the woman with the Scottish accent?" he asked, hearing his own desperation. "You brought her a drink."

"You sent her a drink."

"I did not!"

"Justin said you called and ordered it. It was really something. Even the guy at the bar commented on how impressive it was, all orange and red." His tone turned accusing. "If we're going to serve it, it should be on the menu. I could have sold six of them while taking it to her table."

"It's not on the menu because we don't serve it. I don't even know what was in it."

"How can that be?" Ryan asked.

"What happened to her?" Rhys demanded.

"She got sick," Ryan said. "Her friend was helping her and then the guy from the bar came to help. He said he'd take them both home." He paused. "It was kind of weird. And Justin kept repeating whatever the guy said."

Chills ran down Rhys' spine. His bartender had been beguiled. "What did this guy look like?" he asked.

"Tall. Good looking in an intense kind of way. Well-dressed. Hey, I've got mains to serve," Ryan said as the bell rang from the kitchen. Rhys could hear that the restaurant was busy. "There's got to be an image on the security camera, though."

"Ask Alexandra to send it to me as soon as she can," Rhys ordered, referring to the hostess who had been working for him the longest of any of the staff and was absolutely reliable. "Tell Justin I want to talk to him. And get those mains out before they're cold."

"Yes, sir. Hope you're having a good break, sir."

Then Ryan was gone and Rhys was alone in the meadow, staring at his phone.

A good break. As if.

Was it a trap? What if Lila wasn't his mate? What if she was? Had she been abducted or was she complicit with the guy at the bar?

Could he ignore what had just happened and live with himself?

No. No matter who she was, his mate or a treasure of the earth to be defended, Rhys had to help her. She'd been captured because of him, and he had to fix it.

All he needed was the gem of the hoard.

Nyssa picked up the shattered pieces of her phone, even though she guessed there was no chance of repair. She'd seen the older man come into the restaurant and had sensed the fire in him. He'd ignored them, though, and gone to the bar, so she'd stopped watching him.

Big mistake.

Was he another dragon shifter? Was he allied with Rhys? She had no idea, but he'd definitely had a plan. She'd only taken the barest sip of that drink and was still feeling dizzy.

Lila had taken a big sip, then another. She'd trusted that it was from her dragon shifter, and maybe it had been. Either way, she'd obviously felt its effects right away.

Then the other man had reappeared, handsome and solicitous. Nyssa had thought then that he had to be an employee or Rhys' partner, given his dark suit and his scent of fire. She hadn't trusted him long, but it had been long enough.

He'd taken Lila so quickly that Nyssa knew it had been arranged in advance. The car had been idling at the curb, a big dark luxury sedan, and had disappeared into the traffic before Nyssa even stumbled to the curb.

Now, there was just the scattered contents of Lila's purse and Nyssa's own broken phone. Nyssa had picked up Lila's coat from the back of her chair and hugged it closer. At least Lila had her skin, because it hadn't been left behind. That meant she had a chance to fight back or maybe even escape. Nyssa spotted the battery for the phone and the microchip when she was picking up Lila's stuff. Maybe some whiz kid could get Rhys' number off it. One thing was for sure: she was never going to forget that guy's face.

Maybe someone at Bones would know who he was.

Or better yet, where to find him and Lila.

CHAPTER THREE

knew I'd sensed a firestorm," Alasdair murmured when Rhys had told the *Pyr* everything.

"I'm not sure it's real," Rhys said again.

"That's Embron," Rafferty said, tapping Rhys' phone. The image had come through from the security camera at the restaurant, and even though the man had been turning away, Rafferty clearly recognized him. "He came to my shop, wanting to buy the gem of the hoard."

"But you had it then," Kristofer said. "Why didn't he take it?"

"I lied. I told him it was sold." Rafferty smiled. "I implied that Maeve had acquired it."

If Embron had allied with Maeve, that couldn't be good news for anyone, to Rhys' thinking. He cleared his throat, but his fellow *Pyr* continued to talk about Embron as if Lila wasn't in danger. To his thinking, every moment counted and they needed to *move*.

"But Embron couldn't tell that you were dishonest with him, or that the amber wasn't there?" Erik asked.

Rafferty shook his head. "Apparently not."

"How curious," Erik mused.

"But that makes perfect sense," Bree said. "He didn't know that I threw a stone instead of the gem of the hoard. That was how we got away with it."

"And he didn't know you had it all those centuries," Kristofer added.

"So, he can't sense it," Erik said with an approving nod. "That's one thing in our favor."

"I don't care about the details," Rhys said, impatient with the discussion. "I need the gem of the hoard and I need it now."

That got Erik's attention. "You can't mean to surrender it to him!"

"He can have it, if that's what releases Lila."

"I thought you didn't believe she was your destined mate?" Rafferty asked softly, his eyes glowing.

Rhys flung out his hands. "Either way, she's a treasure of the earth to be defended, and you're all just standing around, talking. I need the gem and I need to find her, and I need to do it right now."

"I don't think I've ever heard you raise your voice like this," Hadrian commented.

"Well, if you all keep being so obstructionist, you'd better get used to it," Rhys snapped. He held out his hand. "Look. The sparks are flickering. She's in danger. What if he kills her?"

"If the firestorm's a spell, that could be part of it," Kristofer noted. "They could be trying to lure you in."

Drake spoke with measured calm. "They'll expect you to charge in immediately. Any trap set for you will rely upon that."

"Then what do you suggest? Abandoning her to Embron?" Rhys asked with exasperation. "I need to fly down there and locate her while we can..."

"You need to plan," Drake interrupted firmly. "We need to approach slowly and discern as much as possible about her situation before revealing ourselves."

Rhys' heart sank. "We're not going to fly down there."

"It's hardly subtle," Erik noted.

"It would mean a lot of beguiling to be done," Alasdair said with a shake of his head.

"But driving will take hours," Rhys protested. "Hours we don't have!"

"You said yourself that the might be a fake," Balthasar noted.

Rhys heaved a sigh. "What if she *is* my mate? What if Embron kills her?"

"He will not kill her until you come," Drake insisted. "The gem of the hoard is his objective, and she is his means to gaining it." He lifted a finger. "The true peril will be when he can grasp the gem of the hoard and perceives that she is no longer useful."

Ronnie caught her breath and averted her gaze. Rhys thought he saw her shiver, but Drake caught her hand within his own.

Quinn cleared his throat. He was standing with his arms folded across his chest, listening with a frown between his brows. "What exactly does this gem of the hoard do? Why does he want it?"

"It's supposed to control all magick, but I'm not sure why," Kristofer said. "Embron wanted it badly, though. He dove into the sea after it, then evidently sought out Rafferty to get it."

"But how did he even find Rafferty if he can't sense the gem?" Bree asked.

"He followed my scent, I'll guess," Rafferty said. "I was there after you brought him down." Bree and Kristofer nodded as one. They both looked a little spooked, and Rhys couldn't blame them. The plan to leave the gem of the hoard in their custody seemed like an even bigger invitation to trouble now. If Embron had followed Rafferty's scent, he could follow Kristofer's.

"All the more reason to give me the gem of the hoard," he said, but no one seemed to hear him.

"Do you think Embron found Maeve?" Alasdair asked.

"I thought she was trapped in Fae and all the portals were closed," Rhys said. The night felt colder and more filled with menace than it had just hours before. The last individual he wanted to see again was the Dark Queen who had compelled him to dance endlessly. His feet still had sores on them and he'd started to wonder whether they'd ever heal.

"I'm thinking he must have looked for her," Hadrian said. "Otherwise, he would have followed Kristofer's scent and ended up here already. He must have conferred with Maeve to have even found Lila."

"He followed her scent from the beach where the firestorm sparked," Rhys guessed. "I don't even know where it was."

"I'll bet Maeve did," Hadrian said. "We had gone through the portal at Bones, after all." Rhys met his gaze for a moment, and knew both of them were recalling that painful dance. "Either you met Lila in Fae, or you went through another portal to wherever she was."

"Maybe it was where she works," Kristofer suggested.

"Maybe. But where is she now? How do we find her and save her?" Arach asked.

"The firestorm," Rhys whispered, looking at the faint glow around his hands. "I should be able to track her."

"Even if it's not real, that might work," Kristofer noted.

"We might be able to follow his scent from the restaurant, too," Hadrian said.

"I think we should locate Lila and worry about Embron later," Rhys said with urgency.

"But you could be walking right into their trap," Balthasar said.

"I have to do it, though," Rhys said. "I can't abandon her, whether she's really in danger or whether she's under a spell."

They all nodded, none of them surprised.

"You can't go alone," Alasdair said.

"No." Erik's lips tightened into a grim line. "Give the gem of the hoard to him, Kristofer," he ordered softly. "There can be no feint that Embron will believe. The dragon prince will want to examine it before he releases his hostage. He won't be tricked again."

"And we can't trick him because we don't have magick," Arach said with some bitterness.

"No one has much anymore, because Embron has seized most of it," Bree noted as Kristofer went to his hoard to retrieve the stone. He returned and surrendered it to Rhys without comment. Bree frowned. "He must have chosen to release Maeve from Fae, in order to ally with her."

That hardly sounded like a good thing.

Rhys turned the gem of the hoard in his hand. He didn't like the feel of it, which said something. He had an affinity to the element of earth, just as Lila had guessed, and most stones felt welcome in his hand. Not this one. It was a piece of amber, not quite perfectly spherical, about the size of a tennis ball. Inside its golden depths, there was a spider in the act of killing a wasp, trapped in that deadly pose for all eternity. The amber was cold in Rhys' palm, cold enough to make him shiver.

"Too bad we don't know how to use it," Balthasar said.

"You won't master magick in that short of a time," Bree said. "Sorcerers train for centuries, eons even."

"Too bad we don't know one, then," Quinn said and Melissa gasped.

"But we do," she said to Rafferty. "That woman we met in Edinburgh said she was a witch. She knew Embron. Eithne was her name."

"But she's in Scotland," Hadrian protested.

"No," Melissa said. "She's from Manhattan. She went to Edinburgh to visit the old lair with Embron, but she must be home by now." She pulled out her phone and began scrolling through it. "She gave me her number."

"One solar day isn't a lot of time," Drake reminded them all softly. "We need a plan."

"I'm going after Lila," Rhys said.

"I'm going with you," Hadrian said.

"We're all going with you," Alasdair said. Arach and Balthasar nodded agreement. "Saving Lila has to trump our plans to find Theo."

"If Maeve is allied with Embron, finding Lila might lead us to Theo,"

Rhys said.

"I'll seek out Eithne with Melissa," Rafferty said. "She might know something of use."

"What about the book?" Drake asked. "We might need something to barter with Maeve."

"Arach and I will find the vampire, Sebastian, after we rescue Lila," Balthasar said. "Maybe we can convince him to part with it."

"Good luck with that," Kristofer said wryly.

"I might be able to beguile him," Arach mused. Rhys knew that Arach had apprenticed to Lorenzo, the illusionist and the best of the *Pyr* at beguiling.

"You might," he said, encouraged.

"I promised to stop at Bones on Monday," Alasdair said. "The Others might know more by then."

"We might know more by then if we get moving," Rhys said, trying to urge them along. "We need to drive back to the city now."

"Let's stick to our plan of staying here a few days longer," Erik said to Quinn and that *Pyr* nodded agreement.

"Absolutely," Quinn agreed. "If Embron comes after Kristofer, he and Bree shouldn't be alone." He reached out and took Sara's hand. "Who knows? We might have a prophecy soon, too. A firestorm has sparked, after all."

Sara nodded. She was the Seer of the *Pyr* and prophecies about firestorms often revealed themselves to her, or to Erik. "I'll do my best."

"We'll start by fortifying the dragonsmoke barrier immediately," the leader of the *Pyr* said. "If Embron has any kinship with our kind, he won't be able to cross it."

Rhys looked down at his hand and watched the light of the firestorm flicker, as if it might go out. He caught his breath and the others followed his gaze.

"She's in grave danger," Rafferty said.

"Or it's a lure," Kristofer said, folding his arms across his chest.

"Either way, I'm answering the summons." Rhys headed for his truck, pulling out his keys. "I'm driving," he said to Hadrian.

"No one is going to get in your way," that *Pyr* agreed.

"I will join you," Drake said. "I have a favor to you, Rhys, to repay." He shook hands with Rhys, then kissed Ronnie, advising her to remain at Kristofer's lair with the boys.

Meanwhile, Arach, Balthasar, Hadrian and Alasdair all rose to their feet. "Six against one," Alasdair said with satisfaction. "I like these odds."

Rhys was reassured to have so many dragons at his back. Embron was old and powerful, and might be allied with Maeve. Even so, he dared to be optimistic about their chances.

He just hoped they reached Lila in time.

A Firestorm.

Lila opened one eye and regretted her choice immediately. Even the shadowy light of her prison made her head pound. That drink should have been called an Atomic Bomb. It had hit her hard and fast. She'd only had a quarter of it, but its influence was impressive.

Maybe there'd been more in it than fruit juice and alcohol.

At that realization, Lila forced her eyes open and looked around. She was in a basement room, judging by the small high windows. They were made of glass blocks so there was no chance of opening one. The walls and floor were unfinished concrete but the ceiling had been finished with acoustic tiles. There was one lightbulb hanging from the ceiling at the far end of the room but it wasn't turned on. The light was coming through the window, which meant at least one night had passed.

She examined her hands, but the orange glow of the firestorm had faded to a glimmer. Rhys wasn't close, then.

Lila wasn't sure whether that was a good thing or not.

Her purse wasn't with her, of course, or Nyssa's phone. She didn't even have her jacket anymore—it was probably still on the back of her seat at the restaurant—and the room was cold. There was just an old mattress on the floor, which was where she'd been lying. There was a bucket in the opposite corner and as Lila realized the hopelessness of her situation, she feared she might need it. There were no stairs, but there was a door in one wall.

She tried to keep from freaking out that she was trapped, her worst nightmare, and was managing pretty well until she realized she didn't have her skin. She went through her own pockets frantically, even checking her favorite hiding place inside her bra, but it was gone. Panic rose within her like a cold wave.

She tried to scream, but no sound came out.

Her terror rose a definite notch. Lila's heart raced at the realization that *this* was her worst nightmare.

Trapped and silenced, without her skin.

And too many hours away from the soothing caress of water.

She tried to stand up and had to push herself to her feet, hanging on to the wall at the same time. Her stomach roiled at just that effort and she leaned against the cool concrete for a long moment, waiting for the room to stop spinning.

Maybe they should call the drink a Sneak Attack.

Why would Rhys send her such a drink? Why did he hate her so much? It was one thing for him to be suspicious, but quite another for him to actively wish her ill.

Let alone have her locked in a basement prison. The prickle of fear seemed to accelerate her body's reaction to dry land. She'd spent hours in transit, almost a full day, and now this. How long had she been here? It could be the next morning, Sunday. It could be Monday. She had no idea.

And there wasn't a drop of moisture to be seen.

Maybe Rhys had wanted to ensure she didn't disappear. If he knew anything about selkies, he might have prepared for that—and she knew he hadn't been pleased with her comment about kids.

Still, this choice seemed extreme for him. She had a feeling he'd just call her and talk to her, trying to change her mind with logical arguments.

He'd probably have them all arranged in order of relevance. Maybe draw up a spreadsheet to tabulate them accurately.

Or maybe he'd just ignore the firestorm. He wouldn't try to hurt her.

He was orderly. Reasonable. Temperate, even when annoyed. She didn't sense violence in him.

Not like her captor, who simmered with hidden fire. Lila shuddered.

She felt dirty as well as frightened and the taste in her mouth was terrible. She reached up to push her hair back from her face, wishing she had a comb.

That was when she saw the red string tied around her wrist. She hooked a finger under it and tried to break it, without success. It wasn't just strong string, though—she could tell it was magick by the way it left a burn on her finger and on her wrist. It seared the flesh when she tried to break it.

Magick.

A spell would explain why she couldn't make a sound.

Lila dismissed any wishful thinking and faced the truth. She was a prisoner and she was doomed. The Fae could just leave her here, without water and without her skin, and she would wither and fade to nothing within days. It was the easiest murder in the world—and there was nothing she could do to fight back, not without her freedom or her voice. There would be one less selkie in the world, as easily as that.

But was Maeve her captor? This sure didn't look like Fae. There was no silver light, no music, no dancing at the high court. There was no wine to tempt her to take just one taste, a sip that would trap her forever. There were no companies of loyal followers of the queen. There was nothing pretty or festive about this place.

Where was she?

Lila made it to the door, leaning on the wall most of the way, and tried the knob. Of course, it was locked. She leaned against it, trying to force it open, but no luck. It was a metal door, steel, which also made her doubt that she was in Fae.

Magick but not Fae. The combination didn't make any sense, not since Maeve had snared all the magick centuries before and claimed it for her own. Was someone challenging her?

Who was her captor?

What did he want?

Lila leaned back against the door and surveyed her prison. There were no clues within it. Somehow she had to defeat this plan, whatever it was. Somehow she had to escape. Maybe Nyssa would be able to help. She took three deep breaths and tried to calm her fears, even though she didn't believe things would be okay.

"New Jersey," Rhys muttered as they crossed the state line. He was driving faster than usual but couldn't quell his sense of urgency. They'd made better time than anyone could have expected but it wasn't good enough. It was dark and the stars were out, the lights of Manhattan gleaming ahead of them. Snow was swirling around the truck, sparkling in the light of the headlights, and drifting across the road, but there hadn't been any accumulation yet.

The sparks of the firestorm emanating from Rhys' fingertips suddenly pulled hard to the right. "This exit." He cut off a tractor trailer and ignored the trucker's horn. Hadrian, he knew, was gripping the edges of his seat but wisely keeping his mouth shut.

The firestorm's light flickered, dangerously close to extinguishing itself as they plunged down the ramp. Rhys' heart stopped and he heard Hadrian catch his breath. Suddenly, the sparks flared again, sputtering like wet wood touched with a flame. The gem of the hoard seemed to get a little colder and a little heavier in his pocket, and his heart felt like a rock in his chest.

He had a very bad feeling about Lila's condition.

"That can't be good," Hadrian said quietly. "Does this thing go any faster?"

Rhys put his foot down to the floor. The tires skidded a little and he guessed there was a bit of ice on the road. He ran a red light, following the flames of the firestorm, and didn't care.

Lila needed him.

"Maybe you could breathe some smoke," he suggested to Hadrian.

"That's the extent of your plan?"

"So far, yes. Find her. Do whatever is necessary to get her back. Retreat to my lair and breathe a dragonsmoke barrier. Then satisfy the firestorm so no one can follow it to imperil her ever again."

"That getting-her-back part could be tricky."

"That's why I brought you," Rhys said and they shared a grim smile. A spark shot off his fingertips, the firestorm brightening to a pale orange flame. "Down this street. I think we're getting closer."

Hours passed and the light was fading when Lila heard the creak of footsteps overhead, then the sound of a door opening.

Footsteps descended a staircase.

Heavy measured footsteps, like those of a man.

Maybe even one who simmered with hidden fire.

Lila stepped away from the door. She flattened herself against the wall beside the knob, bracing herself to attack, hoping that the element of surprise was enough to make a difference.

She should have guessed that her plan would be foiled.

As soon as the door to her prison began to open, she jumped at the man who had unlocked it. She intended to claw at his eyes, but never made contact. There was a shimmer of brilliant blue as he shifted shape, then a dragon breathed a torrent of flame across the basement room. The mattress caught fire as a huge claw locked around Lila, trapping her arms against her body.

She was hauled out of the prison and slammed into a concrete wall in the larger basement room. She hit her head so hard that she was left dizzy, then the dragon's eye was beside her face. He was so large that he filled the basement, his tail trailing up the stairs to the main floor above. There was no sign of the man whose footfall she'd heard on the stairs and she'd seen the blue shimmer of change.

Her captor had to be a dragon shifter. In his dragon form, he was as black as anthracite, scaled from head to toe, and his eyes shone with fire and malice. Smoke rose from his nostrils and he bared his teeth, showing her how large and sharp they were.

There was also smoke coming from the burning mattress in the other room.

"You can't surprise me," he informed her in a low rumble. "My partner can read minds."

No, not the Dark Queen. Not here. Not now.

"Of course, the Dark Queen," a woman said. "How does it feel to be powerless, Lila?" Maeve came down the stairs slowly, picking her way around the dragon's tail. Her dark hair had some threads of silver and her face was lined. She looked a lot younger on television as reporter Maeve O'Neill, so Lila wondered what had suddenly aged her. She still wore red spike heels, though.

Was her youthful appearance maintained by magick?

Or was it just make-up on television? Lila couldn't believe her appearance could be changed that much by make-up.

Maeve's aura was still silver, but it flickered as if she was injured or sick. Was her appearance affected by the loss of at least some of her magick? Lila glanced down at the red string on her wrist, remembering that magick was finite and that sorcerers had to choose where to use theirs.

She risked a glance at the dragon and saw the simmer of red magick in his eyes. He had the magic now. Had he taken Maeve's?

Maeve moved into the other room with a fire extinguisher. Lila felt a little bit sorry for her being stuck with the dirty work. There was a strong smell of chemicals and enough dark smoke to make Lila choke, then Maeve returned to smile at Lila.

Any sympathy she felt for the Dark Queen vanished when Lila saw the malice in her eyes.

"Finally silenced," Maeve said with satisfaction. "I must say, I like selkies much better when they can't charm." She shot a glance at the dragon that was almost resentful, but his gaze remained fixed on Lila.

Lila looked pointedly at the red string on her wrist, inviting a confession.

Maeve's smile broadened. "Mine, of course." She flicked a quick glance at the dragon and Lila glimpsed hostility in her eyes before it was dismissed. Lila guessed that the dragon was in charge and Maeve didn't like it. There was a gleam of red in his eyes and a faint glow around him, as if he'd laid claim to the magick and was radiant with it.

If these two were having a turf war, the last place Lila wanted to be was caught in the middle.

Nevertheless, it looked like she was.

The dragon shifted shape and Lila closed her eyes against the shimmer of blue light. When she opened them again, he was the same man who had captured her at the restaurant.

His aura was as dark as a thundercloud, one that might obliterate the sky. This one was wicked to his marrow and nothing could heal that.

She gauged the distance to the stairs and Maeve laughed. "Don't waste your time. Embron wants something from you and you'd be smart to play along. Since I'm in his debt, I might not argue your case if you prove...troublesome."

Embron was his name. It meant nothing to Lila, but she'd remember it.

She looked between the two of them and tried to manage her thoughts. Maeve was said to be able to read minds, and she didn't want to reveal everything she knew.

Lila chose to wonder what Embron wanted from her.

Maeve immediately proved that the rumors of her mindreading skill were true. "The gem of the hoard, of course," she said, as if Lila had asked her question aloud.

Lila recalled that she hadn't seen it in eons. She pointedly thought that she didn't have it and didn't know where it was.

"Ah, but you see, the *Pyr* do know where it is. You have the misfortune to be the destined mate in the first firestorm that sparked for one of them since they took possession of it." The Dark Queen smiled. "They'll do anything for the sake of the firestorm, even step into an obvious trap to try to save the mate. You are his weakness. It's just a matter of time."

Embron looked down at Lila's fingertips and smiled slowly. Lila didn't have to look to know what he saw. She could feel the firestorm heating slightly, burning with greater insistence, and understood that meant Rhys was closer. She guessed that there were sparks lighting at the tips of her fingers and glanced down to see that she was right. Rhys had done nothing to deserve a reckoning.

It was this Embron who should pay the price. She was so horrified that she didn't hide her thoughts quickly enough. He met her gaze and there was something unsettling about his cool confidence. She knew with fearsome certainty that he didn't care about any other creature but himself, and that he would do anything to achieve his goal.

If that objective was possession of the gem of the hoard, then there was no telling what he'd do once he had it. The gem would give its master control of all the earth magick. The adept who knew its spells could draw all that power to himself, and Lila doubted this dragon shifter would use it for the benefit of anyone else.

She looked away but not quickly enough. He caught her chin in his hand, forcing her to meet his gaze. "You will tell me all that you know," he said, speaking in a low seductive voice. His voice wound into her thoughts with curious ease and blended with her desires, twisting them. She wanted to tell him, but she knew the impulse wasn't her own. "You will remember the entire history of the gem of the hoard."

Lila thought that she didn't know it. Not all of it.

"Then you will tell me what you *do* know," he continued. Flames appeared in the pupils of his eyes and Lila closed her own eyes. She knew an unnatural ability when she saw one and didn't trust that trick.

To her surprise, he released her and she peeked to find that he had stepped back. He smiled coldly as he put a copper bowl on the floor. Maeve stood back, also smiling in an unsettling way. Embron produced something from his pocket and tossed it into the bowl.

It was Lila's skin.

She lunged for it, unable to stop herself, but he seized her again, holding her captive just a few feet away. Lila kicked and struggled, but she might as well have been fighting a man of stone. She panicked, horrified, as Maeve struck a match and dropped it into the bowl.

The pain was immediate and excruciating. Lila felt her toes burning, as surely as if they'd been pushed into the flames. A scream rose in her throat but she couldn't make a sound, her cry trapped so that she thought it might choke her. Dark smoke rose from the skin as it burned and her thoughts filled with entreaties for mercy.

"Remember what you know about the gem of the hoard," her captor invited.

Yes, yes. Lila would do that. She would do anything to stop the pain. She would tell him anything. She would tell him everything.

"Excellent choice." Maeve flicked her wrist and conjured a jug of water. She poured it into the bowl and the fire sizzled as it went out. Lila sagged in relief as the pain subsided, trembling to her very core. Her skin was still intact, just a little singed around the edges.

Maeve poked in the bowl with one manicured fingertip, then pulled out the skin. "Imagine if we let the whole thing burn," she mused, then turned a glittering look on Lila.

She wasn't going to give them any reason to do that.

The gem of the hoard.

"Start at the beginning," Maeve invited, and Lila did.

Rhys located the house in the wee hours of the morning. He'd driven past a suburban house in New Jersey and knew immediately that he'd found the place where Lila was being held hostage. The brilliant flare of the firestorm when his truck was alongside the house couldn't be denied, nor could the scent of dragon.

Hadrian hunkered down in his seat, looking grim. "He'll smell us. He'll feel it."

"I had to be sure," Rhys argued and his friend nodded once.

Rhys found a high school with a deserted parking lot six blocks away. He parked there and turned off the truck, hoping that distance would dim the firestorm's flame. It looked like his strategy had worked. The flames glowed like embers at the ends of his fingers, but there were no sparks.

Early on a Sunday morning, the parking lot was empty. The other *Pyr* pulled into the lot and parked their vehicles alongside his truck. Balthasar was the first to get out and he stood beside Arach's car, studying the sky. The night was overcast, with a brisk wind from the west. The neighborhood was quiet, and the sound of the turnpike was so distant that only the *Pyr* could probably hear it.

Rhys was struck by the power of the firestorm even in its subdued state. It hummed in his veins and slid over his skin, turning his thoughts to passion and feeding his desire to shift. He wanted to defend his mate with every fiber of his being and knew that he would fight with brutal efficiency this night. He eyed the glow around his hands, thinking it should be brighter with such close proximity. Was that a measure of Lila's welfare or a sign that it was a trick? He wished he knew.

Drake came to stand beside him, that *Pyr's* eyes narrowing as he considered the orange glow on Rhys' fingertips. His lips tightened and he didn't comment, just surveyed the sky and took a deep breath. "The sun will rise soon," he said finally, his voice deep. "We must wait for the cover of darkness."

Rhys turned on him with horror. He meant to wait an entire day?

Arach was studying the houses that backed onto the football field. There weren't many windows facing the park, which was a good thing. "Not many potential witnesses," he said softly. "Good choice, Rhys. We can shift here tonight."

"We'll meet again, here at dusk," Drake said with finality.

"But my mate!" Rhys protested.

"Is the bait in the trap," Drake reminded him. "Your arrival is anticipated, but we must learn more before we reveal ourselves." Rhys was impatient with this logic, even though he saw the sense of it. He reassured himself with the simmer of the firestorm—that it still burned meant that she was alive—as Drake assigned tasks to the others. They would explore the neighborhood and learn as much as possible by the time they reconvened at sunset.

Rhys was sent home to rest, the better to diminish the firestorm's light, and knew he would spend the day chafing with impatience instead.

CHAPTER FOUR

ila closed her eyes and thought the story she knew so well.

Before we speak of the gem of the hoard, we must consider the Isle of the Blessed.

Once, when the world was young, the gods descended from the heavens to mingle with men. The children born of these unions were so beautiful that they were easily distinguished from those of either lineage. They lived longer than mortals, and were often given additional gifts. They could change their physical form, switching from the skin of a human to another creature. Some of these shapeshifters controlled their transitions by choice; others were compelled to change by an outside force, like the phase of the moon. Some of these shifters preferred one skin over the other, and many lived most of their lives in one form or the other. Over time, those often lost their ability to shift between forms.

There were those, both mortal and immortal, who resented these beings, because they were seen to be endowed with too much advantage. As a result, the children born of the union of gods and men, regardless of their differences, joined together. They called each other the Blessed, for truly, they believed they were. Many of them hid their gifts in an attempt to blend into mortal society, but this did not halt their persecution: their innate beauty revealed their truth.

Eventually, the Blessed realized they had to choose. Dissatisfied with the societies of mortal men, yet having no desire to retreat from the physical realm as the immortals did, these children born of both kinds decided to create their own realm. They boarded ships and sailed away from the cities of men, full of hope for a new future. The Old Man of the Seas took them in the palm of his hand—for there were many of his daughters and his only son in their ranks—and guided their ships safely to an island that was a natural paradise. Some said he had created it just for them. The Old Man of the Seas was much concerned with justice, after all.

The Blessed explored their new home from one coast to the other and were very pleased with their good fortune. They convened a ruling council in which each of their thirteen kinds was represented and each voice was heard. They divided the island to give each kind a domain suiting their needs best. They built a capital city where there was a natural harbor and agreed to work together for the common good. They chose a king from the ranks of their fellows, one Evenor, the son of the Old Man of the Seas who had shown them such favor, and he vowed to rule them to the best of his abilities.

The Blessed prospered in this place, and their affluence and influence grew over the years. They each used their gifts to create fine goods or to cultivate crops, providing for themselves then trading the remainder with the cities of men. Their cloth was reputed to be more finely woven and more richly hued than that found anywhere else in the world; their wine was both sweeter and more potent than any other; their grain was hardier and its flour made bread more delicious and more fortifying. Their women were renowned for their beauty and their soldiers for their valor. It was as if all their worldly endeavors were graced by the divine favor of their forebears. Over time, the cities of men began to regard the Isle of the Blessed as a magical and mystical place. That Evenor did not allow mortal men to set foot on the island only increased its allure.

It also fed the envy and lust of mortal men.

The palace of Evenor, which overlooked the harbor, was a large and graceful residence. Its walls were carved of the white stone found only on the island, a stone that was both uncommonly strong and light. The spires of its thirteen towers—one for each kind—were said to rise so high that they touched the clouds, and birds soared around them. The highest tower was the residence of the official oracle, who brought the council of the gods to Evenor and took the prayers and blessings of his subjects to the gods. In the beginning, there was regular communication.

The qualities of the white stone meant that the walls could be built tall, but also that they could be thin, so thin that reliefs carved in the surface were illuminated by sunlight. To walk from the harbor to the throne room was an opportunity to see the entire history of the island displayed in intricately carved images, in which each kind was shown in its greatest glory.

The Blessed returned from their trading journeys with gifts and tribute from other cities. All was carried up that long road and presented to the king in the throne room. The gifts were then stored in the treasury, which occupied the top floor of the large central tower. The walls of the treasury had thirteen large windows, which were not truly openings. In those spaces, the stone had been carved so thinly that the sunlight pierced it and shone on the hoard piled in the room.

There were coins from every society, gold and silver and bronze. There were cups and chalices, some studded with gems, buckles and brooches and pins. There were loose gems and crystals, some with fire in their depths. There were stones set in jewelry, crowns and bracelets, necklaces and rings. And there were pearls, the glory of the seas, in all their various hues and shapes and sizes. It was said that it took a year and a day for Evenor's clerks to inventory all the contents of that room, and more was added all the time. He ornamented his palace with gems and draped his queens in jewels. He shared tribute with his commanders and presented gems to his advisors, so that the leaders of each kind of the Blessed were adorned in ways that enhanced their beauty.

It is not known how long this realm prospered, because the exact date that the magick came to the island is uncertain. Perhaps it came with tribute, a spark tucked into a gem, a curse engraved on a sword, a spell entangled in a string of pearls. But a shadow came to the island and it touched the heart of Evenor first.

The magick began simply. It made Evenor's voice a little sharper when he was disappointed, then over time honed his words so they cut deeply enough to draw blood. He stepped onto the path of doubting his fellows and trust eluded him. First, he wondered if he had been told the entirety of the truth—and because he showed displeasure so readily, some of the truth was hidden from him by those who feared his reactions. From that, he came to believe others conspired against him. It was an easy progression to fear that his luck was turning, that he had been betrayed, and thence to the conviction that his entire court was in league against him. The blessings offered to the gods diminished until they were forgotten entirely, then the gods did not reply to his queries. Evenor became bitter and angry, unpredictable and fearsome to those who had loved him. He remained in his chambers or locked himself in the treasury to review the inventory there.

By accident or design—one can never be certain with magick—that was when the Envoy arrived and brought the gem of the hoard to the Isle of the Blessed.

Rhys was first to arrive at the parking lot that evening, bristling with impatience. He was glad to see his fellow *Pyr* pull in behind him.

Hadrian inhaled deeply and seemed to shimmer as he came to stand beside Rhys. "There won't be much snow tonight," he predicted as flurries spun out of the sky toward him.

Of course, the falling snowflakes were attracted to Hadrian, who was an ice dragon. They clung to his auburn hair as if they couldn't resist him and he smiled as he lifted a hand, watching the snowflakes fall on his palm. They melted and Rhys thought he heard a sigh of contentment from each one, as if it had found home.

Alasdair got out of his rental truck and grimaced. "I hate driving on the wrong side of the road," he muttered, just as he always did. His eyes glinted as he surveyed his fellows and he obviously tried to lighten the mood. "I thought one of you would be brave enough to ride with me."

"You're better off-roading than on the interstate," Arach teased.

"Avoiding sheep is his gift," Hadrian added.

"Never mind city traffic," Arach added. "I'll never ride with you there again."

"It's a nightmare for me," Alasdair admitted and they laughed a little together. Rhys knew they were trying to ease his concerns by making easy conversation. He might have joined in the spirit of it all, but he was too tense.

Drake arrived and shook hands with them, and Balthasar shared what he'd noticed about the house. It looked abandoned, but he'd smelled *Pyr* when he walked by and there was a red glow of magick, too. Hadrian had learned that it was a rental property and Arach that a woman had rented it just days before. Alasdair hadn't been able to confirm who had moved in, only that there hadn't been any moving trucks. There was said to be a dark sedan parked in the garage.

It was precious little information and Rhys resented the delay of a day to gather it.

"We need to be ready for anything," he said. "There might be a portal there." The other *Pyr* nodded agreement and he felt them bracing themselves for battle.

"How is she?" Drake asked and Rhys held out his hand, showing the steady flicker of the firestorm.

"Then let's do this thing already," Balthasar said.

In that moment, the light of the firestorm went out. In the darkness of that parking lot, none of the *Pyr* could miss the change. It didn't light again. It no longer hummed in Rhys' veins, filling him with urgency and need.

It was gone and he shivered in the darkness, even as he knew what it meant.

Rhys didn't waste time on words. He leapt into the sky, shifting shape in a brilliant shimmer of blue, and flew directly to the house. His fellow *Pyr* were right behind him: he could feel their sense of purpose and hear the beat of their wings.

He only hoped they didn't arrive too late.

In the basement, Lila continued to recall the story. She felt an increased simmer in her veins and dared to hope that meant salvation was finally on the way. When her desire sparked, she knew for certain.

Rhys was coming to help her, and somehow, she had to ensure they both escaped.

He might not anticipate the Dark Queen's presence. Lila studied the queen through her lashes, noting that Maeve was only a shadow of her former self. Embron must have claimed her magick, maybe surrendered just an increment to her. She was rationing what she commanded, expending magick on the curse to keep Lila silent, even at the expense of her own youthful appearance.

Maybe Lila could work with that. She let a measure of charm slide into her thoughts, hoping to lull the pair into complacency, and refused to think of Rhys.

The Envoy was not one of the Blessed who resided on the island, and so he should not have been permitted to set foot on the island. But when his ship arrived and he stepped onto the dock, his red cloak flicking in the breeze, those guards who should have halted his progress found they could not move. They might as well have been struck to stone.

Evenor witnessed this failure from the high tower of his palace: he raged down to the harbor to set matters to rights. He was convinced that his sentries had willfully chosen to defy his orders, and the red glow in the air seemed only to feed his suspicions. He stormed through the city to the harbor, where the Envoy awaited him with a smile.

The Envoy explained that he was immortal but had been born of a union between two of his kind. He was not a god and he was not a man. He was not one of the Blessed. He was his own kind, one who called themselves the Fae, immortal yet rooted in the earth, and that was why he believed he belonged on the island. Indeed, he believed his rightful place was at the side of Evenor, for he could teach him so much. He had a talent for making his desires come to fruition which he called magick. He indicated the stonestruck guards as proof of his skills.

The Envoy also brought Evenor a gift, a sphere of amber unlike any gem Evenor (or even his clerks) had ever seen before. It was large and filled with flecks, like much of the other amber in the treasury, but this specimen had snared two creatures in its formation. A spider was in the act of killing a wasp, both of them trapped for all time in the heart of the sphere. It was both fascinating and horrifying to look upon the moment when two predators battled for supremacy. When Evenor gazed deeply into the globe, he spied a swirl of red light circling the pair. The stone was cold, always cold, yet it fascinated Evenor. He caught glimpses of a red light where the heart of each creature should have beat, and sought always to see it again.

The Envoy called it the gem of the hoard and said that red light was the magick that it commanded. He confessed to Evenor that it was his skill with magick that made his dreams come true. He offered to teach Evenor what he knew, the better to make Evenor the greatest and richest ruler in all the world, in exchange for a place at his court.

Evenor was intrigued. He welcomed the Envoy as his guest and advisor, and the trouble in his court began in earnest.

In the days of the Isle of the Blessed, my kind, the selkies, dominated the north end of the island. We were fishermen and sailors, but also weavers and knitters. The knots we made remained tied forever, giving value to both our nets and our sweaters. We harvested mollusks from the seabed as well as pearls. We collected coral and we dried seaweed in the sun. We gathered shells and pebbles and composed songs that carried the rhythm of the sea.

We found magick in the sea, a gentle magick of encouragement, one that ebbs and flows. We were the ones who put an echo of the ocean's waves in every seashell. We were the ones who learned to seed pearls. We were the ones who saved drowning sailors, or gave sweet dreams to those we could not save. It was said that the oldest among us could whistle up a wind or summon a storm. It was known that one or two of our kind, in such close union with the god of the seas, could turn away a storm. We slipped into the sea often, returning to shore to bear our young, to make merry, to take a reprieve.

Our closest neighbors and allies were the mer-people, whose beauty remains legendary and whose loss we still mourn. They preferred to stay mostly in the water, and loved the depths of the seas. We took their tribute to Evenor for them, and conveyed their goods for trade. We polished their pearls and taught them our songs, and the bonds between our kinds were strong. Our land was ruled by the oldest son of Evenor, Nereus, who was a selkie himself. His younger brother, Arcado, was a merman and ruled the mer-people, our neighbors. The sons of Evenor had been dismissed from the court of their father for petty misunderstandings, but if they had suspicions of greater trouble, they shared them only with each other. We believed all was well in the capital.

In those days, there was a great bell hung in the harbor, gracing the entry to the city from the docks. It was only rung to call the Blessed to the city for council with Evenor, and when it was sounded, it could be heard from one end of the isle to the other. It rang and we went, as bidden, to find this Envoy at the right hand of Evenor, commanding his fleet, whispering in his ear. Evenor kept the gem of the hoard grasped in his hand, hiding it from our view, but the red glow that emanated from it crept between his fingers. Nereus and Arcado were silent but we knew them to be troubled.

Evenor told us that the Isle of the Blessed would be attacked by mortal men, that our former trading partners had all become our enemies. He told us to prepare for war. He commanded my kind and the mer-people to show favor to our ships and destroy those of the men who came to attack. I remember how the Envoy smiled, so pleased with the words of Evenor that he couldn't hide his reaction. Someone asked about advice from the gods, but Evenor had locked the oracle in his high tower. The Envoy had warned against false prophecies, reminding Evenor that we were different and thus, required to defend ourselves from all. Evenor believed this, for he thought the gods no longer favored his kingdom.

A shiver slipped through the crowd at the Envoy's declaration. The mermaids had friends among mortal men, sailors who had become favorites by bringing gifts of mirrors and combs. Shifters of all forms were half human themselves and reluctant to conspire against those they saw as kin. Evenor would not listen. He said the die was cast. He retreated to his palace with the Envoy, leaving us to fight the battle he had begun.

Over time, it became clear that he had insulted our trading partners. He had cheated and he had lied. He had deceived those who trusted him, and this war, was their vengeance upon Evenor.

The war came, just as we had been warned, but it was more brutal than any could have envisioned. The seas turned as dark as wine with shed blood, then the mortals stormed the harbor. The air glowed red with magick as they took the palace and Evenor was dragged from his throne to be slaughtered before all.

The savagery of his death was shocking, but the Envoy laughed.

The mortals were filled with a bloodlust that couldn't be satisfied, turning on each other once most of the palace guards had been slaughtered. The streets ran with blood as the invaders cried for the treasury to be opened to them. The fine white stone of the palace was stained red, and the tower of the oracle crumbled to dust, falling in on itself. The air was red with the fury of magick.

Just when the survivors thought nothing could go more wrong, the Old Man of the Seas rose from the depths in fury. He pounded his trident upon the ground, sending the seas into a frenzy and making the earth quake. He roared and he bellowed, outraged that war had come to the isle he had created, furious that Evenor had so betrayed his divine trust.

The earthquakes made the ocean boil and the hot fumes from the fissures opened in the sea floor made birds fall out of the sky. Fish were cast onto the shore in great quantities and left dying as the island heaved. The Old Man of the Seas strode into the courtyard of the palace and lifted the corpse of Evenor into his embrace. It was said that he wept for the loss of his only son.

The Envoy appeared then atop the tower of the treasury, holding the gem of the hoard high, and challenged the Old Man of the Seas. The storm crackled and snapped, and they say lightning fell into the stone. It was said to have filled with red light so brilliant that all had to close their eyes against its brightness. It was said to pulse with fire and drive the attackers to madness. It was said that many who looked upon it in that moment were blind forever after.

The great god seized the gem of the hoard, even as a bolt of red magic emanated from it and struck him. The Envoy was said to have smiled as the great god stumbled in shock. The divine scream of anguish echoed through all the world as the gem burned brilliant red and hot. The Old Man of the Seas dropped the gem and it fell into the sea. He dove back beneath the waves, and all assumed he pursued the magnificent gem. He took the corpse of Evenor, abandoning his trident to hold his son.

Nereus, leader of our kind and the eldest son of Evenor, claimed the trident for his own. The Envoy snatched after the gem, but it was too late: the sea boiled where it had splashed into the water. Nereus silenced the Envoy forever with one blow of the trident, a fitting return for his treachery.

With Evenor and the Envoy dead, with the gem of the hoard and the Old Man of the Seas vanished beneath the waves, the sea stilled. The air cleared. The earth fell quiet. The red haze of furious magick was extinguished, leaving both mortals and Blessed looking about themselves in wonder and shame.

It was too late, though, for the Isle of the Blessed. The island began to sink that very day, like a ship taking on water, and nothing halted its progress. Nereus summoned scholars from all over the Isle and even from the world of men, but the slow sinking could not be stopped. It took a year and a day for the tallest remaining tower of the palace to disappear beneath the waves, and within a decade, even the sharpest-eyed sailor couldn't spot the ruins any longer. The island sank and kept sinking, all the way to the bottom of the sea.

The gem of the hoard had done its worst and the Isle of the Blessed was lost forever. It survived solely in the dreams of men, and the memories of the Blessed who survived.

"But where was the gem of the hoard?" Maeve demanded.

"Lost on the bottom of the sea," Lila thought and shrugged. *"The great god may have it."*

"No," Embron said. "No." He stood up and paced. "It ended up in my twin brother's hoard, hidden even from me." He leaned closer, emanating malice. "I want to know every creature who touched it, every one who possessed it. I mean to retrieve every shred of magick it shed on its route, as well as claim the stone itself."

"I don't know," Lila admitted, although she noticed the flash of Maeve's eyes. What did the Dark Queen know?

"That's not all of the truth," the man growled. He lit another match, sparing Lila a smile as it flared. "But we know how to prompt your memory." His voice was low with threat and she began to scream in her thoughts even before he tossed the burning match into the copper bowl, even before she felt as if she'd been set afire.

This time, he didn't extinguish the flame. This time, he let it burn until Lila knew she couldn't bear anymore. She had nothing more to tell him, though, nothing she could confess. She heard the crackle of her skin burning and there was nothing she could do to save herself. The world dimmed around her as her terror rose.

Time passed in a blur of torment, of the fire being lit and then extinguished, of more questions she could not answer, more demands, then a match being struck again. It was not long before Lila realized she would die in this dry basement room and no one would ever know the truth.

It was many hours before she surrendered to the pain.

Embron planned it that way.

The house was dark. The neighboring houses were dark. There was a stillness in the air that fed Rhys' sense of foreboding, but he couldn't have stayed away from Lila's prison to save his life.

He breathed fire as he descended upon on the house, setting the roof aflame. He and Hadrian tore it off on one side, flinging the burning shingles and trusses into the barren backyard. Rhys was garnet and silver in his dragon form while Hadrian was emerald and silver. They were both large and deadly fighters, muscled and powerful, partly due to their shared affinity with earth. Rhys did not care who saw them or if their battle was documented.

Lila might already be dead.

Arach and Balthasar descended into the shadows of the house and smashed down the walls. Arach always looked like a precious treasure to Rhys, with his scales of glittering aquamarine edged in silver. His elegant grace made it easy to underestimate his fighting ability. Balthasar was citrine and gold in his dragon form, slender and sinuous but fierce. Alasdair, hematite and silver in his dragon form, followed them into the ruined house and breathed fire in every direction, trashing the walls and rooms as they sought Lila. Drake hovered above them, imposing and dark against the night, as he beat his massive wings and breathed a sanctuary of smoke. Rhys knew that the older *Pyr* would set the permissions on his dragonsmoke so that only their DragonFate team could cross its protective barrier.

When the house was ripped open and the walls shredded, the doors hanging askew, Rhys couldn't believe his eyes. There was no sign of habitation. There were no furnishings. No people. No dragon prince, no Fae queen, and no Lila. The house appeared to be deserted.

Then he saw a quicksilver flash of light, illuminating the perimeter of a door. Rhys was reminded of the portal to Fae that Kade had created in the wall of Bones. The house had a basement! He ripped off the door, only to be greeted by a plume of dragonfire. A dark dragon, ancient and wily, a dragon that had to be Embron, erupted from the basement. He was so large that he broke the framing on the door, shattering the wood and part of the subfloor. He soared into the sky and breathed a torrent of fire at the clouds, his red eyes gleaming with malice, then he dove back amongst the *Pyr* to fight.

"Leave him to us," Hadrian commanded in old-speak and Rhys descended to the house. He shifted shape quickly as dragons battled overhead. He felt their collision and heard a roar of pain but continued downward.

There was smoke in the basement, silvery smoke that obscured his vision and made Rhys wary. His heart pounded when he reached the concrete floor and he tried to survey the space. It looked like there were two rooms, just as empty as the house above.

No. There was a bowl on the floor. The smoke rose from the bowl like a silvery snake, diffusing into the air. Rhys choked on the smell of burning skin and eased closer to the bowl, bracing himself for surprise.

There was something in the bowl, something that could have been a length of fabric folded on itself, or a pelt. It had been burned but Rhys guessed it was skin, the skin of a seal. The flippers were burned and the length of it singed. His heart was heavy with the certainty of whose skin it was and he reached to retrieve what was left of Lila.

The firestorm flared to sudden light as he touched the skin, the entire basement illuminated with its golden glow. He felt a presence behind him in the same moment that his feet began to ache again. Rhys seized the skin and spun to confront an ancient crone. She raised her hands to hex him, but no light came out of them. She swore then stumbled backward on her red heels, tripping over a fallen form in her haste to get to the stairs.

Lila. He hadn't even seen her.

Rhys dropped to his knees beside his mate and hated how pale she was. She was unconscious, if not worse, which made Rhys' heart stop then race. He bent close and relief flooded through him at the faint whisper of her breath. He gathered up his injured mate and raced up the broken stairs.

"Rhys!"

He looked up at Drake's warning in old-speak, only to find the large dark dragon closing fast, talons raised and eyes glowing with rage. Embron looked ancient and formidable. Smoke rose from the old dragon's nostrils and sirens sounded in the distance. He took a deep breath, an indication that he was going to breathe fire.

Rhys surveyed the situation, noting that Alasdair was pursuing the hag down the street: her very high heels slowed her down and Alasdair would certainly catch her. Balthasar was wounded. He'd fallen in the backyard, his dragon form draped over the remnants of the broken roof. He was breathing, though, and Rhys could hear his heartbeat. Drake was still breathing smoke high above the house and Arach had joined him, the pair of them making a cocoon for Lila.

The *Pyr* couldn't communicate in old-speak, not without Embron hearing. Rhys exchanged a quick glance with Hadrian, who was hovering behind him, hoping his old friend anticipated his choice.

"Looking for something?" Rhys taunted Embron in old-speak, then passed Lila to Hadrian. That *Pyr* caught her and soared toward the sphere of Drake's dragonsmoke. Drake carried her within its protective barrier, and Rhys had one less detail to worry about.

Embron roared and took flight, pursuing Hadrian. Rhys shifted shape with a roar, snatched up her skin and tucked it beneath his scales for safekeeping, then leapt into the sky to lock talons with Embron. The force of impact sent them tumbling end over end, their claws locked in the traditional preclude to battle.

"Too late for your mate," Embron taunted. *"I thought you would show more enthusiasm."*

"I had to get what you wanted," Rhys replied, thumping Embron hard with the weight of his tail. The older dragon grunted, but didn't retaliate.

His eyes glowed as he leaned close to Rhys. *"Do you have it? Do you have the gem of the hoard?"* His gaze roved over Rhys, as if he would be able to spot it that easily.

"I won't trade a treasure for a corpse," Rhys scoffed. *"You made a mistake, as the old and feeble are inclined to do."* He smiled slowly. *"Too bad, Embron. Now I have the gem of the hoard."*

"No!" the other dragon roared. *"It belongs to me!"* He tore his claw free with such astonishing power that Rhys couldn't keep a grip on him. He was like a massive serpent in the sky, wily and strong beyond any opponent Rhys had faced before. He slashed at Rhys, but Rhys guessed his intention and ducked. He wasn't quite quick enough. Embron's claw cut through the air like a knife, with remarkable speed. He caught Rhys' side, his talons digging deep, then leaned close to whisper. *"Surrender it to me."*

"You broke the deal," Rhys managed to reply. *"You injured my mate."*

Embron chuckled. He shoved his claws deeper into the wound in Rhys' side, a jab that stole Rhys' breath away and made him falter in flight. He felt his own blood slide over his scales and the world spun around him. He saw people on the street below, watching the fight, and couldn't summon the energy to care.

He needed all the power he had to fight back.

Rhys saw Hadrian approaching Embron from behind and let his eyes droop to slits. He took a ragged breath and deliberately lost the rhythm of flight. He felt himself fall and waited until Embron pulled his claw free. That was almost as painful as the blow had been.

Rhys heard Hadrian hit Embron from behind and the old dragon roared. Rhys soared upward before he reached the ground, coming at Embron suddenly from the underside. He hit him hard enough to knock him across the sky. Hadrian dug in his claws and ripped the old dragon's wings, which made him bellow and bleed. Embron pursued him and Hadrian retreated as quickly as he could. Embron flew a short distance, then Rhys whistled.

"Looking for something?" Rhys had pulled the gem of the hoard from beneath his scales and tossed it in the air now, taunting Embron with a glimpse of it. The old dragon's eyes shone and he shot toward him, his wings beating hard against the night.

Rhys raced upward into the cloud of dragonsmoke. Embron followed him and snapped with his great mouth, obviously thinking he could just bite the gem out of the air. His mouth closed instead over dragonsmoke, dragonsmoke that had been breathed without granting him access, and he screamed as the dragonsmoke stung and burned the inside of his mouth. Rhys winced, knowing how much it could hurt. It had been a long time since he'd been burned by dragonsmoke and he remembered it being a savage pain.

When Embron raised his head, his eyes were orbs of fire. He flew around the haven of dragonsmoke in a tight circle, so big that his tail almost touched his nose. *"She's not dead,"* he muttered in old-speak. *"You owe me, Rhys Lewis, and I will collect."* He smiled then, a dangerous deadly smile. *"I know exactly where to find you."*

Rhys' blood ran cold.

But Embron was finished with him, at least for the moment. The old dragon surveyed the people gathered below them and Rhys heard his low chuckle. He feared then what Embron would do and guessed just before he did it. Embron roared and flew directly at the gathered crowd of onlookers, breathing fire down upon them. He breathed a long hot plume of crackling fire. The adjoining houses caught fire, as did the trees in their yards, flames shooting into the sky just as the fire department trucks came around the corner.

Embron smashed the fire trucks, tipping them over in the street as if they were toys, snatched up two fistfuls of people and laughed as they screamed. He then flung them down, breathed fire on Arach and Hadrian for racing to catch them. Embron then sailed into the sky. He flew high, until he disappeared through the clouds, and Rhys feared for a long time that he would return and make things worse.

He was gone, though, at least for the moment.

"We have work to do," Drake said in old-speak as he surveyed the chaos beneath them. He surrendered Lila to Rhys again. *"Take her home. Ensure she can't be targeted again and we will do the rest."*

Rhys would have been glad to help his fellows, but he saw the wisdom of Drake's suggestion. He caught Lila close and flew back toward his parked truck. It would be easier to slip into his apartment in his human form and the *Pyr* had plenty of beguiling to do already on this night.

At least Lila was alive and safe with him.

He set her gently in the passenger seat, reassured by the crackle of the firestorm and the orange glow of its light.

And that was when he saw the red string on her wrist.

His heart stopped. The mark of a Fae curse was something he never wanted to have in common with anyone—and this one made him wonder anew whether the firestorm was genuine. But as he stared, torn between his choices, the red string twinkled and disappeared.

He blinked, but he hadn't imagined it. There was still a burn on Lila's skin, a red line marking the flesh where the string had been bound. Had Maeve released her? Why?

Rhys didn't know. He no longer cared.

Just as Drake had suggested, he had to take Lila to the safety of his lair.

ila dreamed.

She was floating through the sea, powerless to affect her course. She was caught in an undercurrent, one that drew her down into the depths against her will as surely as if there was a rope bound around her waist. She battled against it, to no avail. The water was strong and the current relentless. She guessed that she was being summoned and surrendered to the sea.

As she drifted ever deeper, she saw the pillars of the lost city rise before her. She was pulled to the square before the harbor, drawn through the gates of the submerged palace. It was impossible for her to be so deep in the ocean, so she knew she dreamed. Her heart ached to see the legendary murals on the walls of pale stone, but the dream gave her no opportunity to stop and examine them. She was pulled to a polished circle that gleamed like a mirror.

The dark mirror. It was legendary on the Isle of the Blessed, an instrument of divination that showed something different to each viewer. The tale was that it showed each what he or she needed to see.

Lila had never seen it with her own eyes. She had never been privileged to enter the treasury and had been only a child when the Isle of the Blessed had sunk beneath the waves. She didn't want to look into it now.

What would the dark mirror show her?

Why had she been summoned to it, even in a dream?

She had to look. It was only a dream.

When Lila leaned closer to the smooth surface of the dark mirror, she saw a child. A little boy, with hair of brilliant orange and eyes the color of a summer sky. A little boy who smiled and laughed, his cheerful disposition never swayed by anything. A little boy with too many freckles to be counted. She smiled as she remembered them trying to do so, how he laughed when he was tickled, how his eyes sparkled with joy.

She saw a little girl, hair as dark as a river, eyes as fathomless as Lila's own. A little girl, quiet and shy and sweet. A little girl with a heart as big as the moon and a gift for knowing what would happen next, just before it did.

Lila's throat tightened as the little girl seized her hand and the mirror seemed to disappear. They walked on a beach together, the wind cold and sharp, the sea dark and smooth. The little boy ran down the pebbled beach ahead of them. She felt the prick of old tears as she looked out to sea and yearned for what was no longer her own.

Trapped.

Then the boy brought Lila a stone, a pebble with a fossil in it, and she was overcome with sadness. She sat down on the beach and cried, unable to stop her tears. She wept for the poor dead creature whose body had created the imprint in the stone, and she wept for herself, fearful of her own fate. She was dying inside and she knew it, denied her rightful due and powerless to change her situation.

The stone also had a hole worn in it by the sea, a hole that her thumb rubbed, seemingly of its own volition. She had an empty space where her heart should have been, a hole worn in her body by the choice that had become a prison.

Then the sea darkened in hue and swirled between Lila and the mirror, obliterating the children and the beach. There was only water, in a thousand hues of indigo.

She felt a different hole in her heart, one caused by loss and grief.

A glow of orange light sparked behind her, then burned with greater power, defying all she knew to be true. It lit the depths of the sea and warmed the cold waters, and Lila turned in surprise. An orb of fire burned red-hot, then turned orange as she reached for it. It turned yellow as she was drawn ever closer, and white when she swam ever closer.

It emanated from a man, a man with dark eyes and a penetrating stare, a man with fire in his soul and a question in his gaze. She knew he was garnet and silver in his dragon form. She knew this fire burned between them with an intensity that could not be denied and that it did so for a reason.

Destined mates.

She wanted all he had to give.

Lila shed her skin and shifted shape, unafraid to show him what she was, unafraid to risk sharing her truth. She watched the slow smile dawn on his lips, saw the admiration light his eyes, then she reached to frame his face in her hands.

As she kissed him, the light flared to incendiary heat, making the sea boil around them and a swirl of bubbles rise toward the surface. It surrounded them like a radiant halo, searing the injuries of the past and giving her newfound hope for the future. As he deepened his kiss, catching her close, Lila felt a curious conviction that she had finally found a safe harbor, the one she hadn't even known she'd been seeking.

Alasdair chased Maeve down the street, amazed that she could make such good time in those heels. The portals to Fae were closed and the Dark Queen was without allies. She was visibly aging, right before his eyes. She stumbled a few times, but kept picking herself up and carrying on. Clearly, she wanted to reach someone or something. He guessed that Embron had given her just enough magick to keep her alive.

She was driven by something and, even if it was just ambition, Alasdair wanted to know more. He could have snatched her up, but he trailed her instead, flying at a steady pace. Distance and the falling snow would obscure him somewhat, but he called to the fog and the mist that he commanded and tugged it around himself like a shroud.

What was her goal?

Maeve never glanced up. When she slowed down to a walk, Alasdair drew a little closer. Her heels clicked loudly as she walked, but there was no one on the streets to see her. The town was sleeping as the snowflakes tumbled lazily out of the sky and melted on the pavement.

Maeve turned down a street and then another, ducking under the awnings of shops and restaurants, heading steadily in the same direction. Alasdair thought of the people who had taken pictures of the dragonfight and knew he should go back to help his fellow *Pyr* with the beguiling—or to deal with Erik's outrage.

First he'd learn what Maeve had planned. She reached an intersection far below him just as the lights turned red. There were no cars coming and no people around. She didn't hesitate, but walked right to the middle of the road and stopped.

Was she taunting him?

Alasdair hesitating, sensing a trap.

Then he smelled a fellow *Pyr*.

Kade!

Now, he turned up! Alasdair was ready to give Kade a stern talk about playing for the team.

A lime green Mustang lunged out of a side street, its tires squealing as it spun to a halt in front of Maeve. Kade bounded out of the car and left the driver's side door open. He was shimmering blue, on the cusp of change, and looking up.

Straight at Alasdair.

Alasdair recognized that Kade intended to defend the Dark Queen. She really had him under her thumb, then. He lunged toward Maeve, intending to snatch her up, but Kade shifted shape. The shimmer of blue that accompanied his change was blinding in its intensity and he blew dragonfire as he launched himself at Alasdair. Kade was a lithe dragon with amber and gold scales and his hide glittered in the glow of the dragonfire. Alasdair was well aware that the other *Pyr* was younger and more agile than him.

Maeve meanwhile flung herself into the car, then gunned the engine. The Mustang roared out of the intersection like a shot, fishtailing as it disappeared into the darkness.

Alasdair breathed a plume of dragonfire at the departing car, but the tail lights were already disappearing. Kade leapt into the sky and raised his talons in the old challenge, his eyes shining with malice as he confronted Alasdair.

"We're on the same side," Alasdair protested.

"Not any more," Kade retorted. *"I've been pushed aside and ignored long enough."*

"You can't mean to fight me for her," Alasdair argued, even though he could see that was the case. He needed a plan to outwit the other *Pyr.*

"Just defending one of the treasures of the earth," Kade countered. *"Give my stylus back and we'll call it a night."*

"I don't have it. I gave it to Rhys to follow his mate."

"But he found her here. He doesn't need it anymore, and I do." Kade beckoned with one hand.

"Why do you need it? Maeve is here, not in Fae. You don't need a portal."

"But she does, and I'm on her team now." Kade smiled with confidence. *"We have a thing."*

"A thing," Alasdair scoffed. He was sufficiently outraged to seize Kade's talons and lock claws with him. *"Her thing is to eliminate all shifters, including us. She won't make an exception for you."*

"Believe what you need to," Kade replied, more cocky than Alasdair had

ever seen him. *"I'm not in any danger from her."* His eyes glowed red as he leaned closer and Alasdair feared the other *Pyr* was in Maeve's thrall. *"I serve her in every way."*

"You can't!" Alasdair roared, punctuating his disgust with a hard blow of his tail. Kade caught his breath and breathed fire again. They were in such close proximity that the scales on Alasdair's chest were singed, which infuriated him. *"You don't know what you're doing."*

Kade laughed. *"I know exactly what I'm doing."* He slashed at Alasdair with his back claw, obviously not holding back.

If it was a fight to the death, Alasdair was in.

He raged dragonfire, burning Kade's wings, and beat the younger *Pyr* hard with his tail. They tumbled through the air together, talons locked as they slashed and bit at each other. Kade was sneaky and fought hard, but Alasdair was more strategic with his blows—each one of them hit home. He thought he was getting the upper talon as Kade obviously weakened, and moved in to take the other *Pyr* down. He wouldn't kill his fellow dragon shifter, but he'd teach him a lesson, one that was apparently overdue.

Suddenly, Kade twisted, as slippery as an eel, and slid out of Alasdair's grasp. His weakness had been a trick. He retreated a short distance, then reared up, spreading his wings wide as he breathed a river of dragonsmoke and flew straight at Alasdair.

Kade targeted his dragonsmoke to strike the wounds on Alasdair's feet, the ones that refused to heel since he'd been trapped in Fae. The pain on contact was excruciating, and it only got worse as the dragonsmoke eased deeper into the wounds. Alasdair tried to retreat. He tried to outrun the silvery tendril of dragonsmoke, but it followed him, persistent and accurate. It bit at him like a snake, sinking into the sores so that he thought he'd lose his mind. It seemed to be locked around his ankle, like a rope that would follow him anywhere, and he couldn't break the stream. It was more like a braided cable than a tendril of smoke and he felt a reluctant admiration for Kade's skill. Alasdair could have been dancing in Fae again, dancing endlessly and against his will. There were daggers in his feet and a haze of dragonsmoke clouding his thoughts.

He knew the very moment that Kade began to use the dragonsmoke as a conduit and started to suck the energy from him. Alasdair realized he was fading. He feared that Kade wouldn't hesitate to kill him. Alasdair tried to call out to his comrades in old-speak, but the words were garbled and his cry too faint to carry the distance. He lost the rhythm of flight as the tendrils of dragonsmoke encircled him like a cage. They struck him in a thousand places, siphoning off his power, turning him into a shell of himself. Kade grew brighter and seemed to be larger with every passing moment, his scales shining brilliantly against the night sky and his eyes burning with that red inner fire. He laughed but didn't ease his assault.

Alasdair roared in frustration when he realized he couldn't stay aloft, then he fell.

He never hit the ground, though. Kade swept him up and carried him off triumphantly. The other *Pyr's* wings beat hard, carrying his prey away from the suburb where Lila had been held captive. The air was colder and there was wilderness beneath them, with a road snaking through the darkness of the trees. Alasdair glimpsed the lime green glimmer of the car far below. He shifted shape against his will and heard Kade's grunt of satisfaction that he was easier to carry. He struggled to stay conscious but soon wished he hadn't.

Because even the bite of dragonsmoke was nothing compared to the horror of Maeve invading his mind. Once they reached her home in Philadelphia, she read his thoughts like he was an open book, her fingers prying loose his memories and secrets with relentless force. Her assault was intrusive and penetrating. It left Alasdair feeling violated and nauseated, and then as Maeve wrung his secrets free, it became painful.

At that moment, Alasdair would have promised anything to make her stop.

He did.

Rhys cooked, putting the energy of his agitation to good use.

As soon as he'd gotten Lila to his place, taken off her dirty clothes and put her to bed, he'd called down to the restaurant for supplies. He lived in an apartment on the top floor of the same building that housed Everyman Epicure, a situation that did nothing to curb his tendency to work all the time. Usually, his apartment was a refuge, albeit one where he seldom did more than sleep—and that only for a few hours at a time. If Rhys was a workaholic, he was a happy one. His apartment kitchen was well-equipped, even though the restaurant was close, and he was glad of it.

On this particular night, he was restless as he never was.

What if Lila wasn't his mate?

What if she was?

Either way, she'd been abducted and abused by Embron and Rhys wanted to avenge her. He wanted to hunt down the dragon prince and demand a reckoning, to battle him to the death in retaliation for what he'd done to Lila.

But the firestorm wasn't satisfied.

And Lila needed his protection.

Rhys was torn between his desires and his responsibilities in a new and unwelcome way. The orange glow of the firestorm seemed to heighten his feelings and amplify his concerns. He felt more protective of her than he'd ever been of anyone before. He hovered on the cusp of shifting shape, ready to protect her at an instant's notice. Rhys didn't like feeling on edge. It wasn't like him. He was the steady and consistent one, not the one who jumped at shadows.

But that all changed with Lila in his bed. The firestorm flickered and he saw peril in every corner. He heard danger in every creak of the wind and groan of the old building, even in the sound of traffic on the street far below. He stood at the kitchen counter and told himself to get a grip—then someone knocked on the door and he nearly shifted shape and breathed fire instead of just answering the door.

It was Justin, bringing the delivery from the restaurant. The usually confident bartender was almost as rattled as Rhys, desperate to apologize for what he saw as his mistake with the drink—and what Rhys knew had been Embron's beguiling.

"And Ryan said their bill was unpaid," the bartender confessed. "It's not like they were trying to trick you out of a meal: they barely touched their plates."

"That's fine," Rhys said. "It only makes sense given what happened. I'll take care of it. Were the other patrons upset?"

"Not for long. Ryan said she'd gotten some bad news." Justin pushed his hand through his hair and looked exasperated, even though Rhys was nodding approval. "I really don't like when you're off and the place is busy. It's tough when things go wrong."

"I don't like it either," Rhys admitted and they smiled at each other. "What happened to her purse?"

"Oh, her friend took it, the woman who was with her. She just ran out after her."

Nyssa Macleod.

Justin frowned. "Do you think she'll be all right? It drives me crazy that I made her sick, or served her a roofie without realizing it."

"It's not your fault." Rhys reassured his employee: he even had to beguile him a little bit, because Justin had a very strong sense of responsibility. Rhys didn't feel a bit of guilt about that. He finally sent

Justin back downstairs and told him to go home. It was past two in the morning, after all.

Then Rhys leaned back against the door and exhaled.

In his agitated state, he could have fried one of his best employees. He had to calm down. If nothing else, his uncharacteristic tension was a good reason to try to satisfy the firestorm. If it was real and Lila conceived, he could try to change her mind about their son later. If it was real, satisfying it would eliminate its flame, which would make it harder for anyone to find them both.

If it wasn't real, he had to think it would be a great interval even so. He liked Lila's honesty and how direct she was. He had no doubt she'd tell him exactly what she liked—and the prospect of delivering to her expectations roused the glowing embers of the firestorm.

Rhys closed his eyes and listened to her steady breathing. She was in his bed. He'd stripped her nude since her clothes were dirty and wet, then tucked her in. She wore a stone on a silk cord around her neck and he'd left that, even though he didn't know why she'd chosen such a token. The stone was dark grey with a fossil in it, and the hole looked like it was a natural one. He sensed that it was important and didn't interfere. He'd put her clothes into the washing machine in the small closet by the bathroom. There was something satisfying about knowing she was in his lair, in his bed, sleeping as if she trusted him. Maybe she was just exhausted, but Rhys had a hard time caring as the firestorm crackled between them.

He also had a hard time staying away from her. He could smell how own sweet scent as well as the salty tang of the sea from her skin. The smell of burned flesh was impossible to ignore. He put away the groceries quickly, then lit candles around the apartment. Their glow soothed him, even though their flames undulated back and forth, caught in the crackle of the firestorm between himself and Lila.

What if it *was* real?

He went to the bedroom door and looked in at her, feeling a stab of desire that wasn't entirely due to the more insistent burn of the firestorm. Her features were serene in sleep, as if she was relieved to be out of that place. Rhys could believe it. He held out his hand and smiled at the sparks that danced between them. The evidence of the firestorm reassured him in one way: at least it was back.

Lila wasn't dead.

Even better, she was smart. She was brave. She had to be old, maybe as old as him, maybe older. She knew what he was, too, and had powers of her own. He'd never met a female shape shifter before. He went to the side of the bed and looked down at her as the firestorm burned brighter with proximity. She had a talent for surprising him, even for challenging him, and Rhys liked that more than he might have expected. She'd come after him, intent on putting the firestorm behind them. She wasn't big on kids, but maybe that would change.

Maybe she'd had a bad experience in the past.

He could think of what it might be. There was one persistent story about selkies, the one about the mortal man who had fallen in love with one and taken her as his bride. The man had hidden her skin from her, so she couldn't return to the sea, and she'd been his captive as well as his wife. That didn't sound like any kind of love to Rhys.

Was that her fear? Being trapped? If so, Embron's abduction would have been terrifying.

At least he had her skin. Rhys filled a bucket with water and added some salt, then put her skin into it. It appeared to be dry as well as burned, and he wondered whether it was his imagination that it looked better once in the water.

He'd be sure to give it to Lila so she understood his intentions.

And there was, of course, her physical assets. Rhys knew he'd never seen a more beautiful woman. She was lovely, sleek and beautiful, and she moved with the fluid grace of the water. There was something otherworldly about her, a quality he would have noticed even without knowing that she was a selkie. He thought about that kiss on the beach and caught his breath as the firestorm crackled with newfound heat, as if approving of the direction of his thoughts. He thought of the way she'd teased and provoked him on the phone and found himself smiling. He remembered how powerful she'd been underwater and how quickly she'd been able to swim.

If only he could believe in the firestorm. He had to wonder whether Lila would risk her own survival to trick him. It probably depended on what Maeve might hold against her, or how strong Maeve's magick was. At least the red string was gone. Rhys pulled up the duvet, and eyed the slight burn on her left wrist.

She had to be snared in the Dark Queen's web, just as he had been. Rhys wanted to believe that Lila wouldn't have done that by choice.

But he wasn't sure.

He went back into the kitchen, which was his favorite place, and breathed dragonsmoke to defend his lair. Rhys knew that he wasn't in the right meditative state to do a good job. Not only was he jumpy from a combination of the firestorm's insistent demand and his uncertainty of its truth, but he didn't trust Embron to leave him and Lila alone, not with the gem of the hoard sitting on his kitchen counter. Rhys didn't feel safe. His thread of dragonsmoke broke repeatedly and even though he wove in the ends, he knew it wasn't the best barrier he'd ever created. Fortunately, there was already dragonsmoke encircling his lair, and even though its power faded over time, even the remnants were better than no defense at all.

"I'll sit watch," Hadrian said in old-speak, just as Rhys heard his friend settle on the roof overhead. He was relieved when Hadrian began to breathe smoke, slowly and deeply, making a barrier faster and thicker than Rhys had been able to do. Hadrian wove his dragonsmoke into Rhys', buttressing what was there, filling gaps and increasing the thickness. Within moments, the lair felt more secure and Rhys felt some of his concern fade.

Now he could cook. Lila had barely tasted her dinner before Embron's interference. She had to be hungry and Rhys could solve that. He checked the ingredients he'd requested, then had a hot shower while he made his plan. The wounds in his side were fierce and deep. He cleaned them up as best as he could, smearing them with one of Sloane's unguents. They stung, but he knew the mixture would help him heal. Then he bound the wounds and dressed.

It was snowing outside and the wind buffeted the window. He'd turned on the gas fireplace when he'd changed and surveyed his lair with satisfaction, his anticipation rising.

Was it his imagination that a red light flicked in the heart of the gem of the hoard? Rhys picked up the cold piece of amber and looked into its depths, but was only able to see the two creatures trapped forever in its depths. He shuddered, then left it on the end of the counter. He hadn't ever believed in magick. Even if recent events showed that he'd been wrong, Rhys sure didn't trust it. He had no idea how to command it and he didn't want to learn. The sooner it was extinguished the better, and the only unfortunate thing was that surrendering the stone might make Embron or Maeve even more powerful.

He wondered what Lila knew about magick and the gem of the hoard, and resolved to ask her.

Cooking, though, was a process that Rhys could command. He controlled all of the variables when he cooked and maybe that was why it gave him so much satisfaction.

He reviewed his plan and began to *mise en place*. He chopped and he sliced. He sautéed and he stirred. He listened to Lila's breathing and he strove to time the meal to be ready when she awakened. Slowly, the tension in him eased. He breathed more smoke once his preparations were done, adding to Hadrian's efforts, and dared to hope that Lila truly was his destined mate.

There was only one way he could think of to find out for sure.

Just the possibility made the firestorm crackle with greater vigor.

Lila awakened in a comfortable bed, a little shaken from her dream. A safe harbor? She doubted there was any such place. She would not think about those children. She wasn't sure why she'd thought of them now, except maybe for Rhys' comments about the firestorm.

It had just been a dream, not a portent. She lived in the moment, not in the past, and the future would be pretty much like the present, forever and ever.

Funny how she'd never found that a disappointing prospect before.

Lila sat up with purpose, deliberately pushing away the memories. The room was such an improvement over her prison that she thought she might be dreaming again. It was clean and comfortable. The pillow was real, and so were the smooth sheets. She was clean and almost naked, wearing a T-shirt that had to belong to a man.

She liked the exposed rafters overhead and the hardwood floor, the brick walls and the thick rug beside the bed. She wiggled her toes in it, and made a pretty good guess as to which man's bed she occupied. The bedroom wasn't much bigger than the bed and she saw a walk-in closet on the wall opposite to the window. The blinds were down, but she could hear traffic and guessed from that and the dimensions of the space that they were back in one of the most expensive cities in the world. She sensed that she wasn't alone, and when she smelled food cooking, she smiled.

Of course. Lila lifted her hand and studied the glow of the firestorm, burning around her hand. It was brighter than it had been, closer to yellow than orange, and was shooting little sparks into the air. She felt its heat slide through her body and licked her lips, her imagination filling with ideas of better things to do in bed than sleep.

That was, after all, what she'd come for.

"I thought you were awake," Rhys said. She jumped a little to find him in the doorway watching her, his eyes dark and his expression inscrutable. He looked as if he'd had a shower because his dark hair was damp. He was wearing a T-shirt that was tight enough to reveal how muscled he was, jeans and a pair of kitchen clogs. His shirt was probably the same size as the one that was hanging around her in folds.

His aura had changed, though, from the last time she'd seen him. It still had that shadow upon it, the one she thought had been caused by grief, but she looked closer and saw more. The aura was fragmented around his feet and she knew he'd sustained an injury there. The halo of red-gold light that surrounded him was also cracked on one side of his torso. That was new.

Rhys was wounded, and by the effect on his aura, his wounds weren't small.

"Why?" she asked, instead of immediately offering to help. She wasn't very strong herself in this moment, and surrendering her energy to heal would only make her more vulnerable. She'd be sure she was safe first.

Rhys lifted his hand. "It brightened." A spark jumped from his fingertip to Lila, striking her in the chest. She gasped, feeling like a bolt of lightning had hit her in the heart, but then the tidal wave of desire that followed made her simmer to her toes. The spark seemed to bounce, because it then returned to Rhys, slicing a white arc of heat through the shadowed bedroom. He closed his eyes and took a step backward when it collided with his chest, then inhaled sharply. She saw him grip the doorframe and knew he was as affected as she was. His eyes glittered a bit when he opened them and his gaze fell to her wrist where Maeve's red string had been.

Lila frowned as she touched the burn on her skin. "It's gone. Did you take it off?"

Rhys shook his head. "Only she can remove it. It disappeared. I thought maybe you would know why." His gaze was searching.

"How so?"

"I wondered what you traded for your freedom."

Lila shook her head. "Nothing. I had nothing to trade. That's why he was going to kill me." She shivered. "Maeve must have undone the curse. She must have needed her magick for something else."

"I don't understand."

"Magick is finite." She tried to think of an analogy he'd understand. "Like the number of burners on a stove. If you have four burners and five pots, you have to choose."

Rhys nodded. "What was the curse?"

"I couldn't make a sound." She shuddered at the memory. "She silenced me. It was awful."

"Why would you be silenced?"

"Probably because selkies can charm. They wanted to make sure I couldn't, even though I'm not very good at charming, and those two are hardly average mortals."

"Is charming like beguiling?"

"I don't know. What's that?"

"It's similar to hypnosis. A *Pyr* creates flames in his eyes, which fascinates the subject and compels them to look deeper. It also makes them more suggestible."

"That's what Embron was doing!"

Rhys was visibly indignant. "He tried to beguile you?"

She nodded. "When they wanted to know everything I knew about the gem of the hoard. I closed my eyes, but his words still twisted my thoughts."

He nodded. "I think Embron beguiled Justin and Ryan to have them deliver that drink to you."

"You said it wasn't you. I should have believed you."

He shrugged. "It might not have made much difference."

"Promise never to beguile me and I'll promise never to charm you?" Lila suggested.

"I'm not very good at beguiling."

"And I stink at charming. Something else we have in common."

Instead of smiling as she'd hoped, Rhys frowned and looked at the floor. "My memories of having a red string on my wrist aren't a lot of fun either."

"What did it do to you?"

"I couldn't shift and I had to dance." His dark gaze met hers.

Lila's mouth went dry with sudden understanding of his injured feet. "Not the dance. I've heard it's terrible."

"The rumors are all true," he admitted and looked weary at just the memory. "It was relentless and I couldn't do a thing to stop it." This time, he shuddered.

He'd been compelled to dance until his feet blistered and the skin broke, until they bled—and still he'd had to keep dancing. Lila hugged her knees to her chest, but stayed in the bed. She had the urge to reach for Rhys, to touch him and console him, even to heal him. First she had to know where she stood, before the firestorm complicated everything.

Maybe it already had.

Healing him, though, would complicate things even more.

"Is it common for the firestorm to be fake?" she asked.

Rhys shook his head. "Not as far as I know. The last firestorm was a Fae spell and it was the first fake one I'd ever heard of."

"In how long?"

"Five hundred years, give or take."

"Youngster," she scoffed but Rhys didn't smile this time either.

"That's what we followed into Fae." He swallowed. "Four of us went through a portal together then somehow were separated. I met you, then was struck by that lightning."

"Wait. You went through the portal *before* we met?"

Rhys nodded, his eyes dark.

That wasn't good news. Their encounter and the firestorm could have been contrived by Maeve. "She did get you then?"

Rhys nodded. "Even though you warned me."

"And one of the *Pyr* is still there."

"Theo never came back and he wasn't with us. I have no idea where he is."

"Trapped in Fae," Lila guessed and Rhys nodded.

"I ended up with Hadrian, dancing, then Kristofer and Bree saved us." He frowned again. "We were planning to find Theo when this all happened."

This news made Lila want to get back to North Rona as soon as possible. It couldn't be good for her to be alone with Rhys, generating this light show that pinpointed their location, when both their kinds were hunted by the Dark Queen.

And he'd entered Fae *before* they'd met on the beach. Maeve didn't usually let anyone leave Fae, not without demanding a toll. What if the Dark Queen had let him go, in exchange for something else? What if the firestorm was a spell to trap *her*? There were a lot fewer selkies than *Pyr*, from what Lila could see, and she guessed that Maeve liked to tidy things up quickly when she got close to eliminating a species.

One thing was for sure: it had been a really bad idea to come to New York.

CHAPTER SIX

ila was well aware that Rhys was waiting for her to say more.

"She's relentless in her hunt," Lila said and swung her legs out of bed. She felt weak and more than a little parched, but she had to leave.

Rhys took a step closer. He stopped before her and put his fingertip beneath her chin when she averted her gaze. The contact sent a surge of fire through her, obliterating the thought of everything except pulling him into the bed with her.

He was dangerous and so was this firestorm.

She moved to step past him. "I've got to go home."

"You can't leave until you rebuild your strength. What do you need to recover?" His voice was low with concern and she instinctively believed that he did care about her welfare. "I don't know much about your kind."

She dared to meet his gaze. He really only had to know one thing and Lila couldn't see her skin anywhere. It couldn't have been lost, because that would have killed her. She knew it had been burned, because she could feel the effects of that. Its absence made her fear that she was trapped in a much more familiar way than being locked in a basement room. A lump rose in her throat as she realized why she might have dreamed of the children.

It was happening again. Panic sparked within her and she wanted to run.

Rhys lifted a dark brow and she realized he was waiting for her reply. He wasn't going to move out of her way without one, and he was a lot more formidable than her.

"Water," she admitted.

"A glass?"

"A tub. A pool would be better. Do you have an ocean in the closet?"

He smiled and gestured to the door. "I can offer a tub. I'm more the shower type myself, so you'll be the first to use it. Do you need salt, too?"

Lila nodded, liking that he'd guessed that part. How many times had she needed to contrive a story to explain her need to bathe in salt water? It was kind of nice not to have to lie—but not nice enough to let down her guard. She would be able to think more clearly once she felt the water again. She had no choice now but to accept this dragon's help.

She took a step, but wavered on her feet. She would have reached for the doorframe, but Rhys swept her into his arms instead and carried her out of the room. The firestorm didn't miss a chance to flare brighter, to burn with more insistent heat, to tempt her to invite him into the tub with her. Rhys halted and caught his breath as it blazed around them, proving he was shaken by its power, too.

"Is it always like this?" Lila asked when she could manage to speak.

"I don't know." He smiled down at her. "We only get one in a lifetime, so it's a first for me, too."

"Five hundred years is a long time to wait," she said.

Rhys' dark gaze dropped to linger on her mouth. She felt the low rumble of his voice in his chest when he spoke. "There's only one way to stop the flames and one way to know for sure," he murmured. She remembered him telling her as much and her heart clenched. Rhys slowly bent and brushed his lips across hers, holding her captive against his chest, his gesture so gentle that Lila was surprised. She guessed that he was asking permission. Her heart thundered and she yearned for him, just with that fleeting touch.

The firestorm lit to blazing intensity with his caress, feeding her need for him and incinerating her reservations. Lila closed her eyes, forcing herself to focus. She'd come for sex, pure and simple, but there was nothing simple about the prospect of sex with Rhys Lewis. She had to be sure of his plan.

"Just sex satisfies it?" she asked, and heard how husky her voice had become.

"Yes and no. It's the conception of that heir that douses the flames." His lashes swept down as he surveyed her and she noticed how thick and dark they were, how well he hid his feelings, how intensely she was aware of his desire for her all the same.

Her desire for him wasn't easy to ignore either.

"That could take time," Lila whispered.

Rhys shook his head. "The story is first time, every time." He took a deep breath, one that made his chest press against her. "Once does it."

"That's hard to believe."

"There are a lot of things that are hard to believe right now," he said roughly. "The firestorm is the least incredible of all of them." His gaze clung to hers. "If we made love and the flames were extinguished, then we'd know the firestorm had been genuine."

"And I'd be carrying your dragon son or daughter."

"We don't come into our powers until puberty," he said, his tone matter-of-fact. "And it would be a boy. The *Pyr* always have sons."

Lila was as skeptical of that as of first-time-every-time. "Always?"

He held her gaze, his conviction clear. "There's one female *Pyr* at a time, who is supposed to be a prophetess. Erik has a daughter, so that role is taken."

"Only boys, then."

"Only boys." Rhys frowned. "But you need water. I apologize for being distracted." Lila couldn't fault him for that since she was pretty distracted, too. He strode out of the bedroom, carrying her into a compact bathroom, all white tiles and grey stone, with a big mirror. There was a glass-walled walk-in shower, but even better, the large and deep tub he'd mentioned. He set her down on the side of it and eyed her with concern. "You okay there?"

Lila must look a wreck. She watched him survey the burns on her legs and the darkened flesh of her toes then saw his lips tighten.

When had someone last been protective of her?

His attitude was seductive, but Lila knew better than to succumb.

She'd made that mistake once and she wouldn't make it again.

The firestorm made it very tempting to just hang on to Rhys, maybe for good. Maybe even do a little more than hang on. Lila found herself studying his mouth and knew she had to put some distance between them.

"Well, I'm not going to drown," she said, trying to make a joke. She felt a lot weaker than expected and that worried her.

Rhys almost smiled. "I guess not. I'll get the salt." When he stepped away, moving with his characteristic purpose, the flames of the firestorm dimmed a little and Lila was able to gather her thoughts again.

She looked around, liking the tidy economy of his home. The small window in the bathroom was high and frosted, admitting light but no view. She thought from the hue of the light that it might be from streetlights or the moon.

She'd glimpsed a larger room and leaned forward for a better look. It was simply furnished, too, the focus on a kitchen that took half the space. There was a counter between the kitchen and the living room, with a couple of stools pulled up to it. The apartment had to be in a converted warehouse, because the ceilings were high, with exposed beams and pipes. The floors were heavy wood, polished smooth and honey gold in hue. It reminded her of the restaurant, both welcoming and organized, and she took an appreciative sniff of whatever was cooking.

Rhys returned with a box of salt and put it on the side of the tub. He pointed around the bathroom, acting as if they were strangers—or as if the firestorm wasn't sizzling between them, taking Lila's thoughts straight to the gutter. He was taller than her and superbly toned, a little bit tanned, his hair short and his shoulders broad. She watched his hands, liking their powerful grace.

That ruptured aura made her want to touch him even more.

To heal him.

He was one tempting dragon shifter.

"Towels there. Soap there. Let me know if you need anything else." Rhys snapped his fingers before Lila could reply and reached out of the bathroom. He lifted a bucket and met her gaze with an apologetic smile. "Sorry I didn't know how to mend it or fold it. Actually, folding's not my best trick, especially things that aren't square. It took me ages to learn to fold my scales away. I was the class dunce." He smiled, looking like anything but a slow learner, his gaze so intense that Lila's mouth went dry.

Her skin. It had to be her skin.

Her chest tightened.

Rhys put the bucket down beside her and Lila's tears rose when she saw its contents. As charred as it was, it was still a tremendous relief to see her skin again. He'd even put it in water and she could smell the salt.

"I wasn't sure..." he began when she didn't say anything.

"Good guess," she said, casting him a smile. "Great guess. Thank you."

He stared at her as if dazzled, then nodded once and straightened.

Lila reached down and caressed the skin's silky fur, forgetting herself in her relief. She exhaled and a burned spot shimmered beneath her hand before disappearing, the skin healing beneath her touch. She realized a bit late that she'd revealed her ability, but kept her hand over the spot as she looked up at Rhys. Maybe he hadn't noticed the mist of her healing breath.

"One thing I do know about your kind is that story," he admitted, his voice a low growl. "If you stay, it will be your choice, not mine."

Oh. Lila's heart fluttered and she couldn't look away.

Then a timer sounded in the kitchen and Rhys glanced in that direction. "That's just prep," he said quickly. "Take your time."

"You're cooking at a time like this?"

"You didn't have time to eat your dinner," he said, his smile broadening and becoming a little crooked. He was incredibly handsome, and his smile made him look both younger and less stern. Lila's heart skipped a beat.

But he was *Pyr* and she was selkie.

Their kinds didn't belong together.

Worse, if they were together and she chose to conceive, that son would be another creature of mixed ancestry for Maeve to hunt and kill.

All the same, Lila didn't want to argue with Rhys, not right now.

She also didn't want to tell him that first-time-every-time wouldn't necessarily work out that way between them.

"And you guarantee every bite," she recalled, feeling an answering smile curve her lips.

"Cooking is my stressbuster. You're lucky I didn't cook for the multitudes tonight."

"Would I have to eat it all?"

"I'd hope you'd at least taste it all."

Lila laughed, watching his slow smile of satisfaction light his features—then the timer rang again. Rhys headed for the kitchen, pulling the door closed behind himself and leaving her to her bath. Did cooking trump everything in his life? Lila didn't know, but the fact that he'd surrendered her skin left her inclined to give him the benefit of the doubt.

A commitment to their work could be another thing they had in common.

Lila turned on the taps, dumped in all of the box of salt, then lifted her skin out of the pail as the tub filled. She was trembling deep inside, shaken by the knowledge of how close she had come to losing her skin. She ran her hands over it, remembering how Embron had deliberately burned it and felt a bit sick all over again.

She locked the door, not wanting to be disturbed, knowing Rhys could break down the door if he chose to do so. Her breath healed the worst of the burns and she hugged the skin close, savoring its familiar scent and feel. Her healing breath filled the small room with a soothing pale mist, one that caressed her all over and calmed her thoughts, too. Lila felt a lot more serene by the time she slipped into the full tub. She held the skin against her chest, then slipped beneath the surface and pulled it on.

Rhys had given the skin to her, because he knew its power. He understood that having it in her own possession was her heart's desire.

Lila decided that she would surrender to this firestorm in return. If she chose to conceive his son afterward, she'd give him the boy. It wouldn't be like the other time. It wouldn't be a sacrifice. It was a rational and willing exchange, one heart's desire for another.

Perfectly rational.

Even if this simmer of need didn't feel rational at all.

"Do you mind?"

Rhys turned at the sound of Lila's question. She had a sexy voice, low and sultry, and spoke slowly, as if she had all the time in the world. Her Scottish accent worked for him in a big way, too.

To his relief, she looked a thousand times better than she had when he'd brought her home. Her dark hair was long and loose, and it shone a bit in the candlelight. She was barefoot, dressed in one of his chambray shirts, the sleeves rolled up and the hem falling to her thighs. He wondered whether she was wearing anything underneath at all.

The sores on her skin had vanished as surely as the burn from the red string. She was almost glowing with good health.

How had that happened? Something in the water? Maybe it was a selkie thing.

Lila smiled at his survey and gestured to the shirt. "I put my things in the dryer and literally have nothing to wear."

"No, I don't mind. Not at all," Rhys said, as casually as he could. He took a good long look before he could check himself, noting the lean strength of her legs. The shirt could have been just a little shorter, to his thinking, or open, instead of hiding the rest of her curves.

When he met Lila's sparkling dark gaze, she smiled, as if she'd guessed his thoughts and didn't mind. The firestorm burned with a golden glow, echoing the light of the candles and filling his place with light and heat. It simmered in his veins, making him think of her back to the bedroom and getting rid of that shirt, of exploring her from head to toe and taking her to the cusp of pleasure...

There was a loud sizzle and the smoke alarm sounded, jolting Rhys back to reality.

"Something's burning," Lila said.

Rhys had already spun to find smoke rising from the grill. He swallowed a curse and quickly moved pans around, turning off the heat and doing his best to save the grilled vegetables. One look at them smoking in the pan and he chucked them in the sink. They sizzled in the bit of water there and he put the pan aside. He surveyed the result of his distraction and tried to plan an alternative that would be ready at the same time as the fish. He failed.

Then the firestorm crackled as Lila laid a hand on his shoulder. He closed his eyes, feeling its insistent sizzle, and turned to see her eyes narrow. Her gaze swept over him, her expression so grim that he wondered what he'd done or said wrong.

"You're hurt," she said with quiet conviction, then met his gaze.

Rhys was surprised she knew. He thought he'd hidden the damage pretty well. "How can you tell?"

"It's your aura," she said, her tone pragmatic. "And I'm a healer. I look for it."

"You didn't say anything earlier."

"I saw it right away."

But she hadn't done anything. Rhys understood immediately. His return of her skin had been exactly the right thing to do.

Lila smiled and flicked a fingertip across his mouth. "And this firestorm of yours is a little distracting." Sparks danced between her fingertip and his lips and she watched them as if mesmerized, their light mirrored in her eyes. Then she looked up at Rhys, their gazes locking as his heart nearly stopped. He felt as if a barrier had been dissolved between them and was glad he'd thought of the skin.

"It is," he managed to agree, and could have drowned in the darkness of her eyes.

"Where are you hurt?" she asked, giving him a fierce look. "Or would you rather I found the injuries myself?"

"It's just a rip or two," he said, trying to make light of the damage Embron had inflicted. "The usual result of a dragonfight. It'll heal."

She raised a brow. "Without treatment?" She was already lifting the hem of his T-shirt and the firestorm crackled between them with dizzying intensity.

"I put some of Sloane's salve on it," Rhys managed to say. "It works pretty well."

"Sloane?" Lila bent to look at his side, placing her hand against the bandage he'd bound around himself. She shook her head, then unfastened the end of his makeshift bandage. She looked as disapproving as Sloane might have, but Rhys had found it hard to treat this particular injury because of its location.

"The Apothecary of the *Pyr*. He makes herbal potions for us."

Lila inhaled sharply when the cloth fell away. "No salve will fix these, at least not soon." Even Rhys was surprised by the deep gouges and had to avert his gaze.

He lifted Lila's hand away, not wanting her to think he was an invalid. "It's fine. It'll heal," he said. "Let me serve your dinner."

"No. I'm going to fix this first," she said with authority. Rhys opened his mouth to argue, but she shook a finger at him. "Are all the villains vanquished? Could Embron come back for another round? What about the Dark Queen? Is she locked safely back in Fae?"

Rhys sighed. "You're right. It isn't over."

Lila's smile was fleeting. She flattened her hands against his skin, pressing her palms against the open wounds. Then she leaned against him and closed her eyes. Rhys caught his breath at the lick of the firestorm against his skin, then the cool touch of her palms against his injuries.

"I don't think..." he began to protest.

"Don't think," she said, then bent and exhaled right beside his wound.

Rhys' eyes widened when he saw something swirl from her mouth. It was blue or maybe green, like a mist rising above the sea. It flowed from Lila's mouth to his injuries, and instead of the spark of the firestorm, he felt a coolness wherever it touched. The ocean might have been lapping against his side, each wave of salt water easing the pain a little bit more. He sensed the intensity of her concentration and understood that she was giving him a gift. The rhythm of her breath and the relief made him lean back his head and close his eyes.

It felt so good.

Selkies could heal, or at least this one could. Rhys hadn't known that, but he had no doubt of Lila's powers. He felt the muscle knitting together again. He felt the skin growing so that the wound closed. He felt the burn of the injury fade and even the swelling disappear. By the time Lila straightened beside him and tossed her hair over her shoulder, he knew what his exploring hand would find.

His side was healed, as if he'd never been injured at all.

His mate had chosen to help him.

Rhys' doubts about Lila's intentions were completely dismissed. She had to be his mate. The firestorm had to be real.

He looked down, awed and amazed. "Wow. Thank you."

Lila didn't reply, though. She looked down at his feet, then dropped to one knee.

"They aren't healing," he admitted. She eased off his kitchen clog with gentle hands then grimaced at the sight of his injured foot.

"These wounds aren't from a dragonfight," she said, glancing up at him. "These are from Fae, from dancing."

Rhys nodded.

Lila winced and ran a fingertip along the side of his foot. "Blisters that rose and broke, then bled. I'll bet the bottoms of your feet are almost raw."

"It's not pretty," Rhys admitted.

She moved her hand toward the wounds and away from them again, frowning at something only she could see. "There's still magick in them."

Rhys was reassured that they'd come to a similar conclusion. He usually recovered quickly and while he was making some progress with these injuries, they should have been completely healed by now. She asked to see the other foot and Rhys removed his other clog, watching as she studied them.

She knelt before him and breathed her healing mist, the relief so intense that Rhys felt tear prick when he closed his eyes. He could feel the coolness against his feet, and once again, he felt the wounds closing and the skin healing. The pain receded so that it wasn't at the fore of his thoughts anymore and gratitude flooded his heart.

Lila stopped then and frowned down at his feet. They weren't completely healed, but the improvement was remarkable.

"Thank you," Rhys said.

She stood, bracing her hands on her hips. "I don't want to seal them completely before the magick is evicted." She smiled at him. "I have to think about this," she admitted. "Magick is complicated."

She'd proven that they were stronger together than apart. They would have a partnership, even if it took him nine months to convince her.

He could start right away.

"Better thinking on a full stomach?" he asked, feeling lighter and more like his usual confident self.

Lila smiled, a brighter and happier smile than he'd seen so far, and stood beside him. "Did I earn dinner for improving those wounds, at least?"

"You don't have to earn dinner," he began to protest, but Lila silenced him with the caress of her fingers across his mouth. The firestorm surged between them, making the air crackle with heat, feeding Rhys' need to give her pleasure.

"Don't worry about the vegetables. I mostly want the fish," she whispered, then kissed the corner of his mouth. He closed his eyes against the flare of light, then watched her, mesmerized. "Maybe a little salad." She kissed the other corner of his mouth, sending a tide of desire through him that left his knees weak.

Rhys lifted her against him, then seated her on the counter. She immediately wrapped her legs around him, holding him tightly against her heat. "We don't have to eat at all," he said, noticing that he sounded breathless and rushed. "Or not right away."

"Great minds think alike," she whispered, reaching to replace her fingertips with her mouth. "In fact, I have an appetite for something a little more substantial." Her eyes lit with mischief and she surveyed him with a smile. "Are you guaranteed to please, too?"

"Of course."

She laughed then framed his face in her hands and kissed him, teasing him with the brush of her mouth over his and sending sparks flying into the air. Then she sealed her mouth over his and Rhys forgot everything but the glorious woman in his arms.

And the firestorm that demanded to be satisfied.

Each kiss was better than the last.

Rhys locked his hands around Lila's waist, leaning against her so she could feel his erection. He could have been carved of stone, every muscle taut, every bit of him pumped. Lila ran her hands over him, locked her fingers into his hair and opened her mouth to him. Rhys didn't hesitate: he angled his head, deepening their kiss and swallowing her gasp of pleasure. His kiss turned wicked and provocative, teasing and tempting her, proving that she'd been right about his attention to detail. The weight of his hands on her was perfect. His kiss was the ideal combination of sweetness and hot demand. The firestorm crackled and burned around them with such intensity that Lila had to close her eyes against its bright light. She felt a trickle of perspiration slide down her spine and tasted salt in their kiss, but she didn't care.

This kiss was so wonderful that she didn't want it to end.

Rhys' hands slid under the hem of the shirt she'd borrowed from him and she heard his little growl of pleasure when he discovered that she was naked underneath it. He lifted it to her shoulders and she raised her arms, letting him push it over her head. His eyes glittered as he surveyed her, nude on his counter, and he cast the shirt to the floor.

Then he took a step back. He peeled off his T-shirt and Lila was the one taking a close study. There was a dragon tattoo on his chest, one that wasn't nearly as magnificent as he was in dragon form. The sparks of the firestorm seemed to dance around the ink, illuminating it with inner fire. Rhys kicked off his jeans and she inhaled in anticipation as he returned to kiss her again. She wrapped her legs around his waist and her arms around his neck, claiming his mouth with another demanding kiss. One of his arms locked around her waist and the other slid beneath her, lifting her off the counter.

He carried her to the bedroom without breaking his kiss, then laid her on the sheets she'd left rumpled. Before she could protest, his mouth slid down, kissing the underside of her chin, the side of her neck, the hollow of her throat. His lips left a trail of fire as the firestorm sparked and burned with increasing heat and Lila thought she might melt with desire. He cupped her breast in one palm, his thumb sliding across her nipple in a gentle demand that made her catch her breath. Then his mouth closed around her nipple, teasing it to a tight peak with his lips and teeth and tongue. He had one arm locked around her waist and his other hand slid between her thighs to caress her.

Lila moaned and surrendered to pleasure. Rhys stretched out beside her and she hung on to his broad shoulders, letting him torment her with his touch. When her nipple was tight, he turned his attention to the other one, even as he rolled her clitoris between his finger and thumb. He pinched it lightly and Lila dug her fingernails into his shoulders, burning with a need to have him inside her. She made an incoherent plea and felt the breath of his laughter, then he eased two fingers inside her, his thumb still driving her to distraction.

Every sweep of his fingers over her body left a line of sparks in its wake and she soon felt as if her skin glowed with desire. She felt radiant from his sensual touch and she saw the halo of light that the firestorm created around them. It danced on the ceiling, an aura of their mating, and she smiled that it was both bright and whole.

She caught his face in her hands again and kissed him, letting her fingertips trail into his hair and down his neck to his shoulders. She felt the line of fire left in their wake and knew they coaxed this fire to burn together. Lila poured everything into her kiss, wanting it to be persuasive and potent, slow and sensual, as well as filled with the urgency of the firestorm.

He'd waited five hundred years for this. He'd never experience it again. Lila wanted this night to be a touchstone for him, a potent memory of the birthright of his kind.

She was pretty sure she'd remember it forever.

She opened her mouth to him and Rhys accepted the invitation, demanding more from her with every breath. Lila once again wrapped her arms around his waist, wanting to feel his heat inside her, and rocked against him. He was hard and thick, as impressive as she expected a dragon shifter to be, and she couldn't wait. The storm was rising inside her and she knew she was close to release, but she wanted them to ride that wave together.

"Not yet," he whispered, catching his breath.

"Now," she demanded and rolled him to his back. She tossed her hair as she sat astride him, smiling down at him in triumph as she took him inside her. He closed his eyes in the same moment that Lila tipped her head back with satisfaction.

So good.

"So tight," he whispered and flexed his fingers, gripping her waist. When he opened his eyes, they were gleaming, and his smile was slow and wicked.

Lila lowered herself over him, letting her hair fall in a curtain around them, crushing her breasts against his chest. He surveyed her as his hands roved lower and he gripped her tightly then drove even deeper. She held his gaze as she rolled her hips, watching him inhale sharply, her lips parting as he rubbed against her.

"You're blushing," he murmured.

"I'm burning up."

He grinned and rubbed against her, making her lips part with pleasure. "Let's kindle this fire," he said. "Let's make it burn white-hot and forge everything new."

That was an invitation Lila couldn't refuse.

The firestorm sizzled beyond any fire Rhys had ever experienced. It burned and it cauterized; it cleansed and it purified; it made everything simple and clear. Lila was his mate. They would have a son. They would build a family and a future together, and the moment he had awaited his entire life had arrived.

The firestorm marked the beginning.

Its heat surged through his body, filling him with power and purpose, and the conviction that his destiny was just as foretold. The sight of Lila, her smooth fair skin, her long dark hair, her eyes filled with a thousand invitations, was more than he could resist. That she'd healed him was so much more than he'd ever expected in a mate. She moved with a sensual grace that he knew would always fascinate him. He liked that she was clever and outspoken. He liked that she was accustomed to taking care of herself.

He knew they'd make an incredible team.

She was atop him, her hair flowing out behind her, her lips curved in a smile. The firestorm burned around her like a brilliant corona and Rhys felt its fire in his veins. He would never forget this moment. She bent over him and speared her fingers into his hair, holding him captive to her hungry kiss. Her breasts were pressed against his chest and he could feel the beat of her heart.

His own matched its pace, and the sensation made his head spin. He closed his eyes and surrendered to the demand of the firestorm, its pulsing heat, its urgent insistence on satisfaction. He moved within Lila's slick heat, then eased a finger between them to caress her clitoris. He felt her gasp as if he had made the same sound himself. His breathing matched hers and the thunder of his heart was her own. He knew as she approached the summit of her pleasure and was right with her. When he felt the storm launch, he pinched her and she roared with pleasure as her climax swept over her. The brilliant halo of fire brightened around her, flashing white with her release.

Rhys heard himself roar as he followed suit, and his pleasure seemed to last a thousand years. He closed his eyes, his heart thundering in the aftermath, then she collapsed atop him, still trembling. Rhys could have run a marathon, judging by the thunder of his heart and the simmer beneath his skin. He smiled at the sweep of her silken hair over his lips, then opened his eyes. She braced her weight on her hands and smiled down at him.

"Wow," she said, then licked her finger and touched his shoulder. She made a hissing sound. "Hot stuff."

But there was no golden spark of the firestorm, not anymore. It had been genuine, and now it was satisfied. Rhys exhaled and felt his heart slow, then he reached up to spear his fingers through Lila's hair. The long strands tangled over his hand and her smile broadened as he pulled her down for another long slow kiss.

The firestorm was satisfied, but he still had to convince his mate of the merit of their partnership. Rhys intended to take his time—and be persuasive.

This night might be his only opportunity and he was going to make it count.

CHAPTER SEVEN

ila awakened to bright light.

She thought at first that it was the firestorm, then realized there was a beam of sunlight shining across the bed. It was warm and golden, autumn sunlight, and its color reminded her that she should get back to the island. The blinds were open and she could see frost on the window, sparkling in the sun. It would be a cold day, which made her yearn to linger in bed.

It would be even better if Rhys joined her.

Lila rolled over and stretched, unable to keep from smiling after their night together. Rhys had been every bit as attentive to detail as she'd expected. She couldn't remember when she'd had so many orgasms in rapid succession.

Dragon shifters really did have stamina.

He'd been more than worth the trip from Scotland.

Rhys wasn't in bed with her, but the sounds from the kitchen made it easy to guess his location. Lila stared at the ceiling, knowing it was time to make her decision.

Should she conceive Rhys' son?

She'd come to New York ready for sexual satisfaction and nothing else. Rhys' faith in the firestorm and his desire for a son was more persuasive than she might have expected. She could give him what he wanted and had pretty much decided to do so, but without the persistent hum of the firestorm, Lila wondered whether that was a wise choice.

The detail that troubled her was that she'd met Rhys near a beach on North Rona. She'd assumed he'd flown there, following the spark of the firestorm, but he said he'd entered Fae *before* meeting her. That meant either he'd left Fae without realizing it, or that she'd entered Fae without realizing it, and neither option was reassuring. Either meant that there was a portal to Fae closer to Lila's home than she'd realized, one that she wasn't aware existed. Plus Maeve demanded a toll from anyone who crossed the borders of her realm: Rhys had paid one toll but not two, and Lila hadn't paid one at all.

It would be irresponsible and wrong to conceive a child without being certain that infant would be safe.

Lila closed her eyes. She knew Rhys would be disappointed, but she couldn't choose otherwise.

She chose not to conceive.

The firestorm lit immediately, a faint golden glow that slid through her body from head to toe. It brightened to a shimmer and she caught her breath as her desire for Rhys sparked once more. She was surrounded by that yellow light again and so in need of a certain dragon shifter's touch that she might have been celibate for a year.

How was she going to leave him and go home?

She had to find the strength somehow.

She heard Rhys mutter a curse and felt his confusion.

It was time to make her confession, even though he wasn't going to like it much.

Sylvia thought it was Monday.

She wasn't entirely sure and that bothered her. Sylvia liked to be the organized one, the one who knew what day and what time it was, the one who remembered all the details. But she didn't. Not anymore. Her memory had become unreliable since her escape from the Circus of Wonders with Sebastian and she didn't like it one bit.

It had to be Sebastian's fault.

She remembered their wild run across the city, a Fae warrior in pursuit, and Sebastian's deft use of the subways to leave their attacker behind. She remembered being locked in the submarine, the *Growler*, with Sebastian at the *Intrepid* museum. She remembered the sound of the Fae warrior landing on the roof just as Sebastian locked the door and the flicker of silver light around the perimeter of the closure.

She remembered the moment she'd realized she was trapped with a vampire, uncertain when he'd last fed, tingling with the awareness of his intense scrutiny. She remembered her awareness of him, and knew that being attracted to a vampire was a bad idea when she'd make a nice light snack.

Sebastian had a dangerous way of making Sylvia feel as if she was the only woman in the world. The way he looked at her, as if he could read her thoughts and desires—even though he said he couldn't—made her tingle to her toes. She was drawn to him, even knowing that was dumb, and aroused by him, probably by his intention, which was even dumber. She suspected that her sensual dreams of the red room and endless bouts of pleasure with Sebastian were of his doing.

She was unsure whether those encounters had actually happened or not.

She'd lost track of time, thanks to the omissions in her memory. She remembered that she and Sebastian had made a deal in the submarine, and was pretty sure that he'd agreed to answer three questions for her. She had no recollection of what she'd asked, much less what he'd replied. She had about a thousand questions for him so couldn't even guess what she had asked.

After that, everything was hazy and vague, more like impressions than memories. Had she been locked in a vault hidden beneath the antique shop? Where was Maeve's book, the one that Micah had said was entrusted to her? Had Sebastian taken possession of her just to get the book?

Had she and Sebastian gone to Bones together to meet with the Others? It seemed as if they had, but Sylvia didn't trust her memory on that either—especially since the entry about the *Pyr* had revised itself while they were looking at it. That seemed more like a dream than anything that could have actually happened. Could seven more dragon shifters manifest suddenly in the world she thought she knew?

None of it made sense.

The only thing Sylvia knew for sure was that she wanted her own bed and her little apartment more than she'd ever wanted anything else in the world. She wanted to sit in her aunt's courtyard garden and share dinner with Eithne. She wanted to go to work every weekday morning and catalogue books in the basement of the library with a desperation that would have surprised her a month before. If she could have her old dull life back—without enticing vampires, dangerous Fae, dragon shifters, Others or treacherous books—she'd never complain about boredom again.

She'd awakened in the library with heavy velvet curtains, the one that seemed to be Sebastian's room. She'd often wondered about the books that filled the shelves, but when Sebastian was with her, she was more concerned about what he'd do next. He was as unpredictable as a feral cat, but a lot more alluring. For the first time, she was alone in this room, but perusing the collection was the last thing on her mind.

Sylvia drew back the edge of a curtain, only to discover that there were blackout blinds behind them. She looked around one, and smiled at the sunlight that flooded the view. There was almost no one in sight. Some leaves were blowing down the street and the sunlight was fiercely bright and golden. The sky was clear blue. It would be chilly, with a bite in the wind. It must be November, after all.

She'd gone into the submarine with Sebastian on Halloween. If it was Monday, it seemed that too much time had passed for it to be the fourth. Maybe it was the eleventh of November. Surely it would be colder if it was later than that. Sylvia hated that she wasn't sure.

Where was Sebastian?

She went to the door and grimaced when she found it locked. Of course. He left nothing to chance.

She was dressed as she had been that night at the circus and that made her want a long hot shower, too. She walked around the library that was her prison, impatient to escape, and scanned the titles—because there was nothing else to do. A lot of them were collections of folklore and old songs. Fables and stories. Lives of saints. She made a mental inventory of them out of habit, seeking similarities, itching to reorganize them.

If Maeve's Book of Beasts was on the shelves, it was well hidden.

Where was Sebastian? He must be sleeping somewhere, or otherwise hidden from the light. Why not here, in this room she thought was his?

She fought the sense that this was a test or a trick.

Could she open the window? Sylvia pushed back the window coverings again, only to discover that the windows were fixed panes of glass. They didn't open and never had. She spun to survey the room in frustration, then heard a slight sound.

Metal on metal.

She straightened, bracing herself for Sebastian's reappearance. She watched as the knob turned slowly, then the door began to open. It stopped when it was slightly ajar, which wasn't like Sebastian at all. He never hesitated once he'd made a choice. She knew that much about him already.

Her heart pounding, Sylvia crossed the room silently. She looked through the crack into the darkness beyond, but saw nothing in the shadows. She touched the knob and urged the door to open. The hinges creaked and it took an excruciatingly long moment for her eyes to adjust to the darkness beyond. She could barely see the sweep of the staircase, the one that led down to the shop. Items glinted in the darkness there, hurricane lamps and trinkets. She was struck again how it looked like it was from another time. It was more than the antiques—hurricane lamps were used as lighting, and their flames flickered.

A yawning silence rose from the antique shop as well as the scent of dust. She could smell dampness beneath it, as if someone had left open the door to a cellar, and then she heard distant voices.

Men.

Arguing.

Sylvia took a step out of Sebastian's sanctuary. It was Micah and Sebastian who argued. She was sure of it. A woman's decisive voice interjected at intervals. That would be Micah's partner, Rosemary, who gave Sylvia the chills.

She crept to the top of the stairs, wincing when the wooden floor creaked. Were they all in the vault in the basement? Could she possibly make it to the door to the shop and escape? What about the locks?

"Open," a woman said so quietly that Sylvia almost didn't hear her.

She started and spun, spotting the vampire who looked like a teenage girl leaning against the wall behind her. She remembered that Bella was her name. Bella was blond and pretty, dressed in black and pink. She, too, could stand completely still for long intervals, as Sebastian could. Bella smiled at Sylvia as she dropped a ring of brass keys into her Hello Kitty tote bag. Those looked like they should open all the doors in a magical castle.

Sylvia pointed back to the door of the library in question. Bella nodded and smiled, revealing the points of her canine teeth.

Why had she let Sylvia out?

There was something about Bella that prompted distrust.

Bella pointed to the door to the street and Sylvia decided she could get over that distrust if it meant freedom. Even if Bella meant to trick her, maybe she could escape anyway. She started down the stairs.

"Don't forget your book," Bella said softly and Sylvia glanced back to see Maeve's Book of Beasts on the top step. She was sure it hadn't been there before.

She was halfway tempted to step over it and keep going.

Hadn't she been chosen as its custodian? Didn't she want to really look through it, maybe catalogue its contents? If she took it, she could copy its lists.

Eithne had always told her that seemingly random events happened for a reason, that they weren't random at all, so she should trust in them. If Sylvia was attacked by Fae warriors, well, maybe she'd just hand it over. Before she could think about it too much, she bent down and picked up the book. The glamor wavered a little then it looked just like one of the many notebooks she'd bought.

She gripped it tightly and glanced up as Bella gave her a fingertip wave.

That chilling smile was enough to make anyone run. Sylvia took the stairs two at a time, making sure her progress was soundless. The stairs didn't even creak, so someone somewhere was on her side.

Even though she was quick, Bella was quicker. The vampire passed her in a blur and met her at the door to the street, holding out a black quilted coat like a valet. It seemed to be new. Bella's eyes glittered and her features sharpened as Sylvia drew closer, a sign that the vampire might not have fed recently. She opened her mouth and bared her teeth, as if taking Sylvia's scent—and finding it tempting.

The door was unlocked. The sunlight was her only salvation.

Sylvia seized the coat and flung open the door, stumbling into the street as she shrugged on the coat. It was cold, the wind filled with the promise of winter, but she didn't care. She ran and ran, hugging the book tightly against her chest. No one seemed to pursue her, but she didn't slow down. She raced toward her apartment in Eithne's townhouse, her heart thundering and her breath fogging the air.

Sebastian might follow her at nightfall, but Sylvia would make this day of freedom count.

To Rhys' surprise, satisfying the firestorm hadn't eliminated his agitation. As soon as he left Lila sleeping in his bed, his thoughts began to churn again. He had so many questions and not enough answers, plus a pervasive sense of dread.

What if his firestorm was a spell, just as Kristofer's had been? That didn't mean Lila was deceptive—she could be fooled, too. The possibility made Rhys uneasy. After all, selkies had to be on Maeve's list as well as the *Pyr*. Why then was the firestorm's spark extinguished? That must mean it was real.

The firestorm was supposed to simplify things, but instead, he felt that everything had become infinitely more complicated. Even if the firestorm was real, Lila was a selkie and he was *Pyr*: what would their son be? What powers would he have—and which ones would he not inherit? Rhys wanted to respect Lila's choice not to make a partnership with him, but how could he protect her and their son when she was half a world away?

After he showered and dressed, he returned to what he knew best. Lila, again, hadn't had a chance to eat. Rhys cleaned up the kitchen and began to cook breakfast. He had a few things in the fridge and pantry, enough for his breakfast plans. He made himself a pot of coffee and got to work. The rhythm of preparing food soothed him, as it always did, and he dared to hope for the best.

Rhys heard Lila's breathing change as she awakened and put the kettle on for tea. He was trying to prioritize his questions, hoping they wouldn't argue, when the inexplicable happened: the firestorm sparked again.

Rhys stared at his hand, unable to believe his eyes. He blinked but it made no difference. There could be no mistaking the sparks that shot from his fingers or the heat that the firestorm launched within him.

How could it be back?

His mind clouded with desire and he felt the firestorm's power slide through his body all over again, making him burn with need again. This time, though, instead of imagining how it would be to seduce Lila, he knew exactly how it would be. He could remember their night together and that only amplified his reaction. He thought of her smooth skin, her full lips, the way she laughed a little, kind of breathless and husky, when he ran his hands down her sides. He recalled the little gasp she made before her release and the way she completely surrendered to pleasure— and he burned the eggs.

"Oops," she said from behind him, that thread of humor in her tone. Rhys spun to face her and she smiled. "Something burning again." She strolled toward him, wearing one of his T-shirts and not much else, and slipped onto a stool on the opposite side of the counter. She was silhouetted by a corona of fire, one that sparked toward him at intervals and burned vivid yellow. "For a chef, you burn a lot of food. That must affect your restaurant's profits." She lifted a brow and he saw a confidence in her dark gaze, as well as a lack of surprise.

"It's you," Rhys said curtly and held up a hand, watching the sparks fly. "It's this."

"Just as distracting as ever, isn't it?" She spoke lightly and again he was struck by her lack of surprise.

Maybe it was a spell, and she was the one commanding it. The possibility made Rhys feel sick.

"How can it be back?" he whispered.

"Well, it's not for a lack of enthusiasm," Lila said and he frowned. Her smile faded as she studied him. "I could tell you, but you aren't going to like it."

Rhys poured her a mug of tea and slid it across the counter to her, folding his arms across his chest to watch her and wait. He probably didn't look encouraging, but he was annoyed and didn't care whether she knew it.

She said she liked honesty.

Lila picked up the mug and wrapped her hands around it, watching him closely. "I chose," she admitted, then took a sip.

"You chose what?"

"I chose not to conceive."

Rhys blinked. "You can do that?"

"It's one of our gifts."

She called it a gift to deny the firestorm's promise.

Rhys exhaled in frustration and turned back to the stove. He took the warm pan with the eggs, dumped them into the trash, then began to wash the pan. His movements were abrupt, but he didn't want to say too much. She'd chosen. She'd known all along that she could chose yet hadn't mentioned that detail until this moment. He felt cheated and deceived, which should not be part of the firestorm to his thinking.

Yet it remained unsatisfied. It burned with new vigor, but this time, its demanding heat felt both exhilarating and futile to Rhys. He stifled the urge to swear.

Or break something.

He let himself slam pots on the washboard.

"You're disappointed," Lila said after he cleaned vigorously for a few minutes.

"You expected me to be." Rhys glanced her way, knowing his expression was as forbidding as his tone. "You *knew* I would be."

Lila sighed and nodded agreement.

"I thought we were in agreement," he added, his tone hard. "I thought we'd made a plan."

"We were, actually," she admitted, which was a bit of a relief. "But this morning, I reconsidered." She sipped her tea.

She was unapologetic, and while Rhys respected that the choice was hers to make, he wished she'd talked to him about it first.

"You don't think I should get to choose?" she asked and he heard the warning in her tone.

"No. I just wish we had talked about it first." He looked down at the sink, then turned off the water, trying to keep his patience. Lila had to have a good reason for her choice. Well, he hoped she had a good reason. She seemed to be sensible, so maybe there was something he could do to encourage her to reconsider again.

"I don't see what there is to talk about."

Rhys exhaled. "Explain to me what it means for you to choose, please."

"It's the way of our kind. We're immortal and fertile, but we choose when to conceive. Some selkies have lots of offspring. Others have none. Some permit themselves to conceive when they fall in love. Others made dynastic decisions or strategic ones." Lila shrugged as if indifferent, but she was watching him intently.

Warily.

As if he was the unpredictable one, which would have been funny if he'd been in a better mood.

She was immortal. He hadn't been sure. Was that the issue?

"Tell me the truth: did you change your mind, or did you mislead me?" Rhys asked, keeping his tone as neutral as he could. He glanced Lila's way, suspecting that his reaction showed.

"Which do you think?"

"I'd prefer to think that you changed your mind, because otherwise, I don't understand you at all."

"Plus that means that maybe you can persuade me to change it again, especially if you understand me." She smiled. "Although that will mean satisfying the firestorm again, which isn't such a bad idea."

"Isn't it?"

Lila's gaze clung to his. "It was great," she said with soft heat and Rhys felt the firestorm's insistence all over again.

"It was," he agreed, unwilling to look away.

"But that's not it." She put down her mug with purpose. "I reconsidered when I could think straight again. You said you went through the portal to Fae and the firestorm sparked, then you followed it to me."

"Yes."

"But I didn't think I was in Fae, so that means..."

"Either I left Fae or you entered it," Rhys guessed.

"Which means that one of us owes a debt to the Dark Queen, because we aren't in Fae anymore and no one who enters can leave without paying a price."

Rhys glanced at his feet.

"You paid one toll, not two. Both feet count as one price."

He nodded grimly in understanding.

"It also means there's a portal near my home, one I didn't know about, and that's not good news." Lila frowned with impatience. "I can't conceive a child with those uncertainties," she said, her gaze filled with appeal. "I won't bring a child into the world, just to have him hunted down by the Dark Queen."

Rhys could understand that and felt reassured by her concerns. "You're not saying never."

"I'm saying we have work to do first." Lila smiled, her eyes sparkling with mischief. "And maybe it'll improve the second time. Better answer?"

"Much better." Rhys filled up her tea, then handed her the list he'd written out.

"What's this?" She scanned it then met his gaze again.

"A list of the *Pyr* who are my best friends. When you choose to conceive, you can call any of them for help."

She was clearly puzzled. "I'd call you first."

"But if I'm not around." Rhys didn't like talking about the possibility of his own demise, but it seemed a lot more likely these days. Was Lila right that he owed a second toll to Maeve? He didn't want to think about that, but knew he had to. Either way, the *Pyr* were being hunted and anything could happen. "We *Pyr* take care of each other."

Lila folded the list and slipped it away. It disappeared and Rhys wasn't sure where it went. "Selkies don't," she said easily. "We take care of ourselves and often spend a lot of time alone." She smiled at him. "People talk about the challenges of herding cats, but that's only because they've never tried to build consensus amongst selkies."

"Dragons don't agree that readily either." Rhys presented her with eggs benedict with smoked salmon, garnished with fresh fruit.

"Oh," Lila said and her smile lit her eyes this time. "If you're trying to win me over with food, you're totally acing it." She took a bite and visibly savored it, closing her eyes as she chewed. "I thought you said the *Pyr* didn't have magickal powers," she said softly. "This sauce is pure wizardry."

"Butter fat," Rhys said, serving his own plate. "It hides a multitude of sins."

Lila laughed, an infectious sound that prompted his own smile, and Rhys sat down beside her to eat. The firestorm crackled and burned, the tingle of it making him aware of every physical sensation. He could smell the sweet musk of Lila's skin and taste the contrast of the smoked salmon and the silky *béchamel* sauce. The sparks danced along his skin and his breathing matched hers, giving him that dizzy sensation that was so addictive. When she reached to kiss his cheek, he thought the surge of pleasure might take him into orbit.

"What are you feeling?" she whispered and he opened his eyes to find her face close to his, her gaze filled with curiosity.

"Because you're my mate, the firestorm compels my heart to match the pace of yours, and my breathing to synchronize with yours." Rhys shook his head in wonder. "It creates a feeling of union that's almost overwhelming."

"Like coming simultaneously," she said.

"Yes, but better. More intense." Rhys turned to her and was snared by her smile and the light in her eyes. How many times would she choose not to conceive? How many times would they satisfy the firestorm? Even the chance to do it twice blew his mind.

He forced himself to look down at his breakfast and take another bite. They had to figure this out to eliminate her concerns. Rhys agreed with her, and wanted to do his part. "Tell me about the children of your kind," he invited.

"What about them?"

"What powers do they have?"

"It depends," Lila said. "Only a mating with another selkie will create a selkie child. They're indistinguishable from seal pups until they learn to shift, which happens when they're about two years old. They swim with the herd of grey seals until then." She frowned. "Actually, it's humans who can't distinguish our children from seal pups. The seals know."

"How can you tell? Can you communicate with the seals?"

"As children, yes. Some of us maintain that later while others forget. But even so, they treat us and our children differently. We're allowed in the herd, but on the perimeter. It's important that we defer to their leaders to keep the peace, and they vigorously defend the boundaries between us in mating season." She met his gaze. "We don't mate with seals. Ever."

"But you research them."

She nodded. "Seems like a natural fit for a job for me. I understand them a bit better than most researchers and they trust me a bit more because of my nature. They come to North Rona to deliver their pups on the beach and I help."

"That would increase their trust."

"Yes." She finished her breakfast and gave him another stunning smile. "That was delicious. I was really hungry and it was perfect." Once again, Rhys was struck by her sincerity and honesty.

He liked her.

He wanted to be mates in every possible way, and not just because he believed in the firestorm's promise. That meant he needed to find out why Lila was so set against relationships.

Maybe the healer needed to be healed herself.

Rhys got up to refill her tea, thinking furiously. "What happens when you mate with those who aren't selkies?"

Lila sobered. "With men, our children are human. They're mortal. They can't shift shape." She spread her fingers. "They might have webbing between their fingers and some have psychic gifts. Some say they're particularly beautiful or that they're instinctively good swimmers. I'm not sure that's true." She met his gaze. "You said the *Pyr* children are always boys and that they come into their powers at puberty."

Rhys nodded. "They are also always, as far as I know, the offspring of one *Pyr* and one human woman. They're mortal, but have the powers of their fathers. We don't mate with other kinds."

"Or with your own kind."

Rhys blinked. "There's only one female at a time, the Wyvern, and it's taboo to be with her."

"Anyone ever done it?"

"They both died, sacrificing themselves," he admitted softly.

Lila's brows rose. "So, if we had a son, he would likely be *Pyr*."

"But would he?" Rhys had to ask. "Or would he be another new kind?"

"A dragon shifter after puberty, with webbed fingers and a gift of foresight from birth," Lila suggested. Her eyes twinkled. "I expected you to say there's one good way to find out."

"But your concerns are valid. If he's his own kind, he'd be the only one."

Lila frowned. "She'd want to strike him off her list."

"Exactly." Rhys forced himself to say the words. "And it would be pretty easy for fifteen or twenty years. Once he comes into his inherited gifts, he'll have to train to learn how to use them best. Until then, he'd have only you to defend him, or only me, if you surrendered him to me."

"And your fellow *Pyr*."

"I hope so, even though he'd be different."

Lila considered him. "Are you seriously arguing for a permanent connection again, even before I've decided to choose to bear your son?"

Rhys smiled. "Can't blame a guy for trying. I think we're good together."

"I work alone. I live alone. I am alone."

"Me, too, a lot of the time, but I miss having a family." He pointed out the obvious. "If he's not *Pyr*, how am I going to defend a seal pup that I can't distinguish from the others?"

"Do you really think you wouldn't know?"

Rhys shrugged. "I might. We have keen senses. But the fact is that I'm a lousy swimmer and that could be a problem."

Lila smiled. "Maybe I should just teach you to swim."

They smiled at each other and their gazes locked. The firestorm seemed to glow with greater intensity and Rhys found himself thinking of heading back to the bedroom again. But no—when they satisfied the firestorm again, he wanted to know that she would choose to have his son. He started on the dishes. "Is it that you don't have family or you don't want one on principle?"

"Both." Lila came into the kitchen and poured herself more tea. "What happened to your family?"

"Well, the usual thing that happens to mortals. I had a brother, a twin, and I miss him every day."

"Now, there's twins in your bloodline," Lila said with a shake of her head. "Two boys! You should come with a warning label, Rhys Lewis." Her tone was teasing, though, and Rhys didn't take offense. "What happened to him?"

"He died. There was a battle between *Pyr* and *Slayers*, good dragon shifters vs. bad dragon shifters is the easiest explanation. We both went to fight."

"What's bad about *Slayers*?"

"They refused to defend the treasures of the earth, of which humans are one, and were concerned with their own goals instead of the greater good. Some of them advocated eliminating humans completely. They're gone now."

"The Dark Queen?"

"No, we fought against them ourselves. The final battle was long foretold and ended recently: the *Pyr* won. But that fight in the nineteenth century cost many of our best, including my brother." Rhys took a deep breath, the pain of loss as sharp as when it had been new. "He was my constant companion, blood of my heart, breath of my lungs. We learned to manage our abilities together, fought together to hone our skills, shared our hoards and were so close as to be each other's mirror. For two hundred and sixty-two years, he was always there, and then suddenly, he was gone. I still look for him."

"When was that battle?"

"1807."

"More than two hundred years ago," Lila mused and she put a hand on his shoulder. "Most would think that an eternity, but I know it can pass in the blink of an eye."

Rhys nodded and put his hand over hers, appreciating her sympathy. "I was a bit of a mess for a while," he admitted roughly. "Didn't you ever lose anyone?"

She averted her gaze, avoiding his question. "What was your brother's name?"

"Llewelyn."

"Are you Welsh dragons?"

Rhys shook his head. "No. Our father fought as a mercenary across the Mediterranean. He was from Macedonia. He met our mother in Malta, when she took a pilgrimage to Jerusalem. She never made it there, thanks to the firestorm, but I'm not sure she regretted it. She loved the heat and the sun: they settled in Malta and we were raised there. It was only after their deaths that Llewelyn and I went to Wales together. We were two hundred years old before we saw the land our mother remembered to her dying day."

"Did you stay there?"

He laughed a little. "No. We went south, back to Malta, then ultimately west."

"Your mother's sons," she said with a smile.

"That sunshine gets in your blood." He watched the flicker of the firestorm and thought it would be just as hard to forget.

"And you went to war."

He nodded. "I met my friend Kristofer after the battle against the *Slayers*. His brother also flew to war, and the three of us had fought together. Storme spoke of Kristofer often, and when he and Llewelyn died, I slaughtered the *Slayer* responsible then took the news to Kristofer. I was injured myself, as well as heartsick, and Kristofer welcomed me. I stayed with him for a long time, apprenticing to him, and we became good friends. He put up with me when I was a lot of trouble and I appreciate that." Rhys felt Lila watching him but didn't want to review his past sins.

"Does Kristofer live here?"

"Vermont. He was the one who followed the spark of his firestorm into Fae at Bones. The firestorm was a spell, but he and Bree had a real one after their battle with Embron."

Lila moved away at the mention of Embron and her tone became crisper. "I understand that you miss having family, but I can't give you that, Rhys. If we can ensure that he won't be hunted, I'll give you a son, but that's it."

"If you've never had family, how can you be so sure you won't like it?"

"I know," she said with force. "I won't have children..."

"How can you be sure until you try?"

She stared at him for a long moment, her heart in her eyes, and he knew the instant she decided to confide in him. "But I did try," she admitted quietly, her gaze softening. She swallowed, her throat working, then her words fell in a rush. "I had a son and a daughter. I was snared and thought that conceiving them would gain my freedom. He lied to me." Her tone turned bitter. "He kept my skin and he hid it from me. He compelled me to remain in human form and denied me my birthright and called it love. And when I finally found my skin, I left without a backward glance. Family is not for me."

It was that story, the old story, and Rhys hated that it had happened to Lila. That it had also explained a lot of her reservations.

He had to fix this or his firestorm had no chance of a future.

He had to win her trust, no matter what price.

CHAPTER EIGHT

hys looked down at his cold coffee. He knew his question wouldn't be welcome, but he had to know. "What happened to the children?" he asked softly.

"I don't know!" Lila said, turning away from him. "They were mortal. I'm sure they died eventually. I'm sure they forgot me."

Rhys shook his head. "They would never forget their mother. They would never forget you, Lila." He was trying to reassure her, but saw immediately that he'd failed.

She stood up and looked as if she might run. "What difference does it make?"

"Maybe you already have family and you've just lost track of them," he suggested.

Lila was visibly shocked and retreated a step. "No! No one depends on me except the seals, and even they would continue to bear their pups without me. I make no connections. I have no obligations." Her voice turned fierce. "I don't owe anything to anyone!"

That wasn't how Rhys thought of family.

"Maybe we should find out for sure," he suggested. "When did this happen and where were they born? What were their names?"

"No!" Lila said, her eyes flashing. She hurried into the bedroom and returned more quickly than Rhys would have thought possible. She was dressed, and at the door, pulling on her boots.

"You can't leave!" he said and saw her shiver at his words. He pushed a hand through his hair. "I mean, you *can* leave. Of course." She didn't even glance his way. "I'd just rather you didn't. We're destined mates. I've waited for this, Lila, for the chance to have a family again..."

She spun to face him, bracing her hands on her hips. "Don't you think what I want matters, too?"

"Well, of course. But it's not safe with Embron and the Dark Queen out there..."

"I've taken care of myself for as long as I can remember," Lila said, her tone harder than it had been. "I'll be just fine, even without a dragon at my back."

"But where will you go?"

"Back to my island. I'm going to find that portal and lock it forever." She looked resolute.

"I can help," Rhys suggested.

"No." She held out a hand and the sparks flared between them. "This will only make it easy for Embron to find us again, and I'm not going to be an easy target."

"I'd defend you," he said but she ignored him, turning her back on him.

"I lost my coat," she said, opening the closet. "I'll borrow one and send it back." She chose one of his jackets, tugged it on then spun to face him. "Don't follow me, Rhys. If I change my mind, I'll let you know." Then she opened the door and flung herself out of his apartment, moving as if she couldn't put distance between them quickly enough.

"The firestorm isn't supposed to go like this!" Rhys shouted in his kitchen, but there was no one there to hear.

Lila was gone.

If Hadrian was listening from the roof, that *Pyr* gave no sign of his presence. Rhys swore thoroughly, found his boots and took another jacket. He looked in the bathroom before he left, just in case.

Her skin was gone.

Lila wasn't coming back anytime soon.

At least the firestorm meant he could find her.

Rhys growled with frustration and threw himself out the door in pursuit of his stubborn mate. Where would she go? The airport?

No, she'd lost her bag when she'd been abducted and her friend had picked it up.

Rhys pulled out his phone and called Nyssa Macleod when he was running down the stairs. The call went to voice mail and he wondered about the fate of her cell phone. He called directory assistance then, hoping she still had a land line. He was in luck.

There was no sign of Lila in the lobby, though he could still discern her scent. The firestorm had dulled to a faint yellow glow, but Rhys could still follow it.

This time, he'd take his bike. He turned to the garage with purpose.

He'd completely forgotten about the gem of the hoard on his kitchen counter. Rhys just strode by it as if it wasn't even there.

Which was exactly what the magick wanted.

It shone with red spell light as Rhys' bike roared, the sound of the engine echoing in the street.

Hadrian must have fallen asleep.

One moment he was lounging in his dragon form on the roof of the building that housed both Rhys' apartment and that *Pyr's* restaurant, breathing slowly and deeply as he tucked the last stray ends of his dragonsmoke barrier into place. The snow was falling lightly, each flake sizzling then turning to mist as it fell upon his hide, and the stars were bright overhead. He was exhausted beyond belief, his feet were still sore, and he couldn't imagine that Rhys would hurry about satisfying the firestorm. He could have gone back to Kristofer' place or looked for the others, but instead, he shifted shape, huddled deeper into his leather jacket and closed his eyes. The firestorm simmered and burned in close proximity, heating steadily, and Hadrian smiled at its radiance.

He jumped when something touched his dragonsmoke. The clear crystalline peal of the barrier being breached made him shift shape immediately. He was on his feet, ready for battle.

"*Sorry!*" Alasdair called in old-speak and Hadrian relaxed. His cousin was in human form and climbed the ladder to the roof with a weariness Hadrian could understand.

The heat of the firestorm was gone. Rhys must have satisfied it, but its absence left Hadrian shivering a bit.

"Did you catch her?" Hadrian shifted back to human form and watched the other *Pyr* approach. Alasdair really looked worn out, but then Hadrian guessed he didn't look much better himself.

"No such luck," Alasdair said, leaning against a silent air conditioning unit. He ran a hand over his head and yawned. "Someone gave her a ride and I lost the car in the traffic."

"What direction was she going?"

"Out of the city." Alasdair gestured and Hadrian had a strange sense his cousin was being evasive. "West. One of the local *Pyr* might have known better where the road went." He glanced down toward Rhys' apartment. "Where'd they go? Out dancing?"

Hadrian realized with a start that Rhys was gone. His scent had faded. "I don't know. I fell asleep while the firestorm was raging." He was embarrassed by this confession but Alasdair smiled.

"It's okay. I saw him downtown. I was just teasing you."

"Downtown? Where?"

"They went to the vampire's antique shop, Reliquary, for a meeting with the Others. Didn't you hear about it?"

"No." Hadrian couldn't understand why he'd been left out of the loop. The whole story sounded wrong, and if it had been anyone other than Alasdair telling it, he would have been openly skeptical.

Alasdair smiled. "You sleep hard. They must have called me because they couldn't wake you up."

"Rhys called you?" This made no sense to Hadrian and he eyed Alasdair, his suspicion stirring. Why wouldn't Rhys have just called him? Rhys knew he was on the roof.

"Yes, he needs the gem of the hoard. He forgot it, if you can believe that, and left it in his apartment. He gave me his keys, but I can't cross your dragonsmoke." Alasdair held up a set of keys. "Why don't you get it and we'll go meet everyone?"

Hadrian nodded and Alasdair tossed him the keys. They descended the ladder together and went to the door of Rhys' apartment. Hadrian was still puzzling over the fact that Rhys had called Alasdair instead of him, but it must have happened the way Alasdair said—he had Rhys' keys, after all. "I can change the permissions so you can cross the barrier," he offered when he unlocked the door, but Alasdair stepped back.

"It'll take too much time. Let's just pick up the stone and get to the meeting."

"Why does Rhys want it?"

"Why didn't he just take it?" Alasdair countered. His gaze slid away and he frowned. "It must be part of the plan with the Others. I have to tell you, I feel a bit left out this time."

"There must be an explanation," Hadrian said, then clapped his cousin on the shoulder. "There's a lot going on. I doubt anyone is trying to make you feel excluded."

"Maybe." Alasdair shrugged but wouldn't meet Hadrian's gaze. Hadrian decided he must be really upset and resolved to talk to him on the way to the antique shop. He entered the apartment and picked up the globe of amber, which was on the counter.

It was so cold that Hadrian shivered. He thought he saw a flash of red light between his fingers, but when he looked at the stone, it was just a piece of amber.

"Hurry," Alasdair said. "I'd like to get some sleep tonight."

"I could go for a big breakfast," Hadrian said. "Maybe we can find a diner that's open all night." He locked the door of the apartment behind himself. "Should we fly to save time?"

"No, it might attract too much attention. Let's see if we can find a cab." Alasdair had already pushed the button for the elevator and the doors opened. They stepped inside and Hadrian zipped up his jacket as they descended to the street.

He was about to make a suggestion about breakfast but something hit him hard on the back of the head. He groaned as he crumbled to the floor. He heard the elevator doors open a moment later and felt the chill of the street slip around him.

He also felt someone pluck the gem of the hoard out of his hand and heard retreating footsteps.

The amber was gone, and he couldn't sense his cousin's presence.

That made no sense.

But the doors closed, sealing Hadrian inside the elevator as everything went black.

Kade didn't like that another *Pyr's* actions made Maeve smile.

He'd fought and captured Alasdair at her command, hoping to earn her favor again. He'd watched as she reached into the other *Pyr's* thoughts and learned what she needed to know. He'd even driven them both to Rhys' apartment and waited for Alasdair to return. Maeve had become so crippled with age by that point that he'd been horrified by the sight of her. He'd to lift her out of the car and even give her a kiss, but Kade prided himself on his loyalty.

He knew it would be repaid.

Instead, he'd been cheated. He'd caught the barest glimpse of the gem of the hoard as Alasdair surrendered it to Maeve. He'd seen her triumphant smile and the sudden red glow as the magick responded to her summons. He saw the years slip away from her appearance until she looked even younger and more beautiful than when he'd first met her. She laughed, seized Alasdair to give him a kiss, then had disappeared in a brilliant flash of silver light.

She'd taken Alasdair and left Kade behind. He shouted, but she was gone, not so much as a glimmer of Fae light left behind. He had the car. He had his resentment, and not much else. His fellow *Pyr* had taken everything from him that he valued.

Kade stared up at the windows of Rhys' apartment. There was one thing left in this realm that was rightly his that he could reclaim.

The stylus Maeve had given to him. With it, he could open a portal and follow her into Fae, just as he had done dozens of times before.

He locked the car and crossed the street, filled with purpose.

Trust a dragon shifter to see the truth Lila didn't even want to acknowledge to herself.

She was lonely. She'd known it for years.

But that didn't mean she was going to make the same mistake all over again. It was seductive to have a man's attention, never mind his sweet promises—but Rhys wanted something from her, just the way Malcolm Ramsay had. She dreamed about their children, but she didn't dream about Malcolm.

There was always a price.

Lila ran down the stairs instead of using the elevator, all six floors of them. Why did men always have this need to contain their women, wives and mates? Why did they have such an insistence on control? Her frustration rose with every step. She hated that her experience meant that she couldn't trust Rhys and didn't even want to try to—she was afraid that she'd be trapped one more time.

No, no and no again. She wasn't going there.

The firestorm would have to remain unsatisfied. Once she got home, it should be easier to ignore.

When Lila reached the street, she realized she was in front of Rhys' restaurant. She shivered, vaguely recalling how she'd been poured into a waiting car. It must have happened right near this very spot at the curb. It was a timely reminder of how much she hated being powerless and captive.

The restaurant was closed and the windows dark. Lila couldn't help noticing that Rhys lived near his work, just the way she did.

But finding traits they had in common, even *liking* Rhys, wasn't going to help her resist temptation.

There was very little traffic. Lila turned and walked briskly in search of a busier street. Rhys would probably follow her, and she had to muster her defenses first. She knew she was right, but something about this *Pyr* was very persuasive. He was so determined. He kissed so well. He was principled and Lila found that appealing.

The firestorm didn't help, which just meant that dragon shifters were used to winning this battle. Lila was cold, despite having Rhys' jacket, and the smell of him on it didn't exactly feed her resolve to leave him behind.

It had been great.

Maybe the best sex ever.

She flagged down a cab on the cross street and headed for Nyssa's place. Nyssa would have her passport and wallet. With any luck, Lila would be on the next flight back to Scotland.

She was due for some luck.

If Rhys followed her that far, at least she'd be on her own turf. It might be easier to deny him with her memories closer. In Manhattan, Malcolm's croft seemed like another world, or maybe a dream. Standing in the surf at North Rona would make it easier to fight the temptation Rhys offered. She had to be smart enough to keep from making the same mistake twice.

She had to find that portal to Fae, too, and figure out how to seal it forever. The last thing she needed was the Dark Queen having easy access to her work and home.

Nyssa's apartment was way uptown in Washington Heights. It was a long cab ride, but the day was sunny and there wasn't much traffic.

The cab was pulling in at the curb before Lila realized that not having her purse meant she didn't have any cash or credit cards. The fare wasn't cheap, either. She was trying to convince the driver to let her go into the lobby and buzz Nyssa for the fare, but her charm was evidently insufficient. Maybe it wasn't even possible to have enough charm to talk herself out of this. Lila was feeling a bit desperate when she heard the roar of a motorcycle.

It parked immediately behind the cab and a halo of orange fire erupted around Lila.

Rhys.

She was both relieved and annoyed. Maybe she was a damsel in distress once in a while, but Lila didn't have to like it.

The cabbie swore at the sight of the firestorm's flames and she wondered how dragon shifters explained the firestorm to mortals.

Maybe she'd leave that job to him and pretend to be oblivious.

Rhys parked the bike and removed his black helmet, his expression grim. He was wearing a black leather jacket and carried a black helmet.

He looked ripped, annoyed and sexy as hell. He locked the helmet away, then strode toward the cab, exuding masculinity and power. It seemed that anyone would know with a glance that he was a dragon shifter.

It was easy to believe that he could breathe fire.

Lila tried to remind herself of the perils of satisfying the firestorm and couldn't think of one reason to avoid it.

After all, she could just choose not to conceive, over and over and over again. The prospect made her knees weak.

Worse, she couldn't imagine why that would be a bad idea.

She was in deep trouble.

Rhys came immediately to Lila's door and she rolled down the window, narrowing her eyes against the brilliant flare of the firestorm. "You forgot your wallet," he growled, then nodded at the driver. "How much is the fare?"

The prospect of cash distracted the cabbie temporarily from the bright light. Rhys paid the fare and opened Lila's door so she could get out. She stood on the sidewalk and watched as he leaned in the front passenger door, staring at the driver. The driver stared back, as if he couldn't do otherwise. "Funny trick of the light," Rhys said, in a strange melodic tone that caught Lila's attention. It reminded her of something.

"Funny trick of the light," the cab driver said, speaking as if he was in a trance.

"The reflection off the mirror looks almost like fire," Rhys murmured.

"The reflection off the mirror looks almost like fire," the cab driver repeated.

Lila gasped, remembering Embron's attempt to convince her to cooperate. He'd had flames in his eyes and used the same tone of voice. This was beguiling. She didn't interrupt, despite her realization and watched in silence as Rhys shook his head ruefully.

"Just an optical illusion," he said in that same tone.

"Just an optical illusion," the cab driver agreed with a sage nod. He glanced at the road and seemed to recover himself. "Hey, have a good day."

"You, too." Rhys straightened and waved, and Lila stared after the departing cab for a minute.

"Am I right that you beguiled him?" she asked Rhys and saw satisfaction in his smile.

"It went kind of well, didn't it? Maybe I just need the right motivation," he said, his gaze warm as it lingered on her. The firestorm simmered with Rhys' approval and she wondered for the first time whether its intensity mirrored his own enthusiasm.

He reached out and caught Lila's hand in his, then inhaled as the firestorm brightened even more. He made a little growl of satisfaction as he looked at her, his eyes glowing with admiration and a little smile curving his lips. Lila couldn't look away. Her gaze fell to his mouth and her own mouth went dry in memory of his slow, thorough kisses. There was nothing in the world but Rhys and the burn of the firestorm.

He pressed a kiss to her palm and Lila thought her knees might give out. She made the mistake of grabbing his other arm to steady herself and the firestorm's light flared around them with greater brilliance. Rhys tucked her hand inside his jacket, placed her palm over his heart, and she could feel it pounding through the cotton of his T-shirt. She closed her eyes as their hearts matched pace and understood why it made him a bit dizzy.

"Hot stuff," he murmured.

Lila opened her eyes and looked away, trying to compose her thoughts. "Beguiling is like charming, then, and you are better at it than I am." She hated her formal tone, but she had to stop thinking about sex with Rhys. "I tried to convince him to let me get Nyssa to pay the fare, but no dice."

He chuckled and the low sound fed the hum of desire deep within Lila. "If charming really is like beguiling, it's a lot easier if the person wants to believe what you're suggesting." He turned that rueful smile on her and her heart thumped. "I'm guessing most cabbies wouldn't like the suggestion that their customer get out of the taxi without paying."

"Kind of like trying to convince you to abandon the firestorm."

Rhys shrugged and tightened his grip on her hand. "I think defeating the Dark Queen is going to be tough and we should take advantage of strengths wherever we find them." He pressed a kiss to her knuckles and Lila couldn't step away. Then his gaze locked with hers. "I understand your reservations and respect them. I just want a chance to prove that I'm different from that loser who lied to you, whoever he was."

"Malcolm Ramsay," Lila said without meaning to do so. This burn of sensual desire really was messing with her mind. She pulled her hand away, wondering whether there were other ways that *Pyr* could beguile. "Long dead, I'm sure."

"How long ago was it?"

Lila knew she shouldn't tell him, but she was unsettled. If confiding in Rhys would persuade him to stop trying to seduce her, it was a small price to pay. She knew Rhys wasn't going to be shocked by the dates or question her memory, and that was kind of a relief. "He took me as his wife in 1869 and I found my skin in 1875."

"And the kids?"

Lila frowned, seeing them both clearly in her memories again. Her chest tightened. She had loved them so. Leaving Malcolm had been easy. Leaving the children had been wrenching, but they couldn't have survived in the sea. "Thomas was born in 1870, Agnes in 1872." She barely recognized her own voice. It seemed both a million years ago and only yesterday. What had happened to them?

"Did you go back? Just to look?"

Lila shook her head fiercely. "I didn't dare," she confessed softly, but knew that Rhys must have heard her.

If nothing else, the memory fed her resolve. She couldn't do that again. Her heart was shredding all over again and they had to be long dead. Rhys and the firestorm had compelled her to think about those children once more and acknowledge the heartbreak that she'd tried to ignore. She couldn't conceive and bear Rhys' son, then surrender the child and continue with her life alone. Once had been more than enough. Actually, she'd done it twice, because she'd had two children with Malcolm. She marched toward the door to the apartment building, filled with new resolve.

Rhys caught the door and opened it for her, maybe discerning more in her tone than she'd expected. She stole a glance at his profile and couldn't guess his thoughts. His aura was brilliant, though, so vigorous and intact that it was dazzling.

"Is Nyssa expecting you?"

"Not specifically. She's probably hoping I turn up." She studied Rhys. "How did you know where she lived?"

"I remembered her name from the call display and looked her up." He lifted a dark brow, so obviously proud of himself that Lila found herself smiling a little. "She is expecting me."

"You don't have to go up with me. We can go our separate ways right here."

"Not a chance," Rhys said with a resolve Lila knew was unshakable. "I'm looking forward to meeting the King Under the Seas."

Lila's heart stopped. "Not Nereus. He can't be here." She knew from Rhys' confident expression that Nereus was in Nyssa's apartment. "Did she say why?"

"No. Maybe he's looking for you." Rhys scanned the list of occupants and buzzed Nyssa, who immediately let them in.

Nereus probably was looking for Lila. After all, she'd been avoiding him, and hadn't told him of her plans to visit New York. "Oh no," she whispered. She really didn't want to have this discussion in front of Rhys.

Rhys smiled a little when Lila hesitated in following him. "Cold feet?"

"This isn't going to be pretty," she admitted.

"Then I'm glad I'm here to defend you," he said easily, taking her hand in his again. It felt good to have the strength of his grip on her hand, but she knew she shouldn't rely on him. He pushed the button for the elevator, then glanced her way when she pulled her hand from his grip.

"You shouldn't go up there. You can't meet him."

Rhys smiled at her. "Are you protecting me?"

"I'm warning you," Lila said. "He and I have something to settle. It's not your business."

"Isn't it?" Rhys asked, his voice low and silky. He was looking determined again and Lila tried to think of a way to dissuade him.

Lila frowned, not wanting to admit more to Rhys but thinking she didn't have a choice. "You don't understand. My kind are cursed in love. We don't have firestorms and make partnerships like you do. We follow our impulses and remain solitary."

"I got that."

"But our numbers are dwindling and Nereus thinks we should all do our part."

"He likes you," Rhys guessed, his gaze darkening.

Lila didn't know about that. She shook her head. "He wants me to bear his child. I've been avoiding him..."

"And it's awkward." He finished her sentence but didn't seem to be troubled by what she was saying. The doors opened and he stepped into the elevator, evidently not taking her advice. "Forewarned is forearmed," he said and pushed the button for Nyssa's floor.

"You're crazy," Lila protested. "He's going to be difficult..."

"All the more reason to defend my destined mate."

Lila was as agitated as Rhys was calm. She had a definite sense of impending doom. As the elevator ascended, she felt her heart pick up its pace. She found Nereus unpredictable, equally as likely to be charming as violent, and doubted he would be glad of Rhys' presence.

Rhys was standing close beside her, so close that she could feel the heat of him. He inhaled and closed his eyes and the firestorm shimmered a little around them, touched by the blue light that surrounded his body for a moment. The firestorm flared white-hot from every point their bodies were close.

It was going to do exactly zero to improve Nereus' mood.

"The future's so bright, I should have worn shades," Rhys said softly.

Lila smiled despite herself and Rhys captured her hand again with a chuckle. She knew he'd prompted her reaction on purpose.

"I'll leave all the talking to you," he promised. "Just tell me what to do."

"Keeping quiet is a good plan," she acknowledged.

Nyssa opened the door before they even knocked and looked disheveled. Lila was shocked to see in her aura that she was also pregnant.

How could that have happened since Saturday night?

Well, Lila could imagine how...

Nyssa's gaze flicked to Lila and her lips tightened. "I thought you were coming alone," she said to Rhys, her tone accusing. "And I still don't know why." Her gaze flicked to Lila and she was a lot less welcoming than Lila would have expected.

What was going on?

"Who arrives?" Nereus demanded from inside the apartment. "Show yourself!"

He sounded officious and imperious, which wasn't her favorite of his moods. Even so, Lila knew she had to face the King Under the Seas.

Rhys gave her a look, squeezed her hand, and crossed the threshold. Lila lifted her chin, forced a smile, and stepped forward to prostate herself before Nereus.

It might improve his mood.

It might not.

Alex Madison had never been so relieved to reach a destination in her life. She parked the rental car beside Donovan's vehicle and unlocked the doors.

"Finally," her son Darcy said. He was the younger of their two boys and was in the passenger seat beside her. "I thought we'd never get here."

"You and me both."

Alex flicked a glance in the rearview mirror as two scruffy heads popped into view. Malduc and Emyas had been asleep in the back seat, but had evidently woken up as soon as the engine of the car stopped. They murmured to each other as they often did, their eyes darting with suspicion as they surveyed their surroundings. Whatever language they spoke was incomprehensible to anyone else. Alex assumed it was an early variation of Welsh, since they'd been in an enchanted sleep since about 500 AD, but she wasn't a linguist so couldn't be sure.

In a way, it didn't matter. The *Pyr* known as the Seven Thieves could communicate with each other but not anyone else. What Rafferty had learned from them had been with the intervention of his grandfather Pwyll's ghost. He'd explained some of their situation to them, with Pwyll's help, and gotten them modern clothing by the time Donovan, Alex, Marco and Jac had arrived with their sons to take custody of the seven *Pyr*.

Cities flustered them. Cars either fascinated or frightened them. They liked to sing at night after dinner and they had wonderful voices—even if Alex had no idea what the songs were about. (She suspected some of them were bawdy.) They were pretty easy-going as a rule, but she wouldn't have wanted to cross any of them. Their collection of swords and daggers was impressive, and even though the weapons were old, their blades were perfectly honed.

And of course, they were *Pyr*. She hadn't yet seen them shift into their dragon forms and was curious whether their scales looked jeweled like the modern *Pyr*, or whether they were darker, like the Dragon's Tooth Warriors. She wasn't going to provoke them to find out, though.

Rafferty had suggested that they be taken to Bardsey Island, where Donovan had taken over the remote cottage where Marco had slept for centuries. The windswept island had a small population and it was possible the seven *Pyr* might learn more modern Welsh while there. The simpler accommodations and way of life might be reassuring to them, or at least easier than settling them in a city. In the end, they'd formed a kind of caravan of four vehicles. Malduc and Emyas had ridden with Alex and Darcy. They were twin brothers, the younger sons of Pwyll, and Rafferty's uncles.

The pair were visibly relieved to see Donovan's rental car already beside them—or more probably by the silhouettes of Garth and his son Raynald in the back seat.

Alex and Donovan's older son, Nick, rode with his father, taking the passenger seat. He had a newfound affection for maps and had navigated their course from Scotland, ensuring that they kept to smaller roads and towns. Nick had done a great job of ensuring that each day's drive was of similar length and that there was a village with an inn at the end. He and Donovan had conferred in the evening, and Donovan had booked their accommodations in advance.

A third rental car, driven by Jac, parked on the other side of Alex's car. The mate of Marco gave Alex a look of relief and a fingertip wave. Jac appeared to be as tired as Alex felt. Two of Jac and Marco's sons—Powell and their newest addition, Rafferty—were in the back seat, while their oldest boy Maximilian was in the front. It looked like the baby was asleep in his car seat.

Marco parked beside Jac and rubbed his face with his hands. Alex thought him the bravest of the brave, because he had three of the ancient *Pyr* who had recently awakened riding with him. Evrain was in the front passenger seat, in deference to him being oldest and also because he was inclined to car sickness. The brothers Bedwyn and Roderick rode in the back.

Alex wouldn't drive with Malduc in the front seat ever again. She didn't like driving in the UK, especially on small roads, because she was sure she'd drift over to the right side of the road without thinking about it. Having her son in the car was stressful enough without Malduc seizing the wheel to ensure that she avoided a squirrel, as he'd done on their first day of travel. They'd ended up in the ditch and the rodent had been just fine. After that, Malduc got to sit in the back.

Malduc, who had dark hair and brilliant blue eyes, long hair and a beard, leaned forward to peer at her. His beard had been much larger, but he'd trimmed it down neatly. He was fastidious and a bit vain, and Alex thought he belonged to the group of men who thought the male should be the more splendid gender. He could spend hours in front of a mirror, ensuring he looked his best. He tapped his hand on the back of her seat, close to her shoulder. He asked a question, which Alex didn't understand literally but she could guess.

"We'll park here," she said and pointed at Bardsey Island, across the water. "Then we're going over there." She pointed to the ferry, which was pulling into the dock, then gestured across the water.

Malduc's eyes were bright as he followed her gesture, then he nodded and spoke gruffly to his twin. It was funny but Alex could easily tell them apart despite the similarities between the two *Pyr*. Malduc was the more forthright one, and the man of action, while Emyas tended to be the strong silent type. Emyas was more slender, as well. He'd shaved his beard, but she'd seen the difference before that.

Alex got out of the car and stretched, then opened the trunk to get their gear. They'd brought a lot of supplies, anticipating that provisions might not be easily available in sufficient quantities on the island. Malduc pointed to the case of water and commented, prompting Emyas to chuckle. They both helped to take out the supplies and stack them near the ferry dock. It was strange to think of them being more than fifteen hundred years old. With the exception of Garth, the recently-enchanted *Pyr* all looked to be in their mid-thirties, but then, Alex guessed that they hadn't had their firestorms. Garth could have been a mortal man of fifty or so, but he was as strong and vital as the younger *Pyr*.

Dragon shifters really did age more slowly.

An old Volkswagon camper sputtered into the parking lot as they unloaded the cars. It was orange and had European plates. The engine continued to run as one guy got out of the back. He looked like he was in his mid-thirties and dressed casually, his beard a lot more scruffy than Malduc's. He had a backpack that was a bit battered and wore a faded baseball cap. He waved to the couple in the van and they said something to each other. Alex guessed they were wishing each other safe travels. There was laughter, more waving, then the hitchhiker slung his pack over his shoulder and came whistling to the dock as the camper drove away.

Malduc watched him with narrowed eyes and a little bit too much intensity, probably disapproving of his personal habits.

Alex gave Malduc a nudge. "Don't stare. It's rude," she whispered and he must have understood because he turned away.

"Hey," Donovan said, coming to give Alex a kiss. "How much you want to bet that the ferry guy remembers us?"

"If he doesn't now, he will after this," she said and her *Pyr* warrior grinned. "How many trips do you think he'll have to take for just us?"

"Three or four. He'll have a profitable day." Donovan just rolled with the challenge of the seven *Pyr* in a way that Alex wished she could emulate. She was missing her own bed and a house with a lot fewer men around. It was complicated traveling with all these guys and Alex longed for the days when she'd thought being the only woman in a household of four was a challenge.

"Just how much do you owe Rafferty anyway?" she asked.

"What do you mean?"

"I think driving this group from Scotland has got to square you up, no matter how much of a deficit you're running." She softened her words with a smile. They hadn't made love since taking on this task, either, and Alex missed that, too.

"Whatever Rafferty asks of me, I'm going to do." Donovan surveyed the group of ancient *Pyr* who had gone to look at the island and the ferry. They were talking to each other, some with animation and others more gruffly.

"It has to be easier to have them comparatively isolated while they get used to things," he continued. "Fifteen hundred years is a long time to be enchanted."

"But beer is beer," Alex said with a shake of her head. "I'm hoping they don't have a lot of it on the island. Raynald really can't resist."

Donovan laughed. "With any luck, there won't be any women nearby either. Evrain will be chasing them every night."

"And every afternoon," Alex agreed with a smile. She hefted her bag from the trunk and Donovan took it from her, leaving only a small one for her to carry. "What exactly is the plan?"

Donovan shrugged. "We get them to the house, defend them, help them get used to the world, and wait for Rafferty."

"Let's hope he hurries," Alex said. "And I hope you have a cover story for the ferry guy. They're going to be the talk of the island."

"How about this. They've been away, my cousin and his friends, working in mines in southeast Asia. There was a terrible accident. They were among the survivors, but are traumatized. A little peace and quiet is just what they need." He looked at her, his eyes twinkling. "What do you think?"

"It'll only work if they don't all shift shape at once."

"I know. Rafferty talked to them through Pwyll, so here's hoping." He gave her a cocky grin, obviously a lot more confident of success than she was, then went to talk to the ferry guy. Nick was right behind him.

"Tell me I'm not the only one who thinks of them as the seven dwarves," Jac said from beside Alex, making her laugh out loud.

"They are kind of short, comparatively." Alex had noticed that none of them were as tall as Donovan.

Jac nodded. "That's why I told those people in Carlisle that there were auditions for a sequel to the Lord of the Rings."

"How can there be a sequel? The ring is destroyed and the elves have left."

"I don't know, but they believed me. That's what counts."

"Even without beguiling." Alex gave her a high five.

"I know!"

"But here's the thing: who's going to be Snow White?" Alex asked. "You or me?"

Jac made a face. "Not me."

"Not me, either. Driving them is one thing; cleaning up after all of them would be quite another."

"Maybe the creatures of the forest will help," Jac said with a smile. "We can sing."

Alex laughed. "I don't think there's much forest on the island. There might not be many forest creatures."

"Probably better that I don't sing," Jac said then hefted the car seat with her youngest son Rafferty. "You're getting big," she said to him and he laughed, kicking his feet with impatience. He was almost two and Marco came to get their stuff so Jac could walk him up and down the parking lot.

Alex silently wished her luck wearing him out. That boy was a night owl.

"You're Donovan Shea's cousin," the ferry man said, recalling the story Donovan had told him almost ten years before. "Visiting the old white house again."

"That's the one," Donovan said.

"You chose a better day to cross this time," the ferry man said, then smiled at Nick. "And you have grown, boy."

"I have a brother, too," Nick said, indicating Darcy, and the ferry man shook his hand.

"You'll be doubling the island's population today," he said with a chuckle. "It's good you brought supplies." He walked up and down then, surveying their luggage and groceries, assessing the weight of each of them, and began to divide them into groups for the passage.

Alex noticed that Malduc was still watching the hitchhiker, his eyes bright with curiosity. The hitchhiker seemed to be aware of the *Pyr's* survey and amused by it. Maybe Malduc would start offering grooming tips to strangers in incomprehensible Welsh. Alex wouldn't have put it past him.

"Dibs on the bathroom," she said to Jac. "I need an hour alone."

Jac nodded agreement. "I'm right behind you. If the door doesn't lock, I'll sit guard."

"Deal." An hour soaking in the tub would go a long way to improving Alex's mood. So would the bottle of wine she'd snuck into their groceries. It was enough to make her wonder if she could get Donovan alone for an hour, too, and that made her smile in anticipation.

CHAPTER NINE

ara awakened alone in the room she was sharing with Quinn at Kristofer's farm. She almost felt like she was home in Michigan. All she could hear were birds and the distant voices of Quinn and the boys, undoubtedly in the middle of some project. She could smell freshly-brewed coffee and baking, and heard voices in the kitchen below. The sunlight streamed through the big window and the duvet was so cozy that she wanted to stay in bed for a while. The *Pyr* had worked together to breathe a smoke barrier around the house the night before and she was just barely aware of its cool protective shimmer. That reminded her of home, too.

She was in the shower when the verse unfurled in her thoughts.

The gem of the hoard, lost and found;
The fate of Others to it bound.
A Fae treasure, laden with earth magick,
Seized and claimed by a dragon's trick.
All strains of magick share this trait:
None will share, one must dominate.
Dragon flame and selkie tide,
Will diminish the threat if allied.
Their power can destroy just one stone—
Will their choice save their unborn son?

The prophecy! Sara seized a towel and wrapped it around herself, then hurried back into the bedroom. She found her purse and rummaged in it for a pen and paper, then wrote down the verse. As was often the case, she didn't understand exactly what it meant, but the house was full of *Pyr* and they might.

Sara found Erik and Kristofer in the kitchen with Bree and Ronnie. She put the sheet of paper with the verse on the table.

"More YouTube videos," the leader of the *Pyr* growled in frustration, not even glancing up from his phone. Ronnie's lips tightened but she didn't say anything.

"They weren't filmed during the shift at least," Kristofer said mildly, his brows drawing together as he read the verse. Bree came to stand behind him and read it over his shoulder.

"Sounds like there's a battle coming," Bree said and Kristofer nodded agreement. The other mate's hand slipped to her stomach and Sara knew she was thinking about the son she was carrying. They passed the prophecy to Ronnie who read it quickly and looked up, a question in her gaze. Sara shrugged because she didn't understand it either.

"I think we should go back into hiding," Erik said, still watching videos even though they weren't improving his mood. Sara hadn't seen him so annoyed since the Dragon's Tail Wars—and Thorolf wasn't even around.

"I think we have to do whatever is necessary to defeat Maeve," Kristofer said, earning a dark glance from the older *Pyr*. "If we're hunted down and exterminated, there won't be any of us left to hide." He pushed the prophecy across the table to Erik, whose scowl deepened as he read it.

"Magick," he said with disgust. "The world was simpler without it."

"But it was here," Ronnie pointed out. "The Fae just had it all."

"And now Embron has a lot of it," Bree said. "I'm not sure that's any better."

"It sounds like there's more than one stone," Sara said. "If the gem of the hoard is one, then what's the other?"

"Technically, amber isn't a stone," Kristofer supplied. "It's a resin."

"Does that make a difference?" Bree asked and he shrugged.

"What could the other stone be?" he asked instead. "The smoky quartz crystal that was filled with darkfire was shattered to release us from Fae."

"It looks like eliminating one stone, whatever is it, is up Rhys and his mate," Sara said, tapping the prophecy.

"Then their firestorm must be real," Bree said. "He said she was a selkie."

Erik frowned at the verse, reading it again as Quinn returned with all of the boys. He sent them to get glasses of milk and cookies, then Sara felt his steady warmth behind her.

Quinn read the prophecy, too, then wrapped his arm around her shoulders. "Well done," he said quietly.

"I don't like it," Sara admitted.

"You seldom do," he reminded her and she smiled at the truth of that as he kissed her temple.

"This has to be about Rhys' firestorm," Erik said. "At least it's been satisfied. I can't feel it burning anymore." Quinn and Kristofer nodded agreement. "Has anyone heard from the *Pyr* who went back to the city with him?"

"Drake called," Ronnie said, speaking for the first time. "He said Rhys was with his mate and Hadrian was helping to defend his lair. Alasdair had gone after Maeve, and he'd been with Arach and Balthasar beguiling people who saw the dragonfight. He sounded exhausted."

"They didn't get everyone," Erik said with a rueful shake of his head.

"A dragonfight can draw quite a crowd, and in a hurry," Ronnie said, her tone a little defensive.

Erik nodded weary agreement. He looked at his watch. "And Rafferty must still be seeking that witch." Sara knew that *Pyr* and his mate, Melissa, had left the previous morning. They couldn't knock on the door of the witch Eithne in the middle of the night so had delayed their departure. Erik frowned and lifted a finger, but before he could give a command, there was a sound like shattering glass and a roar of fury.

The dragonsmoke barrier had been attacked.

The *Pyr* were immediately on their feet, shimmering blue.

Erik was first to the door and inhaled. "Embron," he muttered and Sara's heart stopped even before she spotted the black dragon overhead. Erik leapt through the door, shifting to an ebony and pewter dragon right outside the house. He shot into the sky with purpose, obviously targeting the dragon prince.

Kristofer was right behind him, shifting to his peridot and gold dragon form with quick power. He was larger than Erik and his eyes glittered more fiercely, but then, it was his lair that was under attack and his pregnant mate was within it. He breathed a stream of dragonfire into the air, then flew high alongside Erik.

"Stay in the house," Quinn counseled, which Sara already intended to do. "Stay inside the dragonsmoke barrier. Sara can feel it, if you're not sure." He gave their sons a hard look. "Listen to your mother." The boys nodded agreement, then he was gone as well. He bounded into the air on the patio, becoming a sapphire and steel dragon as he soared high.

"Awesome," Timmy said as the dragons clashed high overhead.

"When will I be able to do that?" Garrett demanded and Sara held her oldest son closer.

The change would come upon him all too soon, to her thinking, but she couldn't keep him a child forever. Ronnie met her gaze and she saw understanding in that woman's eyes, then they all went to the windows to watch the dragonfight.

To Sara's relief, it was short and sweet—sweet because it ended with the three *Pyr* returning unscathed.

"He fled," Kristofer said with disgust when he had shifted back to his human form.

"He was checking how many of us were here," Quinn said grimly.

"No," Erik said softly. "He changed his plan because he felt the same thing I did." He looked at Quinn who inhaled sharply. Sara watched him close his eyes and saw his confusion.

"The firestorm has sparked again," he said, clearly skeptical. "How can that be?"

"I don't know, but I feel its burn." Erik frowned. "We'd better call Rhys and warn him that Embron is on his way. We can tell him the prophecy, too. It might make more sense to him."

"But how could the firestorm spark again?" Quinn asked.

"Maybe one was real and the other wasn't, or isn't," Kristofer suggested. He took Bree's hand as they all looked at each other, wondering.

"I hate magick," Erik said under his breath and Sara could only agree.

Thorolf was surprised to realize just how much he'd missed Manhattan. The raw energy of the city made it easy to forget a series of long flights with a restless toddler. They'd come halfway around the world in the past few days: after their off-grid vacation in Bhutan, they'd returned to Bangkok to learn about Kristofer's firestorm. Chandra was pregnant again, but as soon as Thorolf had heard that Theo was missing, he'd known he had to help.

It was early evening and the skyscrapers were lighting up. The roads were congested as commuters headed out of the city. The cab made good time, threading through the traffic toward the core. Thorolf opened the window and took a deep breath of the familiar scent of Manhattan. Chandra leaned her head on his shoulder and closed her eyes as they rode, and Raynor finally fell asleep. With each new block, Thorolf remembered more his days as a bike courier in the city. He'd known every alley and every shortcut. He'd loved that job.

So much had changed with his firestorm. There had been a time when he'd thought of nothing except working and partying, when he'd ignored the truth of his nature. Then he'd met Rox, the tattoo artist who loved dragons, and the one who'd taken him on as a project—without much success, he had to admit. Through Rox, he'd met Niall, one of the *Pyr* who had begun to teach him what he could do. Rox had been the first in Manhattan to know his truth, and Niall had been the first other *Pyr* he'd met in centuries. Thorolf was glad they'd put up with him, especially during his own firestorm with Chandra.

And now it was payback time. Thorolf was grinning when the cab parked in front of the Beaux Arts building where he'd been Rox's tenant. It hadn't changed a bit. Chandra lifted Raynor to her hip and Thorolf took the bags out of the trunk.

"You're going to love this place," he told his mate and she smiled.

"If it has a bed and a shower, I'll definitely love it." She yawned. "We're not going anywhere for at least twenty-four hours so don't get any ideas."

"I consider myself warned." Thorolf didn't think it was a good time to tell her that he sensed another firestorm, and that it was burning right in Manhattan. He'd felt a low hum of awareness for the past day and it had flared since they'd landed, a sign that the *Pyr* and his destined mate were close. He hefted their bags and headed for the door, just as Niall appeared. The *Pyr* who had been Thorolf's mentor looked only a little bit older, and his smile was welcome.

"Niall!" They shook hands, then embraced.

"Looks like you're moving in," Niall complained, taking one of the bags.

"We just might. It feels good to be back."

The two *Pyr* exchanged a glance. "Rhys," Niall said quietly, knowing what Thorolf was wondering.

"It's a hot one," Thorolf agreed.

Chandra stopped in the lobby and turned to them, her expression forbidding. "Tell me that there's not a firestorm burning here." Her tone revealed that she'd guessed the truth.

Thorolf grinned. "You know I never lie to you," he said easily and she exhaled.

"Just one night's sleep. That's all I ask."

"No pickles?"

His mate slanted a glance his way when they were in the elevator. "What if I do have a craving for pickles?"

"I called ahead," he assured her. Chandra's appetite for *kim chee* during her pregnancy with Raynor had been a bit of a joke among the *Pyr*.

"Take-out Thai," Niall said. "Lots of it because I remember how Thorolf can clean out a fridge." He led the way down the corridor to the apartment.

"Airport food is seriously depressing," Thorolf said in his own defense. "Expensive, little tiny servings and it all looks like it's been waiting for you." Niall unlocked the door and Thorolf took a deep breath. "It smells amazing, Niall. You're the best." His stomach growled as if to agree and they laughed together.

Chandra wandered into the apartment, staring. The place hadn't changed much since Thorolf had lived there. He remembered Niall and Rox's firestorm, kicking *Slayer* butt in some epic battles, chasing shadow dragons down—even Niall's twin brother Phelan—and breathing dragonsmoke on the building's roof.

"Good times," he said to Niall who laughed a little and started to unpack the food.

The apartment was still simply furnished, although he thought the couch was new. Of course, his bike and collection of spare parts was long gone. The murals on the walls were the highlight of the place, just as they should be. Rox had painted dragons on every surface, dragons in flight, dragons fighting, dragons in all their majestic glory. The murals were just as fabulous as he remembered. Chandra walked around the apartment, studying each one.

"Rox is really talented," she said quietly, then glanced at Thorolf. "And she did these before she knew you?"

"It's why she took me in and made me her project," Thorolf said. "She saw me shift once."

Chandra nodded and sank into a chair at the table, still looking. She beckoned to Thorolf and pushed up his sleeve, examining the dragon tattoo on his arm that Rox had done, then looking at the walls again.

"I'm glad this place is empty now," Thorolf said. "Thanks for letting us stay here."

"Theo had been talking about moving into town," Niall explained. "We were going to offer this place to him, since Rox prefers to live over the shop. It's closer to the boys' schools."

"You don't want to rent it to just anyone and risk damage to those murals," Chandra said.

"Exactly. But he didn't come back from the circus, and worse, he only went there because we asked him to." He gestured to the table and pushed a hand through his dark blond hair. "You eat while I bring you up to date. There's a lot going on."

"Tell me about Kristofer's firestorm," Thorolf said.

"And his mate," Chandra added. "Am I right that the old gods were involved? It sounded like it in the emails, even though nothing was said outright."

"Bree was a Valkyrie," Niall said and Chandra put down her chopsticks.

"There's no Valkyrie named Bree," she said. "There never was. I've known them all, at least in passing."

"Sigrdrifa," Niall corrected. "Bree is the name she was using in human society."

Chandra looked shocked. "Sigrdrifa? You *Pyr* don't bother with half-measures, do you?"

"You know her?" Thorolf asked.

"Less well than some of the others, but I know of her. Who wouldn't? She was the strongest of her kind and the one most recognized by mortals." She took another bite, obviously thinking. "And she gave all that up for love."

"So did you," Thorolf teased and she smiled at him.

"I just find it hard to believe that there's another *Pyr* as persuasive as you. Kristofer is a nice guy and all..."

"But he had the firestorm on his side," Niall noted.

"I thought it was a fake firestorm," Thorolf said.

"It was at first," Niall agreed. "A spell cast by the Dark Queen to trap the *Pyr*, and a plan that almost worked. But when Bree surrendered her immortality to save Kristofer, a real firestorm sparked for them."

"And now?" Chandra prompted.

"Some of the *Pyr* went to Kristofer's place to repair his scale. We stayed in town in case you got in earlier."

"What about Rhys' firestorm?" Thorolf asked. "Is it real?"

"We don't know yet." Niall told them then about the book belonging to Maeve, the list of paranormal creatures that she intended to extinguish. He told them about the bar, Bones, where the Others gathered to try to foil Maeve's plan, and about the vampires of the Coven of Mercy taking possession of Maeve's book. And finally, he told them about the Circus of Wonders.

"And I feel like Theo's disappearance is our fault, because we asked him to check out the Circus of Wonders," Niall concluded. "I had no idea it was filled with Others, but Theo wanted to help."

"And then he went through the portal to Fae with Kristofer, who was following his fake firestorm," Thorolf concluded.

"Rhys and Hadrian were captured there, but Kristofer and Bree managed to free them," Niall said. "Along with the seven warriors who had invaded the lair of Blazion and been put into an enchanted sleep. A lot of them are related to Rafferty."

Thorolf shook his head. "But what about Theo?"

Niall was sober. "He never came back. The bartender from Bones, a woman named Mel, disappeared with him into Fae and no one has seen either of them since."

"Have you tried old-speak?" Thorolf asked.

Niall nodded. "Erik can't sense his presence either." He pushed a hand through his hair. "I keep thinking about those seven *Pyr* who were lost fifteen hundred years ago, leaving no sign of their existence, who just woke up last week. What if Theo's lost for that long? What if we never see him again?"

"And this Blazion?" Thorolf prompted.

"He's the old dragon from the stories," Niall said. "The one slain by Siegfried."

Chandra caught her breath. "Was he awakened again?"

"Kristofer said only briefly." Niall grimaced. "But he has a twin brother, Embron, and he's looking for something called the gem of the hoard, which Bree had taken from Blazion's hoard when she and Siegfried vanquished the dragon centuries ago. She thought it was pretty and had it ever since, not realizing its importance."

"Where is it now?" Chandra asked, her tone so sharp that Thorolf knew she'd heard of this gem of the hoard.

"Rafferty had it. He was going to give it to Kristofer at the scale repair, but Rhys' mate was abducted and Embron demanded the gem of the hoard as ransom. Rafferty gave it to Rhys."

Chandra and Thorolf exchanged a glance. "You have to defend it," Chandra said with urgency. "I'll stay with Raynor. Both of you go to help Rhys."

"You just want all the noodles," Thorolf complained, taking another three bites as he stood up.

His mate smiled. "I'll save the noodles for you. It's this tub of *ajat* that has my name on it." She gestured to the pickled cucumbers, then waved the two *Pyr* out the door.

"Good news," Niall said as they ran down the stairs together. "Rhys' restaurant is right below his apartment. Even though it's closed Mondays, he always cooks when he's stressed."

"Now you're talking," Thorolf said with enthusiasm, taking the stairs three at a time.

Hadrian was sore in places he hadn't even known he had. There was a bump on the back of his head that hurt like hell. He didn't know how much time had passed when he woke up on the floor of the elevator in Rhys' building. He sat up and winced at the brightness of the light, then wondered how it could be so light in the elevator.

He opened his eyes to find himself surrounded by white brilliance.

It could have been ice. He would have felt familiar with that, but it was feathers. Millions of white feathers surrounded him, their tips gently caressing his face. They were so white that they were luminescent, lit with an inner fire. They shone with a silvery gleam, one that was both bright and cold.

He had to be dreaming.

Hadrian reached out to touch the feathers closest to him and was awed by their softness. His fingers slid into them like he'd plunged his hand into a cloud. Then a woman laughed lightly, a sound like delicate bells.

He was entranced.

The feathers moved and her face appeared in the midst of them, which only fascinated him more. She was pretty, with blue eyes and fair lashes, but it was her playful smile that made his heart pound. "Dragon of ice and fire," she said and laughed a little. "I've been looking for you." She leaned toward him, her gaze locked with his, then touched her lips to his cheek. Light flared between them, sending heat through his body, as if her kiss branded his cheek.

Hadrian was amazed. "The firestorm," he whispered, awed by his good fortune.

"Is it?" she asked, her tone surprisingly skeptical.

"It must be," he began but her hand appeared out of the feathers. Her skin was almost as pale as the feathers. On her left wrist was a red string and Hadrian recognized it as being similar to the one he'd worn in the realm of Fae.

He was horrified.

"Not you, too," he whispered but she shook her head, her smile fading. Her fingertips stroked his cheek, as if she regretted something she'd done, and Hadrian felt his skin chill where her kiss had heated it. Instead of a hot brand of a kiss, there was ice lodged beneath his skin. She glanced back suddenly as if startled and he heard footsteps.

"Don't go," he managed to say before there was a brilliant shimmer of light. It was too late. The feathers no longer surrounded him, and she was gone.

As surely as if she'd never been.

A guy appeared and crouched down before Hadrian, and Hadrian wouldn't have been more surprised to see the Devil himself. "I won't go," Kade said with a friendly shake of his head. He surveyed Hadrian. "You look terrible."

"What are you doing here?"

"I came to help with Rhys' firestorm, of course. All for one and one for all."

Hadrian had his doubts. "I thought you had other things to do."

Kade shrugged. "I was wrong." He looked contrite. "I made a mistake and was hoping you guys would give me a chance to make it right."

Hadrian wasn't entirely convinced of the other *Pyr's* motives, but he'd never been one to hold a grudge. Everyone made mistakes.

Even Alasdair.

That made him wince and try to stand up.

Kade put a hand under Hadrian's elbow and helped him to his feet. "You're a mess," he said with sympathy and Hadrian had to nod agreement.

"Isn't it the truth."

"What happened?"

"I'm not sure." Hadrian didn't want to make an accusation against Alasdair before he talked to his cousin. There could have been someone else in the elevator—even though he hadn't seen anyone. Alasdair could be in trouble himself. "I was hit from behind."

"Are you heading up to Rhys' place?" Kade said. At Hadrian's nod, he got into the elevator, too, and pushed the button. Hadrian's head was pounding and he hoped Rhys had some aspirin. He still had the keys to the apartment in his pocket, so that was something. He led the way but Kade recoiled six feet from the door, wincing.

"Awesome dragonsmoke," he said and shuddered from head to toe.

"Maybe I'll just wait out here."

"I can change the permissions," Hadrian offered wearily. He closed his eyes and did so, belatedly aware that Kade hadn't protested it was too much trouble. The other *Pyr* helped him across the threshold and glanced around. Hadn't he been in Rhys' place before? To Hadrian's thinking, there wasn't much to see. It was tidy and minimalist, everything in its place and everything there for a reason.

"If Rhys has aspirin, I'll bet they're in the bathroom," Kade said. "I'll get you something to drink."

"There's a water glass in the bathroom," Hadrian protested but the other *Pyr* ignored him. He winced and went in search of aspirin, vaguely aware that Kade was heading for the bedroom. "This kitchen's the other way," he said with impatience, then checked the medicine cabinet. He found the bottle easily and poured out a pair of pills. He went back into the main room of the apartment with them in his hand.

The apartment was empty.

"Kade?" he asked and turned to look for the other *Pyr*. He couldn't even smell Kade's presence. The outside door was ajar, too. Why had he left so suddenly? Hadrian closed the door, then went to the window in time to see Kade emerge from the building. There was a lime green Mustang parked at the curb, which gave him a bad feeling. That feeling got worse when he recognized the stylus in Kade's hand and guessed what he was going to do.

Hadrian shouted when Kade began to draw a door in the air. Hadrian tried to open the window in time, but fumbled with the latch and dropped the aspirin.

"No!" he roared when the window was finally open. Kade drew the knob and opened the door. A slice opened in the air, giving a glimpse of the silver and red light of Fae. Kade glanced up, as if he'd heard Hadrian, then drove the Mustang through the gap.

There was a flash of silver light and Hadrian's feet erupted with pain. He cried out as agony claimed them again, then fell insensible to the floor.

Kade had lied to him.

Both of the treasures entrusted to Rhys were gone, and it was all Hadrian's fault.

Nothing was as Rhys had expected. Lila had startled him with the confession that the King Under the Seas wanted to conceive a child with her, and Nyssa's welcome was less than friendly. At least Lila's reluctance to have a child was consistent.

The firestorm was burning with insistence, but that didn't disguise the scent of sex in the apartment. Unless he missed his guess, Nereus had been working on increasing the selkie population while he and Lila had been coming uptown.

But Lila thought Nereus wanted her to have his child, too.

Lila didn't belong to him, but she was his destined mate—whether she believed it or not—and Rhys instinctively disliked the idea of any other male trying to stake a claim. He really wasn't fond of the idea of Nereus adding Lila to a collection of lovers, instead of creating a partnership with her alone. To him, it was a lot less than she deserved.

No wonder she didn't believe in commitment.

Rhys was ready to defend her right to choose against anyone who argued otherwise.

Even the King Under the Seas.

The King Under the Seas sat on Nyssa's sofa, holding court over the small apartment. The living room and kitchen were all one space, with a counter between them instead of a kitchen table. The end wall was taken up by a sliding glass door that opened onto a small balcony. The apartment was furnished in silvery blues and greens. There were a few sea shells and a bowl of what might have been sea glass on the kitchen counter.

Rhys disliked Nereus intensely on sight.

Nereus eyed Lila with a little smile that seemed proprietary to Rhys. He granted Rhys the barest glance, apparently dismissing him, but studied the radiant glow of the firestorm. Something hardened in his gaze and Rhys took warning from that.

He guessed that Nereus had followed Lila to New York to collect what he saw as his due and folded his arms across his chest.

He wasn't going to bow before this king.

Nereus looked both ancient and vital. He wore a crown on his brow, a magnificent arrangement of red coral studded with pearls. His silver beard was long and flowed almost to his ankles. His long hair radiated out behind him and was so bright a silver that it was almost white. His eyes were vivid clear blue. His skin was fair, almost like ivory, and Rhys wasn't sure how much he was wearing: the king's flowing beard hid his torso and his thighs. His bare feet were planted against the carpeted floor. He looked like he'd be a bit taller than Rhys in his own human form, and was well-muscled. He'd be a formidable opponent, but Rhys would willingly take him on. Nereus held a trident, a staff of silver as tall as Lila with three sharp tines that caught the light. A faint pearly glow emanated from the ring on his finger, and Rhys guessed it was a mark of his sovereignty.

Lila prostrated herself before Nereus, her hair sliding over her shoulders as she almost kissed the floor. Nereus glanced at him and Rhys inclined his head slightly, just to be polite. He wasn't feeling particularly deferential.

The acknowledgement wasn't enough to please Nereus.

"*Dragon*," he said with scorn. He didn't move his lips but his voice was deep and the words were clear. They echoed directly in Rhys' thoughts, like old-speak. Rhys realized Lila had communicated with him the same way when they'd met that first time and he'd followed her underwater. He wondered how much more this method of communication had in common with old-speak, whether it could be cast at a specific individual or not, and whether it could be used to charm as old-speak could be used to beguile. He wondered whether Others who weren't selkies or subjects of Nereus could hear it, and more importantly, whether Nereus knew that Rhys could hear it.

He kept his expression impassive, just in case. His keen *Pyr* senses might be underestimated by someone who didn't know much about his kind. He wished he could shift, because he knew his hearing would be even sharper in his dragon form. There might be nuances he'd only be able to discern that way.

Nereus lifted a silver brow. "*Another dragon. Is there a plague upon the earth that I have not been told about?*"

"*Not a dragon, a* Pyr, *my lord Nereus,*" Lila replied. "*The* Pyr *are dragon shifters.*"

Nereus made a dismissive gesture. Rhys guessed he had a temper because the Lila he knew wouldn't have found it easy to be so demure.

He hated that she was afraid of the ruler of her kind.

She remained in the same pose. Maybe she hadn't been given permission to rise. Whether she'd been given permission to speak or not, she asked a question, which he thought more like her. "*Where was the other dragon, my lord?*"

"*Perhaps there was only one. Perhaps it was this one that came to rob me,*" Nereus mused, his eyes flashing as he didn't quite answer her. "*Perhaps this is the invader, and you have brought him right to me, a traitor to be tried in my court.*" He raised his trident, but Lila spoke quickly.

"*Perhaps not the same dragon, my lord Nereus.*" It was as if she wanted to keep Nereus from striking Rhys. What could he do with that trident?

She stood up and disapproval flickered in Nereus' eyes. Lila straightened and stood a little taller, as forthright as Rhys knew her to be. She must think Nereus calmer.

"This one has been in my company, my lord Nereus. Can you describe the intruder?"

Nereus sneered. *"He was large and black, powerful and repugnant. He glowed against the depths, crimson with the power of his magick, and his scales shone, like the darkness of the sea beneath a full moon."*

Embron.

Kristofer had said that Bree had cast a stone into the sea and that Embron, believing it to be the gem of the hoard, had gone after it. Had he sought it all the way to Nereus' realm? Where was Nereus' realm?

"This dragon is red and silver, my lord Nereus."

"He came," Nereus continued. *"He came without ceremony or invitation, without asking permission."* Rhys guessed that was the root of the issue. Nereus' tone grew more strident in his outrage. *"He came and rummaged through the remnants of the hoard. He broke the spire of the second tower when he thrashed his tail, and I, I could not confront him because of the diminished number of my subjects."* Nereus rose from his throne and seemed suddenly larger and more fearsome. *"He dared to insult* me, *to ignore* me, *to treat my palace as his junkyard."* Nereus inhaled in fury. *"He ignored and defied me, just as you have done."* Nereus gave Rhys a searching look and his tone dropped low with accusation. *"You know him."*

Rhys held the king's gaze, pretending he hadn't heard the question.

The king leaned back, his expression assessing. *"What is this light?"* he demanded of Lila, snatching at her hand.

Rhys was already shimmering a little, hovering on the cusp of change, and Nereus' quick move took him closer to the shift. Lila must have guessed, because she pulled her hand from Nereus' grip. Nyssa was eying Rhys with obvious alarm.

"It is a light of a dragon's arousal," Lila replied, bending the truth lightly. *"He finds me alluring."*

Nereus laughed. *"And so he should!"* His mood visibly improved. *"He is a discerning dragon, then, one who savors the beauty of our kind."* He patted the couch beside himself and Lila hesitated only a moment before she rose and sat beside him. His smile broadened, though Lila's smile was prim. The king ran a fingertip down Lila's arm and smiled. *"You will surrender to me today, for the good of our kind."* Lila stiffened but, interestingly to Rhys, it was Nyssa who looked more displeased.

"No, my lord. I told you before that I have no desire to conceive now."

"The choice is not yours to make."

Now Lila's tone hardened. *"The choice is always mine to make, my lord. It is the way of our kind."*

"And you will choose as I instruct you to choose."

She stood then, moving closer to Rhys, and the firestorm brightened. Nereus narrowed his eyes against its light and looked annoyed.

Rhys took Lila's hand again, wanting her to know that he supported her choice, whatever it might be.

At that, Nereus rose to his feet. *"I insist that you bend to my will. It is for the good of our kind, Lila."* His words softened. *"It is for the survival of our kind. I entreat you to consider the future..."*

"No," Lila replied calmly. *"The choice of whether to bear a child remains mine to make. If we abandon our principles and traditions, there is no future for us."*

Nereus' eyes flashed and his voice rose. Though he argued for the future of the selkies, Rhys knew he was thinking mostly of his own satisfaction. The way he looked at Lila revealed more than his words. *"I order you to submit for the good of our kind...."*

"No." Lila stepped back and Rhys felt her hand trembling within his grip. *"I'm returning to North Rona now."*

"You will not defy me!" Nereus roared. He loomed larger before them both, his brow as dark as thunder. *"You will do as I command!"* He snatched suddenly at Lila and pounded his trident against the floor in the same moment. Nyssa gasped as the floor shook beneath them.

Rhys immediately shifted shape to defend his mate. There was just barely enough space in Nyssa's apartment to accommodate his dragon form, but Nereus was backed against the wall. At another time, Rhys might have been amused to see Nereus' astonishment. He wanted to breathe fire, but instead he snatched up Lila and held her against his chest in one protective claw, and snarled at Nereus. She gripped him tightly which told him to be ready for more.

"I will not be denied! You cannot expect me to stand aside while you discard our future!" Nereus bellowed and pounded his trident against the floor again. The building shook, and Rhys felt the earth trembling beneath it. Chunks of plaster fell from the ceiling, the walls were vibrating and he could hear people screaming. Nyssa was trying to open the door and there was a distant sound of sirens. The building was rumbling all the way to its foundations and the light fixtures were swaying.

Nereus had started an earthquake.

CHAPTER TEN

Rhys lowered his head and glared at Nereus, holding the king's gaze to let him see the fire in his own. "Don't touch my mate," he growled and watched Nereus glare.

The king drew himself taller and opened his mouth to shout. Instead, Rhys roared, breathing a torrent of fire that made Nereus stagger backward. He pounded the trident one more time and a crevasse opened in the floor, splitting the building all the way to the street.

Rhys felt the building fall away behind him as people screamed. He sheltered Lila with his body and made for the window. A chunk of the ceiling fell, the sliding glass door facing the balcony shattered, and Rhys had to ensure Lila's safety immediately. He bounded toward the broken door and smashed the rest of the glass out with his tail. He lunged onto the balcony and soared into the sky, holding her close all the while.

"Nyssa," she said.

At the single word, Rhys looked down. Balconies were tumbling to the ground, shaken free from the crumbling building. Nyssa was clutching the door to her own balcony, one foot in the air.

"Lila!" she cried.

"You have to help her!" Lila said but Rhys was already sweeping back down toward the other selkie. He scooped up Nyssa, feeling how tightly she clung to his talon in her fear, and the two selkies clutched each other. He caught a glimpse inside the apartment and saw that Nereus was gone, which simplified his choices. Rhys flew high again and Nyssa shuddered as she peered over his claw at the damaged street below.

There was a wide fissure in the road and the pavement was cracked open like an egg. Water shot into the air from broken water mains and something was hissing. People streamed out of the building and lined up on the sidewalk further down the street, clutching cherished belongings, pets and children, as the ground continued to vibrate. The emergency crews were arriving, but his bike was still parked at the curb.

"Where did he go?" Rhys demanded as he flew higher.

"Probably down the crack," Nyssa said, averting her gaze. Rhys saw Lila frown and noticed how she studied Nyssa. "All the way down to the water, then into the Hudson. With any luck, he'll head back to the Isle of the Blessed from there."

Where was the Isle of the Blessed?

Lila gave him a warning look and he saved the question for later.

"He can't swim all that way," Lila protested.

Nyssa smiled. "Oh, don't you know? He has a luxury yacht now. All the perks for our King Under the Seas."

Again, Rhys was aware that Lila was studying her friend, as if skeptical of her words. Then she ran a hand over his scales, sending invigorating fire through his veins. "Thank you," she said, her voice a bit breathless.

Rhys tightened his grip upon her. "It's what we *Pyr* do." Luckily, the Cloisters museum was close with a large park around it, one that would be quiet on a chilly Monday. He flew steadily in that direction.

Nyssa held two purses and gave one to Lila, presumably her own bag. "Occupational hazard of Nereus arriving as a guest," she said with a roll of her eyes. Rhys had the definite sense that she was trying to distract them from something. "I never know whether he'll start an earthquake, just because, so I'm always ready to run."

"It's not the only hazard of having him stop by," Lila said, her voice a little harder. "When did you choose to conceive?"

So, she knew that Nyssa and Nereus had been intimate, too.

Nyssa shrugged. "Sometimes it's easier to just do what he wants."

Rhys was glad Lila didn't seem to agree.

"Where will you go?" Lila asked Nyssa. "Your place is trashed."

"I'll go to Bones. Someone will let me stay with them." She laughed a little. "North Rona has zero appeal so you don't have to worry about me asking you to put me up."

The two selkies eyed each other so intently that Rhys wondered at the history between them. Lila had said that Nereus was in love with her. Rhys guessed that the other selkie was aware of the king's feelings. What did she feel for him? It was way too complicated for him to untangle, with the firestorm already urging him in one direction and Lila insisting on the opposite path.

He said nothing about Embron and couldn't help but notice that Lila didn't either. Did she realize who the black dragon was? How much did she trust Nyssa? Without being sure, he kept quiet for the moment, both about Embron and the gem of the hoard.

He targeted a quiet and secluded corner of the park, landed and shifted shape quickly. Lila's smile of approval gave him a jolt of pleasure, one that was heightened by the firestorm.

"If anyone took your picture over the Cloisters, people would assume the image was altered," she said.

"That was my thinking," Rhys admitted. "I'd rather not have Erik accuse me of indiscretion."

Nyssa looked between them, but Lila waved off any question she would have asked. "Dragon honor code," she said. "Not relevant right now."

"There's a subway station over there," Rhys said and they began to walk toward it. The wind was cool and it looked like it might snow. They almost had the park to themselves, just as he'd hoped. The gardens were past their best, too, and a lot of the plants had been trimmed back for the winter.

It was enough to make him miss the Mediterranean sunshine.

Rhys turned up his collar and set a brisk pace, glad that the selkies kept up. He had a definite sense of urgency, as if something was unraveling almost before his eyes. His phone chimed a couple of times, a missed call and an incoming message, but he had things to do.

He had to get back to his bike, then home to retrieve the gem of the hoard. He'd feel better with it in his pocket, even than leaving it in his lair. He couldn't really believe that he'd forgotten about it, but the firestorm was demanding. He still had to convince Lila about the merit of partnership, too. He wasn't like Nereus, intent on his plan to the exception of all others, and she had to realize that, too. She let him hold her hand, so he counted that as progress.

He'd take encouragement wherever he could find it at this point.

Rhys was simmering.

Lila could feel his protective anger and could just barely see the blue shimmer that appeared when he shifted shape. His reaction to Nereus starting an earthquake was perfectly reasonable in her view, and she had no way to explain the tantrum of the King Under the Seas. It had been a selfish choice and a careless one.

It was also impossible to miss that Nyssa had conceived because Nereus hadn't really given her a choice. That was the exact opposite of Rhys' decision—even though the firestorm was a once-in-a-lifetime opportunity for him, and Nereus could create children whenever he wanted, with whoever he wanted.

Intriguingly, even though Rhys was probably as powerful as Nereus, he was a lot more careful with his strength. He controlled it, because he was protective—not just of her, but of Nyssa, too, and all the treasures of the earth. Nereus thought only of himself. When he was angry, it was usually because he wasn't getting his way, although Lila couldn't think of many others than herself who had defied him.

He could be terrifying and the results of his actions could be worse.

Rhys was different. She impulsively slipped her hand into his, wanting to apologize for Nereus but knowing his actions weren't her responsibility. Rhys gave her hand a little squeeze, then folded his grip around her fingers.

Like she was a prize to be defended.

She smiled despite herself and her heart warmed. "Could you hear him?" she asked.

Rhys nodded. "It's like old-speak. I heard you that first time, too."

"Could it have been Embron who visited Nereus' palace?"

"Embron?" Nyssa asked.

"The guy who abducted me from the restaurant. He's a dragon shifter." Lila saw Rhys look between her and Nyssa and she realized that he wasn't sure whether to speak or not. "You can trust Nyssa."

He nodded agreement and she liked that he accepted her word. "He's black in his dragon form, plus the other *Pyr* said he dove into the sea in pursuit of the gem of the hoard. It certainly could have been him."

"Plus he's nasty," Nyssa said. "I'm glad you got away from him."

Lila shivered. "He's nastier than you think. He made me watch as he burned my skin."

"No!" Nyssa said in shock. "But why?"

"He wanted to know what I knew about the gem of the hoard. I told him the story of the Envoy and the sinking of the Isle of the Blessed."

"The who and the what?" Rhys asked.

"Nereus' kingdom. Well, it is now," Lila explained. "I'll tell you the whole story but the important thing is that I don't know where the gem of the hoard is. That's what they really wanted to know—"

"They?" Nyssa asked.

"The Dark Queen was there, too."

"That alliance isn't good news," Nyssa said with heat and Rhys nodded agreement.

"He said something about tracing every stray bit of magick. He wasn't pleased that I couldn't give him the location of the gem of the hoard."

"So, he tortured you." Nyssa shivered again.

"But I know where it is," Rhys said and Lila turned to him with astonishment. "It was what he wanted as ransom for your release," he explained. "Which is why I have it. The *Pyr* gave it to me to get you back."

"You have it?" She was astonished.

"Why would they do that?" Nyssa asked.

"Because of the firestorm." Rhys spoke as if that was self-evident, but Lila knew it wouldn't be to Nyssa.

"This light is the firestorm. It means I'm his destined mate and can bear his son," Lila explained.

Nyssa eyed the sparks shooting between them. "I was wondering about that, but didn't want to say anything. Are you going to?"

"I chose not to," Lila admitted. She felt Rhys' surprise, but selkies were always honest with each other about matters sexual. She turned to him. "*You* have it? Really?"

"Really."

Lila glanced up at the sky, wondering whether Embron would swoop down on them at any moment. It wasn't an appealing possibility.

"Apparently, he can't sense its presence," Rhys said, which was slightly reassuring. "Neither can I, come to think of it, which is strange since it's a stone."

"Should that make sense?" Nyssa asked.

"It's of the earth," Lila said. "Rhys has an affinity to the element of earth." She turned to Rhys again. "But he can sense the firestorm, right? And if it was the ransom he wanted, he might assume you have it."

Rhys caught his breath, proof he hadn't considered that yet. "We need to get back to my lair," he said, moving more quickly.

"What does it look like anyway?" Nyssa asked.

Rhys looked surprised. "Don't you know?"

"I've never seen it," Lila admitted. "I've only heard about it."

"Me, too," Nyssa said. "I was a glimmer in my mother's eye when all that happened to the Isle of the Blessed."

Again, Rhys looked mystified for a moment. "It's a sphere of amber. I left it on my kitchen counter."

The two selkies stared at him as if he'd suddenly spoken in an incomprehensible language. "You left it on the counter?" Lila echoed.

"It's safe in my hoard, maybe safer than it would have been with me," Rhys explained. "There's a dragonsmoke barrier that no other dragon can cross."

"In either form?" Nyssa asked.

"In any form," Rhys clarified.

"But what about anyone else?" Lila asked.

"Thieves come in all shapes and sizes," Nyssa noted.

Rhys strode more quickly. "It was odd," he admitted softly. "I walked right past it, without even thinking of bringing it."

"What happens when a dragon crosses your dragonsmoke?" Nyssa asked.

"It burns," Rhys said. "It burns like nothing you've ever felt before."

"I think maybe I have," Lila said drily and Rhys glanced at her.

"Yes. I guess you have." They reached the sidewalk and the entrance to the subway. Rhys paused there as if uncertain. "I need to go back for my bike," he said, his gaze clinging to Lila's in silent query.

"I'm going to Bones," Nyssa said and dug in her purse for subway fare.

Lila stood, snared by Rhys' gaze. She didn't want to mate with Nereus, even for the survival of her kind. She wanted another night with Rhys and suspected she always would.

If she chose to bear his son, she couldn't be compelled to bear a child by Nereus for at least nine months. And Rhys, she was starting to believe, would never command her or keep her captive or expect her to surrender her independence to him.

A selkie could get used to that.

And the firestorm's enticing heat had absolutely nothing to do with her thinking. She'd want him even without its insistent sizzle.

Rhys raised a hand, as if he'd sensed that she'd decided, and a cab appeared, heading toward them.

"I'm not going home just yet," Lila said to Nyssa. "Rhys and I have unfinished business."

"I'm sure you do," Nyssa said with a smile.

"Thanks for my bag. Take care."

The two selkies hugged, then Nyssa waved and went into the subway station.

Rhys and Lila didn't speak in the cab. They just held hands in the back, the firestorm simmering and burning between them. Lila wished she did have sunglasses. Rhys beguiled the driver once they were beside the bike, although the chaos in the street was almost enough to distract him anyway.

He'd brought a second helmet, which made her smile. They put them on and Lila got on the bike behind him. Rhys was solid and warm, as hard as rock, and she couldn't resist the temptation to wrap herself around him. She slid her hands around his waist and flattened them against his chest, drawing them together as if she'd fuse them into one.

He felt so good and the firestorm just made that better.

"We'll end up in the ditch this way," he muttered and Lila smiled, knowing he liked it even so. The firestorm burned white-hot and shot sparks in every direction. She felt like they'd become a shooting star when he opened the throttle and let the bike engine roar as they headed back downtown.

"Can you tell me the story you told Embron?" he asked, his voice low through the headset. "It might help us to figure out what Embron and the Dark Queen want with the gem of the hoard."

Lila leaned against him and told him the story, word for word as she'd told it to Embron and Maeve.

The last thing Lila expected was to find a guy on the floor of Rhys' apartment. He looked like he'd passed out drunk there.

"What was all that about dragonsmoke barriers?" she said, surveying the unconscious man with disapproval. "I thought it would keep intruders out and defend your lair." The intruder's aura showed that he'd taken a hit to the head and also that his feet were injured. She narrowed her eyes, recognizing the similarity in the damage to that part of Rhys' aura.

She would bet that this guy had been stuck in Fae, dancing, too.

"Hadrian!" Rhys said and dropped to his knees beside the intruder. He was wearing a leather jacket and jeans, and was quite well dressed. His hair was auburn and wavy and he looked as if he might be as tall as Rhys when he stood up.

Was he another *Pyr*?

Or an employee of the restaurant?

"He's not rotating between forms, at least," Rhys said with relief.

He was *Pyr*, then.

Rhys touched Hadrian's shoulder and that *Pyr* stirred, as if awakening from a deep sleep. Lila saw the lump on the back of his head just as he groaned. Rhys helped him to sit up and Hadrian winced as he tentatively fingered the back of his own head.

"What happened? I thought you were on the roof, breathing smoke," Rhys said.

"I was, until Alasdair came." This dragon shifter had a British accent. Lila stood back and listened, her gaze returning repeatedly to the aura around his feet. She hated the sight of those silver shimmers of Fae light. "He said you forgot the gem of the hoard and asked us to bring it to you at Reliquary."

"I did forget it, but I never saw Alasdair." Rhys frowned. "And I was never at Reliquary." He pivoted to look at the empty counter and his lips thinned.

"Should I know where that is?" Lila asked.

"It's the antique shop in Soho, apparently run by the vampires in the Coven of Mercy."

"Of course," Lila said as if that was self-evident, but no one even smiled. Rhys was helping Hadrian to get up. The other *Pyr* sat down hard on the couch as if he couldn't make it much further.

"Then Kade came, too."

Who was Kade?

"Kade?" Rhys' tone was tinged with alarm. "I thought he was allied with the Dark Queen. I thought he was with her."

Hadrian shook his head, then frowned in regret at the move. "He said he'd made a mistake. He wanted to come in and tell me about it so I changed the permissions on the dragonsmoke...

Rhys swore. He strode into the bedroom and rummaged in a drawer, then swore again. When he came back into the main room his eyes were flashing and there was a blue shimmer around his perimeter.

"Don't tell me he took the stylus," Hadrian said and Rhys nodded.

"What stylus?" Lila asked, but they ignored her.

"I'm sorry, Rhys..."

"Don't worry about it. What's done is done." Rhys was curt. "The question is what we're going to do now."

"You're going to tell me what all of that means," Lila said, wondering whether he would.

But Rhys did. He spoke quickly. "Kade is another *Pyr* who had a stylus that let him create a portal to Fae wherever he wanted. The Dark Queen gave it to him, apparently." Lila felt her eyes widen at this news. "He opened the portal at Bones, and after we were lost in Fae, Drake took it from him. Kade disappeared then and no one knew where he was. The stylus was entrusted to me, to help find Theo, who is still trapped in Fae."

Lila had to sit down. One part of this story was impossible to believe. "You volunteered to cross the threshold to Fae again? Even after what happened to your feet?"

"Yes," he said with a resolve that was becoming familiar. These *Pyr* were all about honor and duty, and defending those they loved. Lila would have admired that more if it had been less likely to put Rhys in danger. "Finding Theo is more important than anything I might have to endure."

The nobility of his nature and his commitment to his fellows amazed Lila. Her fear for him surprised her with its power and stole away any protest she might have made.

Was she falling for this dragon shifter?

Lila didn't want to think about that. "But you wanted to conceive a son," she reminded him. "Is this why you thought you might not be around to defend him?"

Rhys looked contrite. "That's part of it. You know about *her* plan already."

Lila wondered whether she should reconsider her own inclination to satisfy the firestorm and bear that son. It didn't seem as if any of the options available were very good.

Which just meant she had to do what she could to influence the probabilities.

She needed to join Rhys' team.

Embron followed the burn of the firestorm to Rhys' home and inhaled sharply at the scent of the dragonsmoke barrier. He was learning to hate that stuff. He lingered in the shadows of an alley across the street and watched the windows of the apartment, noting the darkened restaurant on the ground floor.

Where was the gem of the hoard? He had to believe that Rhys had obtained it, in order to pay the ransom for his destined mate. The ransom hadn't been paid. Did Rhys still have it?

The light of the firestorm revealed that Rhys and Lila were in the apartment, and Embron heard their voices as they talked with another of the *Pyr*. Three of them. He had no concerns about the selkie, but confronting two *Pyr* in the lair of one of them, after he fought through dragonsmoke, had lower odds of success than he liked.

He kept his hand in the pocket of his trouser, his fingers wrapped around the crystal orb from Regalia. He'd tested the ability of the magick to dissipate dragonsmoke in Vermont and it had failed to make an impact. It was only the one of the two orbs remaining and he was aware that its store of magick was ebbing away. He'd gathered it with such care. Who was stealing it from him?

Whoever held the gem of the hoard was an obvious candidate.

Maeve was another.

He could smell the silver tang of earth magick and guessed that someone in Maeve's thrall had recently visited Rhys' apartment. Had she claimed the gem of the hoard, ignoring their recent alliance? Embron couldn't think of another explanation that fit the situation so well. He'd only trusted her when her magick was in his possession. Now it slipped from his grasp, indicating that she was reclaiming it.

If so, she had the gem of the hoard, she would have retreated to the sanctuary of her kingdom in Fae. He had no means of accessing that realm—which would only increase its appeal to Maeve. The *Pyr* were intent upon stopping her, though. Embron would hide in their proximity and listen.

He waited, then approached the door that gave access to the apartments at the same time as another resident returned home. His smile was beguiling and the young man just glanced over his shoulder, barely hesitating before he let Embron grab the door instead of ensuring it locked. They shared the elevator together, Embron choosing the fourth floor after the young man chose the third.

It was a small building with only three or four apartments on each floor. When the man got off the elevator, Embron pushed the button for the fifth floor, where Rhys lived. The doors opened and closed at the fourth floor, revealing an empty corridor. Embron smelled toast and heard music. Two apartments were occupied, at least.

The doors closed and the elevator ascended to the fifth floor. The dragonsmoke stung him as soon as the doors opened again. He heard conversation from Rhys' apartment, something about Kade and Alasdair, but couldn't linger to listen, not with the dragonsmoke burning his skin.

He hit the button for the second floor, preparing himself for an exchange with another resident. A surprise encounter could lead to questions and he tried to be ready for them. The doors opened to an empty corridor, though, and he listened, hearing nothing. He stepped into the corridor and the elevator left. Still, the corridor was silent.

The restaurant was immediately below. If Embron took refuge on this floor, he would be able to hear conversation in the restaurant. Surely the *Pyr* might gather there to confer. The unit at the front of the building would give him a view of the street, like that of Rhys' own apartment.

He whispered to the door lock to open to him, and it did so immediately, encouraged by a red swirl of magick. He slipped into the darkened apartment, noticing the pile of flyers on the floor immediately inside. They were coupons and ads for fast food restaurants in the vicinity which had been slipped beneath the door, and the pile was large enough for him to conclude that the occupant was away.

The apartment was neat and sparsely furnished. The shades were partly drawn, but the view over the street was excellent. Embron shifted shape and stretched out across the floor, watching and listening. His senses were sharper in his dragon form and he didn't want to miss a single detail.

He placed the orb on the floor beside him. Though it was tempting to take advantage of the interval and draw magick to it, he didn't want to attract attention. Let Maeve think him beaten.

He watched the orb's glow, narrowing his eyes to note the steady departure of earth magick from its stores, then quietly sang to it, buttressing the Regalian magick snared within it, as he waited.

"Let me see your injury," Lila said briskly to Hadrian and he leaned forward. "How did it happen?"

"Someone hit me." Hadrian braced his hands on his knees. "But Alasdair was the only one with me. I hope nothing happened to him."

Lila didn't point out the obvious. If one dragon shifter could change alliances, then any of them could—and there was the example of Embron, too.

Rhys said nothing. He paced the width of the room, as if getting control of his temper, then pivoted slowly to face Hadrian. "Tell me exactly what happened," he said, his words so crisp that Lila knew more was wrong than Hadrian's injury.

"I fell asleep," that *Pyr* explained. "You know how it is when you're breathing smoke."

Rhys folded his arms across his chest and nodded. "Meditative. When you're tired, it's easy to fall asleep."

"And Alasdair woke me up. You were gone and I couldn't feel the firestorm either." Hadrian looked between the two of them, his gaze clouding with confusion as he eyed the bright sparks burning between them. "I thought you satisfied that."

"Never mind," Rhys said, his tone more insistent. "What then?"

"Alasdair said you wanted the gem of the hoard and that we were to bring it to you."

"At Reliquary," Rhys reminded him.

Hadrian nodded. "He had your keys." His eyes lit and he dug in his pocket, producing the keys and handing them to Rhys.

Rhys eyed them. "This is the extra set from the restaurant, the keys I keep there in case of emergency. I never gave them to anybody."

Hadrian's eyes narrowed. "It was odd," he said slowly. "He said he couldn't cross our dragonsmoke. I said I'd change the permissions, but he told me to just get the stone because we were in a hurry."

"And then?" Rhys prompted.

"And then we got in the elevator and I pushed the button. I had the gem of the hoard in my hand. I remember the elevator starting to descend...and then, nothing." He looked between the two of them.

"Was there anyone else in the elevator?" Lila felt she had to ask the obvious question.

Hadrian shook his head. "I didn't see anyone."

"But there must have been," Rhys protested. He turned to Lila. "Alasdair and Hadrian are cousins."

She wasn't convinced of the other *Pyr's* innocence. "Did he have a red string on his wrist?"

Rhys inhaled and his eyes glittered.

Hadrian's brows rose. "No! I would have noticed that."

Because he'd had one as well, when he'd been compelled to dance with Rhys.

Rhys paced the apartment. "But Alasdair was the one who pursued the Dark Queen when you were freed," he told her. "The last time I saw him, he was chasing that car."

Lila sat down, finding her legs unsteady beneath her. "What if she got him instead?"

"What would she do to him?" Rhys asked. "Other than curse him?"

Lila had to tell him. "I always heard she could read minds and that nothing could be hidden from her. I told her and Embron what they wanted to know, because it's not supposed to be a pleasant experience to have her digging for something specific. I've heard of creatures making deals, just to make her stop."

Rhys' gaze held hers and she knew he was thinking of the torture she'd endured. She wasn't proud to realize that in that moment of anguish she would have given up anything or anyone to save her own skin.

"What can we do to help him?" Hadrian asked, looking between them again.

"Maybe nothing at this point," Rhys said.

"I'm going to guess that the Dark Queen has the gem of the hoard," Lila concluded and Rhys nodded, his thoughts obviously having followed the same path.

"And if Kade has the stylus, he must have followed her into Fae," he added.

"He did!" Hadrian said. "I saw him open a portal on the street, right down there. It was the light from Fae that made my feet hurt again."

"At least the Dark Queen is gone," Lila said. "In Fae, which suits me well enough."

"Maybe not for long," Rhys said. Their gazes held for a moment.

Hadrian was visibly agitated and his aura showed his pain and his uncertainty. Lila found it almost as distracting as the firestorm when she was trying to think.

"Let me look at that," she said.

"It'll just take time to heal," Hadrian protested, but he did as she asked.

She was well aware of how Rhys watched her, admiration in his gaze. She ran her hands over Hadrian's injury and knew it wouldn't heal very quickly. She spared a quick glance at Rhys, checking his reaction to her plan to heal his friend.

He smiled and Lila's heart warmed. "Thank you," he said quietly, and Hadrian looked up.

"Thank you for what?" that *Pyr* said, but Lila had closed her eyes and was exhaling the mist of healing. She felt its cool fingers slide over Hadrian, seeking his injury. She was aware of his nature, the core of fire in his dragon being, and realized he shared Rhys' affinity to the earth, as well. There was a tinge of ice within him, though, and she summoned it, guessing it was key to his nature. The ice mingled with the mist of her breath and she saw hoarfrost on his skin, in his veins, coating each tiny hair.

She also saw the outline of a kiss on his cheek, a purplish blue imprint of a woman's puckered lips. It looked like a bruise or frostbite, but then it shimmered and disappeared as if she'd imagined it.

Hadrian breathed slowly and more deeply, clearly feeling some relief, and the red faded from the bump even as his aura began to repair itself. Lila heard the tingle of a thousand icicles being blown in the wind and she breathed more mist. This time, she thought of the frost that formed on the shore, on the rocks and edges of the beach, the lacy filigree of frost that marked a winter morning, when the sea was silvery grey, its surface as smooth as a mirror. She breathed mist slowly and steadily, feeling the injury heal in increments, losing track of time and place.

She knew she was safe, though, safe in Rhys' lair with a dragon watching over her.

Lila admitted to herself that was a nice change, then concentrated on healing Hadrian.

Sylvia awakened to a persistent knocking.

She rolled over and opened her eyes, halfway expecting to find herself in Sebastian's library again, as if her flight from captivity had been a dream.

Or a failure.

But she was still in her apartment. Maeve's book was on her shelf, glowing slightly red as if to ensure she didn't forget it.

She rolled to her back, thinking of what her aunt had told her the night before over dinner. She wasn't Eithne's niece at all, but had been adopted, chosen by Eithne because of her innate gifts. Eithne was a witch and she was leaving her entire legacy to Sylvia, whatever that meant. Learning that she wasn't who she thought she was, that the story of her parents' unexpected death was a fiction, had shaken Sylvia too much for her to absorb much else. She had more questions.

"Sylvia?" Her aunt's voice carried through the door.

"Aunt Eithne!" Sylvia said before she realized her mistake. She opened the door. "I'm sorry. It's such a habit..."

"I don't mind," Eithne said. "It's actually very nice. Don't change what you call me unless you want to." Sylvia saw that the older woman looked tired. Eithne gestured toward the back of the house, where her courtyard was located. "We've been invited to dinner. I wanted to let you sleep but they're getting impatient."

"They?"

"My guests."

"I'd rather stay here. I have a lot to think about, if it's all the same..."

"It's not," Eithne said with uncharacteristic sharpness. She met Sylvia's gaze steadily. "And bring the book."

Sylvia felt her mouth open in astonishment. How had her aunt known about the book? And why would she bring it? On the other hand, it might not be safe to leave it behind. Eithne was already disappearing down the stairs, her footsteps light and purposeful.

Sylvia closed the door and leaned back against it for a moment. It was evening, which meant it had been an entire day and more since she'd left Reliquary. She'd spent the day of her escape consumed with restless energy and had cleaned her apartment, done her laundry, then gone shopping for groceries. She'd looked over her shoulder the whole time but hadn't seen anyone following her.

She'd had dinner with Eithne, relieved that her aunt had returned, but had been startled by their conversation. She'd been awake most of the night, at first because she was thinking about Eithne's confessions. Later, she couldn't sleep because she was expecting Sebastian to suddenly step out of the shadows or loom over her bed—or that she'd dream of the red room. She'd finally fallen asleep at first light and had evidently slept all day.

Sylvia went into her kitchen and looked down into the garden five stories below. She could see a couple, standing together, chatting and looking at the garden. They didn't seem to be very interested in plants at all and turned with obvious interest when Eithne appeared.

The man had a little dragon over him, a dragon that was opal and gold.

He was a dragon shifter.

She hurried to wash and dress, the presence of one of the *Pyr* in her aunt's garden making her curious enough to almost forget Sebastian.

But not quite.

He hadn't pursued her and she was disappointed. She'd had her arguments all composed. She'd been ready to tell him off. She'd been determined to demand the truth.

But Sebastian hadn't come.

Sylvia had just been useful, and obviously she wasn't any longer.

She didn't have to be glad of that.

CHAPTER ELEVEN

lasdair awakened with a raging headache. He'd never felt such pain, not even after the worst bout of drinking in his life. He felt as if his brains had been tugged out one ear and tossed on the floor, as if someone had rummaged through them, knotted them up, then jammed them back into his head through the other ear. The worst thing was that he couldn't remember where he had been or what he had done to earn this headache. He remembered finding Rhys' mate and pursuing Maeve.

Had the *Pyr* won that dragonfight? Had he celebrated a little too much? He couldn't feel the glow of the firestorm so maybe Rhys had celebrated in the best possible way.

Where was he?

He opened one eye cautiously then closed it again when the bright silver light nearly made his head explode. Bracing himself for that, he opened his eye slightly again, only to realize that he had no idea where he was.

He wasn't alone, that was for sure. He was lying on the ground, cold ground, and he felt bruised all over. There was a woman's high heeled shoe right beside his temple, one with a red sole. That was worrisome. Alasdair turned slightly to look up, way up, to find himself lying at Maeve's feet.

She looked about a million times better than the last time he'd seen her—or maybe he should have said a million years younger. Her hair was dark and glossy again, her cheeks were smooth and unlined. Her lips were full and red, and her dark eyes snapped with vigor. Fortunately, she didn't seem to have noticed his movement at all. Her gaze was fixed on the orb in her hand, a golden orb with something inside it.

The gem of the hoard. Alasdair remembered stealing it from Rhys' lair at her command.

This was not good.

Red light swirled in a maelstrom around Maeve, who was seated on a large silver and red throne, and the prostate Alasdair at her feet. He didn't move, not wanting to attract her attention. The red light wasn't just swirling around her: it was diving into the gem of the hoard. The gem of the hoard pulsed with a power Alasdair hadn't known it possessed.

Maybe it hadn't possessed it, not until Maeve started to weave her spell.

He had a thought then to rise and stop her, but realized he couldn't move. Opening his eyes was the extent of his capabilities. He couldn't open his mouth or make a sound either. He tried and discovered that he couldn't shift shape either. Terror flooded through him at that, and he noticed the red string tied around his left wrist.

He'd been enchanted.

He must be Maeve's captive in Fae, even though he'd collected the gem of the hoard as she'd commanded.

This was really not good.

Why had she kept him?

There was a blinding flash of silver light then and a slash appeared in the air. A Fae warrior stepped through the gap and closed it again, then seemed to revel in the red spell light that spun around Maeve.

"And?" she asked, barely flicking a glance at the new arrival.

"The book is missing," he said.

That got Maeve's attention. She looked at him then and Alasdair respected that he didn't flinch. "Missing?" she repeated.

"The woman entrusted with it has apparently fled the protection of the vampires. She is the one who can see its truth."

"They could have lied to you, Bryant."

The warrior shook his head. "They did not see me, my lady. I didn't reveal myself, but listened first."

She inhaled and sat back. "Vampires don't miss much."

The warrior looked insulted. "I was the heart and soul of discretion, my lady."

Maeve harumphed.

The warrior continued. "The troublesome one says the *Pyr* will have found her..."

"How can he know that?"

"Sebastian is said to have a small measure of foresight, my lady. Although I cannot vouch for his abilities, he does consistently make excellent choices."

"Didn't he surrender the book to this woman?"

"He warned against the choice, my lady. I heard them argue about that."

Maeve nudged Alasdair with her toe. "I know you're awake. Where would we find the *Pyr*?"

I don't know, Alasdair thought, then felt the jab of her fingers in his mind again. He recoiled and couldn't stop the first thought that came to him. *They will gather at the firestorm.*

Maeve bent down and smiled at him, an expression so chilly that Alasdair would have shivered if he'd been able to. "And you can feel the firestorm, can't you? Lead us there and I might release you alive."

He might have protested but she poked deep in his brain and he screamed instead.

Rhys watched Lila heal Hadrian, impressed again that she gave so much of herself to others. Her ability was both gift and curse, because he could see how it tired her. He wondered how she discerned injuries in the first place and wanted to learn more about her gifts. He could see the tension slip from Hadrian beneath the cool mist of her healing breath and was grateful for her intervention.

She seemed to fall asleep, or maybe she'd entered a trance. He got a blanket and tucked her in, then checked his persistent phone.

There was a message from Erik which wasn't a joy to hear. The leader of the *Pyr* was annoyed that they'd been seen in their dragon forms in the battle to save Lila, and Rhys guessed that Drake had heard from Erik, too. Erik also told him about Embron's attack and that the sparking of the firestorm had distracted the dragon prince. And he'd sent Rhys a prophecy.

The gem of the hoard, lost and found;
The fate of Others to it bound.
A Fae treasure, laden with earth magick,
Seized and claimed by a dragon's trick.
All strains of magick share this trait:
None will share, one must dominate.

Dragon flame and selkie tide,
Will diminish the threat if allied.
Their power can destroy just one stone—
Will their choice save their unborn son?

Rhys pursed his lips as he read it. He didn't have an unborn son and didn't welcome the news that he not only had to convince Lila of the merit of the firestorm and conception of that son, but that they were evidently responsible for destroying a stone, too.

The gem of the hoard was amber, which wasn't a stone although people often called it one. What other stone was there? He certainly wasn't glad to learn why Maeve and Embron were at odds, although it made sense. Only one of them could triumph over the other, which meant one would have all the magick. Rhys wasn't sure who he'd prefer to see win.

Could magick itself be destroyed? He had no idea.

Rafferty had been going to see the witch, Eithne. He called the older *Pyr* and learned that they were together, and wanted to meet as Eithne had things to tell them. Rhys invited them to the restaurant for dinner, then called Drake to invite the other *Pyr* in town, too. The restaurant was closed on Sundays and Mondays, so they'd have it to themselves.

Since he didn't know what to do about magick, dragon princes or Fae queens, Rhys pulled up his restaurant inventory and began to plan dinner.

When Lila straightened and opened her eyes, the sunlight was gone. It had to be late afternoon, which explained why she was hungry.

That and the effect of healing.

She was tucked beneath a blanket on Rhys' couch. Hadrian was dozing before her and the bump on his head was gone. Rhys had apparently made a pot of coffee because Lila could smell it and he was sitting at the counter with his laptop. He noticed immediately that she was awake and brought her a hot mug of tea without saying anything. A spark leapt between their hands when he handed her the mug and Lila caught her breath at the stab of desire that shot through her body.

Rhys' gaze was simmering, his eyes so dark and his body so taut that she wanted to drag him into the bedroom and have him all over again.

"Do you have foresight?" she asked, because the tea was perfectly steeped.

"Your breathing changed when you started to wake up," he said with a shake of his head. He smiled, just a little. "Timing is what I do."

Lila wasn't going to argue with that. "It certainly is," she acknowledged with a smile. Their gazes locked and they were captive in a golden moment until she shook her head and looked away. Lila took a big restorative sip of the tea, then wrapped her hands around the mug. She was exhausted but she knew the healing was good.

"You've been thinking," she said, because she sensed that Rhys had decided something.

He nodded and sat down beside her. The strength of his thigh was pressed against her own and the firestorm glowed brightly along the line of contact. It warmed Lila to her toes and turned her thoughts in a predictable direction. Instead of moving away, she leaned against him, drawing strength from him after expending her own, and saw the corner of his mouth lift in a smile. He put his arm around her shoulders and drew her close against his heat. "Are you all right?" It was hard to resist the gentle concern in his tone.

"Healing just leaves me a little tired," she said. "I'll be fine in a minute. The tea is perfect."

"You didn't have to do it."

"I wouldn't have, for one of my own kind," she admitted and felt his surprise. "He betrayed you. If anyone had betrayed me, I would have let them suffer. You're nicer than I am."

"Hadrian was tricked and betrayed himself."

She shook her head. "You *Pyr* give each other a lot of latitude."

"Anyone can make a mistake. Anyone can be deceived or misled. We trust each other and forgive those errors when we can. It makes us stronger together."

Lila felt him looking at her.

"Don't you selkies forgive?"

"Not that easily," Lila admitted. "But we don't work together much either. Will that philosophy hold true for Alasdair, too? And for Kade?"

"It depends, but they're not automatically condemned. They get to explain."

Lila looked into the depths of her tea, knowing that selkies weren't so kind. "Not us," she said lightly and took another sip. "I couldn't do anything with his feet," she admitted. "They have magick trapped in the wounds, just like yours."

He nodded and was silent for a long moment, as if deciding whether it was wise to speak. She guessed that he wasn't thinking about his feet.

"Go on," she urged with a smile.

"Maybe that unwillingness to forgive is why selkies are cursed in love. If you don't forgive or trust, then you're always halfway out the door."

Lila studied her tea, knowing that was true of her.

Rhys continued. "It's like you're not really giving any relationship a chance."

"There's nothing wrong with not wanting a relationship."

"Except it's lonely. I couldn't bear to be without the *Pyr*. They're the closest thing to family that I have."

She was startled by his honesty but didn't doubt his conviction.

"I'd feel like there was a hole in my life again, like I felt after Llewelyn died. Becoming friends with Kristofer wasn't the same, but it filled the void."

Lil was surprised that he chose a metaphor that was so resonant for her, but didn't say as much.

"I can count on them." Rhys met her gaze steadily. "And that's because I trust them. I intend to remain friends with them, I trust them, and I have a commitment to our partnership. I expect it to work, and so do they, and it does. I think those things are all bound together." He sipped his coffee. "Maybe relationships don't work for the selkies because you're always waiting for them to fail."

"Maybe we just have different expectations."

"Maybe you do. I can't imagine a *Pyr* wanting to have sons with every woman who would have him."

"Nereus is concerned with the survival of our kind," she said, feeling obliged to defend him.

"And so am I." He tapped her shoulder. "But you're not, or you would have welcomed Nereus already." He watched her, sure of his conclusions and of her. The sight of his confidence amused her. "I think you're waiting for a better offer."

"Like yours?"

"Maybe." He chuckled and clinked their mugs together. The firestorm flared around them with a heat that seemed more invigorating and comforting than it had before. Lila knew she was drawing strength from him and told herself not to get used to it.

Too late. She knew she already was.

Maybe it was time to put a stop to this. Lila closed her eyes, savoring the warmth of the firestorm, feeling it turn her thoughts in a very predictable direction. She turned slightly and touched her lips to Rhys' throat. She felt his pulse skip, then he pushed to his feet and walked away.

"What about the firestorm?" she asked, hearing the disappointment in her own voice.

"You haven't decided to conceive yet."

"We could satisfy the firestorm over and over again until I do," Lila suggested, keeping her tone playful. "I like sex. Lots of it might convince me."

Rhys shook his head. "No, next time, if there is a next time, will be the last time."

"You really are very principled, aren't you?"

He laughed. "I guess so." Then he sobered. "But I don't blame you for being cautious." He paced a bit, pausing to look down at the sleeping Hadrian. "I was sent a prophecy when you were asleep."

"A prophecy?"

"They're often revealed in conjunction with firestorms," he said, as if this was the most natural thing in the world. He pulled it up on his phone and showed it to her.

> *The gem of the hoard, lost and found;*
> *The fate of Others to it bound.*
> *A Fae treasure, laden with earth magick,*
> *Seized and claimed by a dragon's trick.*
> *All strains of magick share this trait:*
> *None will share, one must dominate.*
> *Dragon flame and selkie tide,*
> *Will diminish the threat if allied.*
> *Their power can destroy just one stone—*
> *Will their choice save their unborn son?*

More talk about teamwork and that unborn son. Lila might have thought this so-called prophecy was just another convenient argument for the firestorm, but she saw that Rhys believed it.

A battle over magick? She wasn't sure she wanted to see that—let alone be responsible for stopping it.

She stole a glance at Rhys and knew, though, that he was going to take the challenge.

In fact, she'd guess that he already had.

"Obviously, we haven't an unborn son," Rhys said before Lila could make that protest. He raised a hand. "And we might not ever have one.

But look at the rest. Do you know what the stones are? It sounds like there's more than one."

Lila shook her head, reading it again. "One must be the gem of the hoard. Maybe Embron and the Dark Queen were working together to get it, each planning to betray the other once they found it. Why would Alasdair ally with either of them?"

"Maybe he didn't have a choice."

Lila shook her head that he defended one of his own kind. "Maybe there was something in it for him."

"I can't see what. We're all on the list because of our nature. I don't see how anyone could be made an exception, no matter what he did."

That made sense. "She resented him when they interrogated me. What if he'd taken the magick and given her only a little bit, maybe to find out what she knew? She looked old, and not having enough magick would also explain her removing the curse on me without demanding a toll."

Rhys nodded. "Because she had no choice. That makes sense. I wonder what the other stone is and where it is."

"And who has it." Lila wondered how something like the gem of the hoard could be destroyed and realized she didn't know enough about magick to be sure.

"How many selkies are left?" Rhys asked after a moment.

The very question was troubling. "Maybe a dozen. I don't keep close track. Nyssa does. There's Sybil and Serena and Salina. Nyssa has three daughters, too."

"All female?"

"Mostly. When Nereus summoned me last, he was bragging that Twyla and Tawdra were both pregnant. He told me that it was my duty to join with him and breed more selkies."

"That's not love," Rhys said, his eyes flashing. "Just like that Malcolm Ramsay who hid your skin to keep you as his wife. That's not love either." He pushed to his feet to pace. "It's no wonder you don't trust the firestorm. You've only known males who were unworthy of trust."

Lila couldn't argue that, but she wasn't sure it was a good time to admit that she doubted there were any males worthy of trust. Would Rhys change once she agreed to bear his son and he had what he wanted from her?

"The funny thing is that I only met Malcolm because I was fleeing Nereus," she admitted instead. "I would never have been on that beach otherwise." Rhys said nothing but he was listening, and that was almost as seductive as the firestorm itself. She cleared her throat and returned to his original question. "There are fewer of us than there are *Pyr*, that's for sure."

There was urgency in Rhys' tone when he spoke again and she felt additional heat in the glow of the firestorm. "We have to fix this, Lila, for the sake of both our kinds. That's the only way it'll be safe for us to bring our son into this world."

"You just want the chance to argue the merit of permanent alliance," she argued, trying to sound as if she was teasing him. "I'm not committing to anything like that."

"No, just this one quest," Rhys said. "I respect your doubts and wishes."

"But you reserve the right to try to change my mind."

He nodded rueful agreement and gave her a little smile. "Spending time with you makes me feel persuasive. I like you. A lot." His gaze filled with warmth. "I see that we make a good team and I want more of that. I like the sound of this prophecy and of our partnership making the world a better place." He shrugged. "Call me a romantic."

Lila would have, but she refused to be seduced just yet. "If you're beguiling me, I'll make sure you regret it," she said and Rhys laughed.

"No flames in my eyes," he reminded her and pointed.

"Is that always the sign?"

"Always," he said with conviction.

"You might be just telling me that to make me susceptible."

He shook his head. "There's the trust thing again." Lila would have protested but he raised a hand. "I understand. I promise never to beguile you, or even try."

Lila felt a glow of pleasure at his vow, but told herself it was a small commitment for him to make. "But if the gem of the hoard is in Fae, we can't get it back."

"Sure, we can. We just have to find that portal near your home then go and get it."

Lila was as startled as Rhys was nonchalant. Hadrian was stirring and Rhys went to his friend, his concern obvious.

"If we find the portal near my home, I want to seal it, not cross it."

"I think we should go through the portal first." Rhys had that stubborn look she was starting to recognize. "It's our duty."

And deep in her heart, Lila agreed with him.

"She'll demand something in exchange for our departure. Those are her rules." Lila knew she'd already entered Fae once and owed the Dark

Queen one gift in exchange. She couldn't think of what she'd surrender, and this would mean giving up two things.

Rhys' expression turned grim. "If we get the gem of the hoard, maybe we can make some rules of our own." He drained his mug. "But first, we need to know everything we can about magick. I've invited the *Pyr* in town to come for dinner at the restaurant to share what they know. If we're going to Scotland, I'll need to close the restaurant for a few weeks, too."

"We?" she asked but he'd offered his hand to her.

"We. I'm not letting you go through that portal alone. Until the firestorm is satisfied, and maybe after that, defending you is my primary responsibility."

"Even above the *Pyr*?"

"Even that. They'd tell you the same thing." He nodded, his decision made. "Let's confer with the *Pyr* and make our plan. Fortunately, Hadrian won't be the only one who's hungry."

Lila was unable to stop herself from liking the sense that she was part of a team. Maybe not being alone anymore was the most seductive element of what Rhys saw as the promise of the firestorm.

Maybe this *Pyr* could beguile her without flames in his eyes.

Rhys led Hadrian and Lila back down to his restaurant. Hadrian had been profuse in his thanks to Lila. He'd then set up the tables while Rhys turned on the stoves and grills. Rhys called several of his employees and explained the restaurant would be closed for a couple of weeks, and made arrangements for them to be paid during the closure.

Then he started to cook.

Hadrian was sitting by himself near the fire, breathing smoke slowly and deeply. Lila hesitated, as if she'd meant to speak to him but realized he was occupied.

"He's breathing dragonsmoke to create a protective barrier around the restaurant," Rhys informed her softly, his fingertip on her elbow. "Leave him to it and come help me."

As the other *Pyr* arrived, they said little, but joined Hadrian and added their dragonsmoke to his efforts. Within twenty minutes, there were four powerful *Pyr*, all sitting with their eyes closed and their hands resting on their knees, exhaling in unison.

Rhys meanwhile had gone through the fridges and made a plan. He set Lila to work dicing vegetables and herbs.

"It's too much food," she protested but he laughed.

"Wait and see about that."

She flicked a glance at the *Pyr*. "Can you tell me who they are?"

"The one who appears older is Drake, leader of the Dragon Legion."

Rhys watched Lila consider the somber *Pyr* with dark hair and dark eyes. He'd surveyed the restaurant on his arrival, as if looking for foes in the shadows, which was characteristic of Drake. He was the most observant of any of the *Pyr*, in Rhys' view, and always ready for anything. Drake had an olive complexion and there was a bit of silver in his hair. He seemed disinclined to talk much and had just nodded at the other *Pyr* before joining them.

"The Dragon Legion," Lila echoed. "Is that a fighting squad?"

"Yes. We fought together against the *Slayers* in the Dragon's Tail Wars." Rhys shrugged. "He's also the ancestor of Theo Stephens, the *Pyr* who didn't return from Fae."

"Not his father?"

Rhys shook his head. "Drake's the father of Eric, who is still young, and he also adopted his mate's human son, Timmy."

"How can he be an ancestor? How old are you guys?"

"All different ages. I was born in 1540. You?"

"120 B.C." She wasn't particularly interested in that or Rhys' surprise, but was busy looking at the *Pyr*.

He told her more. "Drake and the Dragon's Tooth Warriors were enchanted for thousands of years. After they were released, thanks to Rafferty, the darkfire allowed them to travel through time to find their destined mates. Drake had a firestorm before he and his men were enchanted and a son, Theo, and our Theo is descended from him. He was blessed with a second firestorm in our time."

Lila nodded understanding.

"But as a result of the darkfire, the numbers of *Pyr* warriors were bolstered right near the end of the Dragon's Tail Wars. Many of the Dragon Legion are descended from the Dragon's Tooth Warriors. That's why we have a dragon tattoo."

"Phew. I thought you were just afraid you'd forget," she teased, her eyes sparkling.

Rhys grinned. "My forebear, Damian, was one of them. His mate was Petra, an Earthdaughter, who had been trapped in the underworld while carrying his son."

"What's an Earthdaughter?"

"An elemental witch. There were four, one for each element, who were destined mates of the *Pyr* during the Dragon's Tail Wars. Three of them were mates to Dragon's Tooth Warriors sent back in time. I've no doubt there are many more."

"Is your mother's nature why you have an affinity with the earth?"

"I'm not sure. Many *Pyr* do. Hadrian does and Rafferty does. Even Kristofer." He was thinking as he spoke. "And Quinn, the Smith of the *Pyr*. It's almost as common an affinity for us as fire itself."

"What can an Earthdaughter do that a *Pyr* with an affinity to earth can't?"

"Well, it's said that Petra could turn into a pillar of stone or summon an earthquake. I can influence the element of earth but not become it."

"So you could summon an earthquake?"

"I've never tried. Why would I?"

"I guess summoning a destructive force is unlikely to defend the treasures of the earth, including mortals."

"Exactly." A timer rang and Rhys moved across the kitchen to turn over some chicken on the grill and check on a pizza that was under the broiler. He noticed that Lila was looking thoughtful. "Why?"

"I wonder if your lineage gives you specific gifts, that's all. I come from a line of healers, for example."

Rhys granted her an intent look. "I wonder."

She indicated the *Pyr*. "And the others?"

"Arach is the one with dark hair and grey eyes. If you want to know more about beguiling, he's the one to ask. He's amazing at it, but then, he studied with Lorenzo, who is the best of all of us at beguiling. He can even beguile other *Pyr*."

Lila nodded. "I can't think of a selkie who can charm other selkies. That's impressive."

"Are some better than others?"

"Yes, but I think it's practice. Nyssa is really good at it."

Rhys wondered how good the other selkie was at charming. It might be possible for a selkie with exceptional abilities to charm another of her own kind. "Arach's forebear was Alexander, Drake's second, whose mate was Katina, another elemental witch. She was a Waterdaughter, but Arach's affinities are to air and fire."

"There goes that theory," Lila ceded with a smile.

Rhys laughed, then pointed. "Could you make some parsley bouquets for me, please? They're the garnish for this spicy chicken."

Lila did as he asked. "Like this?" At his nod, she continued. "And the fourth? The guy with the man-bun?"

Rhys smiled. "Balthasar. He builds and repairs sailboats, even does some racing."

"Affinities to water and fire?" Lila guessed.

"Exactly. I forget the name of his forebear in Drake's team. Orion, maybe."

"Did he mate with an elemental witch?"

Rhys shook his head. "It was Hadrian and Alasdair's forebear whose destined mate was an Airdaughter, although the story goes that originally she was an immortal nymph. Hadrian and Alasdair are cousins."

"And their affinities?" Lila asked, apparently unwilling to abandon her theory just yet.

"Hadrian's are earth and fire."

Lila made a face and he lifted a finger.

"But Alasdair's are to air and fire."

"Fifty-fifty then," Lila said. "What about the fourth elemental witch?"

Rhys began to plate meals as Rafferty entered the restaurant. "Brandon, a *Pyr* in Australia, is mated to Liz who is a Firedaughter. She's the only elemental witch I've actually met."

The four *Pyr* stood and greeted Rafferty who arrived just then. He was a powerful *Pyr* with long hair and wise eyes. His mate, Melissa, waved to Rhys and there were two other women accompanying them. One was elderly and not strong: the younger one helped her to a chair, her expression filled with concern.

"Rafferty," Rhys said to Lila. "His mate, Melissa."

Lila frowned. "How could I know her?"

"She's a news broadcaster. You might have seen her on television. And she did a series of specials about the *Pyr*."

Lila nodded. "And the other two women?"

He frowned. "I think the younger one is the woman who the vampires entrusted with the Dark Queen's book. The older one must be the witch they said they'd bring."

Lila turned and stared at him. "Surely they wouldn't bring Maeve's book here?"

Rhys froze. "No. Rafferty said on the phone that she'd fled from the vampires. Why would she bring the book when she had no protection?"

Lila was unconvinced and it showed.

Rafferty, meanwhile, was making introductions. He gestured to the older woman. "This is Eithne, who contacted us about Embron's appearance in Edinburgh and led us to the seven sleeping warriors." He indicated the younger woman. "And this is Sylvia, her niece. You all know Melissa, of course."

"Lila doesn't," Rhys said, leading her to meet them all. He introduced her to the other *Pyr*, concluding with Rafferty and Melissa.

Rafferty shook Lila's hand then basked in the glow of the firestorm and visibly drew strength from it. He met Lila's gaze. "I can tell you anything you want to know about this *Pyr*."

Lila smiled and thanked him. The *Pyr* pushed smaller tables together to make one long one and sat down, passing meals to each other like a big family. Rafferty sat at the head of the table, praising the dragonsmoke barrier and asking each of them for news. Sylvia and Eithne sat together at one end, with Eithne at the foot of the table. Lila took the seat opposite Sylvia and asked if Eithne was well.

The older woman's hair was silver and her eyes were blue. There was wisdom in her gaze and an acceptance of her situation. "You are a healer," she said with quiet confidence. "Empathy is part of your gift."

"I would help you," Lila offered.

Eithne patted her hand. "I'm not sure you can. My magick is gone. I gave a lot of it away, but then the rest was seized by my own apprentice. I am fading, but it is time for me to fade. I have lived many eons."

"Auntie," Sylvia protested, looking as if she might cry.

Eithne seized her hand and gave it a squeeze. "I have one last story to tell, Sylvia, and it's important that you hear it. The story is part of your legacy."

"But..."

Eithne shook her head. "You cannot change what will be. You have no magick yet and must accept whatever comes to you as a result."

"Is that the book?" Rhys asked as Sylvia put a volume down on the table. It looked like a plain notebook, but he couldn't imagine why she'd have brought such a book to the meeting. Hadn't someone said Maeve's book had a glamor on it?

Sylvia started then nodded.

"*The* book?" Lila asked. "*Her* book? The Dark Queen's inventory?"

Rhys and Lila both inhaled when Sylvia nodded again.

"Here and now," Rhys said, looking toward the door with trepidation. Lila had been right to be concerned. He didn't know whether dragonsmoke would dissuade the Fae and didn't want to find out.

"You want to look," Eithne said to Lila, who flushed a little and nodded.

Sylvia passed a hand over the volume and it seemed to shimmer under her hand. Rhys blinked and it had a different cover, an embossed leather one. It looked like a grimoire and he was revolted by the sight of it.

But Sylvia passed it across the table to Lila.

His mate took a deep breath, then opened the book, her fingers trembling. Rhys moved to stand behind her so he could see, too.

CHAPTER TWELVE

t defied belief that Lila was holding the fabled inventory of the Dark Queen in her own hands. She had no doubt that the volume was what Sylvia claimed it to be: it emanated a feeling of malice that couldn't be mistaken.

It had no aura but felt slimy in her hands, like she touched the cold underbelly of evil. She could barely bring herself to turn the pages, but she found the contents horrifying and compelling: once she began to read it, she couldn't stop.

It was also a stretch to believe that she was sitting in a restaurant owned by a dragon shifter, surrounded by his fellow dragon shifters and a witch. She had looked at the auras when Rhys introduced his fellows and was struck by how vigorous they were. The auras of the *Pyr* were bright and richly colored, like gems. Though a few had shadows that hinted at past heartaches—like Rhys—they were clearly a robust group.

Eithne's aura was consistent with those of witches Lila had seen before: it was a constant swirling of pearly hues, like shifting clouds or rising mists. Sylvia, oddly, had no aura at all. Lila couldn't understand that and couldn't stop herself from surreptitiously studying the other woman. Sylvia also seemed despondent and Lila wondered whether that was her character or a recent change. She knew Rhys noticed her curiosity and tried to do a better job of hiding it.

It would be easier now that she held Maeve's book herself. Rhys stood close beside her, also reading it, the heat of the firestorm sizzling against her back.

She looked first for the page with the *Pyr*, hoping Rhys might learn more of the fate of his friend, Theo. It was also easier to look at the names of complete strangers and grow accustomed to the contents of the macabre little volume. Even though she didn't know the deceased *Pyr*, Lila found it chilling to see the names crossed out with dates beside them. She saw the name of his brother, Llewelyn, and that friend, Storme, he'd mentioned.

Rhys had leaned forward and was running his finger down the list of surviving dragon shifters. She felt his relief before he spoke. "Theo is alive, at least," he said and the *Pyr* abandoned their conversations to listen. "And Alasdair. And Kade, too."

"That's better than might have been expected," Drake said.

"I hope Alasdair is okay," Hadrian said from across the table.

"Thank you," Rhys said to Lila, then took the seat beside her. "There must be someone you want to check on," he said, his gaze lingering upon her. "Would you rather I touched it?"

Lila nodded agreement. She felt that the book was drawing strength from her and Maeve's fury wasn't something she wanted to feed. "There were thirteen kinds that made the Isle of the Blessed their home," she said, knowing that Rhys, Hadrian, Sylvia and Eithne would hear. Maybe the other *Pyr* would as well.

Arach was sitting beside Hadrian with Melissa beside him. Rafferty was at the head of the table, Drake on his right and Balthasar on his right, to Rhys' left. They all leaned forward slightly to listen and she reminded herself that Rhys trusted them completely.

"Okay," Rhys said.

"I know the mer-people are gone."

Rhys found that page, with its horrible list of crossed-out names and maps of their locations.

"It says Sheila was the last," he said and met her gaze.

"I knew her and her family," Lila admitted, her heart in her throat.

"Tell me about her," Rhys invited in a low voice. "Bring her alive for us again."

Lila looked up at him, impressed by the suggestion. "She loved to sing and had the most beautiful voice." Her own voice was husky. "I knew her sisters and her mother, but she defied her family."

"How so?"

"She fell in love with a dwarf, a forbidden love since his kind weren't among those of the Isle of the Blessed. She adored him, though, and even talked about giving up her tail to be with him." Lila eyed Sheila's name. "She came and talked to me about Malcolm, seeking advice. She wanted so badly to believe that she and her dwarf could make it work. I wasn't very encouraging."

"I can believe that," Rhys said. "Maybe her dwarf really loved her, though."

"Maybe. That was the last time I saw her."

"Selkies are next," Rhys warned her.

Lila leaned closer, scanning the list, thinking it was far too short, remembering when they had been so numerous. Nyssa was among the living, as were Nereus, Twyla and Tawdra, Salina and Selima, Serena and Sybil. Herself. It was shocking to see her name listed.

Aquinas was crossed out with 2018 as the date beside him.

Lila caught her breath to see Galena, Melita and Ondine crossed out, with 2019 beside them. "Nyssa's daughters," she told Rhys. "I didn't know."

"Maybe that's why she's with the Others," he suggested and she had to admit it was a possibility. She could understand a desire for vengeance—or the need to make a difference by fighting.

"Aquinas was her mate," she confided. "But not the way you mate with the firestorm." She felt Rafferty's smile and saw him take Melissa's hand. "They bred together, no more and no less."

"And now she'll have Nereus' child."

"I suppose that will make another selkie to add to the list." Lila didn't like the thought of bearing a child just to see that offspring hunted by Maeve. The list was chilling and made her agree even more with Rhys about ensuring the world was safe for any son they conceived. She considered the list of selkies again and knew no one was missing. There weren't a dozen selkies anymore. Just nine. It was troubling to see her name listed, but worse to see an X on a map of the world that marked the location of her home. The location of the Isle of the Blessed was marked, too, which she thought was a secret outside of the Blessed who survived.

The combination made her feel targeted and exposed.

The other pages were worse. There were only two medusas left, which reminded her of the one who worked at Bones. Was that why she was there? To help save her kind?

That was the good news, such as it was. There were no centaurs, no unicorns, not a single pegasus. No minotaurs, no satyrs, no griffins, no chimeras, no basilisks. Rhys turned the pages at her request and her horror increased. The last phoenix was gone, along with the *aqrabuamelu.*

"I don't even know what they are," Rhys said, his warmth close beside her.

"Scorpion centaurs. Their kind is ancient and were once said to be the guardians of the sun. They're so warlike that it's hard to believe they were vanquished." Lila took a breath. "Of the thirteen kinds and thousands of individuals, there aren't even a dozen of us left. Nine selkies and two medusas."

Rhys turned back to the page that showed the location of the Isle of the Blessed, his gaze lingering on the X on Westray with her name beside it. "Is this right?"

"More or less."

"Then this must be the beach where we met."

"There's one near my home there. That's part of why I bought the place. The beach is remote and quiet. I like to go swimming where no one can see." She watched Rhys nod, then asked for his phone. She searched for an image of the beach she knew so well. For some reason, she felt compelled to show it to him. There was one on a travel blog and she thought she remembered the backpackers. She showed it to Rhys. "See?"

"But that's not the beach where we met," he said with a frown. "There was a hill back here, and rocks in the sea over here."

It was Lila's turn to frown. "No. There are no rocks there, much less a hill over there. My house is right there."

"There was no house on the beach where we met," he said. "There was a pair of purple sandals. Sparkly ones."

Lila met his gaze. She had no purple sandals, sparkly or otherwise, and no one else swam on her beach. "Are you sure?"

"Positive." Their gazes met and Lila's heart chilled.

She'd been in Fae—which meant she owed Maeve a toll.

Rhys fanned through the book and spoke a little more loudly, his change of tone making Lila realize that the others were watching them. "There's no inventory of portals to Fae," he said to Eithne.

"Because *she* knows where they all are located," Eithne said. "And her magick means she can open new ones for a short period of time wherever she desires. When the Dark Queen possesses her magick, portals can be everywhere and anywhere. Which brings us neatly to the matter at hand." She gave Sylvia a smile, then said Rafferty's name.

"Is it time?" he asked.

"It must be time," she replied. "I already wonder whether I have the strength to tell it all." She did look older than she had on arrival, and Lila could see her fading. There was more mist in her aura and less color with every passing moment.

"Then begin," Rafferty invited. "I thought the meal would restore you and might be worth the delay. Rhys is a talented chef."

"It did and I thank you," Eithne said. Lila looked between them, struck by their formal courtesy, as if they were diplomats from different embassies. "But now I will tell you what you most need to know." At her gesture, Rhys removed her plate then filled her water glass.

"Anything else?" he asked but Eithne shook her head. He left the pitcher with Sylvia, put the plates aside, then returned to his seat beside Lila. Eithne eyed the flicker and glow of the firestorm for a long moment, gathering her thoughts, then she began.

"First, I must explain to you about magick."

But Eithne got no further than that before they were interrupted.

Rhys saw the flash of silver light appear in the air behind Sylvia. It took him a precious second to realize that it was an opening to Fae. Pain exploded in his feet just as a man was flung through the slit between the realms. He heard Hadrian grunt across from him and assumed that *Pyr* felt the same excruciating pain.

Alasdair didn't move after hitting the floor.

"Alasdair!" Hadrian shouted and got to his feet.

The *Pyr* immediately rushed to help Alasdair and confront whoever was coming through the gap. The air was bright with the blue shimmer of *Pyr* on the cusp of change, and the firestorm burned with white heat. Hadrian, who was sitting beside Sylvia, shifted immediately, becoming a powerful dragon with emerald and silver scales. He braced himself over the fallen Alasdair and breathed fire at the slit of silver light, a fierce and powerful guardian.

A Fae warrior suddenly leapt through the slit, slashing at Hadrian with a blade that seemed to be made of silver fire. Rhys smelled *Pyr* blood. Hadrian roared and snatched at the warrior, his movement sending his blood splashing over both of them. Lila gasped at her first sight of his wound and Rhys was shocked, too. The Fae warrior had sliced open Hadrian's chest and even though the *Pyr* was fighting on, he was already fading from the severity of the wound.

What kind of blade was that?

The Fae warrior moved with lightning speed, evading Hadrian and looming suddenly behind Sylvia. He was tall and blond, and looked faintly familiar to Rhys. There was something about his cocky smile.

Sylvia gasped and the Fae warrior took advantage of her surprise to scoop the book off the table. "Just what I need," he said.

"No!" Rafferty shouted.

"Thanks for this," the Fae warrior said to Sylvia with a wink.

"No!" she cried and snatched the book, just barely grabbing onto its spine. The warrior tugged but she held on tightly, the battle over the book pulling her to her feet and sending her chair tumbling backward. She didn't let go. The Fae warrior visibly gritted his teeth and tried to wrench the book from her hands, without success.

"It's mine," Sylvia said with heat, giving the book a tug.

"It's not yours," the Fae warrior replied and gave it such a savage pull that Sylvia stumbled.

She still didn't let go.

Hadrian collapsed beside Alasdair, his blood spreading across the floor. He began to rotate between forms, which was a really bad sign.

Rhys found Lila behind him and seized her hand, before racing around the end of the table where Eithne sat. The witch might have been struck to stone. She was pale and her expression was horrified, but she hadn't moved. Rhys caught the back of Sylvia's dress, but she was jerked away and it slipped from his grip.

Arach, who had been sitting beside Hadrian, had shifted shape, although there wasn't enough room in the restaurant for two dragons, even when one was injured. Rhys suspected he couldn't help himself when a treasure of the earth was imperiled so close to his side. Hadrian shifted to his human form involuntarily and stopped rotating between forms. He was completely still as his blood flowed steadily onto the floor.

Arach, in his aquamarine and silver dragon form, lunged at the Fae warrior, talons extended as if he would tear him to shreds. There was a roar from the front of the restaurant and the sound of smashing glass.

Rhys turned to find Thorolf raging toward them, the blue shimmer of the change surrounding him. That *Pyr* had just barreled through the entry to the restaurant, Niall close behind him. Rhys caught only a glimpse of the tall warrior with his long blond hair before Thorolf shifted to his dragon form, becoming a massive dragon of moonstone and silver. He roared dragonfire at the Fae intruder and Sylvia screamed.

The Fae warrior jumped over Hadrian and Alasdair, moving with that startling speed, and bounded back through the gap. He hauled the book and Sylvia with him.

There was a heartbeat during which Sylvia must have seen what would happen. She could have released the book, but she didn't. She stumbled over the two unconscious *Pyr*, hanging on grimly to the book's spine even as she was pulled forcibly into Fae.

The sliver between realms that was the portal began to close.

Arach hesitated for a second to glance toward Drake, then dove over Hadrian and through the opening, shifting to his human form to fit through the gap.

Rhys understood: Arach was going after Theo. At least one of them had made it into Fae. Thorolf raged closer, teeth bared, but his mouth snapped on empty space.

The opening had been completely closed. Sylvia, the Fae warrior, the book and Arach had vanished, and the restaurant looked just as it had before the flash of silver light.

Except that Hadrian was unconscious and bleeding profusely on the floor, and Thorolf had arrived with his family. Rhys feared it was too late for Hadrian, even as Balthasar rushed to Hadrian's side. Alasdair moaned and stirred, while Eithne buried her head into her hands. She shrank before Rhys' eyes, visibly aging another few decades, and he wondered if she would turn to dust.

Rafferty swore. "She has the gem of the hoard *and* the book!"

"And Kade took the stylus," Rhys added. "We have no way to follow them into Fae." He looked at Lila. "Unless we can find the portal where we met."

Nereus seethed.

He clothed himself in the debris of Nyssa's apartment building, then emerged to mingle with the crowd. He pretended to be another distraught victim but was simmering with fury. How dare Lila deny him again? How dare she choose a dragon over him? Their child would be an abomination, just when the world needed more selkies of true lineage. She would waste a year, if not more, in this folly, when every moment counted.

Didn't she understand what he had done for her?

Hadn't she learned anything from her experience with that fisherman? She would be trapped and abused again, and need to be rescued again. He had given her an entire century to heal, only to see her pursue the same stupidity again.

He hailed a cab and headed downtown, to the dock where his yacht was moored. Its luxuries gave him no pleasure in this moment. He was aboard before he decided how to proceed. He couldn't rely upon Lila to do the responsible thing. He couldn't count on her to deny the dragon, much less to come to him. He'd cleaned up the debris of her errors before, and he would have to do it again.

Nyssa had told him the dragon shifter's name when he had called. Rhys Lewis. He owned a restaurant where they had gone.

He should be easy to find.

And if Lila was with him, she could witness the king's justice herself.

That might drive his lesson home.

The attack had been quick and fierce. Lila had been startled that Arach had entered Fae of his own volition, but it seemed these *Pyr* warriors all shared Rhys' principles. What would it be like to know that someone would help whenever you were in trouble? Lila couldn't imagine having that confidence. She relied upon herself, and knew that if she ever was caught in a situation that she couldn't resolve herself, that would be the end.

But the *Pyr* had come for her when she'd been abducted, because of Rhys and the firestorm. She didn't even want to think about how that situation would have ended otherwise. She had to help them in return.

Drake was helping Alasdair to roll over and sit up. She didn't think Hadrian would be able to rise of his own volition.

"I'm sorry about Sylvia," Melissa said to Eithne and the older woman shook her head. She looked even more weary than she had earlier.

"She must follow her path," she said simply, then sighed. "At least I told her the truth last night." Melissa held her hand and Lila wondered whether she realized how much that helped Eithne. The witch was drawing power from Melissa steadily, and might not have even been aware that she did so.

There was a shimmer of blue light as the moonstone and silver dragon regained his human form. He was very tall and powerful, like a Viking come to life, and his blond hair was in long dreadlocks. He prowled around the place where the portal had been, his annoyance clear as he examined it from all sides. "How the fuck did he do that?" he demanded of no one in particular.

"You owe Rhys a window and a door," the other new arrival said to him with a roll of his eyes. He was blond, too, but his hair was cut short. He was shorter and built like a wrestler.

"Hey, never let it be said that I don't know how to make an entrance," the big *Pyr* said with pride.

"Everyone else uses the door," Rhys muttered. He beckoned to Lila and as she moved closer, the firestorm burned a little hotter. The big *Pyr* took a deep appreciative breath and held up his hands, as if to bask in its radiance.

"Killer firestorm," he said with enthusiasm.

Lila didn't think it tactful to tell him how close he was to the truth.

"Lila, this is Niall Talbot, the DreamWalker of the *Pyr*." Rhys gestured to the smaller of the two newly arrived *Pyr*. He nodded to her and she sensed that he wasn't one to waste words. "He and his mate, Rox, live in town and have two pairs of twin boys."

"More twins," Lila murmured with a smile and Niall grinned.

"They keep us busy."

Rhys gestured to the big *Pyr* who had shifted shape. "And this is Thorolf, apparently returned from Asia in time to trash my restaurant."

"I was trying to help!" Thorolf protested, then grinned and offered Lila his hand. "Some firestorm you've got going here."

"I didn't exactly start it," she said.

He laughed as her hand disappeared in his. "But you haven't stopped it either." He winked. "Maybe you just like the burn."

Rhys cleared his throat. "Niall, Thorolf, this is my mate Lila. She's a selkie and a healer."

"Don't mind him," Niall said in a confidential tone, gesturing to Thorolf. "He's always like this."

Niall's aura was royal blue, as steady and bright as looking into the heart of a sapphire. Thorolf's aura was gold and powerful. Lila had the sense that he wasn't just vital but very old.

Niall moved to crouch at Alasdair's side, surveying the injured *Pyr* with concern. Was he a healer? Alasdair seized Niall's hand, apparently realizing he was there, and began talking in an insistent undertone. He might have been making a confession or a report, but his words flowed in an incoherent babble. His gaze wandered, his eyes out of focus. Niall listened to him, then looked up with a frown. "Do you know what's wrong with him?" he asked Lila.

"*She's* been in his thoughts," Lila said softly and Rhys glanced her way, obviously hearing her concern. "I can't help him." She shook her head. "I'm sorry but he may never be right again."

"No!" Rhys protested, but she met his gaze steadily.

"I saw it once before. The damage to the aura is unmistakable." His aura was green but it was burned, as if acid had been poured on it. There were gaps and ragged holes where there should have been steady light.

"It means, though, that you were right about him, Rhys. He was compelled to betray you. If he chose to do it, it was to survive."

"Torture," Rhys murmured and she nodded.

"But how did he betray Rhys?" Niall asked even as he tried to soothe Alasdair, who was becoming more agitated. "Feel free to bring me up to date."

"He stole the gem of the hoard from my lair for the Dark Queen."

Niall nodded even as he frowned a little. "He probably feels guilty and is trying to explain himself. Can you tell me any more about what she does or how she does it, even anything about the effects?"

"In the case I saw before, the individual had persistent nightmares," Lila said. "I think he relived the violation until it drove him insane."

"A selkie?" Rhys asked.

"A centaur. One of the last. It was said that the Dark Queen compelled him to reveal the locations of his remaining fellows."

"Maybe that was what drove him to madness," Rhys suggested. "He felt that he had betrayed his kind."

"Niall does dreams," Thorolf interjected. He must have been to the kitchen because he was eating a sandwich that Lila knew Rhys hadn't made. It was too big and too sloppy. It was also disappearing very quickly.

"Hey, stay out of my kitchen," Rhys said. "You'll leave it a wreck."

"Hey, I'm starving. Breathe dragonsmoke around it if you want to defend it. Or cook for me."

Rhys snorted.

Unchastened and unapologetic, Thorolf turned to Niall. "Can you dreamwalk Alasdair?"

Lila was intrigued. Niall could walk in someone else's dreams?

"I'm going to try," that *Pyr* replied. "If I can find the thread of his sense of guilt, I might be able to unfurl things. It's worth a try. Let's get him to a quiet corner and I'll see what I can do."

Dreamwalking was something Lila would like to witness. She rose to follow Niall.

"If nothing else, this attack proves that the Dark Queen has the gem of the hoard," Rafferty said quietly from behind her. "She has enough magick to open portals again."

Lila had to agree.

She was going to follow Niall and Alasdair, but glanced at Hadrian first. What she saw stopped her cold. Balthasar was treating Hadrian's chest wound, his expression grim.

"Balthasar has studied with Sloane, the Apothecary of the *Pyr*," Rhys told her quietly. "Sloane makes herbal ointments and salves specifically to treat the battle injuries of the *Pyr*." Lila nodded, remembering that Rhys had used them. Balthasar had already slowed the bleeding and was preparing to stitch the wound closed.

She didn't want to interfere but hadn't Balthasar seen the mark on Hadrian's cheek? She'd thought she'd imagined it before when it had faded away, but it was back and darker than ever. The purple imprint of a woman's kiss was spreading a taint through his aura. The hue of it and the way it grew, relentless in its progress, told Lila what it was. She'd heard of a kiss of death before but had never seen one. That was why she hadn't recognized it earlier. Left untreated, she knew it would kill Hadrian.

She glanced at Rhys and saw his concern for his friends. It wasn't her place to judge the *Pyr* and their commitment to each other, the trust they granted so readily, but she wanted to help Hadrian.

Because Rhys cared for him.

"Can I help?" she asked impulsively and felt the weight of Rhys' quick sidelong glance. He was surprised and obviously had guessed that she was using her talent as a gift to him.

"I think I can manage, thanks," Balthasar said lightly. "It's a deep wound and it's clean..."

"No," Lila said, wondering how he could ignore that mark. Maybe he couldn't see it. "There's something else. Don't you see it?"

"See what?"

She pointed to Hadrian's cheek. "There's the imprint of a kiss there, one that I noticed before. It's darker now than it was. And it's spreading a taint into his aura."

"A kiss?" Balthasar asked and his tone revealed he didn't see it. "A taint into his aura?" He turned to look at Lila. "Should I know what that means?"

"No, because it's magick," Eithne said. "It's a Fae spell," she clarified. "Sometimes called the kiss of death." Lila nodded.

Balthasar looked mystified. "What does it do?"

"It condemns the recipient. He sees a woman of beauty and is enthralled, especially when she gives him a kiss. It burns a mark on his soul and will eventually kill him." Eithne shook her head. "He will think he has died of love for her, but the truth is that she chose to kill him."

"But why?"

"Perhaps for the spark of his soul, in *Pyr* terms. Life is the root of magick and its origin. Taking a life is one of the crudest ways to obtain more magick." She snapped her fingers more imperiously than Lila would have expected, maybe to keep Lila from saying anything more about that kiss of death.

Eithne had shared only a part of the truth. Why?

The witch snapped her fingers imperiously. "I need a stone. Any stone. The more plain and unremarkable it is, the better."

The *Pyr* looked at each other. Obviously none of them carried a stone.

Lila indicated the one that she wore on a cord around her neck. She didn't need it to remember Thomas. Maybe she wouldn't be haunted by dreams if she gave it away. "What about this?"

"Even better!" Eithne said with a smile and extended her hand.

Why was it better? It was just a stone and she'd asked for a stone. Lila hesitated for only a second before she surrendered it, then told herself it was the right choice.

She felt odd without it, almost naked, but that was foolish. She shook her head then glanced up to find Rhys watching her.

What did he see?

What had he guessed?

"A hag stone embued with Fae magick," a man said, his tone sardonic. "Possessed by a selkie in the middle of a firestorm. What could possibly go wrong?"

Everyone looked around and Rhys doubted he was the only one surprised to see the vampire Sebastian lounging in the doorway to his cellar.

"Sebastian," Drake muttered even as Eithne bristled.

"Your kind are always so critical," she informed the vampire. "You might try to be part of the solution instead."

Sebastian blew her a kiss.

Lila eased closer to Rhys, her hand sliding into his, and Rhys simmered, both from the heat of the firestorm and the potential threat to his mate. His heart was already aglow that she'd intervened to help with Hadrian's treatment. He knew it wasn't her inclination to worry about the team.

She'd helped Hadrian for him, and Rhys knew it.

But what was the importance of the stone? Lila had both wanted to surrender it and wished to keep it. Rhys had felt the conflict within her. Sebastian had called it a hag stone. What did that mean? Rhys doubted it was a reference to Lila's age. The stone was important to Lila and he had no idea why.

And why was the vampire suddenly in his restaurant?

Sebastian was dark-haired and handsome, with eyes of cool clear blue. There was something predatory about him, something that Rhys didn't think was simply due to his nature. The vampire's watchfulness and his ability to move quickly made Rhys suspect that Sebastian had always been a hunter. Sebastian was dressed in dark jeans and a black hoodie, his dark clothes just making his face look more pale and his eyes more blue. Rhys wondered how often he had to feed and whether he had done so recently.

The other *Pyr* seemed to share his doubts. When Sebastian's tongue slid across his lips, Balthasar moved between Hadrian and the new arrival; Rafferty tucked Melissa behind himself and stood before Eithne, his posture protective. Niall and Thorolf similarly barricaded Alasdair from view.

Sebastian surveyed them all with thinly veiled amusement. "A little too late to be defensive, don't you think?" he asked and eased into the chair that Rafferty had abandoned. He templed his fingers together and braced his elbows on the table, watching them all with glittering eyes. He didn't seem to be quite real.

"One of the vampires," Rhys murmured to Lila and she nodded as if she'd already guessed.

Sebastian inclined his head slightly, an indication that he'd overheard. He was taut and emanated a chilling anger despite his lightly spoken words. Rhys guessed that he was furious about either the loss of the book or of Sylvia and wondered which it was.

"Your wine cellar is admirable," Sebastian said to Rhys. "Perhaps if I had not been so lost in admiration, I might have arrived in time to avert disaster." He shrugged and leaned back in the chair. Though his pose was casual, he looked ready to pounce and Rhys couldn't ignore his annoyance. "Perhaps not."

Sebastian's gaze lingered on the unconscious Hadrian, then on Alasdair, who was still muttering quietly. Niall and Thorolf had gotten him into a booth and he was barricaded between them, shaking his head as he ceaselessly talked nonsense.

Sebastian lifted a brow, as if surprised that the *Pyr* could be wounded, then nodded at Eithne, who was still holding Lila's stone. "Don't let me interrupt. I do love story time, especially if there are magick tricks, too." He widened his eyes mockingly, his disdain clear.

Why had he turned up at all?

"I will tell the truth, not a story," Eithne said fiercely. "It will be the last thing I do."

Sebastian inclined his head. "Is that why you dither over the telling? Because you don't want to die?"

Color touched Eithne's pale cheeks. "I was taught that it was forbidden to speak of these matters to those who were not adepts. It's not easy to overcome old habits."

"But what is being done to your acolyte while you wallow in indecision?" Sebastian asked coolly.

Was Sylvia the witch's apprentice? If so, Rhys had missed that part.

"She is not my acolyte."

"Believe what you need to." Sebastian was dismissive and mocking. "Maybe you could find encouragement in the prospect of increasing her chances of survival, regardless of her role?"

"Of course, I do."

Sebastian waved a hand, then looked pointedly at the large clock on one wall. "Tick tock," he murmured, those eyes glinting. Rhys wondered what he knew and doubted he'd share. He had the sense that Sebastian was worried about Sylvia, which surprised him. He didn't think vampires cared about mortals, other than as a food source.

He didn't think vampires cared about anyone but themselves.

Eithne took a deep breath and turned Lila's stone in her hand. She whispered to it and there was a quick flicker that Rhys might have imagined. The second flicker was longer and more vehemently red. He knew he didn't imagine that. She continued to speak softly, her words indistinguishable to him even with his keen *Pyr* hearing. Maybe they were in a language he didn't know. Rhys bent closer, trying to listen, but still couldn't make out the words. He saw Rafferty leaning closer, eyes narrowed, as well.

Silver flickered on Hadrian's cheek, like electrical sparks. At first they seemed random, but then they gathered momentum and Rhys saw the outline of a kiss, like a lipstick stain, on Hadrian's face. It was purple at first, then lightened to blue as the sparks were drawn out of it. The sparks turned red when they collided with the stone, endlessly rolling in Eithne's hand. Her words flowed like a lullaby and he understood that she was summoning the magick out of the kiss.

Everyone was silent and transfixed.

Suddenly the kiss flared red. Hadrian's skin looked particularly pale around it. Rhys saw a jolt of silver light leap to the stone. The kiss shone then, like skin that had been burned, but the color had been drawn from it.

"That is the best I can do," Eithne said, her words faint.

Was it enough? Hadrian's breathing changed and his color improved. Balthasar looked at Lila and she nodded agreement. He bent then and began to stitch Hadrian's wound. Lila frowned, though, and Rhys knew there was more to the wound than that.

Someone applauded slowly, and Rhys could guess who it was.

"Brava!" the vampire said with sarcasm and stopped his clapping. "Perhaps we could pick things up a bit and get to the good part."

Eithne granted him a poisonous glance.

"Will there be snacks?" Sebastian asked, unrepentant.

"I doubt I have anything on the menu you'd like," Rhys replied.

"I doubt you do," Sebastian agreed with a laugh. His fangs showed and maybe his point had been to remind everyone of his nature. Rhys doubted any of them would forget. He had a distinct scent, at least one the other *Pyr* would discern as clearly as Rhys did. He smelled hollow and almost dead, like bones bleached in the sun. He glanced at the wounded *Pyr*. "I've never had a taste for dragon, lucky for all of you."

Eithne straightened in her seat and cleared her throat. "I was taught that magick is the ability to anticipate, influence, alter or control the future," she said and the *Pyr* moved to assemble at the table again.

Hadrian had awakened while Balthasar had been binding his wound. Balthasar and Rhys helped him to the seat Sylvia had occupied; Balthasar sat beside Hadrian, vigilant. Alasdair remained with Niall in a booth against the far wall, but seemed calmer. Lila and Rhys took the same seats they had occupied earlier, Lila beside Eithne, and Rhys beside her. Drake moved to sit at Rhys' left. Rafferty took the chair to the left of his original seat, now occupied by Sebastian, and Melissa sat between him and Balthasar. Thorolf swaggered to the table, glared at Sebastian, then sat between the vampire and Drake.

Sebastian smiled. "Don't tell me you're afraid."

"Bite me," Thorolf retorted and Rhys bit back a smile.

Eithne cleared her throat, then resumed, her voice no more than a whisper on the wind. "You may be surprised to learn that magick is found on almost all sentient planets. Magick is linked to life itself. Perhaps it is an innate urge in all creatures, great and small, to control the future, to influence their own situation, to affect change in their environment, to make their universe a little better. We find magick in many various manifestations but it is always there: the urge is key. Each planet, each society, each life form, has its own variation."

She took a sip of water and fell silent for a long moment. Then she began to spin the stone on the table, holding it in place with her index finger. She murmured her charm again and Rhys felt a strange tingling in his feet. He looked down to see silver sparks emanating from him, as well as from Hadrian's feet.

Lila watched as if fascinated.

Sebastian mimicked the ticking of a clock.

Eithne's eyes flashed but she spoke again, continuing to spin the stone on the table top. "Earth magick originates here, on the planet you call Earth. It was developed or discovered by those beings innate to this planet. It is of the Earth."

"Is that important?" Thorolf asked.

Eithne nodded. "Magick generally does not transfer well to systems other than the one where it was developed. This is because the imported magick doesn't derive from the essence of that system or mirror that society's assumptions."

"So, we're talking about alien magick, too?" Thorolf said when she paused again. "Like, from space?"

"Your own prophecies list three kinds of magick," Sebastian said with impatience. "What do you think the difference is between them?"

"The creatures who developed them?" Rafferty guessed. "There's earth magick, dragon magick and darkfire. That's Fae, Embron and Blazion, and the *Pyr*."

Sebastian shook his head. "It's origin, all right, but not by species." His eyes shone as if he would challenge them with his assertion. "By planet."

"Whoa," Thorolf said. "You're shitting us."

Sebastian glared at him. "I do not *shit* anyone, thank you very much, dragon boy. Such bodily functions are no longer my concern."

"Right," Thorolf muttered. "Because sucking people dry is so much less disgusting."

The pair glared at each other, then Eithne pointedly cleared her throat.

"He is right," she said. "Earth magick is from earth. What you call dragon magick is actually Regalian magick, from Regalia, which I brought to this system, and the twin princes, Embron and Blazion, released here."

Rhys blinked. Embron and Blazion had come from another world? His fellow *Pyr*, with the exception of Hadrian, looked less surprised than he felt. He assumed they'd heard at least part of the story already,

probably while he and Hadrian were in Fae.
He had to catch up.

CHAPTER THIRTEEN

learned the origins of magick when I was an acolyte at Nimue, sent there from my home planet of Regalia because of my natural abilities. I was distinct among my kind for my ability to anticipate future events. This marked me as one to be trained further and ultimately resulted in my being accepted at Nimue. There I learned and trained in the manipulation of possibilities and probabilities, and honed my skills. I should have known after all my training that to share my magickal power was wrong, to bring it to another system was wrong, and to surrender it to those who had not been trained to wield it, could only result in disaster. And so it has."

Sebastian yawned elaborately, but Eithne ignored both him and the little spinning motion he made with one finger. "We don't need your *curriculum vitae*, darling," he drawled.

Eithne pinched her lips together but didn't reply to that. "I have told Rafferty about my journey from Incendium as the custodian of the twin royal princes Embron and Blazion, who were exiled for the crime of being related to a jealous tyrant of a king. It was a long journey and I chose to give them each a gift, these two handsome dragon shifter princes of whom I convinced myself I was fond."

"You surrendered your magick to them," Sebastian said and held up his hands. "Big mistake. Epic. Super-sized."

"We get it," Thorolf told him and they glared at each other again.

"Maybe I should try dragon again," Sebastian threatened softly. "Just to be sure my tastes haven't changed."

"Go ahead and try," Thorolf replied.

"You can argue later," Rhys reminded them. "Listen now." Eithne looked more frail than she had and had shrunk in the telling of her tale. She was paler and more wispy somehow. Rhys was reminded of an elderly bird.

She continued to spin the stone and the silver flashes of light continued to be drawn to it. His feet already felt a million times better.

"The truth was I knew very little of their characters—and less of their inclinations. When we reached earth, Blazion immediately used his innate powers for ill. He acted like one of your ancient gods, seizing whatever and whoever he desired, casting away what he no longer wanted, wreaking havoc for sheer pleasure. Embron released the magick I had given him, loosing it on a world unprepared for alien sorcery. I thought he was simply curious and naive about its effects. Blazion, inspired by his brother, did the same and between the two of them they turned this world upside down."

Eithne ran a hand over her hair and Rhys saw new lines on her face: was she aging before his eyes? "Regalian magick is infinitely more sophisticated than earth magick, or at least it was at that time. Earth magick was overwhelmed by the powers of the twin princes and driven underground along with the Fae. When the *Pyr* decided to control—or attempt to control—Blazion and Embron, their earth magick merged with what had come to be called dragon magick to create the force of darkfire."

"This is where the Cantor enters the tale," Rafferty said.

"He does," Eithne agreed. "The Cantor of the *Pyr* was the most sophisticated wizard of your kind and among the most skilled on Earth. Pwyll was the first Cantor, but his oldest son, Myrddin, exceeded his father's capabilities. Myrddin's son, Uther, was said to be even more powerful than his father and so he led the *Pyr* who set out to destroy Blazion. They didn't succeed, despite his abilities, because Blazion turned Uther's own spell back upon the *Pyr* company."

"They were the warriors trapped in an enchanted sleep in Blazion's lair in Edinburgh," Rafferty said.

Eithne nodded. "Which you awakened with darkfire." She said this last word with gusto and spun the stone a little faster. Rhys was sure she was smaller than she had been, and even more pale. Sebastian looked vital in comparison to her.

"Wait a minute. I thought there were seven of them in Edinburgh," Rhys noted and Rafferty nodded agreement. "Eithne just said there were eight in the company."

"Uther was not among those enchanted," Rafferty said, counting off the seven thieves on his fingers. "There was Malduc, Emyas, Garth, Raynald, Evrain, Bedwyr and Roderick."

"Maybe you should find Uther," Sebastian said, as if that might be readily done.

Eithne shook her head. "A wizard who hides isn't easily found, as he has already proven. It has been fifteen hundred years and none of you know anything of him."

"*Touché*," Sebastian said, bowing his head to her.

"But isn't Uther dead?" Rafferty asked, looking between the vampire and the witch.

"What difference would that make?" Sebastian asked, impatience in his tone again. "You talk to Pwyll, don't you?"

Rafferty was visibly startled. He probably hadn't thought the vampire would know such a thing.

Thorolf shook his head. "This is getting weird," he muttered and Sebastian chuckled.

"Wait for it," the vampire advised. "Or maybe I should say 'hold my beer', to speak in the vulgar idiom you best understand."

Thorolf put his fists on the table. "If you've got something to say..." he began but Rafferty gestured for him to sit down. He did, but folded his arms across his chest, and shot dark glances at Sebastian. The vampire appeared to be amused. He bared his teeth and Thorolf's eyes flashed.

"You were telling us about magick," Rhys reminded Eithne.

Eithne nodded again, her eyelids drooping. She seemed to be fighting exhaustion, but kept spinning the stone. It moved more slowly now and her voice was so soft that everyone leaned closer to hear her words. "There is no reason for magick to have a physical manifestation in its own right. It is an impulse, an energy, a command or a manifestation of desire. Yet in many systems, magick does impact the senses. It may appear as a glow of red light or a shimmer like starlight."

"Or a flash of silver light," Sebastian said, then sighed with tolerance. He made the spinning motion with his hand again.

"It may emanate a sound like falling snow or tinkling bells. It may change the ambient temperature when it is at work. It may cause another reaction in particularly sensitive individuals in the vicinity—"

"By the pricking of my thumbs," Rafferty said with a smile.

Eithne inclined her head in acknowledgement of that. "Exactly. Or shivers, what humans call someone walking over their grave. There is no reason for this, except that perhaps the magician wishes his or her influence to be known. I would argue that the most insidious and terrifying magick is that which leaves no sign and cannot, in fact, be discerned at all."

Once again, Sebastian yawned elaborately. "Wake me when you get to the point," he muttered.

Eithne frowned down at the spinning stone. "One commonality that we find in many societies with regards to their magick is that it can be stored in natural receptacles." Everyone else looked at Lila's stone, too. "On Regalia, quartz is used to store magick, quartz like the orbs in the pommels of the daggers presented to the twin princes. I poured my magick into those orbs to give it to them, and Embron retrieved one from Blazion's lair in Edinburgh."

"Two? Where's the other one?" Rhys asked, thinking of the prophecy.

"It must have shattered. Embron summoned all of my magick into the orb in his possession. That could only be done if its twin orb was destroyed."

"How?" Rhys asked.

"The forceful withdrawal of its magick might have broken it." She sighed. "It was a magnificent spectacle. He was stunning. I would never have imagined..." Her voice faded and the stone stopped spinning.

Was Embron's crystal orb the other stone mentioned in the prophecy?

Eithne continued. "Here on Earth, the Fae used amber as a receptacle for magick. The gem of the hoard is a particularly marvelous specimen of amber and became the greatest receptacle for their magick.

"And the Cantor used quartz crystals for the darkfire," Rafferty said. "We used a smoky quartz crystal recently to re-gather the darkfire."

"Yes," Eithne said. "When the stone receptacle is shattered, the magick is released. It scatters throughout that world and only a powerful sorcerer can gather it back together again, if it can be done at all. It's never destroyed. It's dispersed and gathered, over and over again." She nodded at Rafferty. "Your Cantor had a potent command over the darkfire."

"He did," Rafferty acknowledged.

"But there's one more thing you must know," Eithne said, her voice raspy. "There was a time when the Fae poured their magick into the gem of the hoard, concentrating it so that its power could be harnessed and held by one individual. At the same time, Blazion strove to gather the dragon magick from Regalia again, although he had to compete with

Embron for it. There were those of us concerned for the fate of all kinds when magick might be commanded by a few. So, we used the affinity of magick for stone to empower certain talismans. We couldn't give the receptacles much magick, but we gave them enough for prophecy, so that the Others could warn themselves and choose their paths more wisely. Each kind had its talisman, and though each kind had a tale of how that talisman came to be in their possession, the truth is that they all came from this secret confederation of sorcerers who feared the battle between the Dark Queen and the twin princes."

"But we *Pyr* don't have such a talisman," Rafferty protested.

"Have you lost the Dragon's Egg?" Eithne asked, and the *Pyr* were visibly startled.

"It's shattered," Drake said.

"But when it was whole, you used it for prophecy."

"Erik did," Rafferty acknowledged and looked shaken. "We believed it was a gift of Gaia."

"And in a way it was." Eithne gestured weakly to Lila. "And your kind have the dark mirror."

"Not the dark mirror," Lila protested with alarm and Rhys was surprised at her reaction. "No one has approached the dark mirror in centuries. It might not even exist any longer."

Eithne lifted the stone by the silken cord, smiling as it spun before her.

"Impossible," Lila protested. "It's lost forever, sunk beneath the seas."

Eithne shook her head. "You saw it."

"That was just a dream," Lila protested.

"It awaits you," Eithne insisted.

"What's the dark mirror?" Rhys asked. "Where is it?"

"It's in the treasury of the palace in the sunken Isle of the Blessed," Eithne said. "It was given as a gift to Evenor, many centuries ago. Some said it was a scrying glass. Others called it a portal."

"It's wicked," Lila said hotly. "It has a will of its own."

"Of course, it does," Eithne acknowledged wearily. "It was made with Regalian magick."

A quick glance was exchanged around the table.

"Are you going to tell them how Regalian magick is more sophisticated?" Sebastian prompted in a silky purr. "It's not the adjective I would have chosen, but you are the storyteller today."

Eithne composed herself with a visible effort. "Earth magick mirrors the desire and the influence of the magician: it does, mostly, what it is commanded to do. The exceptions are invariably the result of poor spell-casting. This is typical of many more rudimentary systems of magick. Regalian magick, in contrast, has been cultivated for so long that it has become a force onto itself. Regalian magick is sentient."

Rhys was shocked. He saw Lila nod a little, her expression wary. That was what she didn't like about the dark mirror. A will of its own. How would that manifest?

He wasn't sure he wanted to know.

Eithne continued, her voice shaky. "It has its own impulse, its own desire, and its own agenda. It is not uncommon for Regalian magick to take command of the sorcerer and invert the expected balance of power. I believe that is part of what happened here, with my magick. I believe it wanted to be free of my constraints, to be unfettered, and so it coaxed me into making a gift of it on that long journey between the stars."

"But what does it want now?" Rhys asked.

"What we all want," Sebastian said, rising to his feet. "Or at least what all rulers and despots want, and what most wizards want—more power. *All* power. Looks to me like the Dark Queen is getting close if she's got the gem of the hoard back and her book, too. I'll guess Embron has the only surviving orb of the pair."

Eithne nodded.

"Forgive me if I don't want to let the fate of all Others rest on the outcome of that inevitable battle of wills," Sebastian said. "I think I will have to call in a favor."

One minute he was standing beside the chair, and the next he was at the doorway to the kitchen. Rhys didn't even see him move.

"I apologize for the disappearance of the 2014 Romanee-Conti Grand Cru," he said, inclining his head slightly to Rhys. "I could never resist a good red wine." Rhys caught a glimpse of his smile and then the vampire was gone.

"Hey!" Rhys protested, standing up in his outrage. "That was a gift!"

"A splendid one," Sebastian said from the cellar of the restaurant, laughter in his voice.

"The wine is gone," Eithne said, her words no more than an exhalation.

"It can't be. It's under lock and key," Rhys said, marching toward his wine cellar to check even though he suspected what he would find. There was a whiff of stale air in the cellar, although he was sure there was no access to it from anywhere but the kitchen. He saw a wet footprint on the floor and traced it to one wall, then discovered a seam that he'd never noticed before. The wine cabinet was still locked, but the lock was hanging at a slightly different angle, and the bottle in question was gone.

Rhys swore.

"Fancy stuff?" Thorolf asked, appearing at the top of the stairs.

"It's worth about fifteen thousand dollars," Rhys said, hearing his own annoyance. Thorolf whistled in admiration. "I was saving it for a special occasion."

"I'll bet," Thorolf said. "Like hey, satisfying this firestorm." He whistled again and winked at Rhys. "It's hot stuff."

"That's up to Lila," Rhys said, then climbed the stairs back to the restaurant.

"I've got to think that getting rid of that vampire dude is worth the price, though," Thorolf said.

"If he's really gone," Rhys replied, to that *Pyr's* obvious dismay.

In the restaurant, the *Pyr* were talking all at once, and Eithne's eyes sparkled as she stared at Rhys. She twisted the cord and the stone spun rapidly.

There was a moment of sharp pain in Rhys' feet, as if the magick left him with reluctance, then it was gone. The stone flashed, then was dark again.

The firestorm crackled between him and Lila again, sending one of those orange arcs of flame between them. Rhys didn't know how he'd stand it. He stared at Lila and she stared back, and there was no one else in the world for him. The firestorm sizzled and crackled, building to the force of an inferno, but he couldn't look away from the dark promise of her eyes.

He crossed the restaurant like a man in a daze, then bent, because he couldn't stop himself, and touched his lips to hers. Lila sighed and parted her lips beneath his, welcoming him. He heard the simultaneous gasp of the *Pyr*, who had all felt the surge of the firestorm, and closed their eyes against its incendiary heat.

"You will need this," Eithne said, her voice faint and raspy. She had aged beyond belief, her skin pale grey, her hair turned to silver, her figure bent and shrunken.

Rhys watched as the ancient woman offered the stone to Lila again. Lila hesitated for a moment, then accepted it.

"The magick is yours to command, but there is not much," Eithne whispered. "Choose well, Lila selkie."

Then the cord passed from her fingertips to Lila's grasp, and Eithne crumbled. Before Rhys' very eyes, she dissolved into pale grey dust, as insubstantial as a mist. Lila gasped aloud as a little breeze swept the ash into a whirlwind and it vanished.

Eithne was gone forever.

Marco, formerly the Sleeper of the *Pyr*, stood outside the cottage on Bardsey Island and breathed deeply of the night. It was impossible to forget that he had slumbered for centuries in this very place, enchanted by Pwyll for his own safety. His defense had been entrusted to Rafferty and then to Donovan. He wasn't certain when he had been brought to the island, but he knew it well. The sound and smell of it, the rhythm of it, was woven into his very marrow.

The cavern where he had slept had collapsed. The *Slayers* had been defeated, including the one who had invaded that cavern. Marco'd had his firestorm and he smiled that his mate, Jac, and their sons slept so deeply in the cottage behind him. This place remained a sanctuary. He tipped his head back and savored the sight of the stars, so many stars, so bright that he felt he could reach up and take a handful. The wind was brisk off the seas and there would be clear cold days ahead.

He felt the flicker of darkfire and wondered at its source.

Marco shifted shape and stretched out across the cool earth. His dragon form was black as night, but his scales were touched with a blue-green shimmer evocative of darkfire. He slowed his breathing and blended with the shadows, so still that only the glitter of his eyes would reveal his presence to an observer. His senses were sharper in his dragon form, his vision more keen, his hearing more acute. He saw the distant sparks of darkfire and realized they were gathering.

At first he thought the darkfire was coming to him, but then he heard an old familiar chant, a summons that was being sung softly—and not by him. He peered more deeply into the shadows on the hill behind the cottage and discerned a figure.

The hitchhiker from the wharf. Yes, there had been something about him. That man held the pieces of a shattered crystal in his cupped hands and sang to them. The darkfire flowed to his hands, glinting in the pieces of stone, gathering with ever greater speed.

Another voice joined the song, a deep voice that came from the cottage. Marco saw the shadows shift as Malduc stepped into the night and walked toward the hitchhiker in the hills. He sang, his chant joining that of the hitchhiker, buttressing the summons with his own song. The darkfire gathered more quickly, a flurry of blue-green sparks circling those broken pieces of stone.

Interesting. Marco wondered how many others Pwyll had tutored in his time.

The hitchhiker didn't look up at Malduc's approach, but his song became a little more insistent. Marco might have guessed he was Uther but was certain only when the singer began to rapidly shift shape. He became a dragon, a deer, a lion, an eagle—the transformations were quick and dizzying to watch, the shimmering halo of blue light never fading completely before he shifted and it flared again. In each form, he held the broken crystal in his hands or his claws.

And the darkfire sparks danced with joy as they approached him, as if reunited with an old friend.

Marco heard Emyas come out of the house, following his brother Malduc and joining the song. He didn't wait to learn whether the other *Pyr* in the cottage would join in, but began to sing himself. Malduc was startled by his voice, his gaze searching the shadows until he spotted Marco. But Uther simply smiled, then shifted and sang even more.

The darkfire gathered with greater speed, the stars shone down upon them, and Marco knew all would be right.

Unlike his fellows, Marco trusted the darkfire completely.

It was snowing outside when Rhys finally led Lila out of the restaurant. Big white flakes were tumbling lazily out of the sky, as if in slow motion. The street was quiet, especially after most of the *Pyr* departed. Niall and Thorolf had taken Alasdair and Hadrian back to the apartment where Thorolf was staying. Hadrian was going to stay in New York for a bit to supervise the repair to the restaurant door and window. They'd nailed plywood over it for the time being. Drake was going back to Kristofer's place to bring Erik up to date. Balthasar, Rafferty and Melissa were going to meet Rhys and Lila at the airport in the morning to fly to the UK.

Each had a job and a responsibility, and Lila understood that each would do his best to fulfill it. Rhys had his arm draped over her shoulder as they waved farewell and she enjoyed the increased heat of the firestorm in his close proximity, especially on such a cold night.

"Brrr," Rhys said with a shiver and Lila smiled at him. "It's nights like this that I miss Malta."

Rafferty paused before getting into the cab after Melissa. "Maybe there's something you should do to warm up," he suggested with a teasing glint in his eyes. "It would make travel a lot easier."

"I have you and Balthasar to help with the beguiling," Rhys said easily. "And we picked seats apart from each other." He squeezed Lila's shoulders. "It'll be fine."

Rafferty hesitated. "You only have this opportunity once, Rhys," he said softly, reminding the other *Pyr* of something Lila was sure he hadn't forgotten.

"Having a child is a big commitment," Rhys replied. "The choice is Lila's since she has to do the hard part."

Rafferty looked between the two of them, his doubts clear. "I wonder..."

"I know what you wonder," Rhys said gently. "But I have only one chance to get this right. You taught me that."

Rafferty nodded then and got into the cab, leaving them standing on the sidewalk in front of the restaurant.

"Are you trying to be my champion?" she teased and Rhys chuckled as he led her toward the elevator.

"Not really. I just want more than sex. More than one night."

"We could have lots of sex," Lila suggested again. "Like I said, I could choose not to conceive every morning and we could satisfy the firestorm over and over again. It would be fun."

"I admit it's a tempting idea," Rhys said and pushed the button for the elevator. He smiled down at her but his eyes were serious. "But I want so much more."

"Why? Sex is good. Sex is great. It can be more than enough."

Rhys shook his head. "Sex is not what I've been waiting for. You can find that kind of satisfaction anywhere. I want a partnership. I want a family. And that means I need to help you trust me."

Lila opened her mouth to say that she did, then thought the better of it. She was too tired to think straight and the firestorm had a way of making her want to charm Rhys into giving her more than a good night's sleep.

"Thank you for helping Hadrian," he said. "I know you weren't sure of his motives."

"But you were. I was glad to help."

They stepped into the elevator. He'd grabbed a box of salt from the kitchen of the restaurant after cleaning up and gave it to her.

"Since you used up the last one," he said as they ascended.

Lila hugged the box and smiled back at him. "Thanks." It would be easy to get used to having a dragon shifter in her life, a protective one who anticipated her needs.

It would be easy to get used to having Rhys in her life.

"What did you think of dreamwalking?"

"I couldn't see exactly what Niall was doing, but he explained some of it to me. And I could see how he was healing Alasdair by the improvement in his aura." Lila frowned. "I guess each kind has their own healing rituals and processes. It's fascinating." She didn't say anything about learning more because that was fraught with implications—and promises she wasn't ready to make.

Rhys nodded, then the elevator doors opened and they stepped into the corridor.

She thought of the *Pyr* and how readily they worked together as a team. She thought of the list Rhys had given her, just that morning, of the *Pyr* she could call to help with their son: the dragon shifters she'd met were on that list and she knew he trusted them completely.

Her son, if she chose to conceive him, would have a dozen fathers, no matter what happened to Rhys. He'd have a community and a family, one that was prepared to do whatever was necessary for his good.

Lila couldn't help feeling a little bit jealous of that.

Rhys' apartment felt like a haven, especially lit with the welcoming glow of the firestorm. The snow swirled outside the windows and he didn't turn on any lights. She wondered whether the firestorm was meant to cast a romantic light. Rhys didn't seem bent on seduction, though. He went into the bedroom, evidently expecting her to head to the bathroom. Lila stood and watched him, hugging the box of salt.

"Are you going to pack much?" she asked, wanting to linger with him for a minute.

Rhys came out of the bedroom with something shiny in his hand. "All I really need is this and my passport, but take your time. I can sleep on the couch tonight."

"I thought you'd want to snuggle up on such a cold night," she teased.

Rhys gave her a simmering look. "I know my limits." He put down the shiny item and opened a closet, removing a blanket and pillow.

Lila was curious. "What's this?" she asked, picking up the token hung on a gold chain. It was beautiful, a gold L studded with pearls, with a large ruby on the end of each arm. It looked as if a gem was missing from the point where the two arms met. An L. "Something to remember Llewelyn?"

"Something like that," Rhys said, lifting it out of her hand. He ran his thumb across it in a caress he probably wasn't aware of, then put it gently down on the table beside his passport. "It was my mother's."

"Did she have an R, too?"

"No, it's not an L." Rhys turned it, as if he'd never thought of that before. "It's half of her crucifix."

"You said she was on pilgrimage when she met your father in Malta."

Rhys nodded. "And this was the cross on her rosary. It was just plain gold then, but my father had it studded with gems after she agreed to marry him." He smiled a little in reminiscence and Lila felt another stab of envy. "She was a widow and her marriage had been barren. Her husband blamed her and when he died, she was afraid to marry again. He'd been a lot older than her, and she wasn't sure that any new husband would be kinder. So, she went on a pilgrimage to ask for the Lord's blessing."

Rhys touched the talisman gently as Lila watched him. His eyes were dark with memories. "She was kneeling in the church, saying her prayers for the night, when the firestorm sparked. My father was a man-at-arms and he earned his keep as a guard when there were no wars to fight. He'd been guarding the treasury of the church when she came to pray." His smile broadened. "The story was that he fell in love at first sight, but that she was more cautious."

Lila bit back a smile of her own.

"What?" Rhys asked, meeting her gaze.

"Are all you dragons smitten quickly?"

"We understand the import of the firestorm. We trust that it has chosen the right mate for us."

"Even if mates are cautious?"

He chuckled. "Maybe we teach each other the merit of being persuasive."

Lila could believe it. She found Rhys and his constancy very persuasive.

He looked at the gem again. "My father escorted her around the city, showed her the sights, and courted her so ardently that she missed the departure of her ship."

"By accident or design?"

"I don't know. But she missed the next three she could have taken, and then she agreed to marry him."

Lila smiled, finding it easy to imagine that a persistent *Pyr* suitor would be hard to resist. "And they had twin sons, thanks to the firestorm."

Rhys nodded. "Llewelyn was a few minutes older than me." He sobered then and she knew he was thinking of the loss of his brother.

She wanted him to smile again. "Will you tell me about him?"

"Well, you can guess what he looked like. We were twins." He gestured toward the dragon tattoo on his chest. "Only the tattoo is a recent addition. He never had one. He would have liked being part of the Dragon Legion, though. He was always a good fighter."

"But you said he died in that war."

"He did, but it was because he intervened for me. It was a big fight and the air was filled with smoke as well as dragonfire. I didn't see the *Slayer* coming up behind me and I didn't sense him at all. I'd taken a few hits and was bleeding a bit, but I shouldn't have been so inattentive. I thought we'd won the battle. But this *Slayer* soared in behind me and Llewelyn spotted him in time. He shoved me out of the way and attacked the *Slayer*, but that meant he took the blow intended for me. It was a hard slash, one that would have torn my wings off if not more, and he took those talons right across his stomach. His guts—" Rhys winced and shook his head. "I'm sorry. It was awful."

Lila put her hand on his arm, almost feeling his pain. "He died instead of you."

Rhys nodded. His throat worked. "He was dead in the blink of an eye. There was no question of getting help in time. It took Storme and I both to finish the *Slayer*, and Storme was fatally injured by then, too. I couldn't believe that I would be the only one to survive, since I was the one who had fucked up in the first place."

"But you were."

"I was." Rhys' voice was husky. "I saw them both exposed to the four elements, because my father had always been superstitious about that and it seemed like the least I could do. Then I left the battle and sought out Kristofer to give him the news about Storme." He fell silent for a minute and his lips tightened. "They'd argued about going to the battle and had parted badly, so at least I didn't have that burden to bear. I'd just caused Llewelyn's death by not paying attention."

"It was a war," Lila said, thinking that guilt might be the reason for the shadow on his aura.

Rhys shook his head. "It was a mistake. I'll never forgive myself for it and that's okay. It was a big mistake. I shouldn't ever make one like it again."

Lila didn't think about her own mistake. She'd learned from

surrendering to Malcolm and knew that satisfying the firestorm with Rhys wouldn't be a repeat of her error.

"And thus began your lost years?" she asked lightly, still trying to prompt his smile.

"Not right away. First I went looking for Gwendolyn."

"Who?"

"The woman Llewelyn loved. She was part of the reason we went to war."

"She refused him?"

"No, not that. She wasn't his destined mate." Rhys shook his head and led Lila back to the kitchen. He put on the kettle, then leaned on the counter, facing her. "You have to understand that my father was a great romantic. He loved the idea of the firestorm, and was adamant that a *Pyr* should commit to his destined mate forever. He believed that the firestorm offered the one opportunity in a *Pyr's* life for stability and happiness and also to create a legacy. He believed that the firestorm was always right, and that its spark always led a *Pyr* to the woman who was the best possible complement for him. Kind of like Rafferty."

Lila nodded understanding.

"So, even though it's not forbidden for *Pyr* to be with other women, my father believed it was wrong. A fleeting union was something he could ignore, but for a *Pyr* to pledge oneself to a woman who was not his destined mate was unforgiveable in his eyes."

"But why? You live long. You might wait several human lifetimes for your mate."

"That's true. But we never know when the firestorm will spark. A *Pyr* could pledge himself to a mortal woman, then have his firestorm spark the next day, the next week, the next year. And he would be obliged to follow its heat, to satisfy it and to conceive a son. I don't actually think anyone can resist it for long."

"But people get divorced all the time," Lila had to comment. "Isn't it similar?"

"No, because they don't get married with the assumption that they'll get divorced. They really hope it'll be for the duration. At least, I hope that's what they think when they marry. Otherwise, I'd expect the match to be doomed."

"They'd have one foot out the door," Lila said, remembering his earlier words.

"And a *Pyr* knows that a union with a woman who is not his mate could end at any minute—or that he could be compelled to be unfaithful, which was also not acceptable to my father. My father always said that the mark of a warrior is in his kindness, and that those least worthy of respect are the ones who are cruel without cause." Rhys held her gaze. "He thought that making such a pledge would be unfair and unkind."

"But Llewelyn disagreed?"

"No, Llewelyn agreed completely. He just fell in love and couldn't do a thing about it. He decided to leave Gwendolyn without making a promise, and so we joined that war together. I confess that I was afraid he might turn back, which was part of why I went with him. He loved her so much. It was hard for him to make that choice, and I wanted to support him in it."

"It doesn't seem right to deny love."

"No. It didn't." Rhys sighed. "We had a good example in my parents. Their love was impressive, constant, powerful. I think it only grew stronger the more years they were together."

"How does that work?" Lila asked. "The *Pyr* are long-lived, so did your father survive your mother for a long time?"

"No. There are those who say that in cases of a great love between a *Pyr* and his destined mate, his body matches pace to hers. A *Pyr* will often get his first grey hair after his firestorm, for example, though for all the centuries between then and his coming of age, he might change very little. I've looked like this since I was thirty-five."

"Except for the dragon tattoo," Lila reminded him with a smile.

"Except for that," he agreed with a smile of his own, then continued when she thought he might fall silent. "My father had a little silver at his temples when my mother's health failed. She would have been in her eighties by then and at the end, she was a bit confused. She had a fever and was weakened by her illness. I remember when the physician shook his head, took his fee and left her. She was shivering then, making no sense, and my father's heartbreak was in his eyes. It was terrible to watch her fade away." The kettle boiled and he turned to make tea, his movements less graceful than usual.

"And she died then?"

"Not quite. She was suffering, though. My father shed his boots and his sword and climbed into her bed. He gathered her into his arms, and told her a story of a widow who had stopped in a church to pray on her way to Jerusalem on pilgrimage, a woman whose womb was barren and whose heart was swept clear of hope. He told her about the spark of the firestorm, reminded her of how its glow had lit the chapel like a sunrise. He told her how its warmth filled the heart of the *Pyr* warrior and lit the features of the widow as she turned to look at him in wonder. He told her of their courtship and their marriage, of the birth of their sons and the joy they found with each other. He told her how much he loved her and he wept a little after she fell asleep in his embrace."

Rhys shook his head and his throat worked. His voice was husky when he continued. "I remember the crackle of the fire on the hearth and the rasp of her breathing, the distant sound of the sea and the low murmur of my father's voice. The mood of the room had changed completely. She was at peace and they were together."

"Forever," Lila said, her yearning for a bond growing steadily.

"We left them, at his instruction, and when the sun rose the next morning, my mother was dead. My father's hair had turned as white as snow during the night and he had aged greatly. He made all the preparations for the funeral and I remember him setting his affairs in order. She was buried in that church where they had met, as she had requested, and I was shocked that her crucifix was missing from the rosary in her hands."

Rhys picked up the jewel and let it swing on its chain, catching the light. "Back at home, my father gave us each half of that crucifix, which he had asked a jeweler to split. He explained that my mother once asked that it be divided between us, for we were two halves of a whole and it was all she had of her own to give. The stone that sat in the center of the crucifix, a cabochon sapphire, was on the half that Llewelyn had. My father joked that it would have been a crime to slice such a fine jewel in half." He frowned and sighed. "He died that very night. He had made arrangements for his own burial beside her, so within a week, they were both gone."

"And this is typical? That the *Pyr* dies after his mate?"

"It's not uncommon from what I understand." Rhys was staring at the half-cross as it swung from its chain. "And the example of their love is why Llewelyn and I both knew he couldn't make a vow to Gwendolyn, because he couldn't be certain that he could keep it. He met her in Wales, when we finally journeyed there to see my mother's homeland."

"You weren't quick about it."

Rhys shook his head. "No. I think we knew that when we left the house in Malta we were unlikely to ever return. We had a good childhood there and a good life. It was only natural to linger and savor."

"But you went to Wales."

"And there was Gwendolyn. So we went to war. When Llewelyn died, Kristofer was in Norway, then, and I went to him first with the news of

Storme. But once that was done, I believed Gwendolyn would want to know that Llewelyn had truly loved her, and I thought I owed him that errand. But I couldn't find her."

"Had she moved away?"

Rhys raised his gaze to hers. "She'd died. It was said that she had killed herself, that she had filled her pockets with stones and walked into the sea, never to be seen again. It was said that she couldn't bear the grief of losing the man she loved." He spun around to pour her tea, reaching for a mug from the shelf.

"Did she know his nature?"

Rhys shook his head without turning. "Llewelyn insisted he'd never told her."

"What happened to his half of your mother's crucifix? Was it lost when he died?"

"No. I looked for it. He didn't have it."

"He couldn't have lost it. It was too important to both of you."

Rhys put the tea down in front of her. "I think he gave it away." He held her gaze, his own hot with unshed tears. "They said that Gwendolyn wore a gem from her lover when she walked into the sea. That was one of the reasons so many people tried to find her body, but she was never found." He coiled the chain around the gem on the counter. "Now you know all my secrets." He might have turned away, but Lila reached to cover his hand with her own. She could see that the shadow on his aura was receding, a sure sign that telling the story of his lost brother was helping him to heal.

She wanted to finish the job. If he was determined to go into Fae for his fellows, he was probably going to have to fight. Lila wanted him to be as strong as he could be.

She didn't want to lose Rhys just yet.

"You should wear it," she suggested. "Instead of keeping it in a drawer. That way, your family will be with you all the time."

Rhys considered the gem for a long moment before he nodded agreement. "I think you're right," he said quietly. He put the chain over his head. Lila smiled that the gem was right over the heart of his dragon tattoo. Rhys met her gaze and they stared at each other for a long hot moment, the firestorm crackling between them with irresistible heat.

"Thank you for sharing that story with me."

"It was easier than I expected." His smile was rueful. "Maybe it was time to tell it."

"Maybe you needed to entrust me with it," Lila suggested, knowing what she had to do. Her path was absolutely clear, and it had nothing to do with evading Nereus and his scheme for creating more selkies. She reached out to Rhys, putting her hand on his chest so that the firestorm flared white between them. She was going to miss it. She raised her gaze to his, aware that he was utterly still. "This way, I can share it with our son, in case you can't."

He stared at her, his shock obvious.

Lila smiled. "I will choose to conceive, Rhys, if you want to satisfy the firestorm again."

"Lila!" he whispered with a wonder that once again made her feel precious. His eyes lit and he came around the counter in a flash, scooping her up and swinging her around so that she laughed aloud at his pleasure.

"Are you sure?"

Lila nodded. "Positive."

Rhys was deadly serious when he put her on his feet, his gaze filled with a wonder that made her heart pound as much as the firestorm. His gaze searched hers as he framed her face in his hands. "Thank you," he whispered and kissed her to silence before she could reply.

His kiss was right. The firestorm was blazing, heating her to her toes. This was why she had come to New York, and Lila would have no regrets.

CHAPTER FOURTEEN

ila's offer was a gift unexpected. Rhys had halfway expected she would retreat to her island and leave their firestorm simmering forever. He was determined to ensure that she didn't regret her decision. He poured everything into his kiss and loved how she responded to his touch. She wasn't shy and that was part of why he found her so perfect. Her arms were around his neck, her fingers in her hair, her grip on him both seductive and demanding. She pressed against him, the imprint of her curves lighting fires within him and taking his desire to a fever-pitch.

It was more than her physical allure that made him want her. She was so giving and generous with her healing skill. She'd helped the *Pyr*. She'd added her efforts to those of Balthasar and Niall and done it so readily that he guessed she yearned not to be alone any longer. She'd been disappointed and was distrustful of love as a result of her experience, but Rhys would show her that her doubts were wrong.

He'd fallen hard for Lila. He knew he could love her as deeply as his father had loved his mother. He knew that his feelings would only deepen over time—already he couldn't imagine his life without Lila and her smile. The firestorm had chosen perfectly for him, and he wanted to be perfect for her.

This night was the beginning for them both.

When Lila opened her mouth to him in sweet surrender, Rhys caught her up in his arms. He broke their kiss only for a moment, long enough to sweep the box of salt off the counter and into her lap. She laughed and kicked her feet, her eyes sparkling. Rhys bent and swallowed her laugh with a demanding kiss. He carried her to the bathroom, setting her down beside the tub and catching the box as it fell.

"I can do this later," she said, but he knew she needed the restorative balm of the water now.

"Too bad the tub isn't bigger," he said and she gave him a smile. He reached for the tap, but she stopped him with a fiery touch.

"Not yet," she whispered and he was willing to do whatever she wanted.

Lila backed him into the counter, sliding her hands under the hem of his shirt. A sizzle marked the touch of her fingers on his skin and Rhys tipped his head back, knowing he would never again feel desire of such intensity. The firestorm burned, it tormented, it filled him with a desire more potent than anything he had felt before. Everything was about Lila, this marvel of a mate, and her pleasure.

She tugged his shirt upward, pushed it over his head and cast it on the floor. He couldn't help but look as she surveyed him, and he was glad to see her smile of satisfaction. "My dragon," she murmured and Rhys chuckled because it was true. She bent to graze his nipple with her teeth and he caught his breath at the stab of heat. Rhys gripped her waist and lifted her to her toes, even as she tormented his nipple with tongue and teeth. She teased them both, driving him crazy, then traced the outline of his tattoo with the tip of her tongue. Rhys gasped. She created a line of fire, one that made the mark of his nature burn like a brand. His teeth were clenched and his heart racing when she leaned back.

"It's glowing," she said with satisfaction. She lifted her gaze to his. "Like you're filled with inner fire."

"I definitely am." He kissed the side of her neck, trailing kisses to her ear, down her throat, beneath her chin and in the hollow of her throat. He felt her skin warm beneath his caress and her heart skip. His own heart matched the quick pace of hers and he was glad to be leaning against the counter as his world spun.

It spun around his mate.

"I'm going to miss the firestorm," Lila confessed in a sexy whisper, rolling her hips against Rhys and making him catch his breath. "I like how it makes everything more intense."

Rhys could only agree. He swept his hands down her back and under the hem of her sweater. It joined his shirt on the floor, then he unfastened the front clasp of her bra with his teeth. She was so smooth, so beautiful, that his breath caught at his good fortune. He cupped her breasts in his hands and Lila leaned back as he teased one nipple with his teeth. He ran his tongue around the taut peak, creating a line of fire on her flesh and she moaned with pleasure.

Her eyes were dancing as she shook out her hair, then she framed his face in her hands. "The shower is big enough for two," she said, her tone teasing.

"Yes." Rhys speared his fingers into her hair and drew her up for another long kiss, wanting to both make this interval last and yearning for immediate satisfaction.

"You're huge," she whispered, giving him a bold caress.

"Complaining?" Rhys teased and she shook her head, laughing, her hair once again seeming to flow like a river. She held his gaze as she unfastened his jeans, and he savored the feel of her hands as she pushed them down. She caressed him then bent and took him in her mouth, making him shudder with need.

Rhys couldn't wait. He lifted Lila away and stripped off her tights, holding her against his chest as he turned on the water. He carried her into the glass-walled shower and backed her into one corner. He kissed her thoroughly, then eased down the length of her, kissing her neck, her breasts, her belly, then finally lifting her knees to his shoulders. Lila whispered his name when he closed his mouth over her and arched her back, spreading her thighs wide and then moaning deeply.

Rhys braced her against the wall of the shower and ate her slowly, taking her to the brink of pleasure, then easing away again. He tempted and teased her, feeling how taut she was, loving how wet she was. He took his time, not caring how long it required to ensure her pleasure. He gripped her buttocks, holding her captive to his caress and she rocked against him, gripping his shoulders with her fingers. The hot water flowed over them, the firestorm glowed and he wanted her to remember the satisfaction of the firestorm forever.

Rhys knew the moment when she was on the cusp of release and this time, instead of withdrawing, he drove her to her release. She cried out in pleasure, rocking against him as the tide swept through her. She was flushed and her eyes were sparkling when she looked at him, and Rhys saw resolve in the line of her lips.

She spun and backed him into the same corner, then hooked one leg around him as she pulled his head down for a consuming kiss. Rhys lifted her up and she wrapped both legs around him, pulling him against her silky heat in silent demand. He gasped as she took him inside her in mercilessly slow increments, his heart nearly stopping with pleasure.

And that was nothing compared to how she rode him. She tormented him as deliberately as he'd teased her, moving with that enticing rhythm until he was certain he'd lose control, then slowing or even stilling completely before beginning her amorous assault again. She was slick and smooth, powerful and seductive. The firestorm burned with new brilliance, so white and hot that even though the water should have turned cold, the shower stall was filled with steam. The water sizzled, the room was filled with radiant light, and Lila smiled as she took Rhys to the cusp of release again.

This time, he couldn't stop. He turned so that she was against the wall and buried himself inside her, moving with power against her clitoris so that she flushed with her arousal. They stared into each other's eyes, transfixed as they conjured the storm together, then shouted as one with satisfaction.

Rhys closed his eyes and sagged against the wall, his breathing hard. Lila leaned her head on his shoulder, then tapped a fingertip on his tattoo. Rhys could feel that there was no spark, and he knew the room had become dark.

The firestorm was satisfied.

He took a breath and looked down at Lila. She smiled at him. "I choose," she whispered, and he kissed her again, overwhelmed with gratitude for the firestorm's gift.

He loved Lila, and his love would last through the end of time.

Fascinating.

Embron had listened to the *Pyr* conference in the restaurant and had learned a bit more from Eithne's tale. He'd known nothing of the tokens of prophecy made for the Others and considered the residue of Regalian magick that must be in each one that survived. He didn't particularly regret the witch's passing—she'd served her purpose to him.

How unfortunate that she'd only named two of the talismans. He waited for the *Pyr* to leave and sensed the consummation of the firestorm. When his fellow dragon shifters were gone or otherwise occupied, he left the apartment quietly, darting down streets until he found a deserted lot.

Then he bounded into the sky and shifted shape, turning toward Chicago.

The firestorm definitely lived up to its promise.

And it had been worth the trip, too.

Lila knew she would miss it. No other lovemaking would ever compare. She and Rhys washed each other quickly, because the water was cold. They'd run the hot water tank dry. She dressed in his shirt again when he suggested she wait a bit before taking her bath. "Let me guess. You're going to feed us," she teased and he laughed.

"Nothing heavy. I had oysters sent up from the kitchen and we never ate them."

"Because we need an aphrodisiac now?"

His smile was warm. "Maybe we just need to keep up our strength." They kissed again on the way to the kitchen and Lila was glad to slide onto a stool and watch him work. Even though he was superbly muscled, he moved with a dancer's grace. He was both strong and gentle, principled and reliable.

Lila would miss more than the firestorm.

"How does that work anyway?" he asked as he opened an oyster with a knife. "That choosing bit?"

"What do you mean?"

"Well, how long do you have to choose? Can you change your mind? How does your body know what you've chosen?" He opened another oyster and waited.

"I'm not sure how to explain it," Lila said, watching him work. "It's like a question rises in my thoughts, a question about the choice. It lasts at most a day and a night, but as soon as I decide, it fades away."

"And your choice is what happens?"

She nodded. "I can feel the difference."

"And if you don't choose?"

"I've heard that the body chooses, but I've never taken that chance. I like to be in charge of my own fate."

Rhys smiled. "I can relate to that."

"And once the choice is made, it's done. I can't change it. I can see the change in the auras of other selkies."

"Like Nyssa."

Lila nodded.

"What do you know about this dark mirror?"

She shivered. "Only that I'd rather avoid it."

"Why?"

"It has a bit of a reputation of tricking those who look into it."

"That Regalian magick."

"Maybe."

"You said something about a dream," he reminded her, punctuating it with an intent look.

Lila sighed. "I dreamed that I looked into the dark mirror. It must have been when you were bringing me here."

"And what did you see?"

Her throat tightened. "The day Thomas gave me this," she said, lifting the hagstone on its cord. "He found it on the beach. He loved the beach, they both did, but he had this collection of treasures he'd found." She smiled in reminiscence. "I made him a little bag and he carried it everywhere."

"It's a good idea to keep the hoard close," Rhys said with a smile.

"I guess so," Lila agreed.

"But here's what I don't understand," Rhys said. "You said that the Isle of the Blessed has sunk so that it's too deep to reach."

"Yes."

"But Nereus complained about Embron invading his treasury and that he could only watch. They must have both been there." He looked up, a question in his gaze, and Lila realized the discrepancy.

"Maybe it's not as deep as it used to be."

"What would make it rise again?"

Lila shrugged. "An earthquake?" She braced her chin on her elbow. "Or maybe they both have extra powers."

Rhys nodded. "Maybe." He slid a plate of oysters across the counter to her, garnished with half of a lemon. The rind had been cut to curl across the cut surface of the lemon in a playful swirl.

"That's pretty." Lila said with appreciation.

"Just a little something extra. There's an old saying that one eats also with the eyes." At her nod, Rhys squeezed the juice over the oysters with a flourish. "Maybe you should tell Nereus you've conceived and piss him off enough to start another earthquake. Then we could get to the treasury more easily and check out that dark mirror."

Lila froze in the act of taking an oyster. "You don't want to do either of those things."

"Oh yes, I do. We need to find that portal and seal it shut."

And he wanted to go after Theo and now Arach. Lila felt cold. "I'm not sure he would be angry."

Rhys gave her an intent look. "I don't have a single doubt."

They didn't have a chance to argue about it, though, because there was a quick shimmer of blue light from beneath the apartment door.

Someone knocked and the deliberate rhythm sounded imperious to Lila.

Rhys inhaled sharply, his hand dropping to her arm even as he came around the end of the counter. His eyes glittered and he was tense. The blue light outside had vanished, and Lila wondered whether she'd imagined it.

She wasn't imagining that Rhys was on the cusp of change himself.

He reached for the door, waited a heartbeat, then opened it. Lila smelled salt, the salt of the sea, and knew that Nereus had sought her out.

But why?

Arach awakened in a place of brilliant silver light. There was sand beneath him and it reflected the light with blinding intensity. He rolled over, realized he was in his dragon form, and discovered that he couldn't shift shape. There was a red cord tied around his ankle, one that burned where it touched him.

He couldn't breathe fire either and that spooked him.

Worse, somehow he'd ended up in an arena, one with high white walls around the circle of white sand. At the summit of the walls were rows and rows of spectators, all cheering and clapping, as if they'd come for a spectacle. They were Fae, with wings and fair skin, with tattoos and sparkling laughter. They were so delicately made that they didn't look real, and their gazes were filled with bloodlust.

Arach had a bad feeling about that.

High above there was only darkness, and Arach didn't know whether that was a roof or a starless night.

To his right, there was a structure that sheltered a group of seats, one that made him think of the private boxes at sports events. A red and silver striped awning hung over what could only a throne, and Maeve was seated upon it. She was dressed in red and held a golden orb in one hand. Her smile was filled with satisfaction and he guessed that she held the gem of the hoard.

Even from a distance, Arach could see the red light that circled her like an army of glowing fireflies. A familiar Fae warrior stood slightly behind her and to her left. The librarian Sylvia sat at her right. She didn't look pleased about her situation and Arach guessed she didn't have a lot of choices.

A woman with dark hair sat at Maeve's left hand, her expression mutinous. Arach realized with a start that it was the bartender from Bones. Mel was her name, if he remembered right. She was silent and he wondered whether that was by choice. He narrowed his eyes and saw the red strings on her wrists. She'd had one before, but now she had two.

He saw Kade sitting just outside the royal box, his expression sulky. It was good to see that there hadn't been any benefit to betraying the *Pyr*.

Was Theo here, too? Arach sought his fellow *Pyr*, but there was no sign of him. There was a gate directly opposite him in the high wall, and something moved restlessly behind it. Something big and orange that caught the light at intervals.

Arach knew that Theo was carnelian and gold in his dragon form. He rose cautiously to his feet and the spectators shouted. Eggs and stones were thrown onto the sand, several of them striking Arach and he looked around himself in horror.

"Let the games begin!" Maeve cried and the crowd roared approval, stamping their feet and clapping their hands. Sylvia looked grim. That Fae warrior smiled. "Let them fight to the death!" the Dark Queen added and the spectators were deafening in their approval.

But who did Arach have to fight? And how could he fight without all of his powers?

The gate opened slowly and Theo lunged onto the circle of white sand. He breathed fire at the sky, pawed at the ground like a wild beast, and slashed his tail through the air. The crowd bellowed their approval. His carnelian and gold scales caught the light and it seemed to Arach that there was a red glow beneath them all.

It was Theo, though. His first thought was that they'd make a feint and both escape. Somehow they'd save Mel and Sylvia and...

But in that moment, Theo turned his glittering stare on Arach and dread filled Arach's heart at the hatred in his friend's expression. There was a red string around Theo's leg and hunger in his snarl.

And not one glimmer of recognition in his eyes.

Theo bellowed and charged, and Arach wondered which of them would survive.

Then he feared neither of them would.

Lila could see that Rhys didn't appreciate Nereus appearing at his apartment and lair. He was protective and she understood that. She liked it, actually. To tell the truth, she wasn't happy about Nereus coming after her either.

Nereus was dressed this time, wearing jeans, a deep blue anorak and a white knit aran sweater. She didn't doubt that he'd attracted some attention on his way, because he was handsome and fit. He exuded vitality and charm.

"I've come to take Lila home," he said with a smile, but Lila heard the thread of steel in his tone.

She felt stalked and didn't like that. Nereus had cornered her before, but she'd hoped that his seduction of Nyssa would have taken the edge off his desire to breed more selkies.

No such luck.

"I thought a king would be too busy to play courier," Rhys said, bristling on her behalf.

"I have so few subjects left." Nereus surveyed Lila and she saw the gleam in his eye. "I can't help but be protective of every one." He ignored Rhys then and spoke only to Lila. "I see you're ready. I have the yacht here and am heading back to Ireland myself. It will be no trouble to take you home."

Nereus had a plan and Lila could guess what it was. Nyssa had said the yacht was luxurious. He must be planning to seduce her on the crossing.

Lila was fiercely glad that she had decided to conceive Rhys' son already. Nereus wouldn't be able to force her to submit to him. He'd be displeased not to get his way, but then he'd calm down.

It would be better if he discovered the truth when they were far from Manhattan. Another earthquake wouldn't be a good thing.

Nereus came to her side and leaned close to speak to her. His eyes were very blue and his expression intense. "It's time to go home, Lila," he said softly and she found agreement in her heart. "You need to finish your work for the season."

Lila opened her mouth then closed it again, a conviction that he was right filling her thoughts. Her concerns about his intentions faded so quickly that she almost forgot them.

"I know what it is to fall in love," Nereus whispered, understanding in his expression. "But you and I both know our kind are cursed in romance."

Lila stared into his eyes, knowing he was right.

She couldn't give Rhys the relationship, the romance, and the family he wanted. It wasn't in her. Just because she was tempted to try, she knew she couldn't really trust. Their relationship was doomed in a dozen ways. Rhys didn't like the cold, but her life and work were close to the Arctic Circle. He loved his cooking and his restaurant: there was no call for either on North Rona or even much on Westray. He said he wasn't much of a swimmer and she could have spent her life in the water.

They were badly matched.

The firestorm had gotten it wrong.

Or it really had been just about sex.

"You're right," Lila said to Nereus. She shrugged into Rhys' jacket again as Nereus watched with approval. "I'll send it back to you," she promised as Rhys stared at her, then picked up her purse.

"I thought we were going to Scotland together."

"There's no need. If Nereus has his yacht, that will be simpler."

"But..." Rhys looked at Nereus and fell silent. She suspected he wanted to ask about the Isle of the Blessed and the dark mirror. "You're sure?" he asked instead.

He'd support her choice, whatever it was.

That would ensure that he and Nereus didn't fight, which had to be a good thing.

"It only makes sense," Lila said lightly, then kissed Rhys' cheek. "Thanks for the great meals, Rhys. Give my best wishes to the *Pyr*." She walked past him to leave the apartment,. "Let's go," she said to Nereus. "You probably want to catch a tide."

Nereus matched his step to hers. Satisfaction oozed from his every pore and she saw his aura brighten. He took her elbow and she couldn't think of a polite way to pull away. It was a small gesture, really. "It's not so important with the yacht," he told her. "It has so much power. I never have to wait for tides anymore. And so smooth. You won't believe it. You can hardly tell that you're on a boat..."

Lila was well aware of Rhys watching her go. She sensed his disappointment but knew it was probably better sooner rather than later. Their partnership had no future.

The situation was perfectly typical of selkies in love.

Lila could give Rhys a son and she would. He'd given her some potent memories.

That would have to be enough for both of them.

Lila had gone willingly with Nereus.

She'd abandoned Rhys, apparently without a second thought.

Even though she'd warned him that selkies were all about pleasure and living in the moment, that they were selfish and didn't make lasting bonds, Rhys couldn't believe it.

He'd been so sure that she was beginning to believe in the merit of a permanent bond. He'd been positive that they were good together and couldn't accept she didn't see as much. He watched until Lila and Nereus got into the waiting cab and then he paced, fighting his indecision. He was torn between the need to protect her and his commitment to defending her choices.

He didn't like Nereus or trust him, which didn't help.

What if she'd been charmed?

It had happened so fast, but then she didn't believe it was possible for selkies to charm each other? Rhys didn't doubt that Nereus would use any tool to get what he wanted.

Was it wrong that he wanted to be sure Lila was okay? Rhys decided it wasn't. He grabbed his coat and followed them.

A luxury yacht preparing to go to Ireland. It couldn't be that hard to find.

The yacht was every bit as luxurious as Lila could have imagined. It was large enough for a dozen people and outfitted with every amenity. There were large screen televisions and leather-upholstered furniture, as well as a kitchen sufficiently well-equipped even to impress Rhys. There was a dining room, a bar, and a big deck at the back that had a pool. It looked strange in the snow, like a mirage conjured from the Mediterranean.

That made her think of Rhys and his fondness for Malta.

Everything made her think of Rhys. She knew that whenever she saw a mention of New York, she'd think of him. Food and restaurants and kitchens would bring the memory of him cooking into her mind. Then there were the obvious associations: fire and flames with the firestorm, dragons obviously with the *Pyr*, and garnets would always make her think of his dragon form. She knew he'd admire the sleek stainless surfaces and smoked glass panels of the yacht, the polished wooden floors laid in a herringbone design, the modern spiral of the staircase. The spare design with good materials reminded her of his home and his restaurant.

An hour apart and she missed Rhys already. Lila told herself that it was for the best, but she was regretting her decision with all her heart.

She'd seen eight staff members so far, and was a bit concerned that they all had that glazed look of people who had been heavily charmed. They were like automatons, not people, and fulfilled their duties with both efficiency and unwavering smiles.

They gave her the creeps.

"What do you think?" Nereus asked, obviously filled with pride. He was happy, expansive even, since she'd gotten into the cab with him and Lila knew that was because he was unaware of her pregnancy. Male selkies couldn't read auras, and only the healers among the females could read them as well as Lila. What Nereus lacked in those skills, he clearly made up in charm.

"You should give me your skin," he suggested as they walked down a more narrow corridor toward the staterooms.

Lila tried to hide her horror at the suggestion.

She obviously failed, because Nereus chuckled. "I had a chamber made for keeping skins at their best," he informed her as he unlocked a cabinet. She realized that the smoothly paneled wall actually hid a lot of storage. Nereus showed her clear units filled with water inside the compartment, though only one held a dark grey skin. "Look, mine is there. It's in the perfect balance of salt and nutrients, better than ocean water."

It did look particularly healthy. "How can that be?"

"No pollutants," he said. "My skin is in better shape every time I retrieve it from here, as sleek as if I were a thousand years younger." He opened an empty unit in invitation. "It's like the fountain of eternal youth. Give it a try."

Lila hesitated.

"Lila," Nereus chided in a playful tone. "I'm your king. I would never ever betray you or any of our kind." He rummaged through his ring of keys and removed one. "Here. I'll give you a key of your own to the compartment, if that makes you feel better."

"It does. Thanks." Even with the key in her hand, it still wasn't easy for Lila to surrender her skin. She put it into the water herself and was reassured as it seemed to blossom as soon as it was submerged. She felt cool and soothed herself.

She'd become too suspicious, probably a result of living alone and communing with seals and introverted researchers.

She remembered Rhys' comments about those who didn't trust having one foot out the door, then forced herself to push the memories away.

"You've been working too hard," Nereus scolded, his tone almost paternal. Lila wasn't going to tell him about Embron and Maeve's treatment of her skin. It didn't matter anymore and it would only infuriate him. "Come and get some rest. My chef is preparing dinner, but you can get settled while the yacht leaves the harbor. I never eat until we're on the open seas. It's so much more tranquil that way." He swept open a door and Lila blinked at the sumptuous room revealed.

It was almost a half-circle, with floor to ceiling windows around most of the outer curve. The wood was golden and smooth, and she suspected the paneled walls concealed storage, like that in the corridor. The floor was dark wood laid in a herringbone design and a king-sized bed was against the wall opposite the windows. The lamps were lit on either side of the bed, their golden light making the space welcoming. She could see a large ensuite bath on the other side of the bed. Nereus touched a switch and blinds descended over the windows, one after the other, hiding the open sea before them. He touched another and a large television rose out of the floor opposite the bed. Another switch started some light classical music and yet another turned on more soft lighting.

"I never would have expected this on a boat," Lila said as she turned around to look.

"Exactly! It's almost too luxurious for a king." Nereus stroked the fur covering on the king-sized bed, as if he was amazed by the yacht, too. If he'd bought it, though, why would he be so surprised by it? It would be like Nereus to specify every detail.

"How did you get this yacht?" Lila asked.

Nereus chuckled. "Toll of the seas. The owners were stranded. They ran out of fuel and abandoned ship, then died, floating in the middle of the ocean in their lifeboat."

"Did you know them?"

"Of course not. They were mortals." He was scathing, as if their death had been the inevitable outcome of their nature. "The yacht was abandoned, spoils for the first to find it." He smiled and stroked the fur again. Lila had the definite sense that he was glossing the truth. "The glory of the seas, ripe for the taking."

Lila turned away so he wouldn't see her doubts. "Lucky for you."

"Lucky for me," Nereus agreed. He took off his jacket and snapped his fingers. One of his crew appeared in the doorway, then bowed his head and took the jacket. He touched a panel in one wall. A door opened, revealing a closet full of clothing.

Men's clothing. The crew member hung up the jacket, closed the cabinet and retreated. A chime rang somewhere and Nereus glanced up.

"They'll be wanting me," he murmured. "I'll see you at dinner."

"Wait. Is this *your* room?" Lila asked.

"Best one aboard. They call it the Captain's Suite." Nereus smiled. "I call it the King's Chamber."

"Where's my room?"

"Right here, of course."

"You don't have to surrender your room to me."

Nereus paused in the act of leaving the room and glanced back. He held Lila's gaze steadily. "I'm not." Their gazes held for a long moment, his intention crystal clear. There was only one bed, after all, and she could see the heat of desire in his eyes.

"I don't think sharing is a good idea," she said, bracing herself for his reaction. She might as well get this part behind her.

"Why not?" Nereus asked. "We need more children, another generation of our kind. I've explained it to you, repeatedly, Lila."

"But I'm already pregnant," she confessed.

Fury blazed in his eyes and she thought for a heartbeat that he might strike her. A veil was torn away and Lila saw the savage truth of the King Under the Seas. She took an unwilling step back, realizing that she hadn't made the choice in Rhys' apartment on her own.

"You charmed me," she whispered.

"I saved you from making another mistake," he said through gritted teeth.

Lila felt like the hollow in her life was yawning wider. She should have believed Rhys when he'd suggested it might be possible for a selkie to charm another selkie. She should have been prepared to defend herself against Nereus' will.

Would Rhys ever forgive her?

Would she have the opportunity to ask for his forgiveness?

Nereus took a long breath, his gaze simmering when he eyed her again. "I suppose it's another abomination?" he asked, his voice quivering with anger.

Lila was startled by his choice of words. "I don't think so."

"You never think so!" he snapped. He flung out a hand. "You surrender what is precious to those who don't deserve it. You willfully create children that are mongrels, instead of adding to our numbers, and you consistently, persistently, deny *me*!"

"I can stay in New York," Lila said. "I don't have to remain as your guest..."

"Of course, you will remain. It is time you learned the consequences of your actions."

"I'm going to have a child, a *Pyr*, who will be raised by Rhys. That's the consequence of my choice."

"Your child will be half-selkie," Nereus said, his tone poisonous.

"You think you're creating life but you're bringing death to another creature. Such mongrels must die."

"The Dark Queen might not find him," she dared to suggest.

"Then I will give the child to her."

She was shocked by how fierce Nereus was. "You can't mean that..."

"Of course, I mean it," he retorted. "It's the way of every kind to eliminate the weak and the wounded, to sacrifice those who are damaged or impure. You've lived among humans too long. Think of the seals. Think of the pups they leave to die because there's something wrong with them."

"They don't..."

"They do! And you have refused to take responsibility for your choices, leaving me to repair the damage."

"It's not the same."

He glared at her. "It's exactly the same, and once again, I'll clean up your mess."

Lila felt cold. "What have you done?"

"What had to be done. What was right and just." Nereus tugged a second smaller key from his ring. He tossed it at her, the gold flicking in the light as it flew toward her. Lila caught it instinctively. "Look upon the consequences and reconsider the wisdom of your choice," he said, his voice soft with threat. "I'll give you time to come to your senses."

He spun on his heel and left then, slamming the door behind himself. Lila heard the lock click, but seized the doorknob anyway and tried to open the door. It was secured against her, just as she suspected.

She pivoted and leaned back against it, surveying her fine prison. Trapped again and charmed into it. Plus the staff were charmed into following Nereus' orders without question. Her skin was locked away and out of her reach, and she felt the engines of the boat throb underfoot.

They were leaving New York.

Lila dug in her purse for her phone, but it still had no service. She surveyed the stateroom, fighting her fear.

Then she remembered the key, still clutched in her hand. What did it unlock?

The consequences of her choice.

Did she even want to know?

CHAPTER FIFTEEN

he harbor master says there's a super yacht," Balthasar confided when he met Rhys at the docks. "He's annoyed because the paperwork isn't right."

It was cold, even though the wind was calm. The snow was gaining momentum and Rhys could think of a dozen places he'd rather be than on Manhattan's docks. The smell of fish and brine was strong and the dampness made it seem colder than it was. He'd called Balthasar to help because Balthasar knew boats. "How so?"

"He thinks something might be forged. But every person he sends to investigate comes back without an answer. He's convinced they've all become incompetent."

"No," Rhys said grimly. "They've been charmed."

"What does that mean?"

"It's like beguiling, but it's what selkies do."

"That would explain it. It's docked down here," Balthasar said and they strode together toward its berth. "You sure about this?"

"I need to be sure that she's glad to be with him. She chose so suddenly. I wonder whether she's been charmed." Rhys shrugged. "One word from her and I'll stand back. I just want to know that she's safe."

Balthasar nodded understanding, then gave a low whistle as they approached the berth. "Now that's a yacht," he said softly.

Rhys stared. The boat in the berth looked more like a spaceship than a yacht. It was sleek and silver, shining as if it was made of stainless steel. Its shape was streamlined and it looked expensive. It was also enormous, though he imagined that the kind of people who traveled like this didn't pack themselves into little staterooms.

"It's got to be three hundred meters long," Balthasar said in wonder. "You don't see these yachts often in New York."

"Why not?"

"They're for cruising and partying. There are a lot of them in the Mediterranean, and a bunch in Australia. It probably has at least one pool, a bar and dining room..."

"And a kitchen," Rhys said. "Do you think you could get us on board?"

Balthasar smiled and redid his man-bun, tidying it up a bit. "I've been looking for the chance to try out a beguiling tip from Lorenzo that Arach shared with me. This looks like the perfect opportunity."

"If I can help, just tell me what to do."

"We'll figure out who's in charge of the staff and I'll focus there. If you're going to be in the kitchen, I should probably work my way up to the bridge." Balthasar nodded. "Try to take care of anyone I miss."

"Deal. I just want to see her. If she tells me to leave, then we'll be gone."

Balthasar nodded. "The engines are starting. We'd better move fast."

Lila found the lock that fit the key. It was in a cabinet opposite the closet where Nereus' clothes hung. She guessed it had been designed to hold a woman's accessories, because of the position of the shelves. She could imagine designer shoes in the smaller sections and purses arranged in the larger ones. It would be almost like a store display, the way she'd seen fancy closets online. There were drawers that could hold sunglasses and jewelry, but none of those accessories were stored there.

The shelves and drawers were filled with little tokens, carefully arranged in rows. Most of them were metal, and she was struck by a sense that they were the detritus of many lives. The styles of the jewelry were all different, as if it had originated in different eras. There were rings, bracelets and brooches, a sextant, carved tusks and necklaces. There were hair combs and clouded mirrors, several compasses, and even a hook that might have been a replacement for a man's hand. There was a silver picture frame, the photograph damaged by water beyond recognition, and a cigarette case with an elaborate monogram.

It could have been a display from a junk market or a thrift shop, but each item was given its own space. Some looked as if they had been polished. Lila stared, unable to make sense of the collection, if that was what it was. Why was it locked away?

What was it?

Then she spotted Malcolm's pocket watch. It was in the middle of the top drawer, displayed like a prize, and she immediately reasoned that it wasn't Malcolm's watch at all. It must just be a similar one. His pocket watch had been plain, after all, less expensive and ornate than many of its kind. Just a plain pocket watch in a plain gold case on a simple chain. She remembered how the gold had been worn away, revealing the grey metal beneath.

This one showed similar wear.

It had a slight dent in the lid that covered the face of the watch, proof that such protection was needed. Malcolm's watch hadn't had a dent. She was sure of it.

But it had been a long time.

The chain was the same, much cheaper than the watch, with the same clasp. She picked up the watch and listened to it, not at all surprised that it wasn't running. Malcolm's watch had been broken, too, broken after Thomas played with it one day.

She closed her eyes in memory of Malcolm's fury with the boy and refused to remember the lashing he'd been given. The watch had belonged to Malcolm's older brother. Duncan had been dead by the time she met Malcolm, all of his possessions passed to his younger brother. Malcolm had been alone, which she'd thought explained the sorrow tinging his aura. She turned the watch in her hand, remembering Malcolm's resentment of his older brother, and wondered one more time just how Duncan had died.

It couldn't be the same watch.

Lila opened the case and read the inscription.

For Duncan—
With every good wish for a prosperous future.
—Father

She closed the lid with alarm. It *was* the same watch. But what was it doing here?

"He was wicked," Nereus said in the speech of their kind, his words flowing into Lila's thoughts.

Lila heard the door unlock behind her but didn't turn. She tried to hide her reaction to Nereus' return. *"I never wished him ill,"* she said. *"I just wanted to be free."*

Nereus came to stand behind her and she felt him looming over her. One hand closed over her shoulder and she feared his intentions. He slid her hair to one side with a gentle fingertip before gripping her other shoulder with that hand. He pressed a kiss to the back of her neck and her heart thudded a warning.

"Because you are gentle and a healer," Nereus said quietly. "That is why you must be protected."

Lila kept her gaze fixed on the watch and fought the force of his charm.

"He abused you," he breathed against her skin. "Why would you mourn him?"

"Because he's dead, of course. I tried to heal him," Lila said, keeping her tone mild. She remembered the damage to Malcolm's aura. "I wanted to help him."

He'd been a handsome man, muscled and well-proportioned, with pain in his grey eyes and honey on his tongue. She'd thought she could heal him. She'd thought that she'd ended up on that beach because he needed her, because she could make a difference. For a while, she'd thought she was making progress, but the children fed his fury.

He'd been hard on Thomas and had ignored Agnes. She remembered the incident with the watch, just a curious boy playing with a trinket. Thomas hadn't meant any harm. She blinked back tears in memory of that cheerful little boy, his relentless curiosity and his sunny nature. She hoped he had lived long and had many sons. She hoped he had prospered in her absence, and Agnes, too.

"You have to recognize the limits of your own powers," Nereus said. "You can't make a man whole who is broken beyond repair."

Lila turned in his grip to meet his gaze. "You seem to know a lot about Malcolm. I didn't think you'd met him."

Nereus smiled, his gaze warm upon her. "I had to avenge you. You must see that." He bent and touched his lips to hers even as Lila recoiled. "It was my duty to protect you."

Lila stepped out from under the weight of his hands and retreated until her back was against the cabinet. "You killed Malcolm?"

Nereus folded his arms across his chest, his expression less seductive. "He was taken by the sea. He was claimed by me." He pointed to the watch. "That is a trophy of justice done."

The hair crept on the back of Lila's neck. If the entire collection was similar tokens, then Nereus was much more violent and vengeful than she had realized. "How?"

"He was a fisherman," Nereus said. "They die all the time, especially if they head out to sea alone." His eyes flashed. "He was easy pickings."

Lila had never thought about Malcolm dying. He'd been so vital. "When?"

"After your escape," he said with satisfaction. "I gave him a year."

"But what about the children?" she demanded. She'd assumed they'd be fine, that Malcolm would raise them among his kind, but they would have been alone.

Nereus scoffed. "I took the boy the first time he ventured into the sea alone." He smiled. "So easily done." He opened the next drawer and Lila spotted a blue cloth bag that made her catch her breath. She'd sewn that little calico bag herself, sewn it by hand for Thomas to store his treasures. His hoard, Rhys had called it. She reached for it with a trembling hand, feeling the stones and shells inside it.

"He was never parted from it," she said, knowing that she could list the contents. There was a black stone with a fossil in it. A spiral shell worn down by the sea so that only a filigree lattice remained. The beak of a seabird. She remembered each discovery, remembered him running to show his latest find each time. She'd never let her children go onto the beach alone, but now she realized she'd had no idea what to fear.

Or who.

"He was in the end," Nereus said, his tone reasonable. Lila steeled herself against him. "You have to realize, Lila, that they were unnatural. They couldn't be allowed to live."

"What about Agnes?"

He shook his head. "She never came to the sea. I tried to call her, but she refused. I claimed her son, though." He pointed to a small jet pin carved in the shape of a leaping fish. "Her husband gave her this on their wedding day and she gave it to the boy on his." Nereus smiled as he caressed each item in his collection and Lila took a step back.

"I have to leave," she said.

"Too late. We're underway."

"I can't have your child. I've already conceived. I've already chosen."

Nereus' gaze turned cold. "There are ways. You know that as well as I do." Then his easy smile returned. He locked the cabinet and claimed the key, gripping her elbow and guiding her toward the door. "But there's no need to argue now. I came to tell you that dinner is ready."

"I'm not hungry."

"But I am, and I insist that you join me."

Anger and rebellion rose within Lila, but Nereus was resolute and his grip was relentless. She chose to pretend to be convinced.

He led her to a dining room dominated by a large round table. Once again, the lighting was soft and luminous. There was music playing and the blinds were closed against the winter night. A long line of fire crackled in the modern fireplace set into one wall. There was an ice bucket with a bottle of champagne within it, and a pair of champagne flutes on the table. Lila sat, wondering how she would escape, as two staff members appeared.

They were attractive but so slender that Lila found it hard to be certain of their gender. They were dressed in clothes so simple that they could have been a uniform: black trousers and white shirts. They worked with silent efficiency and Lila noticed that their eyes were glazed, as if they were drugged.

"A little charm is the best motivation," Nereus said as one popped the cork. The other held their chairs and offered their napkins.

Lila knew then that the staff would be of no help to her.

How was she going to escape?

The champagne flowed into the glasses, bubbling as it was poured. The glasses were set before them, then the second staff member re-appeared with two large plates. He set down one in front of each other them. They were oysters, a dozen on each tray, with half a lemon garnishing each plate.

Half a lemon with the rind cut in a distinctive curl.

Rhys was aboard! Relief swept through Lila, but she knew instinctively that he wouldn't charge in to rescue her. He'd want to know what she wanted. That was Rhys' code of honor and in this moment, Lila appreciated it—and him—more than ever.

Nereus waved the staff members away. He raised his glass of champagne then eyed Lila. "You look startled. What's wrong?"

"Nothing, it's just so pretty," Lila said. "But I couldn't possibly eat a bite."

"Shall we drink to the future instead?"

"It might be bad for the baby," Lila said, unable to forget his words about there being ways to be rid of Rhys' son. She pushed the glass away slightly, feeling Nereus' annoyance rise. She had a thought then of how she could alert Rhys to her choice. She smiled at Nereus and used their style of speech. *"It would be so much easier to relax in your company if I didn't know you'd killed my son."*

Rhys had been able to hear their speech before.

Lila hoped he could hear it now, because Nereus put his glass down hard and wrath flashed in his gaze. Then he shook his head, composed himself, and turned the full weight of his attention upon her. His voice dropped and Lila knew he was going to try to charm her again.

She only hoped she could resist.

"It would be so much easier to relax in your company if I didn't know you'd killed my son."

Rhys was stunned when he heard Lila's claim. He abandoned the rest of the meal preparation and went to the door of the kitchen, opening it slightly to watch Nereus and Lila. There were two crew members in the kitchen, standing to one side and awaiting orders, apparently lost in their daydreams. It was eerie how unaware they were of their surroundings and how they could be stirred by a command.

Balthasar said the charming was intense and must have been sustained over an extended period of time. The two *Pyr* had been hard-pressed to get aboard, even working together, and Rhys was still wary of being revealed.

He didn't trust any of them.

If Nereus had killed Lila's first son, the King Under the Seas wouldn't have any qualms about killing the second. Rhys fought against the shimmer of blue light that revealed he was on the cusp of change. His instinct was to defend Lila, but he had to wait to be sure—and remain disguised while he did so.

"Lila, Lila, Lila," Nereus said, shaking his head. His tone was filled with disappointment as if she were a wayward child. "I only did what had to be done." His tone was persuasive. "I told you as much already. I did the responsible thing. Our lineage must be kept pure..."

Lila was staring at the table, her entire body taut with her resistance. "Then you can't blame me for protecting my unborn son."

"You have to see reason, Lila," Nereus replied in that soothing tone. Was he trying to charm Lila? "It's for your own good, Lila, as well as the good of our kind. Even if you manage to deliver this abomination, you can't defend the child forever." He sighed with apparent regret. "It's fated to die."

"No, he isn't." Lila insisted.

"How do you imagine that?" Nereus asked. "If I don't do the responsible deed, then the Dark Queen will hunt him and do it for me."

"You said you would deliver him to her," Lila said with heat.

Nereus smiled. "His destiny is an unkind one, Lila. The child has no future. It would be kinder to end this madness now, before it has progressed very far."

"No." Lila insisted. "I have chosen."

"And I invite you to choose again." Nereus rose smoothly and went to the bar. He took a bottle from a locked cabinet and poured its dark contents into a glass. He returned to Lila and placed it before her. "This will see the situation resolved by morning," he explained. "It will be as if you chose correctly in the first place. We need never speak of it again."

Lila took a breath and stared at the glass. She had to know it was an abortifacient. Rhys wanted to shatter that glass and ensure no one could ever drink its contents. Lila, to his relief, seemed to agree.

"Lila, Lila," Nereus cooed. "This is for your own good. Look at me!"

She looked up with obvious reluctance and even Rhys could feel the weight of the king's will pressing upon her.

"It will be best," Nereus insisted. "It would be kind, Lila. Imagine the agony endured by the victims of the Dark Queen."

Lila frowned and seemed troubled. "I couldn't heal that damage," she whispered and Nereus sat down beside her.

"It's hard to admit our shortcomings, Lila, but we all have them. You trust too readily. You see the best in others. It's your gift. You are gracious and kind, but you must think of the future." He slid the glass closer to her hand. "Drink this and we'll put this incident behind us forever."

Lila sighed and wiped away a tear. "Of course, you know best, my lord," she said in a meek tone that Rhys couldn't reconcile with her character. She lifted the glass and for a heartbeat, he feared she'd been convinced—or charmed.

Then her eyes flashed and she flung the contents of the glass into Nereus' face. "I won't let you execute another of my sons!" she declared and jumped to her feet. Her chair fell backwards behind her but she scrambled over it in her haste to retreat.

Nereus roared and snatched for her.

Rhys shifted shape as he leapt across the dining room floor, breathing a fearsome plume of fire in defense of his mate. He saw Lila's smile of relief and knew he'd made the right decision, then Nereus pivoted to fight. He'd seized his trident, though Rhys had no idea where it had been hidden, and the silver tines flashed as Nereus struck the first blow.

It was remarkable to Sebastian that despite all he disliked about mortal society, he kept returning to it. It was more than a need to feed and survive. He was drawn to humans in a way that annoyed him.

Perhaps he was addicted to them.

If that wasn't a troubling realization, he didn't know what was.

Despite his hatred of air travel and congested public meeting places, of artificial light and of being cloistered with strangers for periods of time, he'd taken a commercial flight to Ireland. He was hungry and more than a little bit irritable when he strode down the cobbled streets of Dublin late on the night after his arrival.

He fed quickly, without lingering over the choice, and the city had one less homeless beggar. He would tell Micah that he had put the man out of his misery. Maybe that would mitigate Micah's inevitable annoyance about Sebastian's abrupt departure. His victim's blood had been thin, redolent of alcohol and some venereal disease that disgusted Sebastian. The vermin of human society were so much junk food—accessible, cheap and ultimately dissatisfying.

Maeve's townhouse was easy to find, given the faint glow of red magick emanating from it. The back door, in the dark yard, had a lock that was ridiculously easy to pick. He'd expected more of a challenge from the Dark Queen, but apparently she was careless.

Or she had other alarms in place.

Sebastian slid into the shadowed interior and listened for long moments, scarcely breathing, as silent as only a vampire could be. Nothing. The house was as good as abandoned. He narrowed his eyes at the bottom of the stairs and scanned them, noting the faint beams of the motion detectors. He chose a path instinctively then followed it, ducking beneath one beam and leaping another, moving like quicksilver. He paused at the top of the stairs, listening. The alarm system hiccupped, reset, and remained silent.

He moved so quickly that the system discounted the input from the sensors as a glitch. He was following a path mapped out and taken by another, one who had paid the ultimate price for his transgression, and Sebastian knew it all too well.

He felt followed by a shadow.

Or a ghost.

Sebastian reached the top floor of the townhouse quickly and identified the bedroom by the red radiance showing beneath the door. There were no alarms here, as it was assumed any intruder would have been caught on the ascent. Maeve's bedroom was a boudoir, in every sense of the word, red and silver and lush. Satin and fur, pillows and toys.

Sebastian thought it frivolous.

One mirror was broken, which interested him. He found a broken crystal orb on the carpet beneath it, and poked it with a fingernail. It was devoid of magick, no more potent than the emery board left on the dresser. It had to be one of the orbs held by the dragon princes.

He straightened and turned, letting the magick reveal itself. There was a portal here, in this room, a way for Maeve to move easily between the realms. He'd come to her Dublin home expressly to locate it and use it.

The one who had come before him had found it, which was proof that it existed.

Sebastian stood and waited, still as death, then he saw the faint pulse of red. There was an armoire on the far side of the room, a massive piece of antique furniture. The red pulsed as if there was a light inside it. He opened the doors, pushed back the clothes and smiled at the outline of a door in the back of it. The red light came from behind it.

Sebastian opened the door and stepped through the opening into a smaller room, one hidden behind the bedroom. It had to be fitted beneath the gables of the roof, as dark and sinister as the bedroom was light and feminine. There were spiders and the wood was unfinished, the rafters bare. In striking contrast, there was a beautiful display cabinet built into one wall, a remarkable piece of workmanship in a place where no one would see it. He found himself drawn closer to examine its contents.

Ah, a unicorn horn. It couldn't have been anything else with that pearlescent hue, so long and straight, encircled by a chain of faded and dried daisies. A centaur's hooves rested beside it, then a scale of glittering topaz and gold that looked the right size to have fallen from a dragon's hide. He saw a mermaid's mirror and what must have been one of her scales, smaller than the other and iridescent green. He peered at something dried and horrible and concluded it might have been pointed ears, once upon a time. They perched beside a harp. The case was crowded but not full, and Sebastian guessed that these were Maeve's trophies from the last of each kind she eliminated.

There was nothing that hinted at vampires. There was a white feather, one that might have fallen from an angel wing, and he eyed it thoughtfully. He wondered at that dragon scale, then reminded himself to hurry.

The portal to Fae itself had to be in this room. He didn't expect it to easily reveal itself, but the faint glow of red troubled his vision. The shadows looked both deeper and less substantial in its light. He ran his hands lightly over the inside of the roof and along the floor, disturbing cobwebs and sending mice scurrying. He finally found the portal by feel, the silver light icy cold as his fingers slid over the crack, as if an arctic draft blew through the hairline gap.

He found the latch then, knowing it had to be there, and hauled open the door. The Fae warrior standing guard on the other side was even more surprised than Sebastian when they suddenly were confronted with each other. That increment of preparedness was just enough: Sebastian seized the warrior's weapon from his scabbard and sliced him open before he could move.

The Fae warrior gasped as he turned to a cloud of silver mist. His physical form dissipated like fog, right before Sebastian's eyes, and his garments fell empty to the ground. Sebastian could hear a crowd roaring in the distance, like they were at a sporting event. He grimaced, not looking forward to mingling with immortals any more than he liked mortal companionship.

And crowds were the worst.

If there was a party or celebration, though, Maeve would have taken Sylvia there. The uniform and the weapon might prove very useful.

Fortunately, this Fae warrior had been of similar size to Sebastian.

He refused to see that coincidence as ominous.

Nereus was going to kill Rhys.

Rhys exploded from the kitchen in a flash of blue light, shifting shape as he bounded across the dining room. The half-crucifix from his father flashed gold against the garnet and silver of his scales, and his eyes were filled with protective fury.

Nereus bounded to his feet and seized his trident. He jabbed it into Rhys' brow, thrusting with all his might. Lila saw blood flow over Rhys' garnet and silver scales and feared Nereus had been aiming for his eyes. Rhys roared and ducked, his heavy tail swinging hard, as he breathed fire at Nereus. The table and the chairs were swept to one side of the dining room, the table breaking one of the windows when it fell. Lila ran, keeping behind Rhys and out of his way. Nereus tugged his trident free and snarled as he aimed another blow at Rhys.

"You," Nereus said. "You dare to create an abomination with one of my kind."

Rhys roared and slashed at Nereus with his claw. The King Under the Seas darted backward hastily and avoided the blow, but he dropped his trident. Smoke rose from Rhys' nostrils as he stepped over the trident, trapping it beneath his weight.

Nereus circled around him, keeping his back to the wall, but there was no way to get the trident while Rhys stood guard over it. Rhys simply watched and waited.

Lila realized she was backed against the cabinet where Nereus had gotten the dark liquid. She watched Nereus and Rhys as she located the bottle. She gripped it tightly, circling the room slowly, moving toward the broken window. She'd see it destroyed forever. She didn't think Rhys would lose, but this would ensure that Nereus could never compel anyone else to drink the vile substance.

"You have no respect," Nereus said to Rhys. "You have no appreciation for tradition..."

"And you have no interest in Lila's opinions," Rhys replied in old-speak.

Nereus was visibly startled. He narrowed his eyes and stared at Rhys. *"Get out of my thoughts, worm-spawn,"* he replied as selkies communicated.

"Lila says you killed her son," Rhys said aloud and Lila knew from the melodic tone of his voice that he was trying to beguile Nereus. Nereus was staring at him, transfixed.

"I killed her son," Nereus admitted, his voice oddly subdued. Then he shook his head and glared at Lila. She froze, just inches from the window, the bottle hidden behind her back. "It was only right. He was an abomination and should never have existed. Selkies should breed with selkies..."

Lila bristled. "Thomas wasn't an abomination!"

"He was a half-breed," Nereus said with a sneer. "And he shouldn't have been born. You should have mated with me instead of that mortal man. You should have thought of the good of your kind, instead of indulging your unnatural appetites."

"What's the difference between you and Malcolm Ramsay?" Lila demanded. "Both of you thought only of *your* desires."

Nereus' eyes flashed. "I gave you the key to the hiding place for your skin. That's the difference."

"I only met Malcolm Ramsay because I was fleeing from you," Lila said and Rhys glanced back at her in surprise. "I listened to him because you wouldn't take no for an answer."

"Your future is my right to determine! I am your king!" Nereus cried and lunged for the trident.

Rhys snapped at him and caught the sleeve of his sweater in his teeth. Nereus retreated but he was caught. He tugged hard on the sweater and it tore, unraveling as he raced away from Rhys. He tugged it over his head and flung it at Rhys as he threw himself out of the dining room and crossed the deck. Rhys shifted shape in a shimmer of blue to run after him.

"This isn't done!" Nereus cried and dove over the side of the yacht, Rhys in hot pursuit.

"But he'll drown!" Lila said. "He doesn't have his skin." She didn't have hers, either, or she might have dived in after him. She looked back toward the locker and knew that by the time she retrieved it, it would be too late for Nereus.

Rhys gave her a sizzling look. "It would serve him right."

Lila shook her head. "I'm a healer, Rhys. It would be unkind."

Rhys swore, shifted again, and dove over the rail in his dragon form.

They both vanished completely and Lila acknowledged that there was only one of them she was afraid to lose. She spilled the contents of that bottle then flung it into the sea. Once that was done, she clutched the rail, scanning the dark surface of the water until Rhys appeared again. He was still in his dragon form, but took a gulp of air and dove beneath the waves once more.

He'd gone after Nereus for her. Lila knew it and hoped the price wasn't too high.

She hoped she hadn't made a mistake by showing compassion.

Rhys seemed to be under for too long, to her thinking, before he emerged again. He began to swim and she saw that he wasn't accustomed to swimming, at least not in his dragon form. The waves were powerful, though, and if he shifted shape, he might be overwhelmed. The yacht wasn't that fast but it was leaving him behind.

"Help!" she shouted, uncertain who might hear her but hoping someone did. She pulled out the key Nereus had given her so she could retrieve her skin.

"*Balthasar,*" Rhys said in old-speak and Lila realized he hadn't come alone.

Before she could think of where to look for the other *Pyr,* she saw a shimmer of blue light at the bridge above her and a dragon in silhouette against the night sky as he took flight. Lila was glad to see him even though she wasn't sure who he was.

This dragon was citrine and gold, as brilliantly hued as a beam of sunlight, and he dove into the sea without fear, pulling Rhys to the surface. Lila heard a rumble like a freight train and thought she could discern their words, then there was blue light again and Rhys shifted shape. The citrine and gold dragon took flight, carrying Rhys in his talons, and landed gracefully on the back deck of the yacht. Blue light flashed and Lila recognized Balthasar.

She fell on her knees beside Rhys, who was breathing heavily. He wasn't just soaked to the skin but chilled. "I should have learned to swim," he said, his tone rueful and took her hand. He shook his head. "I'm sorry, Lila. I couldn't see him at all. It was like he vanished."

"You tried, though," she said, kissing his cheek. "You tried, even though it was against your own inclination."

He smiled crookedly at her. "Because you asked me to," he said in a soft rumble and Lila's heart clenched tightly.

Did she dare to love him?

When she didn't reply, Rhys offered his hand to Balthasar. "Thanks for that."

"Hey, any time. You might give me a bit of warning, though." They fist-bumped then all three of them returned to the railing and looked across the water. There was no sign of Nereus. The dark surface of the ocean stretched in all directions, and only choppy waves could be seen. In the distance far behind them, Lila could see the glow of Manhattan, already fading from view. There were some lights to the north, perhaps from freighters, but nothing in the seas. The skies were clearer out here and she could see stars between the clouds. There was no snow falling but the wind was icy cold.

"Go warm up," Balthasar said to Rhys. "That wind is bitter."

"Is everything okay on the bridge?" Rhys asked.

"The crew are pretty docile. I think I've got this," Balthasar said, then headed back.

"Are you all right?" Rhys asked as Lila led him toward the cabin Nereus had given her. There were dry clothes there.

She nodded. "Thanks for following me. I didn't realize he was so dangerous."

"Was I right that he charmed you and was trying again?"

Lila nodded again. "I wonder whether he had succeeded a bit. It's forbidden among our kind to try to charm each other. I never even thought he might break that injunction."

"I don't think Nereus believes any rules apply to him." Rhys was emphatic and obviously disapproved of that.

Lila saw that his gaze was still simmering. "Did you come for me or our son?" She had to ask.

Rhys smiled. "Both, but mostly you," he said and she believed it.

"You're just trying to convince me that it's a good idea to keep you around."

He chuckled. "Can't blame me for trying." He peeled off his shirt and shook out his hair. Lila brought him a towel and he rubbed himself down.

"No. And you can't blame me for finding you persuasive, even without the firestorm."

Rhys sobered, clearly surprised.

Lila averted her gaze. "I always thought I liked being alone and self-reliant. I never thought I wanted a bond with anyone, or responsibilities in my life. I certainly didn't want a family. I left the one I had—"

"For the sake of your own survival."

"But I never went back. I told myself that they would be fine." She met Rhys' gaze and saw understanding there. "But I think I didn't want to be tempted. There was something so sweet and comforting about that life, something I did miss, even though I didn't want to admit it."

She took a breath and led him to the cabinet to show him its contents. "When he admitted he'd taken my son, when I saw that Thomas' most prized possession was a trophy, I felt sick and then I was furious." She touched the little bag of treasures and felt her tears rise.

"The bag you told me about," Rhys said quietly, the weight of his hand landing on the back of her waist. "I'm sorry, Lila."

"I am, too." She turned to face him. "I don't know much about being a partner, Rhys, and I know just about nothing about having a family. But I'd like to try to be with you, for more than just the sake of the firestorm."

Rhys was clearly shaken. "If you're going to make my dreams come true, I'll have to try to do the same."

"Is that fair warning?" She smiled at him, liking the sound of that very much.

"I think it is," he agreed. He studied her as if she was the marvel, then bent to kiss her. Lila leaned against him as his mouth closed over hers with that leisurely resolve she was finding very addictive, and she wound her fingers into his hair, drawing him even closer. His kiss turned hungry and he caught her nape in his hand, slanting his mouth across hers to deepen their embrace, and Lila made a low sound of satisfaction.

It turned out that a *Pyr's* kiss wasn't any less persuasive without the spark of the firestorm.

Nereus swam with all his might, fury giving him power. How dare that dragon shifter interfere with his plans for the survival of his kind? Somehow, Nereus would offer him up to the Dark Queen, and make a deal for the selkies. Somehow, he would trap that *Pyr*, using his own nature against him. Somehow he would claim Lila for his own and ensure that her unborn child never saw the light of day.

But first the dragon shifter had to be snared. How? He was powerful. He had Nereus' trident. He was protective of Lila and would probably pursue Nereus all the way to the Isle of the Blessed to finish their battle. The dark mirror was there and offered a portal to deliver the dragon shifter to the Dark Queen, if he could be tempted to approach it, if he could be snared.

Nereus paused for a moment. That token the *Pyr* wore around his neck. He had seen something like it before, in the flotsam and jetsam of drownings and shipwrecks. There was a similar piece in the treasury, Nereus was certain of it.

And if one half was of value to the dragon shifter, the other half would be the perfect bait for a trap.

CHAPTER SIXTEEN

hys was ready to celebrate with Lila in the best possible way, but the sound of knocking interrupted their embrace.

"Lila?" A woman called, her voice muffled. "Lila! Is that you?"

"Up there," Rhys said and they climbed the stairs.

The bridge was at the summit of the ship, with three levels beneath it. Rhys guessed there was at least one more level beneath the waterline with accommodations for staff, supplies and fuel. The dining room, kitchen and the room where Lila had been secured were on the largest level. At the back of the ship on that level was a partly-sheltered patio with a swimming pool.

"Who's that?" Rhys demanded of one of the crew on the next level, who just looked at him blankly. "Who else is on the ship?" The crewmember shook his head, as if bewildered by the question.

"They're all charmed," Lila said. "And they've been charmed for so long that they've forgotten their own will."

The floor above had another smaller deck at the back, a cinema and three more staterooms. Rhys and Lila looked through it quickly, seeking the person who knocked. They climbed the stairs to the third level, which had three smaller staterooms.

Someone was knocking on the inside of the stateroom at the front of the ship.

"Lila!" the woman called and pounded on the door again. "Lila, if that's you, please answer me!"

"Nyssa?"

"Lila!"

The door was locked and solidly constructed.

"His keys," Lila said and Rhys went back to the dining room where Nereus had left the ring of golden keys, leaving Lila talking to Nyssa through the door. They'd fallen to the floor when he'd hit the table, but they were still there, alongside Nereus' trident.

He worked through them on his return to find the one that unlocked the stateroom door. The two selkies embraced, Nyssa almost falling out of the room.

"I was so worried," she said. "He charmed me. I'm sorry, Lila. He was waiting for me when I came out of Bones and said you needed my help, then he locked me in here."

"Come on," Lila said. "Rhys will feed you while you tell us everything." But Nyssa stumbled, too weak to support herself.

Rhys lifted the weakened selkie in his arms and carried her toward the stairs and the dining room.

"He has my skin, Lila!"

Lila stopped and turned, her surprise obvious. "There were two skins," she told Rhys. "He said one was his."

"But it was Nyssa's." Rhys realized then that Nereus would survive.

"He has his skin, then," Lila said. "He won't drown."

"Where will he go?"

"Back to the Isle of the Blessed," Nyssa said with a shake of her head. "He spends his time in the treasury now, trying to figure out what the dragon stole from him. It's a bit of an obsession."

"He can swim that deep?" Lila asked and Nyssa nodded.

"It's some old magick of our kind, he told me. He has it all, so no one can interrupt him there."

Balthasar came down from the bridge then, his gaze sweeping over the trio and lingering on Nyssa. She smiled invitingly at him, despite her apparent exhaustion. "The captain has collapsed," he confided worriedly. "It's like he just fell asleep."

"I'll come and see," Lila said. "He might just have been charmed too long." She hurried up the stairs to the bridge.

Rhys picked up the trident and stood it carefully in the corner, then turned to his fellow *Pyr*. "Can you pilot this ship?" he asked and Balthasar grinned.

"Of course. It practically pilots itself. All the bells and whistles. It's really something." He caught himself, recognizing his own enthusiasm. "I just need to know where you want to go."

"The Isle of the Blessed," Rhys said. "If you can find it. Nereus and I have unfinished business."

Balthasar nodded. "I had a look in the log. This ship consistently returns to a spot in the North Atlantic, just west of the British Isles. That's pretty much the location of the Anton Dhorn Seamount."

"The Isle of the Blessed," Rhys said and Balthasar nodded.

"I'm thinking so."

"Maybe we can get there before Nereus and surprise him."

Balthasar shook his head. "But even if we do, it's too deep, Rhys. The top of the seamount is about five hundred meters below the surface. You can only go that deep with a submersible and that's one thing this yacht doesn't have."

Rhys indicated the trident. "But Nereus was in such a hurry that he forgot his trident."

"Why does that matter?" Nyssa asked.

"I wonder whether he'll come back for it," Balthasar said.

But Rhys was thinking of Lila's comments about his family legacy. "And I'm wondering whether it might work for anyone other than the King Under the Seas." He spared Balthasar a glance. "How far does that seamount have to rise for us to be able to dive to it?"

Balthasar shrugged. "A lot. You can dive to thirty-nine meters, but twenty would be better. Your air doesn't last long on deeper dives."

Rhys spun the trident so its tines caught the light. "Then I have work to do. How long until we get there?"

"I'll figure it out and let you know."

Rhys hoped it would be a few days. He wasn't at all sure how easy it would be to start an earthquake, let alone one in a specific location to create a specific result.

He had to give it all he had, though, for the sake of his and Lila's son.

Balthasar calculated that it would take a week for the yacht to cross the Atlantic at full power. It would burn more fuel that way, but there was more than enough. Since they didn't know what to expect as Nereus' charms wore off, they secured the crew members in their lodgings. Nyssa worked with them, encouraging their recovery, and Lila helped with the healing, too. There was a lot of food aboard, and plenty of gear. Balthasar instructed Rhys in diving technique, when he could use the yacht's autopilot, and each night they all ate together as they planned. They were in unanimous agreement that since Nereus did have his skin, his destination would be the sunken Isle of the Blessed. Lila and Nyssa worked together on a map of it and the palace, based on stories they'd heard. They were pretty sure about the location of the treasury in the palace, and that the dark mirror would be there.

Thorolf and Chandra arrived on the third day after Nereus' dive into the sea. The large moonstone and silver dragon appeared in the skies overhead just after lunch. Even Lila could hear Thorolf cursing as he targeted the back deck of the yacht. It was generously proportioned for humans, but made a comparatively small target for a dragon landing.

"Stay out of the pool," Rhys teased. "You'll empty it."

"I'm trying to stay out of the ocean," Thorolf retorted. Lila saw that he was carrying a woman and a boy. The boy was obviously enjoying the dragon ride and the woman looked resigned to it. "Here goes nothing!"

He dove down, shifting shape in the last minute just before his feet touched the deck. The boy raised his hands and hooted like he was on a roller coaster. The deck was slick with moisture so instead of nailing a perfect landing, Thorolf's boots slipped and he fell hard, sliding across the deck on his hip to collide with the wall. He folded himself around the boy to protect him from injury and Lila assumed it was his son. The woman had jumped from his embrace just before and stood shaking her head even as she smiled at him.

Thorolf's partner and mate, Chandra, was almost as tall as her *Pyr*, with ebony hair that was wound into dozens of braids that wrapped around her head. She was lean and muscled, with a watchfulness that made Lila think she was a strong warrior, too. Their son was five or six years old, and particularly tall, with his father's blue eyes and blond hair.

"To think I surrendered immortality for this kind of travel," Chandra said lightly and Thorolf grinned, untroubled.

Lila was startled by her words. She had been immortal?

"You have no regrets, Chandra, and I know it," Thorolf countered as he got to his feet. "We live each day to the fullest, and that's as good as it gets." He went to her side and touched her belly. "How's the hitchhiker?"

"Used to a little jostling, fortunately, given his father's habits," Chandra said with a smile. "He's fine."

So, she was his mate and expecting another son.

Rhys stepped forward to shake hands with Thorolf. "Thanks for coming. I didn't expect it, since neither of us are big swimmers."

"Hey, I had to see the super yacht." He surveyed the ship with open appreciation. "This boat seriously rocks."

"I'm not sure we have enough provisions," Rhys teased and Thorolf laughed.

"Are you kidding me? I'm not going hungry after that flight." Thorolf poked Rhys. "I was counting on you, dude."

"And you won't be disappointed. Lila, this is Thorolf's mate, Chandra, and their son, Raynor," Rhys said. The woman stepped forward with a warm smile and shook Lila's hand. She gave her son a stern look, distracting him from staring at the yacht like his dad, and the blond boy came forward. She guessed that he was about four years old.

He shook Lila's hand solemnly. "Are you the mate?" he asked. "Was it Rhys' firestorm?"

"It was," Lila said, struck that Raynor was about the same age as Thomas had been when she'd last seen him. She felt that ache of loss again, and knew that leaving her family was a mistake she wouldn't make again.

She wouldn't have to leave them to save herself, not when she was with Rhys.

"Is everyone still at Kristofer's place?" Rhys asked, but Thorolf shook his head.

"You know that Rafferty and Melissa were already heading back to the UK. Now there's something going on with the Seven Thieves that he wants to check out. Donovan called him." Thorolf shrugged. "Then Erik went back to Chicago. Eileen had the heebie-jeebies about something, but it turned out to be no big deal."

"Nothing wrong with wanting your dragon shifter around when things are changing," Chandra said calmly and the others nodded.

"So, Kristofer and Bree are there alone for the moment. Sloane and Sam are on their way from California, and Brandon and Liz are coming from Australia, too." He nodded at Lila. "Liz is a marine biologist, too. She wants to compare notes."

Lila was surprised. "What's her name?"

"Dr. Elizabeth Barrett," Thorolf said in a posh accent, then grinned.

"I know of her," Lila said with delight. "But her work is in more tropical seas, particularly around Hawaii." It was amazing to her that association with the *Pyr* could also improve her professional contacts.

"She's a Firedaughter," Thorolf said, then demanded a tour. "Hey, Balthasar!" he shouted. "I want to drive!" He took Raynor by the hand, the boy as wide-eyed as he was, and Rhys grinned as he led the way.

Lila watched them go, considering the brilliant gold of Thorolf's aura.

Chandra's aura was filled with subtle shadings and seemed to be changing all the time, but it was radiant as well. When she realized the other woman was watching her, she had to ask. "Did you really surrender immortality for your firestorm?"

"There was so much at stake," Chandra said with a nod. "The choice had to be made because I didn't want to imagine a world without Thorolf." She surveyed Lila and smiled. "You're an immortal, too? How old are you?"

"About two thousand years, give or take." She eyed the other woman. "You?"

"I don't remember not being," Chandra admitted.

"Have we met?"

"I might not have been in this guise if we did," Chandra said, obviously amused. "And I might not remember if we did."

"Why not?"

"Because I was divine as well as immortal." Lila knew her surprise showed, but Chandra was philosophical. "Demeter, Diana, Isis, Freya." She shrugged. "Many skins, many shapes, many years."

"Don't you miss it?"

Chandra shook her head. "Time blended together when I was immortal and lost much of its meaning. This way, each day is precious, each hour and each moment. I'm more invested in my life, which sounds strange, but it's true. I treasure life for the gift it is. Everything is so much more vivid, and relationships are both stronger and more potent." Her smile widened slightly. "I don't regret my choice. Mortal life has been a thousand times more rewarding than I ever imagined it might be."

Lila nodded, her thoughts swirling. "Let's find you a stateroom that you like," she suggested. "There are a few choices."

Would she give up her immortality for Rhys? Lila hadn't considered the possibility before, though she was concerned that Maeve would demand some sacrifice from her.

Could she bear to make a partnership with Rhys, knowing that ultimately he'd die and she'd be left behind? If she was immortal, that day would come.

It was already hard to imagine her life without this particular dragon shifter.

They were eating that night without Balthasar when Thorolf pushed away his empty plate. They'd entered an area where icebergs flowed south and it was foggy. Balthasar had chosen to stay on the bridge, making sure their path was clear. He'd slowed the yacht, too, and the engines seemed to throb.

"This might be a dumb question," Thorolf said. "But why did that vampire dude—"

"Sebastian," Rhys said.

"Sebastian," Thorolf said, then cocked a finger at Lila's necklace. "Why did he call that a hag stone?"

"Because that's what it is," Lila said. The others looked at her. She shrugged. "That's what people in Scotland and Ireland call stones like this. Hag stones or witch's stones." She heard her tone change, as if she was giving a lecture. "There's an old belief that stones with a natural hole like this were coveted by witches."

"Why?" Thorolf asked.

"They used them to see the Fae," Lila replied. "It's just a silly superstition..." She fell silent, realizing what she'd just said. She looked down at the stone, wondering whether it was just her imagination that it had a faint red glow about it.

"Eithne did put magick into it," Rhys reminded her, as if he'd had the same thought.

Lila took off the necklace and removed the lace. She held the stone between her thumb and forefinger and looked through it. At first glance, the dining room looked the same, and so did everyone in it, but then she noticed some flickers of blue-green light. All were aligned in the same direction and moving toward the front of the yacht. They reminded her of iron filings in a lab experiment, relentlessly drawn to a magnet.

"What do you see?" Rhys asked.

"I don't know. Light." She gave him the stone and he looked, then caught his breath.

"Is that darkfire?" he asked, passing the stone to Thorolf.

The big *Pyr* looked through the stone, first with one eye, then with the other. "Oh yeah," he said with obvious trepidation. "And it looks like it's going somewhere. Darkfire with a plan. Why doesn't that sound like good news?" He surveyed the dining room, obviously not expecting an answer, and Lila felt chilled. "Is there a way we can talk to Rafferty? My phone has been a paperweight since we got here."

"We're well beyond any cellphone service," Rhys said. "Balthasar might manage something with the satellite phone, but I'd rather he kept his attention on those icebergs."

"No *Titanic* jokes," Thorolf said in agreement.

Rhys stood up and went to pick up the trident, still leaning in the corner. "What if we could solve this ourselves?"

"How so?"

"Do you remember how to sing to the earth?"

"I've helped before." Thorolf grinned. "Think of me as back-up, not as a lead singer. You start and I'll chime in."

"All right then," Rhys said. "Let's see what we can do."

Rhys sang all that night and all the next day. His chant was low and persuasive, filled with power. It started a resonance within the yacht itself, the metal of the structure and the stone of the decor vibrating in response to his call. Lila understood that he called to the element of earth, cajoling it to do his will.

He used the trident, but sparingly, and only tapped it gently on the floor. Thorolf sang with him, matching his chant, and they sang until they were hoarse and exhausted.

Lila did her best to heal them, but Thorolf insisted she help Rhys first.

"It's his rodeo," the big *Pyr* said. "He's the one who needs his strength."

Rhys slept as Lila exuded her healing powers, while Chandra and Nyssa cooked dinner for them. When they gathered again to eat, Lila asked about Rhys' strategy. "You could prompt a quicker reaction if the trident works for you," she said.

"But a violent earthquake will have a big effect," he said. "There would be tidal waves in Ireland and Scotland, at the very least. And on Balthasar's charts, it's clear that the seamount is a volcanic plug. I don't want to start an eruption or a shifting of the continental plates." He nodded and finished his meal. "Slow and steady is the way. It'll still be pretty fast and disruptive to some sea life."

"It's too bad that my second affinity is to air and Balthasar's is to water," Thorolf said. "You could have used some help with earth."

"We'll do what we can." Rhys nodded at Thorolf and they began to sing again.

By morning, new waves rocked the yacht and Balthasar brought news of a disturbance on the ocean floor. They barely took a break for dinner that day and sang long into the night. Rhys' voice was husky and the waves were getting bigger. Raynor became seasick, but his father continued to sing with Rhys.

Lila looked through the hag stone and saw that the glimmers of blue light had changed direction. They were moving toward Rhys, as if he'd become the main attraction. She showed him when he took his break, then breathed her healing mist as he slept.

The next day, he shifted to his dragon form before he sang. The chant wasn't any louder but it was more insistent. The waves grew bigger and began to splash over the rails. The yacht rocked as the two *Pyr* chanted together and they sang as evening fell.

When the sky was dark and the stars were coming out, Lila felt as if they stood on the cusp of something. The two *Pyr* sang, then Rhys tapped the silver trident on the deck. Lila saw a little spark of blue-green fire, then the song changed slightly. The light burned brighter and crackled as it converged on the trident, and the trident itself seemed to burn with blue-green fire. Chandra and Nyssa stood beside Lila and watched. Lila felt the crackle of static electricity and the shimmer of the darkfire stirring in the air. The tension rose as they sang more loudly, then there was a brilliant flash of blue-green light.

The yacht heaved. The ocean roared. The power flickered on the yacht and Lila had a profound sense that something had changed.

Rhys was so exhausted after he shifted shape that he staggered to a chair and fell into it. He was pale and there was perspiration on his brow. "It's coming," he said with satisfaction, then opened his eyes and smiled at Lila. "It's done."

They ate and he almost fell asleep at the table despite the storm that heaved the ship. The waves crashed over them and the world seemed to heave on all sides, but Rhys slept on. Lila breathed her healing mist over him all night long, watching his aura brighten with every passing moment, and hoped they might succeed.

Earthquakes. Sunken palaces with full treasuries. A Dark Queen and an ancient dragon locked in a battle for supremacy—and the *Pyr* caught right in the middle. It was like old times, to Thorolf's thinking, and he wished there could just be a good fight to square everything away. He was ready to get his feet on solid earth again, especially after the tumult Rhys had created.

The sun rose on a sparkling clear day and he went to the bridge. Balthasar said they were getting close and showed off the charts with enthusiasm. Thorolf spotted Chandra on the deck below with Raynor and she pointed to the sky.

A white bird flew ahead of them, then circled over a spot in the ocean.

"An albatross?" Balthasar asked.

Thorolf shrugged. "Whatever it is, I think it's Snow. Is that the spot?" He pointed to where the bird was circling.

"Pretty much." Balthasar turned off the engines and the yacht slowed in the water. Lila and Rhys joined Chandra at the rail, catching their breath in unison as the yacht drifted over white spires in the water below.

"The palace of the Isle of the Blessed," Lila said with wonder.

"Damn," Thorolf said.

"You did it!" Balthasar exclaimed and thumped him on the back.

"Rhys did it." Thorolf counted twelve spires, arranged in a circle. He thought there was a broken one, too. There was a dome in the middle, but it was deep beneath the surface.

"You did it!" Lila cried and kissed Rhys. He kissed her back, swinging her around in front of everyone. Thorolf bounded down the stairs to join the others, Balthasar following more slowly.

"This is the part I haven't been looking forward to," Rhys admitted, glancing down at the palace. He squeezed Lila's hand.

"Better you than me," Thorolf said, knowing that neither one of them was a strong swimmer. "I'll stay here and keep watch over the yacht."

"And I'll monitor your dive," Balthasar said.

"We'll finish what we've started," Rhys said. "That dark mirror must hold the key." He looked at Lila and she nodded agreement.

"We'll do what has to be done," she said and he hugged her again.

"Nothing like teamwork," Thorolf said.

Balthasar had brought the diving gear for Rhys and helped him to suit up, reminding him of his instruction. Lila and Nyssa had retrieved their skins to dive with him.

"I'm coming with you," Nyssa had said earlier. "I've listened to Nereus a lot more. I should be able to help you find the dark mirror more quickly."

"Won't it be obvious?" Thorolf asked. "In prime position in the hoard?"

Nyssa had shaken her head. "The treasury was stacked with riches when the island sank, then there's all the additions Nereus has made from shipwrecks over the centuries. I expect it's a chaotic mess."

"So, the plan," Thorolf said, making Rhys go through it again.

Rhys ticked off the steps on his fingers. "We dive to the treasury. We find the dark mirror. We try to go through it to Fae. If we manage that, we save Theo and Arach. If not, we come back here and make another plan."

"We need to try to find the portal near Westray, too," Lila said.

"First things first."

"And Nereus?" Nyssa asked.

"When you find him, kick his ass," Thorolf concluded and Rhys laughed. They checked their watches, checked Rhys' oxygen and weights, reviewed their signals, then dove.

Thorolf strained his eyes to follow the dark figure of Rhys for as long as he could, his frustration rising when he lost sight of his fellow *Pyr*. He had a bad feeling, but acknowledged that it could just be because he didn't like being on a yacht in the middle of nowhere.

A shadow suddenly crossed in front of the sun. Thorolf looked up to see an enormous black dragon in the sky.

"Embron," Balthasar whispered, then the dragon prince dove into the sea far to their left and vanished from sight.

His arrival couldn't be a coincidence.

How would a dragon defend himself underwater, where he couldn't breathe fire?

They couldn't even warn Rhys.

"This is so not good," Thorolf whispered, peering into the sea. "Is there another wetsuit?"

"Yes, but you don't know how to dive." Balthasar was already shrugging into a wetsuit. "Stay here and keep your eyes open." He buckled on his weights, checked his oxygen, gave Thorolf a thumbs-up that seemed overly optimistic, then dove.

He disappeared into the silvery water and the vigil began.

"I suck at waiting," Thorolf told Chandra.

"I know," she said and slid her hand into his. "Don't worry. I think you'll have a chance to kick butt before this is over."

Thorolf could only hope for the best.

In a way, the dive was wonderful. The water was brighter than Rhys had expected, and he was surrounded by shades of silver, grey and green. It was quiet, like they visited another world, and their movements were slow, like they danced. He descended steadily, timing his dive the way Balthasar had instructed him, the two selkies circling around him with playful enthusiasm. They'd both changed to their seal form and he could only tell them apart by the marks on their skins. He couldn't feel the same joy at being in the water as they obviously did, but he tried to appreciate it.

His heart was pounding a little faster than it should, but he slowed its pace. He tried to eliminate his fear by looking around. Far below them was the roof of a palace made of white stone. The domed roof of the treasury glowed and he couldn't really tell how far away it was. There were spires around it, twelve tall thin towers with windows. As he descended past the tallest one, a school of small fish swam though one window and out the opposite one. Long ribbons of dark green seaweed waved from the towers like banners, and he could see anemones growing on the tower sides, like flowers. The deeper they went, the more life they saw, and Rhys stopped in wonder to watch a school of dolphins swim by.

Lila nudged his hand and gestured toward the treasury. Rhys checked his watch and descended another twenty feet to follow her.

By the time they were at the treasury door, he was feeling more at ease. It was the deepest point of their dive and he remembered all of Balthasar's instructions about timing his oxygen. Lila ducked through the treasury door with a flick of her tail, Nyssa right behind her. Rhys avoided a moray eel keeping guard over the opening, then followed them inside.

It was darker in the treasury, but he could see that Nyssa had been right. There were stacks of loot on all sides—if he'd been standing, the piles would have been shoulder-high. It was all covered with a coating of algae and debris, but when Rhys waved a hand over one pile, a bowl full of glittering gold coins was revealed. He saw pearls and he saw chalices. There were chests with jewelry spilling from them and silver coins everywhere.

Divers would have a field day with this ruin.

But they had to find the dark mirror. The two selkies cleared debris with their flippers and tails, as Rhys used his gloved hands. The water was soon frustratingly filled with floating debris and it was hard to see. Rhys was aware of the press of time and checked his watch repeatedly.

Then he saw the other half of the crucifix he wore. He stared and it caught the light, as if to summon him closer. Rhys nearly missed it, then he could only gape at it. Was he mistaken? Was he dreaming? Had Llewelyn's half of their mother's crucifix ended up here?

It wasn't out of the question, if Gwendolyn had walked into the sea wearing it or holding it. Nyssa had said that Nereus collected treasures from shipwrecks and drowned corpses: who knew how far he went to hunt? Who knew how the currents flowed? Not Rhys.

He looked around but couldn't see either Lila or Nyssa. There was a cloud of muck rising from the other side of the treasury and he assumed that they had found something of interest. The half-crucifix was in a crevasse, as if there was a hole in the floor of the treasury or a crypt beneath it, as if it had fallen through. It would only take him a second to retrieve it, and he didn't want to leave without it. He wasn't thrilled about reaching into that dark hole, either, but he wanted the rest of his mother's gem.

Rhys turned again but still couldn't see Lila. It was against everything Balthasar had taught him, but he thought it worth taking the chance.

He dove, then learned he was wrong.

No sooner had he ducked through the gap into the crevasse than the pile of treasure shifted. It cascaded down behind him, filling the gap, moving with relentless persistence. Rhys seized the gem, tucking it into the pouch at his belt, then turned to stop the cascading treasure. He thought it was only coins and gems, but there were trunks, as well, too many of them for him to stop the avalanche.

He was being buried alive, and no one knew where he was!

"Lila!" he shouted to her in old-speak, hoping she'd hear, but there was no reply. He pushed aside the falling treasure, but there was only more of it cascading down upon him.

Rhys caught the barest glimpse of a hand before his mask was tugged away. He couldn't see for a moment, but he felt that hand grab his respirator. He struggled against his assailant, and spun to see it was Nereus. They were locked together, each trying to control Rhys' respirator when Nereus seized the knife from Rhys' belt and cut the hose. The air bubbled toward the surface with alarming speed.

"Good bye, dragon," he said, eyes glinting with triumph. The King Under the Seas shifted shape in a shimmer of blue, becoming a large sea lion, then turned to dive through a gap that Rhys hadn't seen before. Rhys tried to follow but it was narrow: Nereus slipped through it like a fish but Rhys couldn't make it with his tanks.

On the other hand, they weren't much good to him now. He spit out his respirator, held his breath and grabbed his own dagger, which Nereus had abandoned. He swam hard after Nereus, fearing he wasn't going to make it.

He'd do one last favor for the world, Lila and their son, even if it took his dying breath.

Nyssa had found the dark mirror with only a bit of searching. Lila knew it would have taken her a lot longer to find it, and they needed every minute. The mirror had been buried in rock and treasure, only the top of the frame revealed, and they worked together to clear it.

It took far too long. Lila silently cursed the fact that the mirror was so big. It had to be five feet in diameter, with an elaborate frame. There were anemones by the dozen growing on the frame, but fortunately the surface of the mirror itself was clear.

There was something about it that made her shiver and she avoided looking at its surface. Then she heard Rhys call her name.

She spun, wondering where he was. Nyssa looked at her with alarm and confusion.

"Good bye, dragon." Nereus' voice was the last thing she wanted to hear.

Lila saw the stream of rising bubbles and guessed what had happened, although she couldn't see Rhys. The treasure was shifting and tumbling on the far side of the treasury. Judging by the clouding of the water, that had been happening for a few minutes, but she'd been so fixed on the mirror that she hadn't noticed.

Nyssa gave her a nudge, then swept at the remaining debris with her tail.

Lila understood. She saw Nereus swim out the door of the treasury in his selkie form and swam after him. Rhys shot out of the debris in pursuit of Nereus and caught one of his tail fins.

He didn't have his tanks anymore!

Nereus spun and thrashed, hitting Rhys with his tail hard. Rhys ducked the blow, then slashed at the selkie with ferocious power. Nereus moved in the last minute but the blade found home all the same. A red trail of blood drifted into the water from Nereus' tail. He spun with fury and bit Rhys hard, his teeth tearing through the wetsuit and burying in Rhys' arm. Rhys struggled and Nereus held tightly, even as more blood flowed into the water.

Lila knew they had to move away before predators were drawn to the blood. Rhys shifted shape, though, slashing at Nereus with his dragon claws. Nereus snapped and bit, then shifted shape himself, taking his human form again. The water was bright with the blue shimmer of their changes. Nereus seized the dagger and stabbed at Rhys, tearing a scale loose from Rhys' chest. Blood flowed crimson and mingled in the water. Rhys grabbed Nereus, squeezing him tightly in his dragon claws, then letting his talons dig into the trapped selkie.

Rhys had to be running out of air, but he held on, squeezing Nereus until the King Under the Seas went limp.

Rhys shifted back to his human form in a brilliant shimmer of light, then went limp himself. Nereus flicked his tail and swam away slowly, as if in great pain. The water was full of blood and Lila saw the silhouette of the approaching sharks. She seized Rhys, shifted shape and gave him a breath of air. She felt him stir in her embrace. She assessed the distance to the surface and the speed of the approaching predators and knew they didn't have a choice.

If she didn't take Rhys into Fae, he'd die and Lila couldn't let that happen. She dragged him back to the dark mirror.

Nyssa moved away, revealing that the surface of the dark mirror was completely exposed. Its surface shone like obsidian, glinting as if it would warn them of the perils of entering Fae. Lila knew them all. She'd been afraid of the Dark Queen's kingdom for as long as she could remember, but Rhys needed a chance to survive. She pulled him closer without dwelling on her fears. As soon as she touched the surface, the dark mirror flashed silver. It seemed to ripple, then inhale, because it sucked them in.

She had a sense of a dark wind behind them, as if something or someone followed, then saw a blinding flash of red light.

She and Rhys landed hard on dry earth, both back in their human forms. There was no sign of Nyssa or the treasury of the palace. There was no one else behind them.

They were in the middle of an arena, with sand beneath them. The crowd filling the stands cheered at their appearance. Lila ignored them. She pumped the water out of Rhys' lungs, seeing that his aura was faltering. She breathed healing mist at him and pleaded with him to survive.

To her relief, he coughed and sat up, wincing at the wound on his chest. Lila tried to speak to him, but no words came from her lips.

There was a red string on her wrist.

There was a red string on Rhys' wrist.

She met his gaze in fear as the crowd roared.

"Welcome to Fae," he said, his tone rueful even in old-speak, but Lila had no ability to reply. A dragon bellowed and she turned to see a carnelian and gold dragon breathing fire as he lunged forward to attack. He had multiple small wounds, all of which were bleeding.

Another dragon, aquamarine and silver, bounded to defend them. His injuries were more extensive. Both dragons had red cords around their ankles.

"Theo," Rhys whispered, glancing at the carnelian dragon. "And

Arach."

Lila realized the two *Pyr* were engaged in mortal combat for the entertainment of the Fae, undoubtedly against their will. A woman in a cage at the perimeter of the arena shouted at Theo to stop but the Dark Queen herself, seated on her throne, clapped her hands as she laughed.

Rhys stood up and Lila knew he was trying to shift shape. There wasn't even a faint shimmer of blue, courtesy of Maeve's spell.

"Now things become interesting," the Dark Queen said with glee. "I never watched the elimination of my prey before. I should do this more often." She waved a hand. "Carry on with the carnage."

Theo roared and opened his mouth to breathe fire at Rhys and Lila. Lila closed her eyes, bracing for the worst, but Rhys straightened and turned to Maeve.

"Let's make a deal," he said, to the astonishment of everyone.

CHAPTER SEVENTEEN

Nyssa saw Nereus drop something as he swam frantically away from the sunken palace. Blood trailed behind him in a crimson ribbon and predators were circling. Nereus was obviously trying to make it into the palace itself, and she assumed he could barricade himself in the throne room. How long could he survive there?

She wasn't going to wait and see. She swam down and scooped up the sparkling item that he'd dropped. It was garnet red with gold and shaped like a large scale. It was exactly the same color as Rhys' dragon scales and she sensed that it was important. She picked it up in her mouth, then swam hard toward the surface. Three sharks brushed past her, their eyes and teeth gleaming. Her heart nearly stopped but they swam lower with sinister purpose, following the trail of blood.

Nyssa swam harder, straining to reach the yacht in time. She shifted as she broke the surface of the ocean near the yacht and Thorolf cast her a line. He helped to pull her aboard, working so quickly that she knew he'd seen the cloud of blood.

The sea churned just when she stepped aboard and Chandra brought her a big towel. They all looked as the water boiled, a tide of red blood rising to the surface. Nyssa turned away, then saw Thorolf and Balthasar's expressions.

"It must be Nereus," she said. "He was injured when he tried to kill Rhys."

"And Rhys?" Thorolf asked.

"And Lila?" Chandra asked.

Nyssa shook her head. "They went through the dark mirror to Fae." She shivered and looked at the water again. Then she remembered the scale. She showed it to the Pyr and couldn't miss their dismay. "Is this important?"

"Rhys has lost a scale," Thorolf said grimly.

"It means he has a gap in his armor and is vulnerable," Balthasar said.

"It means he's in love," Chandra added firmly.

But in Fae. Nyssa swallowed.

"We'll wait here, in case they need us," Balthasar said. "Maybe there's still a portal here, or maybe someone will open one."

Nyssa hated that there wasn't much else they could do.

It was perfectly simple, to Rhys' thinking. Lila carried his son and the promise of the firestorm had to be defended as diligently as his mate. He was aware of her fear: once again, she was silenced and unable to change form to defend herself. She'd been afraid of Fae as long as he'd known her, and yet she'd brought him through the portal to save his life. Rhys took that as proof that she was becoming persuaded of the merit of a longer relationship.

He couldn't shift, but he could talk. They'd solve this together.

He certainly wasn't going to be compelled to dance in this place again, not if he could help it. Nereus had tugged a scale free from his armor, but it had fallen with the barest touch. Rhys understood. He loved Lila and now he'd show her—and everyone else—what that meant.

It might make all the difference in the world to her.

The royal box was crowded. In the middle sat Maeve on a large silver and red throne, the gem of the hoard gleaming gold in her left hand. Her precious book was on her lap and a red glow of magick emanated from both the book and the orb. The bartender from Bones was seated at her left hand and looked unhappy about it. Sylvia was seated on Maeve's right hand and didn't look significantly more pleased than the bartender. There were two guards standing slightly behind the Dark Queen's throne: Rhys recognized the one behind Mel as being the warrior who had seized the book in his restaurant. The other wore a helmet so his face was hidden. They stood at attention, crossbows loaded and daggers gleaming in their belts. He wasn't truly surprised to notice Kade seated with the spectators near the royal box, much less to notice that *Pyr's* displeasure. Whatever he'd gotten—or not gotten—for betraying his fellow shifters was his to enjoy forever, as far as Rhys was concerned.

The arena was large and round, with sand beneath their feet and a high wall around the perimeter. The seating for spectators rose beyond that in rows and it looked as if every seat was filled. The crowd was all Fae, their wings sparkling as they drank and ate and gossiped. It was dark overhead, although he couldn't tell if the sky was starless or there was a high roof. The air was filled with red fireflies that had to be magick on the loose, and there was dragon blood in the sand. Evidently, Arach and Theo had been intended to fight to the death and his sudden arrival with Lila had interrupted that. Rhys noted more Fae warriors placed at intervals around the perimeter of the arena, their weapons loaded and ready.

It would take a miracle to get out of Fae alive.

Rhys faced Maeve to make his appeal, Lila's hand in his own. Against every instinct, he turned his back on Theo, who was prowling closer. There was something wrong with his old friend because Theo's eyes were snapping with bloodlust and Arach had considerable wounds. They'd fought, which made no sense. It had to be because of Maeve's spell. Somehow, Theo's intentions had been affected. Rhys hoped Maeve found his suggestion compelling and did so in a hurry.

Maeve, seated on her throne, eyed Rhys for a long moment, then held up her hand. He felt Theo stop, felt the fan of Theo's dragon breath behind him, but didn't dare to be relieved. "A deal?" she asked. "What do you have to offer?" Her tone hinted that he had nothing to tempt her, but Rhys thought otherwise.

"I'll trade you my life for the safe release of my mate," he said and heard Lila catch her breath. He tightened his grip on her hand and nodded at the book on Maeve's lap. "You'll be able to draw a line through my name in your book and move one step closer to eliminating the *Pyr*. It's an easy victory for you."

The Dark Queen was skeptical. "And you'd make this sacrifice, just for the selkie to leave Fae?"

Rhys nodded.

"There's nothing to stop me from hunting her and killing her later," Maeve noted.

Rhys remembered an old story. "If you're going to agree to let Lila leave Fae, there has to be a time of safety for her. I like a year and a day. I thought the Fae did, too."

He felt a nudge in his thoughts and grimaced as something moved through his mind like a bulldozer. He stayed on his feet only with a considerable effort, feeling sweat bead his brow, and staggered a little when Maeve abandoned her search. Lila watched him, her concern clear.

"You actually mean it," Maeve said with some surprise. "You really would trade your life for hers."

Rhys bowed his head.

The Dark Queen smiled and he had a moment to fear what she would do. "Then I agree," she said and lifted the gem of the hoard before herself, cupping it in both hands. She stood and the red light swirled from the globe with renewed frenzy. Silver static spun around it as Maeve murmured, her words lost in the crackle of the mustering magick. She flung out a hand, casting the spell toward him and Lila clutched his hand tightly.

Rhys held his ground and watched the magick hurtle toward him. He only hoped it killed him quickly.

"I love you," he said to Lila in old-speak and felt her fingers tighten on his hand in acknowledgement.

The magick struck Rhys right in the half-crucifix that he wore on a chain around his neck. It felt like an explosion in his soul. It set his dragon tattoo afire so that sparks flew from it, then jolted Rhys' heart hard. He was shaken to his marrow and his body shifted shape of its own accord.

Rhys loved her.

Rhys surrendered his life for her and their son. Lila couldn't believe the magnitude of his sacrifice. There was nothing she could do as he made his wager. She couldn't protest. She couldn't argue with him. She knew Maeve could hear her thoughts but Rhys couldn't—and she couldn't even use the speech of her kind. It was a special kind of torment to be compelled to watch as he threw his life away.

But it was a thousand times worse when the magick struck and he suddenly shimmered blue. He shifted shape, which she knew hadn't been his plan, taking his dragon form in a heartbeat. She was abruptly holding his front claw instead of his hand and his dragon form towered over her.

The crowd roared approval of this spectacle. She remembered his comments about Hadrian and wondered whether he'd rotate between forms, then realized that instead of having garnet and gold scales that caught the light, Rhys was grey. He was utterly motionless.

He'd been turned to stone.

"You're free to go, selkie-girl," Maeve said and lounged upon her throne again, her gaze knowing. "I don't break my promises, after all. I'll catch up with you in a year and a day."

The way the Dark Queen smirked wasn't reassuring. How would Lila hide or defend her son? How would she protect herself? The Fae who were gathered to watch the events in the arena laughed and jostled each other in the stands. Some threw things at Rhys, wilted flowers, gloves and shoes. He didn't respond.

He couldn't respond.

Lila surveyed the perimeter of the arena and couldn't see a door. *"How do I leave?"* she thought and Maeve laughed.

"Oh, you want to leave Fae completely. I thought you just wanted to leave the arena and would spend your year and a day here, amongst us. Of course, that might mean the passing of decades or more in the realm you know better." The Dark Queen leaned forward, eyes shining. "You willingly entered Fae twice. That has nothing to do with your dragon lover's wager. You can't leave Fae until you pay the price. I welcome your suggestions."

The spectators laughed at this, their laughter shrill and annoying.

What could she give? Rhys had surrendered his life for their son. Lila couldn't make the same offer without betraying his trust and condemning their child, but there were two things she could give away.

"I surrender my ability to shift shape," she thought and Maeve nodded approval.

"That would mean you're no longer a selkie, so I'd be able to update my list again. I like that. I'll take it." Maeve opened the book in question and flipped through the pages. Sylvia watched the Dark Queen's movements, her lips drawn to a tight line. "I really should think about allying with the *Pyr*," Maeve mused. "They're doing such an excellent job of promoting my agenda. One less *Pyr*, one less selkie, and no more Valkyries. Imagine if they were following my command." She didn't seem to expect an answer to that but drew a line and made a notation. Lila was certain that she was striking Rhys from her list. "Surrender your skin."

Lila offered it and it was vaporized before her eyes. The sight weakened her knees, then it infuriated her. Maeve would change the entire world to suit herself and cared nothing for the consequences.

"What else?" Maeve demanded. "Make it good."

Oh, Lila would make it good. She recalled Chandra's words and knew the *Pyr* would help her with Rhys' son. She hoped their son looked just a little bit like his father, and she knew he would have the same sense of honor.

She loved Rhys, and that made everything simple.

"I surrender my immortality," she said and there was a stir of agitation in the stands. Maeve looked surprised and one of the guards beside her appeared to be astonished. Wings and feathers rustled and flapped in the stands as the Fae whispered and twittered about this choice. They seemed to be horrified.

Maeve smiled and set the book aside. She picked up the gem of the hoard, cradling it in her hands again. "Granted," she said and her voice boomed over the entire arena.

She took a deep breath and blew on the gem of the hoard, sending a thousand silver sparks toward Lila. They looked almost like the seeds of a dandelion flower caught in the wind. They swirled around Lila though, obscuring the arena from view. They collided with her skin like little pricks of ice and she felt the chill of mortality slip through her body. She shivered from head to toe.

It was done.

To her surprise, the red string on her wrist sizzled and disappeared, leaving a burn mark on her skin. How could that be? She saw a shimmer of blue light from behind her and looked back as Arach shifted to his human form. The other dragon, the carnelian one who Rhys had called Theo, also shifted shape. He staggered a little, as if he'd been released from a terrible burden, and Arach went to his side to support him. Neither of them had red strings bound on their wrists anymore.

What was going on?

What was happening to Maeve's magick?

Lila looked back to the throne to see the dark-haired woman who had been seated beside Maeve on her feet. She looked thrilled and frightened, her hands raised to her mouth. She still had a red string on her wrist, though. Sylvia looked wary, and all of the Fae were alarmed.

A sound carried to Lila's ears then, like a chant, one that made the ground vibrate beneath her feet and sent shivers over her flesh.

Maeve was on her feet, her brow as dark as thunder. The stone statue of Rhys began to shudder and Lila saw cracks appear in its surface. Lila was afraid he would crumble to dust and wasn't sure she could bear the sight.

"No!" Maeve screamed as there was an ominous crack overhead.

"Oh yes," a man said softly from the opposite end of the arena.

Lila turned to look with everyone else. Embron in his human form stood opposite Maeve, a space all around him. He held a crystal orb in one hand, one filled with red light. His smile was as terrifying as it had been in that basement and he held out the globe before himself. It was his spell they'd heard and he began to sing again. His gaze was fixed on Maeve and Lila saw the red magick abandoning the gem of the hoard for Embron's crystal.

It was like the crimson tide receding, or a scarlet curtain being drawn back to reveal the truth. As the edge of the tide moved, the Fae changed appearance, like they were abandoned by a flattering light. Instead of being dressed in red and silver, instead of sparkling and glittering with Fae beauty, they became twisted and bent, brown and black and deepest green. They looked like the dead, found at the bottom of the sea or deep in the woods, gruesome and horrible.

When the line of red light reached the statue of Rhys in his dragon form, the stone crumbled. Lila cried out but in the rubble, she spotted Rhys in his human form, dazed but alive. She fell to her knees beside him, and tried to breathe her healing mist.

That gift she'd retained and she was relieved to see Rhys' color improve and his aura burn more brightly. She fixed her attention on him, wanting him to be as strong as possible.

They weren't out of Fae yet.

Maeve shrieked in the royal box as she visibly aged, her hair turning white and her outstretched hands becoming claw-like. Her nails grew and yellowed; her cheeks sagged, she became gaunt and trembled. Her skin was lined again and she shrank in stature, but she stood on her throne and summoned the magick to return to her.

The retreat of the red tide wavered, and it began to move in the opposite direction again.

Embron's song boomed in volume. The lip of the tide hesitated, then began to move toward the dragon prince again.

It was a war of wills.

A sorcerers' contest.

Embron and Maeve glared at each other, the fury between them making the air crackle with tension.

There could be only one winner and Lila didn't know which would be better.

Sylvia felt powerless and she didn't like it one bit. She halfway regretted leaving Reliquary, although she didn't regret leaving Sebastian. He hadn't even cared enough to come after her. She wanted to mourn Eithne, but first she had to survive.

And she wanted that book back.

It had become a matter of principle.

She watched Embron and Maeve square off in a battle of magick and wished there was something she could do. She wasn't sure she wanted either of them to win, but she wanted out of Fae.

When the stone statue of Rhys was shattered, Maeve's frustration was clear. The Dark Queen had become a hag, using what was left of her magick to summon the rest. She stood up to work her spell and the book fell to the ground.

Sylvia bent slowly, not wanting to draw attention to herself. Her fingers had just brushed the cover of the book when a familiar voice spoke behind her.

"The time has come, I think, to go," Sebastian said softly.

Sylvia glanced over her shoulder in surprise. The guard behind her lifted his visor and her heart skipped at the sight of Sebastian's wicked smile. One of those Fae daggers gleamed in his hand, the ones that could slice openings between realms, and his intention was clear.

Sylvia seized the book in the same moment that Sebastian caught her around the waist. The other Fae warrior snatched at the book and Sylvia gave it a hard tug, even as Sebastian sliced open a portal between the realms.

"Let it go!" he said, which astonished her.

"Not a chance," she said through gritted teeth, giving it a hard tug. The Fae warrior tugged back.

To her surprise, the woman seated beside Maeve jumped up and body-slammed the Fae warrior. "Go!" she shouted to Sylvia.

The Fae warrior slapped her so hard that she fell to the ground. There was a shimmer of blue and a dragon roared from the arena. Sylvia ignored that. The Fae warrior still had hold of one cover of the book. He tugged it hard enough that Sylvia was almost pulled to his side.

Sylvia wasn't going to let go. She heard Sebastian snarl in frustration, then he drew the Fae dagger and it slashed through the air.

The spine of the book was sliced.

The magick surrounding the book winked out, like an extinguished light. The Fae warrior fell back with one cover in his grasp, then Sebastian retreated through the portal he'd opened. The last thing Sylvia saw was a carnelian and gold dragon charging the royal box, breathing fire as he attacked.

Then she fell to the floor in a darkened studio apartment she didn't recognize. There was a skylight overhead and she could see the moon high overhead. Sebastian shut the portal like a zipper, just as she'd seen

Fae warriors do, then shed his borrowed armor as if it burned. He turned the knife in the light, then shoved it into his belt.

"Of course, we had to turn up here," he muttered and seized her hand. "We must be gone when they follow."

Sylvia wasn't going to argue with that. She clutched the remnants of the book and raced after Sebastian. He practically flew down the stairs, then paused to snatch her up and toss her over his shoulder. "But where will we go?"

"Back to Reliquary," he snarled with obvious annoyance. "It's the safest place, unfortunately."

"Why unfortunately?"

"Because Micah and I have argued," he said as they burst into an empty street. "You'll get to watch me grovel for his forgiveness." He raced to an alley then stopped and put her down once they were in the shadows. His eyes were glittering brightly and he looked so pale that Sylvia knew he needed to feed. She backed away, finding a brick wall behind herself, and Sebastian followed as if he couldn't resist. His gaze lingered on her throat for a long moment and her breath caught, then he averted his gaze and swallowed.

"Time, sadly, is of the essence," he muttered, then took her hand and began to run again. "Tell me if you can't keep up."

Sylvia wasn't going to give him the satisfaction of that.

"No!" Arach cried as Theo raged toward the royal box in his dragon form. Rhys realized that one Fae warrior there had struck Mel and that Theo intended to defend her. At least he was back to normal. Lila's healing mist was helping him to recover his senses, but not quickly enough. He saw the shimmer of blue and spun to see Embron shift shape.

The dragon prince became an enormous black dragon that could have been made of anthracite. He looked even more ancient than Drake did, and had thorns on his scales, his eyes burning with inner fire as he took flight over the arena. The Fae spectators stared in awe as his massive black wings beat, raising dust from the ground. He held the crystal orb before himself in one outstretched claw and his chant became so loud that Rhys' bones rattled. The magick was drawn to Embron with greater and greater speed, despite Maeve's attempts to call it back.

She was losing.

When the tide of red reached Embron and swirled around the orb, he laughed and the sound was enough to make the earth shake. There was another crack from overhead, like thunder about to strike, and the Fae fled from the stands of the arena in terror. Maeve continued to call to her magick, but it was clear that Embron would triumph. There were almost no Fae left in the arena and their surroundings were almost colorless.

"Now," Arach said softly and Rhys understood him perfectly. The two *Pyr* shimmered blue as they shifted shape in unison. They took flight with Theo, targeting Embron. Theo was the first to reach the dragon prince, but he was smacked so hard that he fell from the sky. Embron swung his tail with a roar of fury and sent Arach tumbling head over tail toward the ground.

Rhys recalled how Embron had abused Lila and his anger became a cold arrow of motivation. He lifted his claws in the traditional invitation to fight, but Embron only laughed. He breathed fire into Rhys' face, then slashed with one claw then the other. Rhys ducked from one blow, but a talon on the other claw caught him right in the spot where he'd lost a scale. The pain shot through him like liquid fire, but he raged dragonfire at Embron, breathing flames into the dragon prince's eyes.

Embron bellowed and spun to attack, his tail thrashing through the air. Rhys ducked, then sprang upward in the last moment, snatching at the crystal orb. Embron twisted to hold it out of the way and Rhys snatched at his back, grasping the top of Embron's wings. He rode the dragon prince, knowing it wouldn't last long, and bent to gnaw through the tendons at the tops of Embron's wings. Embron roared and spun, struggling to dislodge Rhys, but Rhys held on tight. He managed to make one wing useless before Embron twisted and dove, one claw outstretched to snatch at Lila.

Rhys threw his weight to one side, sending Embron crashing to the arena floor. The dragon prince landed on top of him and Rhys closed his eyes pretending to be more injured than he was. Arach and Theo were attacking together, and he figured he could jump Embron from behind.

Maeve had been spellcasting all the while and Rhys saw that she'd reclaimed some of the magick from Embron's orb. She was looking younger and more confident, and the gem of the hoard was glowing red again. Embron swore and chanted to his orb, drawing the magick back toward him. Again, they were locked in a battle of wills and once again there was a crack overhead.

This time, though, a bolt of blue-green light struck the ground beside Embron with a sizzle. When the smoke cleared, there was a man standing there, a man dressed in jeans with a backpack. He had a beard and looked a bit dusty, like he'd been travelling.

Embron, Rhys, Arach, Theo and Maeve all stared at him in shock. Rhys doubted his were the only eyes to widen when the man shimmered blue. He shifted shape to a dragon of opal and silver, his long tail stretched across the arena and his scales glimmering like moonlight. In the blink of an eye, he shifted shape to become a deer. He was a hare, he was mouse, he was an eagle, he was a salamander, he was a man again. It was dizzying to watch him change and Rhys realized the red light of magick was drawn to him. By the time he completed his cycle of forms again, he was bathed in a red glow of magick.

Embron roared and dove toward him. He was an eagle when Embron snatched at him, and he seized the crystal orb in his talons, wrenching it from Embron's grip. He flew high, shifting to a dragon on the way, tossing the orb to Rhys.

Rhys caught it as the new arrival seized Embron, compelling the dragon prince to watch. It was heavy and hot, pulsing with magick and fury. The new arrival nodded at Rhys and he understood. He raised his claws, trapping the orb between them, and crushed it to dust. A jolt of blue-green light fired from the shattered orb and struck Embron in the brow.

The dragon prince stumbled and fell, his eyes closed by the time he hit the ground. He cycled between forms half a dozen times, but didn't move again.

"The four elements," the new arrival said to the *Pyr*, reminding them that their kind had to be exposed to all four elements when they died. Earth and air were accounted for, and Rhys nodded to his fellows to breathe fire in unison on the corpse of the dragon prince. The new arrival clapped his hands, and there was a rumble above before rain began to fall. Embron's corpse smoked and then it steamed, then chunks of rock began to fall upon the arena.

The Fae had disappeared. Maeve had vanished with the gem of the hoard. The new arrival spun in place, summoning a tornado of blue-green light, and disappeared himself. Rhys saw light far above them, and caught Lila in his embrace. "Hurry!" he called to Arach and Theo, not certain what would happen but guessing it wouldn't be good.

Arach took flight behind him.

"I have to get Mel," Theo said, then disappeared in the shadows below. Rhys only paused long enough to see that Arach was with him, then raced for what he hoped was a portal to the realm he knew best.

He and Lila wouldn't be trapped in Fae without a fight.

Balthasar returned to the yacht shortly after Nyssa, his expression grim. He changed and joined the others at the rail to watch.

"Did you see him die?" Nyssa asked but he shook his head.

"Just lots of blood and happy sharks."

"Rhys and Lila?" Thorolf asked.

"Vanished."

"What about Embron?"

"I never saw him." Balthasar felt like a failure but wasn't sure what else to do.

Suddenly, there was a loud boom, like distant thunder, and the sea heaved beneath them. The yacht rocked precariously as the water bubbled up from the depths. The sea was really dark, unnaturally so, and filled with sand and shells.

Nyssa gasped and pointed at the shards of an obsidian mirror. "It was shattered!" she whispered. "How will they escape Fae now?"

"Is there another portal near here?" Thorolf asked.

"I don't know," Nyssa admitted, feeling helpless.

Something moved in the water, something silver, and they watched as a fish broke the surface. It strained high and something shone in its mouth. It was directly in front of Nyssa.

Balthasar got a net and scooped out the fish.

"What kind is it?" Thorolf asked.

Balthasar shook his head because he'd never seen one like it before.

"A lucky kind," Nyssa said. She pushed back the net and stroked the side of the fish. It opened its mouth, revealing that it carried a ring. Nyssa took the ring, which was set with a large pearl, and the fish flailed.

"Thank you," she said, then lifted it in her arms. "Thank you," she said again then kissed its cheeks. She gently lowered it over the rail and released it into the sea again. Its tail flicked and it was gone, swimming to the depths once more.

Nyssa put the ring on her finger and it shone with a light of its own. A crown of red coral floated to the surface, too, and Chandra took the net to scoop it out of the water. She placed it on Nyssa's brow. The selkie looked regal and remote, and Balthasar exchanged a glance of confusion with Thorolf.

"All hail the new Queen Under the Seas," Chandra said, bowing low before her, and Balthasar understood then that Nereus was dead.

"All hail," Balthasar and Thorolf said in unison.

To Lila's relief, Rhys burst through a barrier and they were suddenly in the sea. They swam toward the light and broke the surface as one. He took a deep gulp of air and she said his name aloud, loving that she could speak again.

The water was cold, colder than the air, but they were alive and in the realm of mortals. She knew because the stars were shining overhead. They were near her home because she could see the Merry Dancers, twisting like a green curtain in the sky. The outline of the hills beyond the beach were achingly familiar and she thought she could even see the silhouette of her cottage.

Home.

Or what had been her home. She understood then that her home would always be at Rhys' side, for the rest of her mortal days.

"Figures," Rhys said, treading water beside her. "One of these days, I should learn to swim."

"One of these days, I'll teach you," Lila replied with smile. "If you teach me to fly."

Rhys laughed. "One is a lot more probable than the other," he said, then slipped underwater again. Lila dove after him and they came up laughing.

"You did that on purpose," she accused and he grinned.

"I like when you save me."

Lila shook her head, amused. "Roll to your back and float. I'll get us to shore." Rhys did as she instructed and she wrapped her arm under his chin, pulling him closer to shore with easy strokes. He was right about trust: it was seductive for him to rely on her without question.

It didn't take long to get close enough to the beach that he could put his feet down and he stood up, tipping his head back to survey the sky. "I have a new appreciation for stars," he said, then smiled down at her. "Did you notice there aren't any in Fae?"

"I did." Lila shivered, then looked back at the dark water. "This must be where I went through the portal and met you."

"Then you know what to do," Rhys said. "Close that portal forever."

"For our son," Lila agreed and took the hag stone off its cord, kissed it, then looked at Rhys. "Maybe we should do it together, as a mark of sharing our futures."

Rhys smiled, his dark eyes filled with pleasure. He fitted his hand against hers so that the stone was trapped between their palms, then wrapped his other arm around her waist. It was like the way he'd shattered the orb, but this was a task they did together.

Lila leaned against him, smiling at the familiar tingle of desire that she always felt when they touched, and Rhys' grip tightened over hers. They pressed their hands together, crushing the stone. The blue-green light of darkfire streamed from between their fingers as the stone was destroyed, then flashed like lightning over the surface of the sea.

"It is done," Rhys said with a sigh of relief. "Although we have no idea where that other beach was."

"Another portal to close another day," Lila said, and tugged him toward the beach. She felt giddy and celebratory, knowing they'd survived and triumphed. She knew that the hole in her life had been filled and she'd never be lonely again. "I'll buy a pair of purple sandals if it makes you feel better."

Rhys laughed, then caught her up in his arms. He carried her to the beach. "Being warm and dry will make me feel better," he countered, then smiled down at her. "Then making love to you all night long."

"You've got a deal, Rhys Lewis," Lila said. "By the way, I love you."

He laughed, his eyes lighting with pleasure, then she pulled his head down for a very satisfying kiss.

Arach lost sight of Rhys in the darkness, but he felt himself pass through a barrier of some kind. It wasn't any more substantial than mist, but it was cold, far colder than Fae had been. His wounds from battling Theo ached more than they had and he was aware of his exhaustion and hunger. He forced himself onward and emerged suddenly in the light of dawn in a rocky place. He shifted back to his human form and wasn't entirely certain it was his decision to do so.

Had he seen more darkfire?

To his astonishment, the bearded stranger and shapeshifter was there, sitting on a rock with a mug of what smelled like coffee. He smiled a greeting, said something in a language Arach didn't understand, then gestured to a white-washed cottage.

Arach figured he had nothing left to lose. He went and knocked at the door as the stranger watched with approval, only to be shocked when Donovan opened the door.

"How did you get to Bardsey Island without me knowing about it?" that *Pyr* demanded, then pulled Arach into the warm and crowded kitchen. There were kids and mates, breakfast and hot coffee, and even a bag of Sloane's healing salves. "You're a mess! Sit down and I'll patch you up as well as I can while you tell me what's happened."

Rafferty appeared and exclaimed over Arach, then Marco and his mate, Jac joined them. The *Pyr* known as the Seven Thieves were there as well and when they spoke, Arach thought it sounded like the same language the stranger had spoken.

But he was exhausted. At least he'd found a safe haven and he hoped the others had done the same. He sank into a chair with relief and glanced out the window, only to see that the stranger had vanished.

After Lila and Rhys bathed, made love, ate and caught up with the *Pyr* on Lila's laptop, Rhys tried to book them seats on the next flight back to New York. There were only two seats left, both in business class, but across the aisle from each other. "We could wait another day," he said to Lila but she shook her head.

"It's only for a few hours." She smiled at him. "Let's go home, Rhys."

That sounded good to him.

"I can put in a request for two seats together, in case it comes up," he suggested. "Someone might have a change of plans."

They flew from Orkney to Edinburgh early the next morning and then to Heathrow. They had a lunch that Rhys found deplorable for the price, and made their way to the waiting lounge in plenty of time for the flight. It looked like a great day for flying.

No sooner had they taken seats in the lounge than a woman stopped in front of Lila.

"Excuse me," she said, her voice soft with a Scottish burr. "Would you mind if I asked you something?" She laughed a little under her breath. "It might be a bit strange to believe."

Rhys noticed then that she was wearing purple sandals. They were sparkly and had high heels, and looked identical to the pair he'd noticed on the beach when he'd first met Lila. He glanced up. The woman couldn't have been thirty years old and she was as tall and slender as Lila. Her hair hung like dark silk to her waist and seemed to flow as she moved. He would have guessed that she walked with the rhythm of the ocean waves. Her eyes were the clear silver-grey of the north Atlantic in the sunlight and when she gestured, he noticed that the bit of skin between her fingers was longer than usual. It extended halfway down the digit, but he didn't find it unattractive. She blushed, noting his gaze, and folded her hand so it was hidden.

"I believe a lot of strange things," Lila said easily and tapped the empty seat beside her in invitation. Rhys felt the tension in her, though, and knew that she'd noticed at least some of the same details.

"It's just that I've dreamed about you," the woman confessed. She shook her head, obviously amazed. "I've dreamed about you all my life, and when I was able to draw you, my mum said she'd dreamed about you, too." She looked between Lila and Rhys, obviously taking their silence for disbelief, then opened her bag with shaking fingers. "Look!" She pushed a sketchbook into Lila's hands.

Lila opened it and Rhys caught his breath. The first image was a woman seated on a rock, the waves splashing around her hips. She might not have been wearing anything at all—it was impossible to be sure, between the water and the cloak of her dark hair—and she was looking over her shoulder and smiling slightly. It was a sad smile and the expression in her eyes was haunted.

As if she was taking leave of someone but had regrets.

Rhys leaned closer and was sure there was a glimmer of tears on her dark lashes, as well as something held in her hand, partly out of view.

But it was Lila. He had no doubt of it.

Neither did Lila. Her fingers trembled as she turned the page. The next drawing was of a man, a man with his hands shoved into his pockets, his gaze fixed on the horizon. He looked to be standing on a pebbled beach and there was resignation, if not grief, in his posture.

"I don't dream of him as often," the woman said.

Lila turned the page quickly and Rhys heard her inhale. A boy ran toward the viewer on a pebbled beach, his bare feet splashing in the surf. He wore knee breeches and his shirt was open at the throat, the sleeves rolled up and his hands dirty. He held a shell in one hand and offered it to the viewer, his eyes filled with mischief. Rhys could almost hear his laughter. He watched Lila run a fingertip above the page, as if she would caress the freckles on his cheeks.

"Thomas," she said quietly, her heart in her voice.

"You know him?" the woman asked, leaning closer. "I don't know his name, or who he is. I usually dream of him like this, or sometimes asleep..." She flicked through the book, showing Lila two more sketches of what was unmistakably the same boy. "Do you know where he is? Do you know why I dream of him?" The woman took a breath. "I thought maybe he was in my future, but if you know him, that can't be true." She raised a hope-filled gaze to Lila.

"I knew a boy once who looked just like him," Lila said, her words husky. "His name was Thomas, but he's been dead a long time."

"Oh." The younger woman was clearly disappointed, then seemed to recover herself. "I'm sorry. I was so excited that I forgot my manners. I'm Kylie. Kylie Tate." She took a deep breath. "I'm going to America. I decided it was time."

"Time for a change?" Rhys asked gently, sensing that Lila was upset.

Kylie sat up straighter. "I'm alone. Everyone in my family is dead." Rhys felt Lila stiffen a little but Kylie didn't appear to notice. "And the night before last, there was a terrible storm with blue-green light flashing on the beach beside our village. The old people said the Fae had abandoned us and it would never be the same. I'm not sure I believe that, but it seemed like a good time to go. I've wanted to go someplace new, someplace maybe luckier." She smiled. "And I've always wanted to go to New York City."

"No boyfriend?" Lila asked and Kylie shook her head.

She lifted her hand, her gaze darting to Rhys, and spread her fingers. "I saw you notice. All the women in my family have hands like this." She swallowed. "They say it's because we're descended from a selkie, and that's why we can't wear a wedding ring. It's her legacy to us, that we can never be trapped in marriage like she was."

"You can be married or trapped without a ring," Lila said.

Kylie nodded. "Yes, but it's a good reminder to be careful about making choices and commitments. My mother said it was because of the selkie that we had dreams. My mother had the Sight, but I just dream of people I don't know." She smiled and made to get up. "I'm sorry to have bothered you. I was just surprised by the resemblance."

"So am I," Lila said warmly. "Tell me where you're from."

"A little town on the west of Scotland. I doubt you've heard of it."

Lila offered her hand. "I'm Dr. Lila Isbister. I study grey seals, mostly on North Rona but also throughout Scotland. I'll bet I do know your little town."

"The seals do haul out there!" Kylie agreed. She named a town that Rhys had never heard of, but he saw that Lila recognized the name. "Nothing else ever happens there." Kylie settled back to chat just as a passenger was paged.

"Mr. Rhys Lewis. Mr. Rhys Lewis. Please identify yourself to the ticketing agent for the flight to New York. Mr. Rhys Lewis."

He went to the desk, hoping they'd gotten the seats he wanted. It turned out that a frequent flier had cancelled and the window seat was available beside one of their aisle seats. Rhys glanced back at Lila and

Kylie, the two of them deep in conversation, and had an idea.

"Would it be possible to buy an upgrade for another passenger?" he asked.

"I have a list of requested upgrades, sir..."

Rhys gestured to Lila and Kylie. "My partner, you see, has just met up with an old friend. They haven't seen each other in years and I know she would enjoy having the flight to catch up."

The ticketing agent glanced across the lounge and smiled. "Do you know the other passenger's name? I'd have to check that she's even on this flight."

"Kylie Tate," Rhys said and put his gold card down on the counter. "It would be my treat."

The ticketing agent nodded when she found Kylie's reservation, tapped a few changes and put the charge on Rhys' card, then paged Kylie to collect her new boarding pass. She was thrilled and impulsively hugged Rhys, which made the ticketing agent smile, then hurried back to share the news with Lila.

Lila looked up as she listened to Kylie's excited chatter, her smile warming him to his toes.

"And I didn't even have to beguile anyone," Rhys confessed in old-speak as he crossed the lounge, liking how Lila laughed at that.

He was completely charmed himself and he didn't mind one bit.

EPILOGUE

Vermont—Thursday, November 28

nce again, the *Pyr* gathered at Kristofer's farm for a scale repair and celebration. Rhys found it hard to believe that less than a month had passed since he'd last been in Vermont. This time, he brought steaks and lobster for their feast, as well as two turkeys and a ham. His restaurant was opening again after the holiday weekend and it felt good to be back in the rhythm of shopping and cooking.

He liked his life even better with Lila by his side. She'd told him on the drive north that she'd decided to cut back her time on North Rona and would only go to the remote island for the annual haul-in of seals that were ready to give birth. She'd keep her census counts and monitor the health of the herd, but would be relying more on her junior research associates.

"Can you feasibly decrease your hours so much?" he asked as he drove. It was a cold clear day, and there wasn't much traffic.

"It was never supposed to be a full-time responsibility. I was just committed, partly because I didn't have other obligations." He glanced over to see her pat her stomach. "I think you've taken care of that." Her eyes were sparkling and she didn't seem to mind the change. "A lot of the researchers are in grad school and need more field experience, so it'll work for everyone."

"Next one of them will want you to retire so he or she can apply for your job."

"Two of them," Lila corrected easily. "Regan even wants to buy my house."

Rhys blinked. "Are you selling?"

"I haven't decided."

He knew that decision was hers to make. "I was thinking, too," he said and Lila laughed.

"It's better than the alternative."

He chuckled. "I could close the restaurant for a month next fall and go with you to North Rona. Our son will only be a couple of months old and you'll probably need a hand."

"I was wondering about leaving him with you. After all, it's going to be cold and wet, which isn't exactly a great environment for a baby."

"Won't you miss him?"

"I know I'll miss you. It seems likely that I'll pine away for both of you." She reached over and touched Rhys' hand. "What if I became a consultant on the project and let someone else take it over?"

"I thought it was really important to you."

"It has been, but I've done it for decades. It's not exactly challenging anymore, especially all the tallying and reporting." She took a breath. "I was wondering whether you needed some help at Everyman Epicure. If I stayed in New York, we might be able to help the Others and the *Pyr* in the battle against the Dark Queen."

"That war's not over," Rhys said.

"And the world isn't exactly safe yet for our son," Lila agreed. "I feel like going back to North Rona would be ignoring the issue. And I did reach out to a colleague at the university here. There's a part-time teaching opportunity that could lead to more. It could be a nice stepping stone."

"You've been busy."

"Researching is what I do."

Rhys pulled over into a rest stop, wanting to be able to look into her eyes. "I'd love if you stayed," he confessed. "I've been dreading the day you leave, although I know your freedom is important to you." He held her hands tightly. "I love you, Lila, and you know I want to build a powerful partnership."

"You make a pretty enticing argument," she admitted, then smiled. "You'll never hide my skin on me. I love you, Rhys, and I trust you. Let's build that future together."

He kissed her and when they finally parted, the windows were fogging up. They laughed as they wiped them clear and grinned at each other as they got underway again.

"I have this idea," Rhys said.

"You're full of ideas."

"No, just one more. I was thinking that I've been working too much and that we should actually take vacations together."

"We're not buying that yacht," Lila said firmly.

Rhys laughed. "Balthasar told me it was being auctioned."

"Let him buy it. Or Thorolf." They laughed together and she gave him a nudge. "What's this idea?"

"Sunshine," he said with a sigh. "I was looking at real estate listings in Malta. There are some old houses, even a castle, for sale, that need some restoration work."

Lila laughed and he glanced her way in surprise. "I wonder whether we liked the same one."

"You were looking, too?"

"Of course. I thought it would be good for our son to know about your family and your past."

"What about yours?"

"Kylie isn't going to disappear anytime soon, and Nyssa is here, too. Plus she's Queen Under the Seas now. With them and the *Pyr*, he's got more family than I could ever imagine." She flicked a glance his way. "Maybe even enough for you."

"Maybe," Rhys agreed, unable to hide his satisfaction.

"I was thinking I could sell my house and put the money toward a home together. I knew it had to be close to the water, for me, and I thought it had to be warm, for you. Malta looks perfect."

"Malta in January *is* perfect," Rhys said. "The restaurant business is slow between New Year's and Valentine's Day. It would be so easy to be away from New York at that time each year."

"Then maybe we should plan a trip and go shopping this January," Lila suggested.

Rhys nodded agreement. "Definitely." He turned into Kristofer's drive. "Have I told you lately how much I love you?"

"I think you've mentioned it," she said with a satisfaction that equaled his own. "Make sure you don't slide into the ditch."

Lila wondered how she could ever have imagined that her life was complete when she was on her own. The *Pyr* were like a big family, and the warmth of their welcome touched her heart. She stood that night outside in the circle of *Pyr* and mates, basking in the radiance of their combined auras. They were so powerful and so filled with love for each other. She could easily understand why their companionship was so important to Rhys.

Their son would grow up surrounded by this circle of support.

Or he would if they defeated Maeve. His right to a future fed Lila's determination to finish that quest as nothing else could have done.

Quinn, the Smith of the *Pyr*, had fired up his forge. He and Sara and their sons were headed home to Michigan after the weekend. The flames were brilliant yellow and shot sparks into the night sky that reminded Lila of the firestorm.

Funny how it didn't seem to matter how many times she and Rhys made love: it always shook her to her marrow and left her marveling at her good fortune to have found him.

But he'd taught her to trust. That was what made it possible to fill the whole in her heart and her life.

Quinn was the first to shift shape, becoming a dragon of sapphire and steel. His son Garrett stood beside him and was obviously enthralled with his father's abilities. His mate Sara stood with their other four sons, each as dark-haired and blue-eyed as their father.

Would their son look like Rhys?

Thorolf roared as he shifted shape and Chandra laughed at him, shaking her head as he became a massive moonstone and silver dragon. Raynor held his mother's hand and looked at the assembled *Pyr* with wonder. He and Lila were the two who were witnessing a scale repair for the first time.

Kristofer was the next to shift shape, becoming a peridot and gold dragon. His scales sparkled like cut gems in the light. Bree watched him with obvious admiration.

There was a shimmer of blue light, then Arach shifted to his dragon form. He was majestic in his aquamarine and silver scales. Balthasar was citrine and gold when he shifted shape. Hadrian and Alasdair shifted in unison, Hadrian becoming an emerald and silver dragon while Alasdair became a hematite and silver one.

They all turned to Rhys, who squeezed Lila's hand before shifting shape himself. His garnet and silver scales shone and only his aura was more radiant with good health and power. He moved into the center of the circle of *Pyr*, inviting Lila to stand beside him before Quinn. She was reminded of a wedding ceremony, except she thought that Rhys' loss of a scale and her contribution to its repair created an even firmer bond between them.

As far as she was concerned, that gap in his armor couldn't be healed soon enough.

Quinn had the scale Rhys had lost, thanks to Nyssa, and heated it on the forge. It changed from garnet and silver to gleaming red, then glowed golden. He held it in his talons, his eyes reflecting the flames, then offered a claw to Lila.

She pulled the token from her pocket, where it had been hidden from view, and gave it to Quinn. She heard Rhys catch his breath and smiled.

"Perfect," Rhys murmured and Lila nodded agreement. She'd had the two halves of his mother's crucifix joined together again by a jeweler in the city, after conferring with Quinn about what kind of token would be best.

"Gold and gems," Quinn murmured as he heated it in the flames. "And even better, love and history."

"Perfect," Rhys said again and Quinn nodded.

He pushed the crucifix into the hot scale and there was a sizzle as they were fused together. Then he lifted the hot scale and pushed it into the gap in Rhys' armor and there was another sizzle as it burned Rhys' flesh.

"Earth!" Quinn cried and the *Pyr* repeated the word. "Gold and gemstones mined from the ground, representing the practicality and reliability of the element, earth."

"Air!" Lila said and the *Pyr* echoed her word. She blew on the new scale, which was already cooling and taking its normal hue. "Air for courage and ideas, for principles and ideals."

"Water," Rhys said, lifting her hair with one talon in admiration. It flowed over his claw and his eyes shone as he met her gaze. Lila thought her heart would explode, for she loved this *Pyr* so very much.

"Water for empathy and emotion," she said, her voice husky.

"For healing," Rhys said.

"And fire," she reminded him with a smile. He chuckled then tipped his head back and blew a stream of dragonfire into the night sky.

"And fire!" the *Pyr* repeated, all of them breathing dragonfire into the darkness. The flames crackled overhead like a living canopy of fire, brilliant orange and hot enough to melt the snow underfoot.

Rhys laughed and shifted shape, swinging Lila up into his arms and claiming a triumphant kiss. His scale was repaired, their firestorm was satisfied, and Lila's heart was healed. There could be no better portent for their future together.

She flung her arms around his neck as the *Pyr* hooted and cheered, and kissed her dragon warrior back.

DRAGON'S MATE
The DragonFate Novels #3

Her kiss will shatter realms…

Dragon shifter and artisan blacksmith Hadrian is determined to strength his fellow *Pyr* warriors in the battle against the Fae by making them talons of steel. He won't be seduced by the sensual promise of what has to be a fake firestorm—even to help a beautiful warrior escape the clutches of the Fae Queen.

Rania is a swan-maiden and Fae assassin, compelled to serve the Dark Queen's will in exchange for her own survival. Hadrian is the last of the dozen assigned victims that will fulfill her revolting bargain, but this dragon shifter isn't easy to kill. It's more than dragon vitality that helps him survive her lethal kiss, but Rania won't surrender to his potent touch for any price when her own life hangs in the balance.

Compelled to join forces against the Dark Queen's deceit, can Hadrian and Rania overcome their distrust of each other to defeat a common foe? Can Hadrian unfurl the painful secrets of Rania's past to give them a future? When worlds collide and barriers are destroyed, can love conquer the obstacles between these destined mates?

Turn the page to read an excerpt from
Dragon's Mate
Coming October 2020

CHAPTER ONE

November 30—Northumberland

adrian MacEwan should be dead.

No one had ever escaped Rania's kiss of death before, but she supposed there had to be a first time. It figured that the failure would happen when she was fulfilling her final obligation to Maeve, when she was on the cusp of freedom. How many centuries had it been? She'd anticipated some kind of Fae trickery, some sleight of hand to keep her from being released—Maeve was deviously clever, after all—but Rania hadn't expected her own abilities to fall short.

Assassination was the only thing she did well.

But not this time. The *Pyr* had recovered, not only from injuries that should have been mortal in themselves, but he'd also evaded the price of her kiss of death.

Was it the selkie's fault? A good healer could counter many charms and undermine many toxins.

Had Rania made a mistake? She'd reviewed their meeting a hundred times. She'd been surprised that the dragon shifter was so handsome, then startled by the flash of light he'd called a firestorm. Had she been shaken enough to make a mistake? It was hard to imagine. She'd become known for her ruthless efficiency.

But it had been tempting to give him more of a kiss, not just one on the cheek. She hadn't even seen him at his best and she knew it. He'd been unconscious when she found him, hit on the back of the head. But there was no mistaking the fire and the ice in him. She'd wanted to slip her fingers into the unruly auburn waves of his hair, to caress the square line of his jaw, to caress the firm line of his lips. He was tall and broad, a warrior even in his human form, and she'd been intrigued even before he opened his eyes.

They were brown, but a thousand warm hues of gold and brown, even with some flicks of gold. There was humor in that gaze and intelligence, too, and his eyes had lit with admiration when he surveyed her own face. The way he had smiled, just a little, had caught at her heart and nearly stopped her from doing what had to done.

When this was over, Rania would seduce a hundred men with brown eyes, even though she had a feeling it wouldn't be the same.

"The firestorm," he'd called it when light sparked between them and there has been awe in his voice. She'd learned since that the firestorm was the mating sign of his kind, the *Pyr*, the mark of one dragon shifter finding the woman who could bear his son. Even then, even when he was a complete stranger and her intended victim, she couldn't disappoint him with the truth.

He had a power to influence her. Maybe that was Maeve's trick. Maybe that was how the Dark Queen would keep Rania from fulfilling the terms of her imprisonment.

But all mortals died. She had to be able to kill Hadrian.

Even though, he still lived, and that meant Rania was still in thrall to Maeve. The Fae spies had said that Hadrian MacEwan would return to his smithy in Northumberland this very day so she awaited him in his own lair.

Impatiently.

A blacksmith's workshop was the last place Rania wanted to be. The only good thing about his home was that it was located in the country. He'd taken over an old mill, converting it to both studio and home, and a river ran merrily alongside it. Rania could hear the birds and the wind, too. She'd never yet adjusted to the modern world, though she supposed she'd have time to do that once her bargain with Maeve was done.

Once Hadrian was dead.

She's manifested inside Hadrian's lair and had already explored it thoroughly. It was simply furnished and comfortable. She concluded that he was a man of simple tastes and pleasures, one with a respect for tradition and history. He was tidy. He lived alone. He read books and did horrible blacksmith things in the workshop she refused to even enter.

She shivered at the smell of iron and ash. That alone should make him easy to kill.

His occupation was why she'd chosen him of all the *Pyr*.

Rania paced and wished he'd hurry. It was already past noon. She was agitated and tried to calm herself.

This time, she wouldn't make a mistake.

When she heard an approaching car, she froze, listening.

When it parked outside the studio, she hid, retreating to his bedroom, and stood silent as she waited.

It would all be over soon. Maeve would cross out the name of another dragon shifter from her inventory and Rania would finally be free.

Hadrian was relieved to be home. As much as he loved his fellow *Pyr*, he'd had enough adventure to suit him for a while with two back-to-back firestorms. He wanted to sleep in his own bed, return to the rhythm of his life and do some solid work that would make a difference. He'd stopped at the post office on his way home, hoping the parcel had arrived from Donovan, and was glad to learn that it had.

He'd heard so much about Donovan's gloves, but had never had the chance to examine them closely. Quinn had told him more about their construction at Kristofer's place, and Hadrian was determined to improve upon them. As far as he was concerned, if the *Pyr* were fighting the Fae for their survival, talons of steel were exactly what they all needed. The Fae couldn't abide steel and after his imprisonment in Maeve's realm, Hadrian was ready for some payback.

He wanted the ability to slice Fae warriors to ribbons and he wanted it immediately.

There was no telling when a Fae portal would open and trouble would start again. Thanks to Lila, Rhys' mate, and Balthasar, his feet had healed, the bump was gone on the back of his head and the slashes to his gut from his fight with Embron were healed as well. Hadrian was determined to stay healthy and whole for the duration.

The mill he'd bought was constructed in an L, which made the division between home and work easy. He's built his studio in the larger arm of the L and his home in the other. At their junction was his office and a formidable barrier of dragonsmoke buttressing the entrance to his lair and home

His lair had one large main room, with a high ceiling and exposed brick walls. The kitchen was at one end, immediately by the door, and there was a big fireplace on the opposite wall. There was an arch on the right of the fireplace, leading to his bedroom, and a door between it and the washroom in the back corner. Windows on the right gave a view of the river that had originally provided power to the mill.

Hadrian paused in the kitchen and took a deep breath. His dragonsmoke was undisturbed, although the protective barrier had faded a bit in his absence. He'd have to fortify it before the end of the day. There was a bit of dust on everything, since he'd been gone more than a month, and he knew that whatever was left in the fridge wouldn't be edible. He'd picked up a few groceries in town for that very reason.

Strangely enough, he had the sense that he wasn't alone. How could that be? How could anyone be in his lair without having crossed his dragonsmoke?

He shook his head, thinking that recent events had made him paranoid. Being tortured by the Fae Queen might do that to a dragon.

Hadrian opened the box on the kitchen counter, only giving Donovan's note the barest glance. He wanted to see the gloves and they didn't disappoint. They were even more amazing than he'd expected. They were made of fine leather, the long sharp talons extending from each fingertip. The steel continued from each finger across the back of each glove for strength, and the talons were hinged, like long fingers. They were also sharp, essentially five blades on each hand.

Hadrian tugged them on, moving his fingers and admiring their flexibility. Sunlight shone through the kitchen windows and glinted on the lethal blades.

Donovan said that he could carry them through the shift, and make them part of his dragon armor. He'd explained to Hadrian that he didn't fold them away with his clothes: in his dragon form, they merged with his claws, lengthening them into swords.

Hadrian couldn't wait to see that. He left the box in the kitchen and moved into the center of the large living space. He called to the shift and savored the brilliant shimmer of blue light that heralded his change between forms. He thought of Donovan's advice and tried to follow it as he shifted. It felt good to be in his dragon form, his tail brushing against the kitchen counter, his wings almost reaching the high ceiling of the lair.

He wanted to roar with satisfaction when he saw that Donovan's strategy had worked. The steel blades were part of his front talons, and when he slashed with one claw, they whistled through the air. Hadrian laughed and slashed again. His first project would be making a dozen pairs of these to outfit the *Pyr*.

Then he stilled and inhaled slowly. His senses were more keen in his dragon form and he knew without doubt that there was an intruder in his lair.

A woman.

Impossible.

But she was there. He smelled her skin.

Then Hadrian felt the faint tickle of a cold flame and desire stirred within him.

It was same light that had sparked when he'd had the vision of that woman at Rhys' place, the one who had kissed his cheek. She'd said then that she'd been looking for him. Lila, Rhys' mate, said that she'd given him a kiss of death.

He'd thought it was a dream, but it was another fake firestorm, just like Kristofer's had been at first.

How dare anyone taint the most anticipated moment of any *Pyr's* life?

Looking for him. She was hunting him, and he wasn't going to be easy prey.

Hadrian took another breath, straining his ears to listen at the same time. She was in his lair. He didn't know how and he didn't know why, but this time, she'd be the one surprised.

He shifted silently back to his human form, keeping the gloves on, then eased toward the bedroom. The light brightened, but it wasn't golden like a firestorm. It was the cold light of a winter morning, and it didn't cast a warm glow either. Its appearance filled Hadrian turned the blood in his veins to ice and that filled him with cold fury.

She'd given him a kiss of death.

It wouldn't happen twice.

Dragon's Mate
Coming in October 2020

Learn more about the DragonFate Novels at
http://DragonfireNovels.com

ABOUT THE AUTHOR

Deborah Cooke sold her first book in 1992, a medieval romance called Romance of the Rose published under her pseudonym Claire Delacroix. Since then, she has published over seventy novels in a wide variety of sub-genres, including historical romance, contemporary romance, and paranormal romance. She has published under the names Claire Delacroix, Claire Cross and Deborah Cooke. **The Beauty**, part of her successful Bride Quest series of historical romances, was her first title to land on the *New York Times* List of Bestselling Books. Her books routinely appear on other bestseller lists and have won numerous awards. In 2009, she was the writer-in-residence at the Toronto Public Library, the first time the library has hosted a residency focused on the romance genre. In 2012, she was honored to receive the Romance Writers of America's Mentor of the Year Award.

Currently, she writes paranormal romances and contemporary romances as Deborah Cooke. She also writes historical romances as Claire Delacroix. Deborah lives in Canada with her husband and family, as well as far too many unfinished knitting projects.

To learn more about her books, visit her websites:
http://deborahcooke.com
http://dragonfirenovels.com
http://dragonsofincendium.com
http://delacroix.net